Queened

⊱Book Six⊰

Mistress & Master
of
Restraint
Series

Queened

Printed in the United States of America
First Printing, 2016
ISBN-13: **978-0692725856**
ISBN-10: **0692725857**

Jaded, thy name is Regina Regal. Enduring a trial by fire, she will be Queened.

Regina Regal wavers between apathetic and destructive because she's numb inside and out. Lost in a sea of ennui, she goes through the motions of everyday life but never truly lives. Happiness is a foreign concept.

In the absence of numbness is pain– a pain so agonizing she would rather stick her head in the sand than feel the devastating loss of the father of her children.

Thrust from Misery Castle, not only losing Grant, she leaves her first born behind. In the ashes of her despair, Regina creates a family for her daughter. But as her eyes open wide, she realizes everything is built on an illusion.

Betrayed. Abandoned. Grieving yet filled with guilt, Regina finally comes to the realization that she has been toyed with as a pawn in a sadistic game Dominion's founders have played since before she ever set foot into Hillbrook. Every move she has made has been orchestrated by the very people she has grown to love and trust. Restraint draws Regina into a whole new world– one that has been at her fingertips but she was too blind to see.

Forced with the task to choose between love and self-respect, Regina learns how if you feel empowered while you're on your knees, no one can tear you down when you're standing firmly on your own two feet.

Dedication

We all go through a period in our lives where we're lost– this is for you. There is always hope.

Six years prior to the present…

Chapter One

"Auntie, look what I made today?" Ella's prim voice flows down the hallway from the breakfast nook to my home office. We live in a modest, three-bedroom house, so I can hear just about everything with no problem. My heart always constricts when I think of Whitt the eavesdropper, so I made sure there was nowhere to hide in my home, and no secrets kept.

Smiling because of my daughter, but shaking because of our visitor, I close my laptop. I believe twenty-hours of work today is plenty, don't you think? Using my balled up fists, I try to rub the eyestrain away, and all I accomplish is making my eyes sting more. After tossing my glasses on the desk, I leave my office in no big hurry.

"Do you think they'll like it?" Eager and sweet, Ella's voice has my smile widening and my pace quickening as I walk down the hallway.

At just shy of nine, my youngest child is trying to emulate her brothers. Since Whitt is the artist in the family, Ella thinks she should have the same talent too. She's too cute to squash her dreams, but she's comically *bad* at art.

Skirting around the partition from the living room to the breakfast nook, I sneak up on them. "It's perfect." I croon, placing a kiss to the top of Ella's blonde head. I hover for a moment, enjoying the feather-soft feel of her wispy hair against my lips and her little girl scent.

Ella always smells like strawberries. Her dad teased when Niel was born about how we had enough blonde and blue-eyed Whittenhowers, and he was proud to cleanse the bloodline with a red-head. As the sweetest form of torture, the genetic lottery gave us another miniature replica of Grant. It's a shot to the heart every time I look at Ella's angelic face, forever missing Grant and Whitt. Looking at my daughter also has me thinking of Daniel– I want to hate him, but I can't, because we all do horrible things in our grief.

When I look in the mirror, I see my lost son.

Watching the scene play out before me, I pour a gigantic mug of coffee, needing the addictive substance to survive. Caffeine addict. With my fix, I sit next to my daughter and her guest.

The day I lost Grant, is the day I lost Adelaide too. Even though she's a major part of my life, I've had to cut myself off from her emotionally. It hurts too much. I hold just as much animosity for Ade as I do love. When I look at her, I see what I've lost and what she still has. I don't mean a life in Misery Castle. It's nothing monetary. It's the sense of family I had in the latter years of living there. It's the connection to Grant she'll forever have. It's the fact that she gets to have unlimited access to my son, to Whitt, and even to Whitney. I don't even know if Kate's second child was a boy or girl, or if she had a third or fourth.

I don't want to know, and I irrationally blame Ade because she's the one who's still in my face. Then the guilt and shame seep in, because Ade has been by my side every step of the way, even if she isn't one of the Whittenhowers I'm missing.

Ade has kept her part of our bargain: I've had no contact with my son or Whitt, and she brings us fresh information. Daniel, Priscilla, and even Kate, have all tried to contact me via Adelaide. But it hurts too much. They aren't my family, and there is no way I'm losing my last thread to Grant– my daughter.

Daniel would steal Ella in a heartbeat.

Albert has spotted me a few times in the city. Kristal is allowed to maintain a relationship with her father, but if she tells him where we live, where I am, or the name of my company, I warned I'd cut her from my life like a cancerous tumor.

My home is owned by Empowerment, but I've done all I can do to hide the creator and owner of my company so no one could find me. Even with Kristal and Fate living with me, we all use post office boxes as our mailing addresses, and our physical address is to a rented, empty office space in the heart of Dominion. I'll do everything I can to protect my daughter, but I do allow her to stay connected to the Whittenhowers via Adelaide.

As long as I have no contact with my son, the Whittenhowers will have no contact with my daughter.

Chatting softly about Niel, Ade tucks this week's photographs into the album Ella decorated with the year in huge, glittery-pink numerals. This is the eighth album filled with picture after picture of Niel and Whitt, copies of all the images Adelaide could find of Grant, along with pictures of everyone in the Whittenhower family.

The worst are the images of Grant and me, but not nearly as painful as the ones featuring Niel, Whitt, and me.

I haven't glanced at a single picture.

That life for me ended the night I left Misery Castle– the night Grant died.

Tightening my hold on my coffee mug, I stare off into space, pretending the tears swimming in my eyes don't exist. I managed to hold the grief at bay over my parents and Jackson, but never Grant. Even after years and years, if I'm not working, I'm impersonating a leaky faucet.

To sit still is to think. To be silent is to feel. Those moments are in my past with Grant, and I refuse to do either ever again.

"Does Whitt like the color blue? He's always wearing blue in the pictures?" Just like any little girl thirsting for knowledge would be, Ella is obsessed with her brothers. Knowing Ella would never see Whitt, I told her the truth. No secrets between mother and daughter. Whitt was Grant's first born, and his last born knows it.

Ella and Ade scour the pictures for similarities, pointing out how they've changed over the years and how much they look like their father, how much Ella looks like them. Ade does this to connect Ella to the family she's never met, not realizing she's torturing me in the process.

I refuse to look at the images, instinctively knowing Whitt now looks exactly like Grant did when I met him. Grant is forever frozen at age twenty-seven. The older Whitt gets, the more it's like Grant is still walking this earth. But Whitt is not my Grant.

While Ella and Ade do their weekly ritual, I devour the comics and drawings that Ade delivers as well. I'd rather know them by hearing their stories and seeing their accomplishments. I don't need to know what they look like, because I'd recognize them out of a sea of billions.

Ella files away all the information she can get– favorite foods, colors, friends, and school subjects. Every week, she makes her own version of a comic book– scrawled words on her best coloring book pages. Ade brings Whitt and Niel pictures of their sister and her *comic books*. In a way, they know her too. They exchange their art, and Ade relays their tales.

"Niel looks different in this picture than the one from January," Ade explains how he has grown stockier and his voice is deepening.

Just like my dad, no doubt. I know my son will go through puberty early, just as I had. Boys usually mature slower than girls, and Ella's going to be an early bloomer too. Niel's almost twelve, and he won't be a child for long. I haven't seen him since he was a few months shy of being a naughty four-year-old.

Rubbing the torturous ache in my chest, I have a hollow spot where my parents used to be. Added to that emptiness is an agonizing pain that represents the four men I've given up because those who love me eventually leave me.

Grant left this earthly plane, but his ache isn't as hollowing as my parents'. I've never truly accepted his absence, because no matter what, I still feel him with me. Maybe it's because of my daughter, having a piece of Grant forever. But I force myself to put one foot in front of the other, because to stop and think, to listen to my emotions… it's debilitating.

My Daniels: my sunshine and my monkey. Someday I'll be with them again, and I hope the loss over these missing years is outweighed by our reunion and spending the rest of our days together as a family.

Roman: I don't even know if he's still on this earth. But the pain isn't hollow, so I believe he may still be with us. I just hope he took my money and started a better life than hanging out in the alley selling drugs. I know he could make a real difference in the lives of children who grew up just as we did. Not knowing if Roman is alive, I've made it my quest in life to make a difference through funding Transcend.

Deep down, there is a large part of me that believes they are all better off without me. With this fear, I surround myself with my girls, doing all I can to help as many people as possible, because there is something tainted, broken yet numb, residing inside me that is seeking redemption.

"Whitt has a new fascination with tattoos." Ade's lips curl into an amused yet indulgent smirk. "I think he started out to annoy Daddy, but he has a real talent for it. Of course, now Niel is begging for some ink." Her throaty chuckle strengthens the ache in my chest. "The oddest part, Whitt doesn't want a tattoo on *his* body."

"Will you bring me pictures?" Ella sits up straighter at the table, chubby cheeks glowing with excitement.

"I'll see what I can do. You know, Whitt's a bit like your daddy was– private."

Pretending I'm not sucking this up like a dried up sponge, I look at my kitchen cabinets, deciding they may need to be refaced. Oak is so 1990s, as Fate would say. Fate has taken to cooking, and Ella is always underfoot, learning as much as she possibly can.

Planning a new kitchen to make their passions bloom would be a good distraction from this tortuous conversation, as would some of Ella's chocolate chip cookies dunked in my coffee.

Hopping up, I make tracks to the cookie jar, trying my damnedest to shut my ears off. Coming to terms with my fate, I bring the jar to the table. "Ella baked these last night," I announce with pride.

A little bit evil, I do this purposefully so skinny-as-a-rail Ade will eat a cookie. Who can deny a grinning little girl handing you a cookie? My daughter is chubby because she's closing in on puberty, and I'm good with that. If Ade ever tries to put Ella on a diet to fit some ridiculous societal standard of beauty...

"Niel–" Ade takes a bite, and I smile on the inside in victory. "That boy is going to be trouble. Mommy and Daddy are planning his twelfth birthday party. You'd think he was a king or something." She shakes her head in dismay, and I know she isn't exaggerating.

A big party to Ade would have more than five-hundred honored guests. Daniel does see his grandson– the heir of the Whittenhower kingdom– as their king. I've no doubt Niel is despicably indulged yet educated, and I just hope it doesn't ruin my son.

"And what does Niel think of this affair?" Unbidden, the words flow from my lips.

Shocked, Ade turns to me with crystalline blue eyes– eyes the same as everyone in the family, except Niel and myself. They are the color of the Caribbean Sea. She gasps when I hold her gaze without flinching. I haven't looked at Ade since my final moments at Whittenhower Estates, with the agony of her soul shining brightly from their depths– an agony I placed there. I never wanted to see their brilliance again, unless it shined from Grant's face.

But Ade's shocked for another reason altogether. Even though I'm starved for information, I've never once asked a single question about the boys. My addiction was fed when Ella was old enough for curiosity. I've always prayed she'd ask the questions I was dying to know. At almost nine, Ella wouldn't think to ask of indulgence.

"Is... is he... does Niel enjoy the attention?" My words stumble out, because asking of him feels so foreign. I break my gaze from Ade's when it shifts to pity. I stare into my coffee mug, tightening my fingers on the handle in a death-grip.

A gentle touch to my cheek brings my gaze back up to Ade. She smiles at me, and then tucks my unruly hair behind my ear.

"No," she murmurs so softly I can barely hear her. I lean forward, trying to hear every word. "I would have soaked the attention up like a sponge. But Niel is patient and quiet while they dote on him. He reminds me a lot of you, never uncomfortable while rolling with the punches. But when he's alone, or when he's with Whitt, he turns into another person. He's like," she breaks off and turns her face from me.

"Who?" I breathe, leaning in closer. I have to know.

"Grant," Ade whispers with a wince, and a stab of jealousy flares through my chest. "When Niel and Whitt are together, he comes alive. They feed off of each other and become mischievous, snarky, and downright naughty. Even with the age-gap, they're the best of friends, either laughing and hugging, or beating the crap out of each other. It's amazing to watch if they'll let you, but it hurts because they're both very Grant-like."

My eyes seek the solace of the oily substance on the surface of my coffee. Watching it swirl around, I try to ignore the intense longing wracking my body.

No matter how hard I try, I can see the pictures in my peripheral. I don't want to caress the images– I want to touch their skin, smell their scent, and hear the timbre of their voices. I want to compare it to the scents, sounds, and sensations locked away in my memory bank. I want to know if they are Grant-like in every way.

I'm starved, for Niel and Whitt, but most of all for a glimpse of the man I lost.

Ignoring the emotions trying to assault me from the inside out, I pull this week's comic across the table, and then leaf through it. As soon as I'm done, Ade will put it in a binder protected by plastic sleeves, so Ella can read it all week without ruining its quality.

The art is exceptional, but I wouldn't expect less than perfect from Whitt. He's a genius with art. Gaining the talents of his father, Niel is the storyteller. Together, their talents are complementary. They create masterpieces, and I'm not saying that because I love them.

Smiling faintly at the style of the artistry, I remember how when I was last with Whitt, he was infatuated with *Manga*. It's evident in his work today that that's still the case. I wonder if he's fluent in Japanese by now.

I wonder if Whitt still hates French. I wonder if he knows Grant was his father, or that he has three more sisters and a brother besides

Niel and Ella. I wonder if he knows his mother was Gwen. I just wonder… about everything.

Shutting down my mind, I hand the comic over to Ade for safekeeping, eyes flicking to my daughter's artwork. Happy for the reprieve, I chuckle under my breath. Ella is her mother's daughter–not a lick of artistic talent. At least not with drawing or writing, but she's a genius in the kitchen and is nutty about bright colors. Biting back the laughter, it's even bad for her age group. Ella's written words are perfect, but the wording is clumsy and awkward. The princess is colored resembling a street-person. A laugh bubbles up my throat.

"Have you put any more thought into *Our Lady of Mercy*?" I shake my head no, heart beating in overdrive. Our Lady of Mercy is Hillbrook's elementary school, only tucked away in another building, sharing the same lot with the rectory little school and the cathedral junior/senior high. Niel's reaching the age where he'll be in the main cathedral. "Regina, you have to at least think about it. Ella isn't getting the education she needs."

I grip our company-logo mug harder. My blunt fingernails go to work etching off the paint. *Empowerment… powering your future.*

"I need to find a better vendor. This one is shoddy. Promoting our business with shit is a bad practice." I avoid Ade by changing the subject.

Ella's registered for third grade at the local, public elementary school. It's a fabulous school since we live in an affluent neighborhood bordering Dominion but close to Crestview. It's nothing like the scary environment I endured.

Ella won't be allowed to fall into the trap the rest of her family was ensnared in.

Entitlement.

We have an issue, though. Ella isn't flourishing. Her IQ was tested last week, resulting in a score of one hundred and seventy three. The faculty politely requested I move Ella to a school that would fit her needs.

Of course, Adelaide wants Ella to attend Hillbrook.

I work my nails until the mug screams out: *own your future*. I smile as I etch away more letters.

Men own your future. That sounds more like Hillbrook's slogan than Empowerment's.

"Regina, focus!" Ade snaps.

Head foggy from exhaustion, I blink at Ade a few times.

If I'm not working or mothering, I have the propensity to leave reality. I'll focus on the inane to occupy my mind.

Reality can suck it.

But since I'm always working, always mothering, always bombarded by reality, I space out often.

Having no shame, "What?" I growl at Ade, hating it when someone puts me on the spot. I'd stop these fucking visits if I could, but my daughter's welfare comes first, and she needs her aunt for access to an unlimited flow of information from Misery Castle.

"When was the last time you took a break?" Concern is thick in Ade's voice, already knowing the answer.

I didn't even take time off for Ella's birth. We were in the middle of launching Empowerment, so I gave birth, then convalesced with my laptop on my lap and Ella at my breast. I didn't allow Ella out of my orbit until her first day of kindergarten.

I eat for sustenance, and because every mother should sit down with their daughter and listen about her day while eating meals. I watch television and movies only because that's what a mother does with her daughter. I play games, mind running the statistics of the win and the strategies on how to make it happen, then I share those with Ella so she can beat Fate and Kris.

My parents were my world, so I mimic my childhood with taco Tuesdays, family game night Thursdays, pizza and movie Fridays, sleepovers on the living room floor Saturdays, and pajamas and TV show Sundays. We have a chore list with gold stars and a list of rewards. We do homework before dinner, and take a walk after we eat. Then after baths, we read bedtime stories and cuddle… then I go back to work.

I do all the things I should, but never anything for me.

Fun isn't in my vocabulary.

My eyes water, remembering the last time I put pleasure above work. It was at Grant's request, and it was our final moments together.

"Excuse me– I have an eyelash in my eye." I stride from the room, knowing Ade saw through my lie. I make it as far as the hallway to the bedrooms.

Leaning forward, I rest my forehead against the glass wall overlooking the backyard and guesthouse. I try to ignore my reflection and focus on Kristal sucking down a cigarette while Fate's thumbs tap away on her Blackberry. Kris sticks her tongue out and waves hello with her middle finger, passive-aggressively pissed yet teasing because I make her sit outside to smoke.

Rolling my leaking eyes, I twist around and slide down the glass until I'm sitting on my heels. Sometimes the backyard isn't big enough to distance me from my ladies.

Just as we were always on Grant slit-your-wrists duty, Ade, Fate, and Kris are on Postal Regina duty. There are always too many eyes assessing my emotional climate. It's a miracle if Ade goes home at the end of the night. Screaming would be an excellent release if I had the energy.

I close my eyes for just a moment and sigh. I simultaneously miss and loathe downtime. Downtime was what Grant needed constantly. Being at rest is a reminder of our epic loss.

"I put Ella to bed." Ade's voice breaks me from my meditation. "I need to talk to you about something, Regina. It's important– even if you don't realize it, something's got to give. You need to get a fucking life."

"Ade, really? I left the house–" Thinking that over, I straighten up with a groan. Darkness has fallen. How long have I been crouched by the window?

"It's been seventeen days since you left the house. I have no idea when you last brushed your hair. You only eat because we are, and I'm pretty sure the best sleep you've had this year was a few minutes ago while crouching in the hallway.

"Fine." Annoyed, like an addict, I'd do anything to get Ade to shut up so I can hide in my anti-reality and go back to work. "I'll enroll Ella into the fall semester at Hillbrook, and then every fucking Whittenhower on the planet will know how to get to my daughter."

"Reg," Ade sighs my name, crouching down to my level. Fingertips trail down my forearm, trying to wake me up while comforting me. "This isn't a war. My father isn't going to steal your daughter."

"Only because I've never taken a daughter from Daniel." My words lash out violently, hitting Ade in the face so hard she flinches. "A son for a son, ring a bell?"

"I can't– I just can't get into this circular argument with you for the billionth time. No one is harming Niel. He's taking his place in the Whittenhower family. If you'd ditch your pride and actually answer my father, you might be surprised. It feels like tug-of-war. Daniel Whittenhower with Niel versus Regina Regal with Ella.

"They're *my* children!" I shriek. "Leave. Please," I beg. "Every time you visit, you bring up shit I'm trying to pretend doesn't exist. I don't have the energy, time, or ability to find an outlet for the fury and frustration I feel right now."

Leaning back against the glass wall, I bang my head a few times, allowing the physical pain to clear the emotional and mental agony plaguing me.

"As for Ella, you've had her for the past nine years– no one could be a bigger influence in her life than you are. My niece should be at Hillbrook, Regina. Even you will admit it was the best education money could buy."

Snapping away, I growl my words. "Never fear, Ade. Both of my children will be properly indoctrinated into your culture of greed and indulgence." Underneath the rage, my voice holds a hopeless quality.

"This said by the richest woman in the state, and New York is a rich damn state." Ade rolls her eyes at me, like I'm being a ridiculous child who can't let anything go.

"I don't keep my money, Ade." I crawl to my feet, swaying a bit now that the anger is abating. "That's the difference– I give more money away each year than the Whittenhower's net worth."

"Rub it in a bit more," Ade teases me in a flirty voice. "But next time, I want you to say that to my father's face… while I watch."

"Knock it off." Mind spinning, I make a decision that will be in my daughter's best interests but not mine. "Fine. Hillbrook. Ella is what she is, whether she goes to private or public school, so it won't change her personality. However, it will change her intelligence level. I do agree with you, but I can't help but fear when Ella comes face-to-face with the rest of her family."

I'm being selfish– I know I am. Daniel stole my son, and then said I wasn't allowed to see his heirs until after they reached the age of majority. *My* son. Grant's sons. The vindictiveness of not allowing any of them to see Ella has been sickeningly satisfying, but it makes me a goddamn worthless person. Basically, I've been waiting until Ella could survive them– could stand with her head held high when they told her she was the product of billionaire's white trash mistress.

"We'll cross that bridge when we come to it." Ade pulls my hand, dragging me to my bedroom. Her bony hand is surprisingly strong, as is her willowy frame, but neither is as strong as her personality. In my emotionally weakened state, Ade sneaks in and takes advantage.

Chapter Two

Riding the sleep-deprivation high, I shuffle down the hallway to my bedroom with Ade spotting me so I don't fall on my face. Utilitarian, my space is everything I could possibly need, and absolutely nothing more. I don't believe in indulgence, but quality is priority. Pale lavender walls, bordered by smoky gray wainscoting, showcase the floor-to-ceiling French doors that lead out to the backyard patio. The floors are white-washed hardwood, as are all of the furnishings.

With lust, I gaze longingly at my plush bedding. We haven't been acquainted in several days. The last sleep I had was almost an entire day ago, and not in my bed. My body had demanded my brain to shut down, and I woke with a keyboard impression inlaid on my cheek.

"We need to talk, Reg." Ade forcefully shoves me onto the bed, and I groan with pleasure when I land. My eyes instantly flutter shut. Bed equals sleepy time– blissful reprieve from reality and anti-reality, since I refuse to sleep until my brain completely shuts down.

"Obviously not tonight, I see," Ade murmurs wryly, gazing down at me with a smirk on her lips. "You need a break, and I need help, so it's a mutually beneficial proposition."

"Hmm?" I murmur, snuggling in deeper. "What more could you possibly need from me? Another heir? A kidney? My beating heart torn directly from my chest?"

"Ah, I'm not a fan of *this* Regina. So melodramatic." Ade huffs a couple of breaths, annoyed with me. "Tomorrow afternoon, you and I have a date to talk. And don't pull any '*I have to work*' bullshit. I'm starting to think you're coding nukes in your spare time."

"Maybe I am." Eyelids slowly opening, I peer out of slits at Adelaide. "Maybe I have a missile positioned to strike Misery Castle when my son is at school."

"Don't go there– you can be such a cunt."

"This cunt has to work tomorrow when you show up, just so ya know," I mutter, enraged but too exhausted to show it.

"Don't act offended when you're just asking for me to beat the shit out of you." Ade's bony ass settles on the bed next to me, real concern infusing her tone. "The girls said you complete projects faster than you get clients, and now you're doing their jobs. The books, Reg? Really? Fate is your financial adviser, and you're not letting her advise you, and Kris is your accountant who isn't allowed to touch the books. They're bored. A bored Kristal and Fate equates trouble. You have to knock that shit off and get a life of your own. Leave the house at least twice a week, not bimonthly."

"Yes, Mommy– but it's more like biweekly." I tease, rolling around my bedding while moaning. "It's like a fucking cloud… and to think, I slept on a couch until ten years ago."

Dreamy smile tugging at my lips, I taunt Ade. How can Ade bitch at me when I throw the disadvantages I lived through back into her face. Two can play emotional warfare.

"Marshmallows and unicorns." I feel like an addict who just got a hit after weeks of withdrawal. I've lived on caffeine and no sleep for the past month. Yeah, I need a damn break.

"You're incorrigible," Ade says in an irritated voice, but her face shows how amusing she finds me. I stretch, flexing my arms over my head, tank top riding high on my belly. Ade closes her eyes, turning away.

I sigh– shit.

"Sorry," I mumble underneath my breath. Crawling under the cloud, I issue a silent thanks that I'm wearing yoga capris and a tank– no need for jammies. I should bathe, but sleep is more enticing.

Closing my eyes, I even my breathing, preparing to sleep like the dead for a few stolen hours. Butterfly wings flutter at my lips, and I open to Ade.

My fault– I treat Ade like shit and she puts up with me when she shouldn't. Knowing how she lusts after me, I used my stretching, and moaning and groaning as a way to punish her.

Allowing Ade to kiss me softly, a moan flows from my mouth to hers when the tip of her tongue seeks mine out. The kiss is warm, pleasant, and connecting, but not overtly sexual. At least it isn't for me anyway. It's pleasurable, and I'll take comfort wherever I can get it.

Adelaide wants more than I can give, so I won't allow it to go any farther than a kiss. I'm sure I would enjoy it, but her feelings don't mesh with mine.

Sharp teeth nip my bottom lip, and my legs scissor underneath the sheets. Ade takes my enthusiasm as invitation. Her fragile hand envelops my breast through the thin barrier of my tank. We both whimper when her palm rubs a slow circle against my eager nipple. My sex pulses, and then dampens my panties. It's closing in on a decade since a hand besides my own touched my breast. Other than a few stolen kisses with Ade, I've been celibate.

Making out with Ade is a mistake, especially since I'm only doing it to feel closer to her brother– I sicken myself.

Turning my face away, I reject Ade. I want to cry for so many reasons. It would be possible for me to make love to Ade, because it would feel really good and I love her. But I don't want Ade the way she needs. I'm not attracted to her. I don't even see her as a sexual being. In my heart, Adelaide is my sister because she's my best friend, and my sister-in-law because I loved Grant and we had two children together.

This is so wrong– destructive. It makes me feel alive for a few stolen moments, but I can't be destructive with Adelaide, not when she's my rock.

Just because it feels good, doesn't make it right.

Turning my back to her, "I'm sorry," I whisper into my pillow.

"You would like it," she purrs directly into my ear, lust tainting her voice where affection should be. Her hand caresses a path under the blanket and settles over my mound. "It feels the same whether it's a man or a woman," she lures me in. "Trust me when I say that a woman knows how to touch better than a man does."

There is no way on Earth Ade would know how to touch me better than Grant did– that man knew how to pleasure every cell in my body.

Mind reeling, I ignore the sensation of her palm rhythmically circling my crotch. My cotton pants are a thin barrier that offers no protection. "Ade," I protest to make her stop.

How do I tell Adelaide that she liked a woman's touch better because she likes women, not because they're better at it? Grant may have taught me about passion, but connection makes everything… more.

"You need this, Regina." Ade's voice rolls throaty yet deep. "It's been years– just relax and let me ease you."

My eyes flick open to find Ade's hand lax at her throat, with a fingertip dipping beneath the collar of her blouse. The fingertip wiggles, caressing her own nipple. Reality crashes. Sickened, I close my eye to the sight of my best friend pleasuring herself because she's getting off on touching me.

"No, Ade." Weak from mental, emotional, and physical exhaustion, I try to push her hand away. "Stop– we can't do this. I don't want to do this with you." I close my legs and roll over onto my side away from her.

Flinching as if I struck her across the face, my statement hits Ade. Hard.

"If one of the other girls offered, you'd take them up on it. I know you would." Insulted. Entitled. Ade straightens, adjusting her blouse. "Why not me?"

"You can't know that. I don't even know that," I stress, disgusted. "And they would *never* offer. Kristal fucks men like they're going extinct, and Fate is– well, Fate is just Fate."

"Trust me when I say that Fate enjoys the company of a female," Ade viciously slaps me with the truth. Haughty arrogance floods her voice, and it helps clear the lust fog from my mind.

I roll my eyes dramatically, sitting up in bed. "So you're going to act like a pissed off husband when his wife won't perform her duty?" I pull the blankets to my neck– no need to give her any more ideas. "I don't owe you anything, Adelaide."

Eyes gone glacial, Ade glares at me. "My first time was with Fate, Regina," she twists my name nastily, and I gasp in shock at her revelation. Ade and Fate couldn't be in the same classroom during high school, so how the hell did they manage to hook up?

"It was the night after Grant passed away. We were just settling in at the apartment I rented, and you were inconsolable. There was nothing we could do to help, and it made us feel powerless. So we gave up, leaving you in the empty bedroom while you screamed and broke everything you could get your hands on. Then we consoled each other."

Ade's words hit me with the force of a runaway train. To throw one of the worst nights of my life in my face. Turning, I scream all of my frustration, agony, and fury into the mattress.

Ade's trying to punish me by telling me this– reminding me of the animal I turned into that night. She's pissed that I wouldn't have sex with her, and now she's admonishing me by forcing me to see that I don't know either of my best friends. It's a classic abuser maneuver– cull the victim from the herd, then make them think they're lost and alone and only you can help them.

Next, Ade will probably tell me Kristal is really a man.

"Just go, Adelaide." I mutter hollowly, exhausted in all the ways that count and then some. "I know you're telling the truth. But if you didn't think to tell me in almost a decade, then why tonight of all nights? To punish me, I assume."

"Why not me?" She repeats.

The real answer: yes, I find Kristal and Fate attractive in a way that would make it possible to touch them intimately. I could see why men would find them irresistible. Would I do it? No. Never. Ade and I are like true sisters– the thought curdles my stomach.

A kiss is just a kiss, everything else is a no.

"Truth. You're a beautiful woman who needs a woman who appreciates you as you are. You're a lesbian and I'm straight, no matter how much you may lust after me."

"Rub it in, why don't ya?"

"I love you, Ade." I roll to face her, but she won't look at me. "I truly do. You're my best friend– you're my sister in my soul. It was irrevocable when Grant and I came together. You're the aunt of my children, the sister of the man I loved. That is why it can never happen between us."

"Then why do you kiss me?" Ade glares accusingly at me, like I'm stringing her along, and maybe I am.

"I apologize, Ade." I close my eyes and try to put my thoughts and emotions into words. "I kiss you because it feels nice and comforting, but mostly because I want you to be happy. When you come onto me, I allow it. But doing so is wrong, because I'm just leading you on."

"Reg–"

"You have Ezra now, and I know things are different in our society when it comes to the rules of affluent marriages. You need to find a real lover who suits your needs." I'm not the sort who offers flowery truths. I always go for brutal honesty– the truth that hurts the most.

Ade covers her face with her hands, and I watch as her small chest moves up and down as she heaves in heavy breaths. I worry that she may be crying, but suddenly she huffs an impatient noise and glares at me.

"You need to live by your own goddamn advice, girlfriend," Ade snarls into my face. "Is there a man tucked under your bed?"

In a dramatic fit, she pulls the dust ruffle up and calls, "Yoo-hoo, anybody under there? Get your horse-cock up here."

"What the fuck are you doing?" Scrambling across the bed, I yank Ade upright.

"Hmm… no one's under the bed, just like I thought." Ade goes on the defensive since she didn't get what she wanted. Same Ade, different day. "Your snatch probably has cobwebs inside it."

"Well, fuck you, too, Adelaide!" I kneel on my bed and seethe. I used to be patient. The keywords are– used to.

"Yeah, see… right there's the problem. No need to lie– I want to fuck the hell out of you. Here–" Ade picks up a book off my nightstand, then tosses it on the bed, almost hitting me with it. "This one's the newest release, isn't it? Are you going to read it while you finger your underused pussy? It's what you always do. The girls and I joke about it, about how the only time you masturbate is to these fucking books."

Ade reaches for the hardcover novel, but I snatch it away and clutch it to my chest.

"I know what they're about, Regina," Ade mutters in a snide, judgmental tone. "You're a naughty girl, aren't you? Is that why you don't want me, because I'm not like that? Was my brother as sick and twisted as you?"

"Stop!" I bellow the instant Ade brings Grant into this. "Get out!"

Face crestfallen, as if Ade realizes how many lines she's crossed, her voice is beyond remorseful yet sad. "I would do that stuff for you, but you won't let me– I would do *anything* for you."

"Yeah, you sound real convincing. '*Regina, I love you so much that I want to make love to you.*'" I mimic Ade's haughty voice. "But what you're really saying is, '*I want to own you, Regina, and I want to fuck you even though I know you don't want it.*'"

Exasperated, "That's not–"

"Then in the next breath, you say my crotch has bats flying out of it, and that I'm a fucking freak for reading these books. Make up your goddamn, cunt-licking mind, bitch. Then get out of my house. I've had it."

"Regina!"

"I just need two fucking minutes to myself. If I find those minutes with this book, then you should be happy for me." I stand on my bed, towering over Ade's willowy frame, screaming my grievances. "It's my life, and I make the cock-sucking rules!"

"I'm sorry," Ade murmurs meekly, cowering.

"No, you're not," I mutter snidely. "Let's be completely honest here. You wanted something, and when I said no, you threw yourself. This is what I don't want my children to turn into. I have every right to deny you something when it's mine to begin with. You all turn into entitled assholes. Not only did you throw a fit because I said no, you tried to punish me as well. Get this through your thick head– no one owns me. Never again will I bow down. Do you understand me?"

Ade smiles at me brightly– her *real* smile. With her blue eyes glittering with pleasure and happiness in my direction, I flash Ade an unfathomable look.

"Why are you suddenly so happy?" I mutter with suspicion, then I remind her. "We're fighting."

Still way too pleased with herself, "You'll thank me later. I'll be here for lunch, and then we will talk."

"Nuh-uh," I mutter indignantly "No more talking. You've keyed me up to the point I'll never get any fucking sleep. Get out!"

"I'll see you tomorrow, Reg. G'night." Ade disappears through the French doors before I can respond. I watch as she traipses across the backyard and enters the guesthouse. Doesn't she ever go home? Fuck, I'd rather be at Misery Castle with my son than stuck here with meddlesome Adelaide.

Multiple lights pop on in the guest house– Oh, Ade has to gossip with the girls first.

I lie in bed, a stew of frustration and anger. I'm beyond the need to sleep, to the point it's affecting my health and sanity. But Ade amped me up, and now it'll be impossible. At the same time, I'm too exhausted to make my way down the hallway to my office, and there is no way I could function enough to work.

The heavy weight of the hardcover beckons me from its resting place on the mattress by my knee. I haven't started this book yet, because I was saving it to savor. My fingers curl covetously around the leather cover.

Shortly after Empowerment was up and running, I obtained my first client– James Atwater, an up and coming author. But I'd rather call Atwater an artist. I formatted his webpage and developed a writing program that suited his needs, and I received copies of his backlist as a thank you gift.

At first, I was thrown off by the dark leather covers, because they reminded me of the upholstery in Daniel's study. Cordovan–

the color of drying blood. Curiosity overcame my aversion. The covers were embossed with a number– No title. No author name.

From the first page, I was ensnared. I couldn't put them down, because it was like the novels were speaking to me. The books became my guilty pleasure, my escape from the world at large. For a few stolen moments, I entered a universe of the author's creation and left my misery behind. The scandalizing content shocked me to my core. I realized it had mimicked parts of the life Grant and I had led, parts I wasn't sure happened behind other's closed bedroom doors. It was a comfort to know I wasn't alone in my fantasies. The books were raw and twisted, and it was exactly what I needed to cope with my life.

Now I receive an advanced-reader-copy every six months or so. Twice a year, I come alive. I never reread the books, fearing I would start them and never reemerge.

Feeling emotions I've long buried, my fingertip caresses the XII. Closing my eyes, I allow my fingers the pleasure of cracking the book open for the very first time.

Without looking, I know what the first few pages say. Expensive, silky paper announces *James Atwater* in a modest font. There is never a title page, or publisher information, or even a list of past works. James Atwater is on page one, and what is on page two always steals my breath away every single time.

With my eyes still shut, my fingertip slides over the *MISTRESS* as a blind-man would with braille. The words are stamped into the paper, not inked. With barely any concentration, I feel the words resonate inside my soul, rather than see them.

My eyes snap open to put myself out of my misery. I can't wait a moment longer. I must transport into the private, hedonistic world of James Atwater's creation.

As with every time I read these books, a flash of memory pulls me under. A vision, or rather, a premonition. Grant gliding smoothly into me, his face lined with sadness. He speaks words of finding me someone to fulfill all of my needs, never believing my protests. My soul screams from its depths how Grant is everything I'd ever need. Everything. Never trusting in me, never having faith in my love for him, the vision warps until a large male is rutting relentlessly on top of me. All I can see is his closely cropped, dark hair.

All I feel is complete and utter apathy. Desperation. Desolation. Destruction.

The reason this comes to me again when I read the books, is because the male in this series always depicts that same man I created from the ether in my vision. A strong man whose nature is dominance and control. A man I aspire to become, not caring that I'm female.

I need to be him, not be *with* him.

Less than a chapter into this masterpiece, my body is on fire– a fire I must squelch. A fire built on the dominance of the main character, not forged through desire but envy. I allow the book to rest open on my breasts. My fingertips flutter down my skin and beneath my pants, wiggling into my panties until they gain access to my flushed core.

I smirk when my fingers impale my swollen flesh. Sorry, Ade– I'm definitely cobweb-free.

It takes all of my concentration to ignore Pandora's Box rattling its chains. I only masturbate while I read these books because the story is strong enough to contain my subconscious. Tonight, my resolve is thin, and visions of pale hair, crystalline blue eyes, and a dimpled smile invade my thoughts.

I press harder to block the image before the sob building releases. I need to have an orgasm– a type of catharses way different than the emotional release through tears.

It's been almost seven months since I've had the solace of pleasure, with no other stress-relievers in my personal arsenal. I pull the apathetic vision I created so long ago, and concentrate on that to suppress Grant from my mind.

Grant equals soft affection, playful seduction, intense longing… unconditional love. None of which I've felt since him.

Apathy would mean not feeling anything, while having the ability to breathe deeply, without fear of my emotions going rampant… to feel alive instead of suppressed, because who I was meant to become died with Grant.

The air fills with the sound of my rough panting, in time with the violent thrusts of the male I conjured in my mind, when in reality it's three of my own fingers brutally jamming into my own cunt. With a guttural shout, I climax, shuddering every few seconds as I flow back into reality.

My breath eases into its natural rhythm as the guilt, shame, and loneliness fills my soul. It's never the same– the release. It doesn't feel as it did with Grant. When I lost my virginity, I told Grant I didn't see what the big deal was about sex. He reassured me it was about connection, and that's why it felt incredible between us. I'm not sure I believed him in the moment, but I do now.

An orgasm brought by my own hand is an empty release. Its pleasure is minimal, the effects are muted, and it never satisfies.

"Feeling better?" a smoky voice purrs from the darkness. I flinch, causing my finger to flex in me, and I whimper at the sensation.

That felt better than my release– not good.

"Shit!" I hiss, scrambling to tear my fingers from my body and to cover myself. "Um… actually, I don't really feel any better." I answer Kristal's question. "Thanks for asking, though," I mutter sarcastically. "I'm seriously going to move to Timbuktu just so I can have two fucking minutes to myself. What could you possibly want, Kris?"

"We need to talk." Impatient, Kristal's tone of voice scares the shit out of me. "And it has to be now."

Chapter Three

Kristal flicks on my nightstand lamp, flooding the room with a soft glow that highlights the flush riding my cheeks and chest. Not shaming me in any way, she settles next to me on the bed with her back propped up on the headboard. She takes number XII from my chest and leafs through it.

"I've been reading James Atwater's books as they're released, but I didn't think this one was out for a couple more months." She quirks a perfect eyebrow at me, and even though it wasn't meant as anything but curiosity, it comes off as seductive.

Speechless, my possessive streak erupts. With a gentle tug, I take the book from Kris, when what I really want to do is yank it free and smack her with the leather-bound tome. *My* book. *Mine.* I don't have many things to my name that solely belong to me, but this book is one of them.

After thirteen years by my side, Kris sees right through me. "In my wildest imaginations, I didn't think you'd be into BDSM." Her ruby-red lips slide into a smirk, looking at me as if she's never seen me before this moment. "But now that I see it, it makes total sense. I bet you don't read anyone but Atwater, do you?" That smirk gets so wide it reaches her ears. Crimson-painted fingertip tapping *my* book, "I bet these are your siren call."

Cunt.

"I don't have time to read for pleasure– I don't have time for pleasure. Period." I mutter, emotions spinning like they used to do when I was pregnant. Since Ella's birth, I can't remember what it was like to be not furious. Primal. "Why are you here? Do you just want to make fun of me?" I grumble and pull myself up next to her. I would have liked to lay in my post-coital tristesse for a few moments without being intruded upon.

"Which do you identify with, Regina?" Her eyes are heated with interest. "I'm curious."

"That's private," I whine. "Don't go there."

"Oh, there's no need to answer that one, because I already know the answer. How deep is your interest?"

"It's private," I mutter defensively– I haven't talked about myself since Grant. Ella is priority number-one, and Empowerment is a close second, with Adelaide, Fate, and Kristal coming before me. "Drop the subject."

"Fair enough." She flashes me a reassuring, understanding smile. "You know, we do care about you, Regina. But fuck if you'll let any of us in. Our friendships are one-sided."

How do you explain to someone who has lived with you for nearly a decade that you can't trust them? Never will trust them. But there is a desire deep inside that demands you take care of them. When I give my emotions freely, I'm setting myself up to be let down. If I give nothing of me, I won't miss anything when they are gone. I'll just replace them with another project.

My mother's words forever haunt me.

"Life is too short. You don't want to be on your deathbed and realize all you've accomplished in life is a series of goals that are meaningless. Goals do not keep you warm at night– they don't hug you, or kiss you, or hold you when you need to cry."

"Kisses won't put food in my belly," I mutter underneath my breath. "Hugs won't put a roof over my head."

Now I have enough money to live off of for lifetimes and lifetimes, but goals keep the demons at bay. Hugs are suffocating when ghosts haunt your every thought.

Smirking at me, Kristal's hazel eyes glitter with mischievousness. I begin to worry, because Kris in this kind of mood is dangerous. Empowerment's resident accountant doesn't look the part. Her glossy, thick chestnut waves are asymmetrically cut, and are now the shade of fresh spilled blood. Her newest tattoo is peeping at me from beneath the sleeve of her black t-shirt. Its eyes seem to follow me. I have no idea what scary creature hides beneath the fabric.

"I need to tell you something." Kristal's sultry voice turns pensive. "Ade's going to make a request of you tomorrow. At first, I didn't think you could do it, but I've changed my mind. You'll be perfect for it. She already has Fate on board, and she enlisted me a few months ago."

"What the hell are you talking about?" My voice is loaded with hostility. I don't like knowing that the women closest to me have been shutting my ass out. Yes, I don't let them into my head, but they aren't allowed to shut me out of theirs. It stings because they've been keeping secrets, which only affirms how I can't trust a single person on this planet.

"You know how Ade is with Ezra– territorial doesn't even cover it. Ezra's into something that's off the grid. She chose me because I'm the obvious choice, but it hasn't worked."

"Quit the pretense and just say it," I grumble, impatient as always.

"Ezra's heavy into the BDSM scene. I thought I'd explain what it meant, but seeing that you're on number XII, I don't think an explanation is necessary. Knowing you, you probably know more than I do."

"Undoubtedly," I murmur, but not as an insult. If anything piques my interests, I learn every single detail I can find. BDSM was no exception.

"Have you heard about that hot nightclub downtown? Restraint?"

"Nope," I pop the P. "See, you know more than me on this subject. You know I never leave this house. I don't even venture to the grocery store."

Chuckling seductively yet wryly, "Restraint is Ezra's creation. Surprising, isn't it? That stuffy weirdo is into BDSM. Who'd a thunk it." Kris pulls an accent out of nowhere, when she speaks elite better than I do. "I went to Restraint on opening night– talk about a siren call." A husky, self-deprecating laugh flows around the room. "Three months ago, I started working as their bartender at Ade's request. She wanted me to have closer access, because she wants to know if Ezra is ever with a woman."

My snort is loud and ricochets. "Ezra's gay. Is Ade fucking insane? Unless Cortez has a pussy."

"It's Ade... so yes, she is in fact insane." Kristal's throaty laugh heats my skin. "Cort most definitely has a fucking *cock*," she stresses, flushing. "A big one."

Shuddering, "Gross," spills between my lips, but I'm shuddering for an entirely different reason. I miss cock, almost as much as I miss Grant. The first guy to offer, I'd probably be unable to say no.

"You know how certain rules don't apply in here–" Kris taps her crimson-lacquered nail on the leather cover of XII. "Just because Ezra's gay, doesn't mean he won't do a woman while riding the high of dominance.

"Yeah..." voice thick, I imagine the man in my nightmares. Only I'm him– the dominant one –and I'm riding the high. No longer apathetic, but alive.

Alive.

"Ade's plan isn't working. No one trusts me since I'm a sub— we're just there, like furniture, until we're wanted. But they don't want to play with me, either. It seems I'm not compliant enough."

"Who'd a thunk *that*?" Unable to stop myself, I laugh so hard I know I'm insulting Kristal.

"Ha-ha, pain in the cunt," Kris snarls. "Ade and her dumbass plan. She wanted Fate to act as a dominant with you as her submissive."

Kris and I share a huge laugh over *that*.

"That was fucking stupid. Does my best friend not understand me at all?"

"No shit— you're about as subservient as a queen, and Fate is about as dominant as newborn puppy. But she's an excellent actress, so as long as nothing is scary, she'll see it as a thrill. Girlfriend has an adrenaline problem."

"Who else is at Restraint? You said *they* don't want to play with you."

"Ezra and Cortez— there's a guy there named Dexter."

Dexter's name goes through me like a lightning strike, because I have no doubt he's one and the same with Dexter Hayes. Ezra is his cousin's adoptive son— family. "Dexter," I murmur breathlessly. "I've never met him, but he was Grant's best friend."

Even though Rebekah Zeitler's grandsons paid for my Hillbrook tuition after she died, and then Marcus Zeitler paid for my college education, I've never met either. I've repaid by donating ten times the amount to Marcus Zeitler's campaign fund via Empowerment.

I will owe no one, because to owe is to be owned.

The cousins were Grant's best friends since birth. Grant would visit with them daily, talk on the phone with them a few times a day, but I never met them— not once. They wanted nothing to do with me, and I never heard from them after Grant's death.

Curiosity and fury make me want to walk into Restraint and head-butt that carnival of a nightmare velvet whorehouse motherfucker.

No longer caring what Adelaide's plan is, I want to do it just so I can look Dexter in the eye and see if he recognizes me.

"Dexter's part owner of Restraint," Kris continues to talk, not realizing fury is buzzing through my system. "He's the only one who keeps his identity. I know Ezra is there, but he goes by the name the *Boss*."

"And wherever Ezra Zeitler is…" I murmur. "Cortez Hunter is never far behind."

"Abernathy," Kris reminds me. "Cort's Cortez Abernathy now, using his pen name everywhere he goes."

"Legally?"

"Don't know– doubt it. Anyway, Ezra and Cortez keep us guessing. I never know which is which. I only know it's them because of Ade siccing me on them. Otherwise, they're completely anonymous. They walk around in a hood– sometimes we have two hoods. It's confusing as hell, and they get a kick out of making us guess when we need to talk to the Boss. When you go to their office, it's always a surprise with which one you'll get. Last night, they both were in the office, and they used the same damn voice– bastards. I didn't know which the Boss was. All I wanted to do was add some new brands to our liquor inventory. They made me beg for it." She gives a sultry growl.

I try to wrap my mind around the kids I met back at Hillbrook running a BDSM night club. Then again, no one knew the fun and games Grant and I liked to engage in.

"Why is Ade worried? Ezra's keeping it anonymous, so it doesn't affect her. I thought– I thought that was the type of marriage she was expecting?"

"When Ade came to me awhile back, she knew I'd enjoy Restraint and she was curious. But something has her scared, and she won't tell me what. Make her tell you before you agree to anything, because I don't want you getting into a situation you can't get out of, and I don't want you regretting anything."

"Regret what?" I challenge, knowing she means this widow routine I've been living. Kris is worried I'll break if I get fucked– in all ways.

Kris gazes directly into my eyes, not taking my shit, which is probably why those dominant men don't want to play with a woman they'll have to prove themselves to first.

"I told Ade how the masters interact with one another on a different level than the rest of us. We're just chattel to them. They don't treat us badly, but they sure as fuck don't respect us."

There's a growl not-so hidden in my voice. "Won't they recognize Fate? I don't want you to be treated disrespectfully, but we both know Fate can't take one negative comment."

"Oh, no doubt Cort will recognize Fate." Kris cackles, the sound evil as it runs up and down my spine. "That's the beauty of the plan. Cortez wouldn't suspect a thing."

"Why?"

Leaning close, Kris whispers conspiratorially. "Um– no one knows this but me, so don't get pissed at the messenger. You know how everyone always assumed that Fate and Faith won't talk because of their family issues. That's not it. Bi, or whatever the fuck Cortez is sexually, Faith was dating Cortez Abernathy throughout Hillbrook. Faith came home from school to catch Fate screwing Cortez on the living room sofa... Faith wanted nothing to do with her *faithless* sister, and disappeared. So, yeah, Cortez knows Fate intimately."

I draw into myself. I know nothing of my friends– the women I chose to spend my life with, to raise my daughter with, and to partner in business. I feel sucker-punched.

"They'll recognize me. I can't risk it. Ella's too important." I'd met both Ezra and Cortez briefly at Hillbrook more than a decade ago, then again at Faith's sweet sixteen birthday party. It was forever ago, and no doubt I've aged enough to where I don't look the same, but the risk is too great. I've avoided all charity events, social engagements, and press releases since I left the Whittenhowers. I couldn't chance my name and face getting out into the public eye and having someone put the pieces together. One look at Niel and me side-by-side, and everyone would know I was his mother. That would be enough fuel for Daniel to take Ella away from me.

A son for a son. A daughter for a scandal.

I'm just a whore– Grant's mistress –and nothing more. I may have more money than the Whittenhowers, but they have political ties and judges in their pockets. They would thrash me morally, and I'd lose my daughter. Ella is my last tie to Grant– the only person keeping me sane.

Completely ignorant to my mental battle, Kris keeps talking as if it's a done deal. "Use an alias. The BDSM community thrives on anonymity. No way would they remember you," she says dismissively.

"Thanks a lot, Kris," I growl, insulted yet knowing it's the truth. I own a mirror. "Why are you playing the submissive? I don't see it." I change the subject. I hate how I don't know my best friends like I thought I did. I thought we shared no secrets and we had each other's backs. I was wrong– so much for trust.

"I'll acquiesce to whoever can make me," Kris says with a challenge lacing her voice. "I make 'em work for it. A lazy dominant doesn't think they need to earn my respect, so they don't get mine. I don't know how the Boss and company treat their subs since they won't play with me, but the club trains dominants to be Masters of Restraint. I'm playing with one right now, and he's so fucking strong it baffles my mind. We haven't had sex yet, because his trainer won't let him."

"Who?" I ask purely out of curiosity, because the awed tone in Kristal's voice piqued my interests.

"No– you'll fuck me up," Kris grits out, sounding genuinely afraid. "I'm positive you'd beat me to death. So it'll be my little secret."

"Secrets, such a foreign concept between us," I mutter sarcastically.

"Ha-ha, bitch. You're stronger than they are, Regina. I mean it– I'm not just blowing smoke up your ass. You need something in your life that is just about finding who you are, and I think you should enter to train."

Voice breathy and thready, because in my heart of hearts, I know I've been a walking corpse. "Why?"

"You need it, that's why. Plus, you'll be in for a huge, pleasant surprise– a surprise that will change your world." She changes the subject– bitch. "By the way, I think Ade has a girlfriend, but she won't say who."

"Who?" I ask again, not so easily deterred.

"I just said I didn't know," she mutters in annoyance.

"I'm not talking of Ade. Who are you stalking?" I worry for the guy– Kristal eats men alive. "Who's my surprise?"

"Wow, look how late it is…" Kris pulls her cellphone from her pocket, then yawns exaggeratedly. "I better get some sleep. I have to be fresh in the morning. My boss is a real task-master. Don't wanna disappoint her."

"Who?" Something is screaming inside me. A long buried instinct trying to rise– I *need* to know who Kris has been playing BDSM with.

"G'night, Boss Lady. I'll start the McAlester account promptly at nine a.m." Kris effectively cuts off our conversation, and I'm tempted to make her answer. She smirks at me saucily, knowing where my thoughts are leading me.

"Kris," I seethe out between clenched teeth.

"Oh, girlfriend, I know exactly what you need. Just say yes to Ade, and you may get what you've always been looking for– what you've lost and need so badly to find."

Yet again, Kris makes me feel like a child. She has a way about her that makes me feel *less*. Kris is three years younger than me, yet she seems worldlier. There will always be a part of me that holds onto my jaded innocence.

"What have I lost?"

"*You*," Kris stresses, looking at me with kindness and pity. "You, Regina. You're the most independent person I've ever met. You don't need a man, yet you lost all of your softness when you lost Grant. But Ade and Fate swear you were a compassionate person way before you met him. You don't need a mate– you just need to find yourself."

Too close to home, I don't comment on any of it.

"Make sure my secretive best friend attends the press release for Transcend in the morning. She needs to present them with the donation on camera for the press. As always, make sure she knows that I don't exist. No mention of me on camera. And please let her know that I love how she fucked Ade and, apparently, Cortez. She's such a *good* sister. We're so close," I say with sarcastic venom.

The potent look Kristal flashes me speaks volumes. She knew of the Ade/Fate tryst, too. I shake my head sadly and leave her sitting on my bed.

Fucking lying by omission bitches.

It's enough that I want to grab my daughter and run away, but I can't leave Niel and Whitt behind. Grant would think less of me if I didn't take care of all of his children, and I can't leave his sister and Whitt's oldest sister behind.

Ruthless in my grief, Kris better not piss me off anymore, because she has no ties that bind.

Furious yet confused, I scrub their treachery from my skin with scalding hot water from my state-of-the-art shower system. It was essential, not one part of its quality workmanship is indulgent. Nope, honest– it's not an indulgence. It keeps me sane and very, very clean as it washes my tears down the drain.

I spend the rest of my night, and early morning, gazing down at the towhead peeking out the top of her Strawberry Shortcake blankie. I bought it for Ella on her last birthday, because it reminded me of her sweet scent. When I was a girl, Dad loved shoving Strawberry Shortcake up to my nose while telling me to take a big sniff. That delicately sweet scent wafted up my nostrils, and that is the exact scent of my Ella.

Ella reminds me of all those I've lost. My mom's name was Ella. Ella looks like Grant, but her scent reminds me of playful memories with my dad. Bittersweet.

As she sleeps soundly, without a care in the world, my fingertips rake through her fine, white strands. They hold a slight curl– my only contribution to her makeup. I'm thankful that she got my dad's curls instead of my wiry mass. I don't know where my hair came from, but I'm glad my beautiful son received it rather than my daughter. A man can pull it off– I'm living proof that a female cannot.

Spending hours a night watching my daughter breathe, I remember the final moments I had with Grant, where he told me he wanted a daughter named Ella, and how he couldn't wait until we had fights over our next born son. Curtis versus Jackson.

Every night, I cry while watching my daughter sleep, because there will never be a Curtis Whittenhower, or another Jackson Whittenhower to walk this earth… not when there is no Grant.

Thoughts shifting, I wonder who Ella will become now that there are no outside forces pushing her in a direction that isn't fluid and natural. Ella will be her own person, shaped by no hand other than her own.

Will Ella be like me, tall and masculine with huge breasts, or will she be waifish like her Auntie Adelaide? Not caring either way, I can definitely wait to find out. I want to keep Ella small and safe, where she has a stress-free childhood. At some point in Ella's future, our lives may collapse. The shifts are inescapable. I wait with bated breath, because the longer the wait, the better it is for my precious miracle.

Breath hitching, Ella's fingertips grip the blankie, and then relax, as she dreams little girl dreams. Her hands are her father's– tapered, elegant fingers and smooth palms. Seeing them is the very definition of bittersweet.

Leaving my post after another night flew by without a wink of sleep, I make our breakfast to begin our day.

Keep putting one foot in front of the other. The dawn never fails to arrive, no matter how dead I may feel inside.

Chapter Four

As I'm crafting the third pot of coffee of the day, I allow the grinder to cover Ade's entrance. I'm pissed at her, and I don't want this conversation to happen. When I'm angry at Ade, I see how one-sided our friendship truly is, and then my fury turns into remorse. She has done so much for me. My children are safe because of her. She's one of three who held me up when my world shattered at my feet. My view of her doesn't change. But, dammit, I'm allowed to be angry at Ade once in a while. I shouldn't have to take all of her shit as repayment for taking care of her brother's grieving mistress and their fatherless daughter.

I grind the coffee longer than necessary in avoidance. The brew will be thick and strong– perfection for the caffeine addict in me. Never sleeping, I have so much caffeine flowing in my veins, it's like I'm tapped into an IV drip.

"It's finished, Regina." Ade yells impatiently from her seat at the granite kitchen island. "I know you know I'm waiting."

I keep grinding– childish, but what the fuck ever. Ade was mean to me last night.

Shouting loudly, "You can't keep up this pace," Ade mothers me, and that's why I'm avoiding her. She's right, and I don't want to accept it.

A smirk pulls at my lips when I stop pressing the button, because Ade continues to yell into the sudden silence for a few seconds. "You're dead on your feet today. If you have a heart attack at age thirty, who do you think will get Ella? Granted, she will be with Whitt and Niel, but she will be surrounded by all three *Daniels*." She stresses the Daniels part.

Right on the spot, I vow to cut back on my caffeine intake. Daniel will have no access to my daughter, because he wouldn't allow her to grow on her own, to flourish into who she was meant to become. Ella may look like a Whittenhower, but she's more Regal.

I dump half of the grinds in the basket, omitting some to deaden the kick the coffee would provide. I gaze longingly at the remainder. *I bet you'd feel good roaring through my veins.* I throw it away, then hit the start button with regret but resolve.

Busying myself, I'm not ready for the difficult conversation to come. I've narrowed down my life to only include the girls in this household. I speak to my clients over the phone, over the internet, and via Skype.

I never leave the house, never dealing with people face-to-face, and I've lost my patience for small talk and bullshit.

I pull the sandwiches I made earlier from the refrigerator: pitas filled with chunked chicken breast mixed with plain yogurt, pecans, and halved grapes. I place a plate in front of Ade, pasting a huge, bright smile on my face.

See, I'm a healthy girl– no worries.

After pouring iced tea into our tumblers, I take my seat next to Ade. "How's your work at the museum fairing?" Ironically, I decide on pleasant small talk. I'll avoid her imminent conversation for as long as I can put it off.

Ade rolls her eyes, but answers because she loves talking about herself. "Great," she mutters enthusiastically, while reaching for her pita. "I want to thank you for buying us the Edvard Munch. We wanted to have a huge gala to show it off, but I knew you'd refuse."

"Have as many parties as you want, just don't invite me to present my donations." I chew thoughtfully, then swallow. "Let me know if you find any more acquisitions, and I'll acquire them for you. Just don't put my name on them."

Turning sheepish, Ade always fears upsetting me. "I had the plaque engraved with Empowerment. I figured you'd be alright with it since that's what you use for all the other charities."

"That's good." I nod my head while chewing. "Do you want Fate to act as our spokeswoman? I'd have Kristal do it, but she doesn't like that shit either, and her tattoos and freaky hair may frighten your elite patrons." Ade shudders next to me from the implications of Kristal crashing a high society party. I chuckle, and take a huge bite of my pita.

Kris would fuck them, both literally and metaphorically.

"God, no, don't ever do that to me." Ade laughs in mock-horror, but she sobers quickly. "You know you don't have to keep buying us stuff. You know that, right? You can keep the money you've earned. It's yours."

"I know." A dozen warring emotions try to rise at once, and I push them back down before they suffocate me. "I have enough to keep twenty generations of Regals happy– or Whittenhowers, whatever. But I want them to earn their keep, to learn and grow, not atrophy with my money."

Face lined with hurt, Ade stares down at her plate. "Is that how you truly see us?"

"No, Ade," I breathe softly. "Earning their keep was not in the monetary sense. You're living your dream, and you're passionate about your profession. That was my point. Whitt shouldn't be in business unless it's his calling. So, as far as donating my money, I can't give enough away with more pouring in daily. I'm not complaining, but I'd rather make a difference in someone's life through education and the arts. Help another dream be realized. Just paying it forward."

"You don't live like you should, Regina." Ade shifts to look me directly in the eyes. "You're living in a tiny house, with nothing personal to your name. You take care of everyone else while neglecting yourself."

"I believe that's the point of my life, Ade. I'm smarter than the average bear, and only a narcissist would use that for personal profit. With my brain, I should be helping everyone, not just myself. And who says I need to live like you do? Why is that a gauge on intelligence, power, and success? Having brands stamped on all of your belongings as if someone other than you owns them? That's not jealousy talking– it's ludicrous to waste money on someone else's name branded on your ass. Having the ability to drink a fifteen thousand dollar bottle of nasty tasting wine is a waste, not a status symbol. Pretentious asshole with no sense of self is what it is."

"Reg–"

"Our home has everything we could possibly ever need. It's soft, safe, and secure, and it houses all of us with room for ourselves. I don't need a misery castle of my own to prove my worth. I don't need to attend galas and spew my achievement. I'm a doer– I do instead of tell. I'd rather let my work speak for itself, rather than speak of work someone else is performing while I take the credit and money hand over fist."

We sit in strained silence as we contemplate the other's stance on life. Adelaide can't fathom someone who's more affluent than her father not wanting to wear their influence like a badge of honor. She would be screaming it from the treetops. I can't figure out why she'd want such a large target on her back. Money brings many problems. The more money you're worth– the deadlier the problems.

I'm worth more money than I can count.

"I didn't mean it like that, Reg, and you know it. You're trying to avoid the fact that you need to do you. Giving money away doesn't mean you can't go to the movies, go to the gym, or go on a date. You're in your prime, but *you* are the one atrophying."

Conversation change. Now!

"How's Ezra?" I ask in preemption to our talk.

"Fine, change the subject– you always do... Awkward. It's always awkward." Ade slumps forward, with her elbows on the island countertop. "I thought we'd eventually form a friendship of sorts, but Ez won't give me an inch. Diane tries to get us to connect, but to no avail. Ezra doesn't know me, and he doesn't want to either." I can hear tears in her voice, and it breaks my heart.

I know their relationship isn't a love-match, but I agree with her and Diane. Ezra and Ade make the perfect pairing: two prominent families combining in an alliance, and with their sexual orientations, neither would feel hurt when the other takes a lover.

"I'm just going to get this over with, but you have to be honest with me for once." I tug Ade, forcing her to look me straight in the eyes. "I know what you want to speak to me about, and I have some conditions and questions. But if you lie, I'll refuse to help you. Do you understand me, Adelaide?"

"Yes, I promise to be honest." She flashes her brilliant smile at me. "You're perfect for this, you know that."

"Why? Why keep an eye on Ezra. It won't change anything between you two. If anything it will create a fissure when he finds out that you're spying on him, especially if he grows to trust any of us. That's rule #1: never change your partner, always accept them for who they are. If you don't like Ezra the way he is, then break it off."

"You don't understand, Regina." Ade slumps back to the counter, and I wait for her to say it's because I don't have a man in my life, haven't in almost a decade. "There's a woman."

"What does it matter who Ezra is playing with? You have lovers, too. So who cares if he has a girlfriend? The one I'd fear is territorial Cortez. Jesus Christ, did you somehow forget choking the piss outta each other?"

"I get it– I do. But I can't explain it. Just know that whoever the fuck this cunt is, she'll destroy all of our lives, especially mine." Ade's eyes glaze with fear and her voice quivers with anxiety.

"You have to explain it better than that, or I'm not helping," I mutter flatly. "We made a deal. I'm either in charge, or your partner in crime. I'll never be the minion."

"Okay." Ade gulps in a huge breath. "I would like to know if Ezra ever takes a woman, because if he does, she is *the* woman. Through Restraint, you need to get close to Ezra so you can get close to Katya Waters. He's gayer than gay, but maybe he'll get off on a masculine woman." Ade eyes me.

"No!" head hitching back, I flinch in disgust. "Fuck you, Ade!" I slip from the stool to cross the kitchen to the coffee pot. I need my addiction to get through this. I grab a mug and the pot, and don't offer any to Ade.

"I know who every one of Ezra's lovers have been. He's been very modest considering his hobbies. I only know of three people he has been with sexually, other than me. Okay, here goes." Ade steels herself. "I'm utterly terrified of this Kat chick. During our last meeting, Ezra made me sign a contract for our engagement. It stated that when Katya Waters agrees to marry Ezra, I must publically break our engagement."

My head jerks to the side to stare directly at Ade. I couldn't have heard that correctly. "What. The. Mother. Fuck? Where did this bitch come from? Poof! Gay man's wet dream?"

With tears pooling in her crystalline eyes, Ade's on the edge of destruction. "Do you have any idea how this makes me feel? I've been betrothed to Ezra for thirteen years. *Thirteen* years, Regina."

"I know," I stress, eyes bugging out. "I've been with you every step of the way, and it makes no sense for a gay man to be this nuts over a woman, especially with Cortez."

"Exactly, that's why I know it's for real." Sighing heavily, "If Ezra will do this to Cortez, after that man has terrorized me for over a decade… There is this anvil hanging over my head, and if I fuck up, I'm finished. Daddy will kill me if I don't land the billionaire, and we both know that isn't an empty threat. Who the fuck is this bitch? Where did she come from? Why does Ezra want a woman in the first place? Is this Kat's cunt gilded in gold?"

I sit in shock and awe, having no idea how to comfort Ade. I'll go to Restraint and do everything she needs because of this. Disrespect, pure and simple. Adelaide Whittenhower is *not* disposable. It's disgusting to keep someone on the hook for over a decade while you wait for something better to come along. They should have never been betrothed in the first place, but that is how their lives function. Ezra knows this more than I do.

Disrespect is a *fuck you* in polite society, and Ade doesn't deserve it.

Restraint. I'll go to Restraint and figure out the how and why. If Ade doesn't end up with Ezra in the end– good. But if she does, Ezra needs to learn his place. Men have *no* right to treat women with disrespect.

I ask without hesitation, "What do you need me to do?"

Adelaide sobs violently and lays her head on the island. I haven't heard those sounds from her since I was told Grant was gone. Bringing up the worst moment in my life, I pull Ade into my arms and hold her while she trembles, trying to comfort her so she'll stop reminding me of torments better left in the past.

"Thank you, I knew you'd do it for me." Ade sniffles, wiping her snot on my shoulder. Being a mommy makes it less gross somehow. "I can't trust Kristal, and she doesn't have the finesse you have. You never fail at anything, and you'll do anything to win. I need that right now. My life depends on it."

"What do you mean?" I pull Ade back to arm's length so I can see her reactions as she speaks.

"Daddy said I had three years to marry Ezra, if I don't manage it… Oh, God," she howls, then runs to the wastebasket to heave what little lunch she'd ate.

I wait while Adelaide cleans herself up at the sink, knowing her pride would get wrinkled if I tried to step in right now. But I do worry, because what could Daniel do that is worse than death.

"Wintercrest asylum," Ade whispers, answering my unspoken thoughts. "If I don't meet Daddy's expectations, he's going to have me committed."

"What? That's not even possible." My mind returns to the past, back to when Jackson and Daniel mapped out everyone's lives and expected their demands to be met. They decimated any type of life I tried to build while they waited to swoop in and take something I wasn't willing to give at the time.

A small part of me can never hate Daniel, because without his meddling, there would be no Whitt, no Niel, and no Ella, and they are too precious to have never been created.

"The woman I'm seeing can't help me– we can't get married because she's already married. Daddy has power of attorney over all of his children until we're married. He'd allow me to marry her, no doubt he would, but she's tied to her husband and would lose everything."

"Wow... you sure do know how to pick 'em, don't you?" I mutter, wishing I didn't sound as sarcastic as I do.

"You don't know the half of it." Ade laughs without humor. "Daddy can do it– he can commit me to Wintercrest if I don't do what he wants." Desperation and terror lace her voice.

"Shit," I spit with feeling. "Daniel is one cold motherfucker. Oh, Ade, I'll do all I can to make sure that doesn't happen. Daniel said three years, right? That's three years to plan." I worry that that isn't enough time. I had five years to plan a getaway from Misery Castle, and Grant's death was my only way out.

"Maybe," Ade sounds hopeless. "Maybe things will change. Maybe my girlfriend will finally leave her husband and be with me. Maybe Ezra will marry me after seeing this chick is a nobody. Maybe Daddy won't be so cold-hearted."

"Maybe," I mutter, doubtful. I ask to change the subject. Just thinking of the eldest Daniel Whittenhower makes me want to visit the wastebasket, too. "Who are you seeing? You tried to have sex with me last night, and I doubt she would appreciate that about as much as I did."

"I can't say who. She's as powerful as my father. Trust me when I say she wants this marriage between Ezra and me to work. There are bloodlines and legacies at stake, and that's why Daddy is so terrified." Face pinking, Ade smiles at me. "As for us having sex, she wouldn't mind– honest."

"Not happening, sister– not even once." I smirk at Ade's poor attempt, but feel mildly insulted. She's engaged to Ezra, has a girlfriend, but all I'm good for is a quick romp to prove she can get with me when she knows I don't want to get with her.

I'm forever destined to be someone's mistress, no one thinking Regina Regal is worth the starring role.

"We need to plan. Will you allow Fate to bring you to Restraint?"

"No– I'm in control, or I'm not doing it. I'll go to Restraint, and bring Fate with me."

"Semantics," Ade grumbles sarcastically while rolling her eyes.

"Take it or leave it, here are my conditions. I'll be the dominant one, because I can't pretend to be anything but. I will not place my body in someone else's hands, and I won't be everyone's meat.

Everything I do will be because I want it to happen. I promise I'll do my best to get as close to Ezra as possible and try to ferret out who this bitch is, and perhaps change his mind about your nuptials."

"Fair enough, agreed." Ade takes a deep breath, like it's the first she's taken in a long while. "You're going to have an issue with my next suggestion, but it's necessary. I need you to play a lesbian, because it's for your own safety. There aren't many women who they would mix you with, but you would be a target for the men. I think I'd puke if you ended up fucking Ezra."

"Not going to happen," I mutter with a grimace. "Ezra is *gay*– I'm not."

"Listen to my intel, and you'll change your mind, Reg. Kris said there are four male Masters of Restraint, and one in training, and a female Master of Restraint who refuses to use the term mistress. The woman is straight, so you're safe there. But that leaves five men, and you'd be the newbie. The newbie who has only ever had sex with my brother. You're a grieving widow, and I doubt you'd ever forgive yourself if they all ended up banging you. Think about what they'd do to a woman like you."

"I hear ya, but I'm guessing your real motivation is that you hope I'll enjoy the female contact." Ade's blush confirms my suspicions. "I'm not fucking a woman. I'll do my best at acting, but I'd prefer a man. I have the same concerns as you, so I'll concede. Plus, I don't want to have sex with Ezra– that would gross my ass out."

"It's not *that* bad, Regina." Ade flashes me a creepy grin.

"What? Having sex with a woman isn't all that bad, or having sex with Ezra?"

"Both." Ade giggles. The grown-ass woman actually giggles like a little girl. "Ezra was rather good at it– very giving yet dominating."

"Holy Shit, Ade!" I squeal. "When? Ez is G. A. Y. You're gay!"

"We had sex the night before our engagement was announced. We wanted to know if we'd be able to get married, since marriage includes kids. We had to know if we could stand to have sex with each other. It wasn't earth-shattering or anything, but it was pleasant."

"Sex should be earth-shattering, Adelaide!"

"It was good enough. We both enjoyed ourselves, got off easily enough. We were together a few times after that. But then Ezra started acting weird, and then he sprung that ridiculous contract on me and this Katya Waters chick."

"When did you guys stop telling me stuff?" Looking Ade dead-to-rights, I feel sick to my stomach. "When did you start editing your lives? I've been in denial, or blind, or whatever... It's like I'm a stranger amongst people who know every single detail about each other, but I know nothing."

Ade doesn't answer me, and I let her drop it because I know the answer to my own question– the night Grant died.

I've been in a fog of despair of my own making.

"Well, I apologize for my absence. But now I'm back, and I have your back. Tell me when, and I'll be ready." My voice breaks with unexpected anticipation and excitement– I almost sound eager. "I have no idea what to expect, but I'm a fast learner."

"Thank you, Regina. You have no idea how this lifts some of my stress. My..." She thinks for a moment. "My girlfriend will be relieved as well. We both thank you," she says in obvious relief.

"If you're going to talk like that, you better confess this chick's name. You're looking starry-eyed when you speak of her. Who is she?"

"No can do." Ade's pale skin turns bright pink. "Go take a nap. Kris has some clothes picked out for you, and Fate will bring them by around eight o'clock and help you get ready."

"I can dress myself." Ade levels me with a look. "I can!" I protest. Another look. "Okay, I can't."

Silently laughing, Ade looks more like Grant than ever, because I always amused him. "Kristal has to work at Restraint tonight, so just act as if you don't know her. The rest is entirely up to you. I need to know what Ezra is up to, any information you can get on the inner workings of the club and its Masters, and dirt on Katya Waters. I know it's a lot, but my future depends on this, Regina."

Chapter Five

I look absolutely ridiculous– like a drag queen with a vagina and real tits. My six-foot-tall body is encased in black latex. The black vinyl skirt barely covers my ass. The lace-up bustier only extends to my ribcage and plumps my large breasts to enormous. I'd worry about anyone noticing my homely face or the tummy fat, but I doubt their eyes will ever leave my tits. Stiletto boots gain me a few extra inches in height I don't need, leaving me to tower over Fate's diminutive figure. My hair is pulled severely from my face and smoothed to the nape of my neck in a twist. My face is made up like a French whore. If I have to pull this charade off in the long term, I'm going shopping.

I glare down at Fate while we wait in the mile-long line, because she's acting like the one who feigned agoraphobia for the last decade when that was me. Clearly I jumped out of the frying pan and into the fire.

Fate holds my hand tightly, like a petrified child on their first day of school, when she's been hitting clubs every weekend since she got her first fake ID. Her eyes are glassy, and her face is flushed. She's scared, but excited to be here. It's more fun for me but more terrifying for her since we are infiltrating Restraint, not just coming for pleasure.

I want to growl at Fate's comfort. The dinky woman is wearing a loose, white shift that leaves nothing to the imagination, but manages to make her look virginal. It also covers everything and looks unbelievably comfortable. I can attest that latex and vinyl are scratchy, and don't get me started on sweating while wearing it.

Bored, I fondle a strand of Fate's hair. Yeah, I seem to have a hair fetish. I don't like the texture of my own, so I feel up everybody else's to compare. Fate's dirty blonde hair falls past her shoulders in a soft wave. It lends to the virginal look she has going on, and it makes me wonder for the billionth time what her goddamn mother looks like.

After having suspicions, Fate started visiting her mother on a daily basis. There isn't much you can hide when you share a life with someone. This was yet another straw about to break the camel's back.

Gwen.

Fate visits with Gwen every day, and when I look at my best friend, I think of Grant being in love with another during our entire relationship, and it somehow taints what I felt about who we were together. Not to mention, Fate is visiting with her biological mother, while my Whitt is still in the dark about who he is, about his true legacy, and I feel like a liar and a thief for never speaking the truth.

So when I look at one of the women I share my life with, my home, my daughter, and my business, I'm illogically jealous because all I see is the woman who Grant loved, the one who left Whitt. But then I remember my own son is being raised by someone other than me.

"Are you okay?" Fate asks, huge pools of watery blue looking innocently concerned. "We can go home. Ade can handle her own shit. Ella and I made banana bread this afternoon. We could watch a movie and snack the night away."

In the face of Fate's hopefulness, I have to shake my head no. The last thing I need to do is sit on my ever-growing fat ass and eat more, while sitting next to the clone of the love of Grant's life.

No, thank you.

There are ghosts haunting me everywhere I look, and there is no escaping a single one of them.

Fate pulls my hand to gain my attention, and looks at the beefy bouncer barring entrance to Restraint. I'm confused since we're behind at least a hundred eager clubbers. But the younger man curls his fingertips in a come hither, and we hither.

I pull Fate behind me, since she keeps trying to drag her feet in fear. Chuckling underneath my breath, I remember Ade thinking that Fate could ever pull off acting like a dominant.

Approaching the stacked bouncer, I attempt to smile at him, trying to hide the fact that I'm out of practice socializing with anyone other than my girls.

We're looking eye-to-eye. The bouncer's a big boy, but my heels make us the same height. His crystal clear blue eyes shine back at me with mirth. Bouncer boy radiates cheerfulness, and I wish his hair was longer than the skull-cut– I'd love to know how it falls. I think it's blond, but it's hard to tell. Handsome, but a bit too young for my tastes– then I realize I'm only asking to go inside Restraint, not date him.

Jesus, Regina. Get your shit together.

"Well, hello there, handsome," I drawl, trying to remember how women talk to men, and for some reason I'm channeling Kris. "What's your name?"

I realize too late I'm supposed to be playing a lesbian, which is a fucking joke. Fate reminds me with the painful dig of her heel into my toes– little bitch. I try to hide my wince, but the bouncer's eyes zero down to my aching foot with the incriminating evidence of Fate's heel still pressed into my boot. I give a throaty laugh to distract him.

Bouncer boy quirks a pale eyebrow and releases a husky laugh. Jesus– that voice is like liquid lust. I'm fascinated by the way his chest moves up and down in his tight, black t-shirt. It draws my attention to the logo of Restraint on his left pec. His masculine hand draws my attention to his full mouth as he covers it with a palm while he laughs at us good naturedly.

"Hmm… your pet needs some discipline." More chuckles spill forth. "Naughty girl. Bad domme."

"I know, right?" My flabbergasted act is not an act– I'm sick of all their shit. "Looking at her, you'd think she was an angel. But I think she likes punishments more than pleasing her master. I think it's time I get more creative and taught my little bitch a valuable lesson."

The opposing reactions my statement elicits is amusing. Bouncer boy's eyes flare with lust, and Fate hides behind me and cowers like a good girl. One of her hands is in mine, while her other grips the back of my skirt like a child at her mother's apron strings.

"My name's Aaron, ma'am." His voice is husky and hits gravel deep. "May I stamp your hand?" I blink at him, eagerly placing my hand in his. I haven't been touched by a man in a decade. I shiver a bit, but it's nothing exciting. Aaron's not my type.

What is my type?

Aaron applies a stamp on the back of my hand with efficient practice. I pull Fate's and my clasped hands for him to mark her, too. She's shivering like a leaf, which I find endearing under the circumstances. I examine our stamps: mine is a paddle and Fate's is obviously a ball gag. I laugh at how embarrassing Fate's stamp is– serves her ass right for being a coward and hiding behind me. Maybe she isn't acting– maybe she really is a submissive. It fits her perfectly. I still can't believe Kris, because that chica is raw.

"Are you ready, my angel?" I decide on the spot that that's Fate's BDSM nickname. The virginal getup mixed with her size and coloring– perfection.

"You have a pleasant night, Aaron," I purr, and I feel up his chest for good measure. It's very brazen, and hides the fact that I'm quaking in my boots and scared shitless.

I drag my sub behind me on an invisible leash. I know Fate will always be a step behind. I'm her protector, her lifeline.

Turning to face her, "Are you ready, scaredy cat?" I smirk at Fate because she's blazing red in her white gown.

"Angel, pfftt– bitch," Fate scoffs at me, not finding her nickname as fitting, or as hilarious as I find it.

"You acting as a dominant– pfftt. Joke," I scoff back. I keep my mouth set in a serious line, and Fate bursts out laughing, and I can't help but join her in our ridiculousness.

"Oh, God. This would have been a disaster if we did this the other way around. Jeez– it would have been awful. I'm so close to pissing my panties."

"Agreed– but no pissing your pants," I tease while grinning down at Fate's bright face. My heart beats out of sync, seeing what Grant must have seen in Gwen. Gorgeous. Innocent. Protectable. Fate is my total opposite. How the hell did he manage to get and stay hard for me?

"From here on out, when we're playing BDSM, your name is Angel and mine is Queen. No telling our real names, and you haven't met Kris before," I caution. "You will be the best damn submissive on the face of the planet. It can't be that difficult– just follow my lead and do as I say. The pressure's all on me, and we both have to be a quick study, or we'll look phony."

"I'll try my best," Fate's voice warbles with fear.

"Don't be frightened, because I promise to protect you." I rub her shoulder, trying to comfort and reassure her. "If you need something, or don't like a suggestion, pinch me twice, and then I'll let you whisper in my ear. Okay?"

"Okay, I can do that. I trust you, Queen." Fate tries the word out for size, then smirks. "I remember Whitt calling you that instead of Regina. Is that why you're using it? Is it in homage to him?"

"Yes and no. In this place, there's another name for someone like me, and I'll be damned before I allow anyone but Grant to call me that– it was for his lips only, and he meant it as every definition of the word."

"Oh, Reg," Fate cries, fingertips covering her mouth. "I'm so sorry I brought it up."

"I'm not a delicate flower, Fate. You guys can talk about Grant. We all loved him in different ways, and we all lost him. I won't melt, no matter how badly I may want to."

"If Grant knew you as the person you are today, he'd be proud." Fate's eyes turn cloudy, like she's thinking of a different time and place. "Very proud. I promise you this."

"Be that as it may, I just hope I don't fuck this up for his sister. Grant would kill me if he wasn't already dead. It's my job to protect Ade from now on since he can't." Unable to continue on with this conversation and stay sane, I pull the Band-Aid off. "Are you ready, Angel?"

"As ready as I'll ever be." Fate flashes me a huge smile, lighting up her eyes. "Ready– you lead the way." She lifts her head and pulls her shoulders back, but her look of confidence is eclipsed by the fact that her teeth are rattling and her hand is scrunching mine.

I shore up my own resolve, and no one would know from the outside that I'm a stew of emotions brewing on the inside. I pull my diminutive submissive behind me and pray that I don't fuck this shit up.

The blood-red metal door opens before us by unseen hands. As soon as we enter, the music hits full force like an unexpected slap to the face, pumping its sounds into our eardrums until our hearts either join the beat or stop beating altogether.

Fate wraps one arm around my midsection and bites her nails into my side. I hope she loosens up next time, or I'm leaving my submissive at home. I can't work with Fate hanging onto me like I'm her security blankie. I'd like that situation better, since I don't trust Auntie Adelaide as a babysitter, always fearing she'll take my daughter on an unexpected visit to Misery Castle when I'm not looking. When Fate babysits, all they do is cook and bake. Win-win.

Another brawny bouncer nods his head in hello, and the door thuds behind us with finality. He has the unseen hands. I nod back to the fellow, then drag Fate down a wide set of stairs onto the sunken dance floor. This club is just a club, yet Fate's acting like it's a slaughter house.

Fate and Kris love talking of their exploits, and they go clubbing every weekend. This is the best location to rack up a few more wicked tales, so I can't figure out what Fate's malfunction is with Restraint.

My fingers pinch Fate's chin to raise her face until blue meets green. "This is just an ordinary club, like every club you've ever entered. My journey back and forth from Hillbrook was a billion times worse than this, and I went through that twice a day for four years. Sex and drugs?" I look around, seeing nothing like I had on the streets. "Pull up your big girl panties, or I'm taking your ass home."

"I'm sorry." Fate's bottom lip quivers.

"Good, play up your need to be attached to me, but don't actually be afraid. It's bullshit, Fate. Do this for Ade– she'd do it for you, and more." I try to drill my need for Fate to comply into her brain. "You're perfectly safe. Got it?"

"Yes, Queen," she whimpers.

"Good girl, now follow my lead. Let's pay a visit to our Chica, and have a drink or ten. Maybe we'll dance for a bit after. We're watching for now. I won't know what to do next until inspiration strikes."

I don't allow Fate to respond. I remove my fingers from her face and try not to notice all the bright-eyed witnesses that are staring at us with lust and hunger. It's as creepy as it is flattering. I bet they love the way Fate's dress is see-through in the strobe lights. Even I will admit she looks lusciously inviting in her virginal white that covers and bares all at the same time. We must make an interesting pair– pure, gorgeous submissive and her hard-ass, ugly domme.

With my taller, larger body, I wiggle us some space, pressing Fate to the bar with me at her back as protection. Restraint is ridiculously packed for a week night, and I wonder what it's like on the weekend. But at the same time, it's also nothing I would expect. The music, lighting, tight-packed bodies, and the ambiance is exactly like any club in the city, if I go by Kris and Fate's stories, because this is a first for me tonight.

As-seen-on-TV is the only visual I had about club life.

The only difference between Restraint and what I've seen or heard, is how the patrons take their dancing one step farther– some are almost mating. I swear a few are actually screwing each other but you can't see anything. The circle of spectators proves my suspicions about a grinding couple on the dance floor– dick has to be in vag.

Glancing around, I look for a booth to camp out in, but they're all full. Apparently, they're also the location for oral sex. That's something you don't see at a regular nightclub– two ladies licking one lollipop. Fate and I both are transfixed by the lollipop. We simultaneously cock our heads to the side in amazement when one of the girls sucks it in until the stick disappears

"Now that takes talent, especially with one that huge." I mutter in appreciation, with a stirring of arousal pooling in my belly, plus a healthy dose of envy since I doubt I'll ever suck another cock in my lifetime. I've had a lot of time to self-reflect in the past decade. Grant did as Jackson said, but that doesn't mean he wanted to. I've come to terms with my lifelong celibacy, and it's not from grief.

Who would want this gargantuan body?

The cocksucktresses begin fighting over their toy, and Fate and I share a nervous giggle. A throat clearing draws our attention from the oral display. Pity, leave it to Kris to ruin our fun.

"Ladies, are you enjoying the show? Can I get you a drink?" It's wrong of me, but I want to correct Kristal and tell her to say *may I*, but I figure I'd get a fist to the face. Kris was a real bear to tutor when she was in high school and college.

"Hi, there– surprise us." I don't drink, never had a beer in my life. By the time I turned twenty-one, I'd had a kid, breastfed, and it wasn't long after I was pregnant again. My twenties are lost, and I'm about to hit thirty any second.

"You sure?" Fate looks terrified for me.

"Yeah, I'm sure." I trust Kristal to totally fuck up my order just to get me wicked drunk. I know I'm in for it when the naughty minx curls her lips into an evil smirk.

Two shot glasses appear before us, and Fate licks her lips in anticipation– maybe Kristal's being nice after all. I watch as Fate tosses back the shot, then I give it a go.

The moment the liquor hits the back of my throat, I know I'm in trouble. Lava can't be this hot. Sputtering, every breath I draw pours fire directly into my lungs.

"Oh. My. God. What the fuck is that? A fire breathing dragon in a shot glass? Are you trying to kill me?" I look over to watch Fate's reaction, and she's having a hard time of it, too. Jesus.

"It's called the Zombie, and it's the most potent drink we serve." Kris looks smugger than usual. "I thought if we started you out as strong as it could possibly get, you wouldn't wimp out on the next drink."

"Diabolical bitch," I hiss under my breath. It still hurts to breathe, but I respect Kristal's reasoning. "Give us something else—something that isn't the unholy union of Satan and the Sun. Ya know, maybe cool it down a few degrees to magma, or an eternity in Hades," I deadpan.

Kristal laughs the entire time she pours our drinks, and the delicious sound is attracting customers like flies to honey. With suspicion, I eye the next round of shots laid before us. Fate's a more trusting sort, but even she picks it up and does a sniff-test first. When her nose hairs don't catch fire, and she smiles, I figure it's safe. I make Fate drink it first, though. I'm not *that* fucking stupid.

"Yummy! Blackberry brandy!" Fate claps, and then eagerly pours the contents of her shot glass down her throat.

When Fate doesn't spontaneously combust into flames, or keel over dead, I follow suit, pouring the drink into my mouth. I close my eyes, waiting for the burn. It's slight compared to the Zombie. I rotate my head on my shoulders and purr as the alcohol invades my system. Mmm-hmm... that's really relaxing. I'd forgotten what relaxing felt like.

"Can I have another?" Eager beaver begs the barkeep.

"No!" Kristal leans over the bar and whispers. "I know you can hold your liquor, but that Zombie is the equivalent of ten shots of brandy. No more for you until later. Besides, I don't think Regina wants to tow you around the club— Hey, is she okay?" I blink when I realize she's speaking to me.

"Oh, I'm fucking fabulous." I rotate my neck again, loving how heavy yet light my head feels. "How come I never drank before? If we could mix it with caffeine, I would drink it night and day. OH! Oh... oh... idea time!" I hop up and down, getting more excited by the second. "We need to make a beverage that has lots of caffeine that would be tasty with liquor. I am so going to market that shit."

"Fuck, she's bombed already." Kristal throws her hands in the air in a gesture of giving up.

"Am not!" I shout.

"Are, too!" They say in unison.

"I'm Queen and this is Angel." Gesturing, I proudly slur to Kristal, trying to get back into character.

"Nice— an old nickname and a deviant stripper name. Great, wonderful to meet you ladies for the first time *ever*." Kris stresses the *ever* dramatically, and I giggle like an idiot. "I'm Kristal, by the way."

I rest my head on the bar and laugh until tears pour from my eyes. Then I bounce out of my seat with super-human speed. "Hi, Kristal!" I shout while hopping in place. My ladies laugh at me, and I don't give a shit. Fate is holding her tiny tummy she's laughing so hard.

Words flowing too rapidly for my ears to track, "Anything happening tonight? Anything that Angel and I may find interesting?"

"Maybe... I may have seen two hooded asshats by the door leading to the dungeon." Kristal's voice sounds extra sultry to my inebriated ears.

I sway to a song of my own making for a few moments. "Oh, there's a dungeon? This shithole isn't it?" I giggle at the expression of outrage on Kristal's face.

"Of course there's a fucking dungeon– this is a BDSM club, you idiot." Offended, Kris growls at me, "And this isn't a shithole."

"Sorry, ma'am," and I'm not sorry at all. Restraint is nothing special. "So how do we get into the dungeon?"

"You have to be invited in."

"So it could take a lot of time to be invited, because I'm socially inept, or I could just break us in. Is it a coded door? I bet I could hack that bitch while two-sheets to the wind." I rub my palms together in anticipation.

I could do it too– I know I could. I want to test my drunken skills. Kris just rolls her eyes in reply and looks at me like I'm an idiot.

"Obviously I have the code, dipshit. I can save you a lot of trouble, but I'm not giving it to you yet. Plus, don't you think it would be kind of obvious when you two are zigzagging around the dungeon and none of the masters invited you in."

"We can be covert, right?" I turn to a smiling and swaying Fate. "Maybe not."

"You need to mingle. I doubt it will take too long before you're invited anyway. If it's not this time, then it'll be the next. You make quite the pair, especially with a drunk Queen. I never thought I'd see you like this. It's amusing as all hell to watch."

"I want to dance. I think we should get our groove on near the dungeon entrance. What do you say, Angel? Oh, wait, you don't get a vote." I giggle maniacally at having total control over another human being.

"This isn't going to end well," Kris mumbles after us, as I drag my sub behind me through the crowd. I find a spot on the floor near a gray door with a keypad. I take a guess that it's the dungeon entrance. There's a hallway with a red exit sign glowing on the far corner. This must be it.

Fate smiles up at me, and I swear under my breath. "You don't know how to dance, do you?" I shake my head no. I spent my teen years studying my ass off. My early twenties were filled with education, childrearing, Grant, and staying one step ahead of Daniel. After that, I focused on building Empowerment, grieving, and raising Ella. I've never had a chance to loosen up until tonight. I've never even been on a date– ever. I was Grant's dirty little secret. No one has ever stamped Regina Regal worthy of keeping.

"Just follow my lead, flow to the music, and pray," Fate mutters snarkily while grinning like a villain.

Dainty and gorgeous, I try to echo Fate's movements and sway with the music. I'd feel better if my tits weren't hitting me in the face, and if the material of my outfit was pliable– uncomfortable doesn't cover it. Where my ass meets my thigh is sweating. I close my eyes and ignore the annoying sensations. Finally, the music roars over me, and I join the crowd in tribute to Bacchus.

Half of my mind enjoys the dance while the other half keeps a constant eye on the door. I nearly piss my pants when the door opens, but I'm disappointed that the man exiting isn't wearing a hood. He's small but stocky, and naked from the waist up. His muscles are evident since he's gracing me with a view of his cut chest and abs. A sheen of sweat glistens on his bronze skin, and I lick my lips in interest.

My libido goes into overdrive. A mass of black curls obscures his eyes from me. As if he senses my attention, he lifts his face and I'm rendered speechless. His whiskey eyes are screaming a command for me to drop my gaze. *Fuck you, not happening, buddy.* I hold his gaze in defiance, and his perfect lips curve slightly.

My eyes take a detour to check out the rest of the tiny man. He can't be more than a few inches over five-feet tall. He wears black leather pants as a second-skin. I go cotton-mouthed as I watch the bulge in his pants grow to an impressive showing. My eyes flick back to his face to see what has created such a strong reaction, only to find his eyes devouring my submissive. I feel slightly rejected that I didn't do it for him, but Fate is a sight to behold.

A pinch to my arm breaks my perusal of the master, and it pisses me off. I glare at Fate, and she recoils.

Rejection, annoyance, and the past few days of finding out my girls lie to me left and right, even by omission, has me acting out of character. "Kneel by my thigh, Angel." I command in a voice I haven't heard in years. Only this voice is deeper, more desperate, and angry.

I've often wondered what Grant saw in me. Now I know– nothing. Men do not like women who can bust their balls. At least not any man I've met except Grant. God, I miss him. Boy, do I feel inadequate right now, to the point I'm disgusted with myself.

Exercise is on my horizon.

"What'd I do?" Fate whines but complies by dropping to the floor.

"Honestly, where do I start? I know– how about we start with you crawling between Adelaide's boney thighs and you never told me." My voice hits the depths of Hell, I'm so pissed they have managed and coddled me for years when I thought I was in control.

I hadn't realized how angry I was at Fate for shutting me out until this moment. How angry I am at all of them. I don't need to know all of their partners, but when it affects all of us, I shouldn't be the only one left in the dark.

Fate flinches as if struck, then she huddles up to my thighs while resting on her heels. Gripping my skirt in her fists, big, blue eyes glitter up at me in shame. "I'm sorry, Queen," Fate pleads. "It was only the once."

"It's not that you did it, or how many times, it's that you didn't think I should know something so pivotal. I'm pissed that you didn't tell me the truth about Faith either. You outright lied to me, and I kept searching for the little girl I used to know. Your sister ran away because you fucked her boyfriend– does Ade know you fucked her fiancé's partner?"

"No," Fate replies, remorse and shame etching across her features.

"This isn't a game, Angel. You have to tell Ade the truth." I grip Fate's tiny chin in my big fingers and drill my eyes into hers.

"Yes, Queen." She whispers, barely moving her lips. "I'll tell Ade the truth."

"Lick both of my boots for being a bad girl." Getting into character, I ignore the eyes watching us. "I'm very angry with you right now, Angel."

I gaze down as Fate's pink tongue tracks a shiny path from the toe of my boot to the zipper that runs up the inside of my calf. I feel many eyes on us, but I don't look. We may be playing D/s, but right now I mean it, and it should lend to our validity.

"Good girl, now the next." I slide my left foot forward for Fate, and she repeats the action while smiling up at me.

Raising slowly, I allow my eyes to finally take in who's staring at us. Where there was one, now there are three. I arch an eyebrow at the hovering Masters of Restraint, and it takes all of my will to turn from them. I can't let them know they interest me.

If the hoods are Ezra and Cortez, which means Dexter is curly locks. Lust abating, stomach roiling, I push away the need to be sick. I was checking out Grant's best friend, and he looked right through me. How can Dexter not recognize someone who was so pivotal in Grant's life?

I can't even contemplate the answer to that question, because it would hurt too much.

Too late– I mustn't have been too important, as I never met Dexter or Marcus, even with how they contributed to my future through tuition. Grant would leave to visit with his friends, and they never once tried to contact me once he was dead and gone.

Regina Regal was a throwaway mistress.

With a deep breath, I pretend I know what I'm doing. Turning to face my demons, "Gentlemen," I purr smoothly in greeting.

Without speaking, Ezra and Cort circle me like sharks scenting blood, because I'm another predator interloping on their hunting ground. I know who they are, but not who is whom since they're both wearing black hoods over their heads. It covers them to the shoulder and has holes cut for the eyes and mouth. Their clothing is identical Italian designer label suits. Even their shiny leather shoes are the same. Their eyes glow like steel ball-bearings from the safety of their masks. The mouths are different– one serious, one snarky– both ruby-red and kissable.

While they circle Fate and me several times, trying to take our measure, Dexter stands in a sphere of his own confidence. Curiosity and grief have me wanting to get to know him to feel closer to Grant, but his affect has me keeping my mouth shut. Dexter is older than me, and I don't mean just in age, but knowledge. Ezra and Cortez feel like babies compared to Dexter.

I'm patient, always meeting their eyes when their path moves them back to my face. I don't follow them with my gaze– I wait.

"Hello," the hood with the serious lips speaks in a smooth, deep tone. I know it's not his true voice, but the one Kris calls *The Boss*. His eyes are kind and assessing, and hold absolutely no judgment.

No one pays Fate any mind as she cowers at my thigh, most likely because they know exactly who she is, seeing as she still runs in their societal circles. As the invading dominant in their midst, I hold their undivided attention. Curly locks is quiet, ever-watchful– a predator sighting its quarry. Snarky mouth is leering at the disgusting display of my tits.

Caught ya, Cortez!

"I seem to be at a disadvantage by conversing with you while you're hooded." I try to get them to out themselves, but it's a longshot. "I can't see you, but you can see me."

"Who are you, ma'am?" Reserved in nature, Ezra treats me respectfully.

"Please, call me Queen." I draw on all of my lessons from Hillbrook to pull me through this conversation. The power in the air is stifling. I wonder if it's difficult for them to be in the same room without having a cage match for dominance. I feel like I'm on *Animal Planet* and the lions are circling.

"Queen, indeed," Cort says snidely underneath his breath, and I wince at the harshness. I turn my head from them, fearing my mortification is visibly written across my face.

I should have gone with something less– less everything. I know I'm strong, but a queen also emulates elegance and beauty. I'm neither. Have to say, tonight has sucked for my self-esteem. First, Dexter not only looked through me, he overlooked me for Fate, and now, Cortez makes fun of me.

Motherfucking lovely.

"What did you say to upset her?" Ezra accuses Cortez.

"Nothing," Cort complains, voice warped with confusion.

"Don't worry about it," I murmur, because the more Ezra highlights the slight, the worse I feel about myself. "What should I call you?" I direct at Ezra, as he seems to be the one playacting at being in charge, and he's respectful enough to actually engage me.

"Please excuse my partner. Words are his profession, and it seems they have failed him this evening. I will apologize in advance for not sharing our names, but this gentleman is Dexter." Ezra gestures to my patron.

Eager to connect with him, I wait for Dexter to shake my hand like a civilized person. But he does not– he actually crosses his arms over his chest in disobedience. This shit is going to be a piece of cake.

I sigh audibly, ignoring the agonizing squeeze to my heart.

Maybe Dexter and Marcus weren't around because Grant knew they would take an instant dislike to me. They must have resented having to pay for my schooling once their grandmother died. They probably see me as an idiot who only wanted a handout, a woman so desperate she'd sell her first born son to the Whittenhowers for an education.

Maybe I hate myself just as much as Dexter must hate me.

"The submissive at my feet is Angel. I apologize, but she's feeling rather overwhelmed with all the power flowing from you guys."

Cortez chuckles, the sound mischievous, and Ezra swats him upside the head because of it.

"Please excuse his behavior. He's only a few days out of training, and I believe Master Dexter isn't pleased at the moment." Ezra pointedly gazes at Dexter, who shrugs in return, apparently not giving a shit how Cortez behaves.

"Your boy already has a black eye– I've cut my losses." Dexter makes a gesture with his hands, and I lean in to get a better sense of what he sounds like when he speaks. Anything Grant experienced is riveting to me.

Being an asshole, trying to demoralize me more, Cortez outwardly leers at my chest, to the point it makes me feel uncomfortable. After going nearly a decade without anyone but Ade lusting after me, I want the floor to swallow me whole.

"If you don't remove your eyes from Queen's décolletage, I'll send you to Master. Would you enjoy that? I know he can get you in hand." Ezra threatens in a voice sounding like broken glass shards sending chills down my spine.

If Dexter, Mr. Short, Dark, & Hung, isn't Master, then who the hell is? Some primal part in me is throbbing to meet this man, like he'll give me my life back.

"If *Queen*–" Cortez twists my name, "–didn't want me to look, she wouldn't be on display." The brat baits Ezra. "What, are you jealous?"

Throat constricting, I push away my need to be sick. I'm supposed to be respectable and taken seriously, not some desperate piece of ass. Kris dressed me as a cliché. I already have a submissive, so I don't need to dress as if I'm on the prowl. Plus, my ginormous body on display would make everyone run, not draw them in. I need the respect of the Masters of Restraint, not be seen as a joke. Hell, Dexter even refused to shake my hand, and Cort is using me to piss off his boyfriend.

I fucked up.

Reaching down, I stroke Fate's hair for a dose of comfort from the familiar. I want to pull Fate to her feet, and then flee this shithole. But I can't let Ade down, especially since her freedom depends on us.

Eyes flicking everywhere, I ignore the fact that Ezra has Cort pressed up against the wall, with a hand wrapped around his boyfriend's throat, and he's growling words of malice. Cortez's eyes glow with mischievousness, and I'm positive that's only egging on his partner's annoyance. Ade doesn't belong in with either of these lunatics. If Adelaide doesn't marry Ezra Zeitler, she'll end up in Wintercrest asylum, when it should be these fuckfaces locked away for Dominion's sake.

It's a cock measuring contest, and I'm short one cock.

Fate's shaking against my leg in fear, and I feel for her. Massaging her scalp, I murmur words of comfort, all the while wishing someone would comfort me instead. But someone has to be in charge, so it may as well be me.

"May I see your sub's face, please?" Cort asks nicely, and his eyes and mouth are serious now. Apparently Ezra managed to appropriately cow the brat.

I assess Fate's demeanor. She knows Cortez well enough to have slept with him. Her sister dated Cortez for years. I'm not afraid of the spoiled brat I met over a decade ago. I tip Fate's face with a fingertip at her chin. I look deep into her glazed eyes to discover she's enjoying the endorphins flooding her veins courtesy of her fear.

"You may," I say to Cort, never breaking Fate's gaze.

I watch Cortez, waiting for recognition to hit. He stares at Fate openly, but doesn't acknowledge her, so maybe we lucked out.

"You're very controlled. Have you trained under the Master in another city?" Dexter watches me as he speaks, and I try not to preen underneath his attention and praise, especially since he sounds begrudging in the first place. "I'd know if you trained here."

Well, that answers that. Dexter doesn't recognize me.

"No, this is my first time in a club, actually." I decide on honesty. I won't tell Dexter who I am, but a lie is easier to remember when it's parallel to the truth. "I was born this way, and I played in private a very long time ago. At the time, I wasn't aware it was a lifestyle choice, so please excuse my ignorance."

"Would you be interested in training?" Dexter watches me like a hawk for my reaction, and I want to smile since he's paying attention to me. But then he goes and ruins it. "It's irresponsible to engage in any BDSM activity without knowledge, education, and training. You could hurt this precious, fragile woman, and you'd have to live with regret for life."

"I...I-I–"

"You need to train," Dexter announces with finality. "Either train, or don't engage in these activities."

"I would very much like to train, which is why I'm here tonight." I answer Dexter truthfully, when I'd rather sink the heel of my boot in his motherfucking bulge. But I have to play nice, because I think I truly need this, because I need something to remove the numb that has deadened my soul.

"Queen will need to apply for membership first, Dexter." Ezra barely covers his curiosity. "We'll need your information and your real names."

"Then I do believe we're at an impasse, gentlemen. I will not release my identity." I gesture at Ezra and Cortez, and their stupid hoods. "Please forgive me, but I would think the two of you would understand the concept of anonymity,"

"We could send her to Master," Dexter offers as a solution. "You would have to tell him your true identity, but it wouldn't go past him." Suddenly he seems eager to have me here, and I'm unsure why.

Maybe Dexter wants to get his hands on Fate.

"No need– I know who they both are." Cort's arrogant words are a shot to the heart. "My partner is playing dumb, because there is no way he doesn't recognize Fate Simpson," he mutters with wry amusement.

Both Ezra and Dexter start choking, but I could care less. I'm just waiting for Cortez to say my name aloud, too. I lock eyes with him, waiting for him to drop the bombshell that will implode my world.

"I don't think Fate would be a good idea for our membership, do you, Boss?" Dexter looks really uncomfortable, like his skin shrunk and caught fire. "This is *not* a good idea. Think of our trainee and the one who blackened Cort's eye."

"Why?" I demand angrily. "Is this because of the reputation Fate's father cast on the Simpson name?" I hiss my annoyance. "It's not appropriate to judge the child for the father's sins."

Dexter and Ezra try to tell me that it isn't why, but Cort cuts them off. "Who in their right mind would trust a Simpson in this city? I wouldn't trust Fate with my money, and there's no way I would trust her with my identity."

"I trust Fate with mine on a daily basis. More than just my money and my identity. My life." Voice taunting with arrogance, Cort brings the worst out of me. "I assure you that my wealth makes yours look like pocket change, and Fate is the only one I trust with it."

Cortez's gunmetal gray eyes brighten, and I realize too late that I answered exactly the way he wanted.

"Shit," I slur with emotion.

I gain the attention of all three men, each looking at me as if I hold the secrets of the universe in my identity. Only Dexter's gaze makes me feel transparent.

"Fate Simpson is the figurehead of Empowerment," Cortez announces. "Masters, I do believe we have the elusive, reclusive creator of Empowerment in our fine establishment."

"Jesus Christ, get her out of here," Dexter snarls, vein in his forehead throbbing, as if he figured out I'm Regina Regal and he loathes me. "Now! Goddammit."

Eyes welling up with tears, I never thought I'd wish to be the Regina of the past who couldn't cry. Fate reaches for my hand and squeezes tightly to anchor me to the here and now.

"Oh, c'mon, Dexter– this will be fun. Fate poses one type of challenge, but *Queen* poses another, and we all love nothing more than a challenge. We let their Chica manage the bar and suck my dick. *Queen* would be fun to have around."

"Stop twisting my name, fuckface," I snarl, on the verge of losing my cool. "And leave Kristal's mouth alone."

"No can do on that delicious mouth." Cort purrs, and Ezra doesn't show any signs of jealousy. "So, who may you be, *Queen?* We're all dying to know." Pure curiosity shines out at me from the depths of Cortez's hood. "No matter how many ways we try to get around all of your dummy corporations to find the real owner, we hit a new roadblock. It's impressive."

"It's a pleasure to see you again, Ezra Zeitler," I say to the correct hood, and his eyes flare like a spooked horse. I grin as I turn to the other hood. "And fuck you, Cortez Hunter… *oops*, I mean Mr. Abernathy. By the way, your books suck." I try for venomous, but it falls short.

Lying isn't in my wheelhouse, and Cortez Abernathy's books are pretty good. Fate clings to my hand as I laugh at the awestruck look on their faces. I expect Cort to retaliate by saying my real name, but maybe he doesn't really know it. Maybe he only knows what I am, but not who.

"It seems my sources are better than yours," I mutter cockily.

"Can we keep her?" Cort's eyes glitter like pure metal. "I want to play battle-of-the-wills with this bitch. Please," he whines to Dexter. "I think you should train her. It would be easier with two females."

"Not a good fucking idea, asswipe," Dexter snaps. "And you know why. It's the same reason training the two of you was a nightmare. I must have done something awful in a past life for this shit to show up on my doorstep." Dexter groans into his hands, and then pulls them through his curly hair.

"I *do* know who she is," Cortez announces.

"As do I," Dexter interrupts.

"Who?" Ezra's stare is intense. "I'm lost."

But Cortez will not be silenced. "Master can't train Queen because of who he's training, where he's training, who owns where he's training, and who lives where he's training. It would be catastrophic. Trust me– you should train her, Dex."

"I don't trust you at all." Dexter looks like he smells a rotten fart. "I think you're trying to make it so you can train her. You're still a toddler– not gonna happen. We will allow Master to choose the correct path."

"Alright, who is she?" Hood covering his face, Ezra's eyes flick back and forth between us. "What the hell am I missing?"

Dexter and Cortez shake their heads no in perfect synchronization. I'm at a loss as well. I look to Fate for some insight, and she shrugs, and then goes back to cowering.

"Give me your cellphone number." Dexter takes charge, ending this horrific encounter. "I'll contact you with Master's response."

Chapter Six

"This is pretty." Ella holds up a lavender dress I bought on a whim. "You should wear this one tonight– no, this one!" My daughter paws through the mountain of clothing lying on my bed.

In anticipation of *Master* calling, I wanted to be prepared. After demoralizing myself with the cliché outfit that made me look like a tranny, I went shopping. Ella is a better sidekick than Kris could ever be. Sometimes it's best to take a modest little girl with you, because it ensures you won't look like a woman dripping desperation.

I'm the founder of a multi-billion dollar corporation, and I will act and dress like it. Deep down, I may be a cheap whore, but no one else needs to know that.

Dignity.

"Hmm… let me try it on first." Ella lounges on my bed with a happy smile playing along her lips while I model the outfits in the floor-length mirror hanging on my bathroom door. "I don't know," I murmur, hating how everything looks… ugh.

"It's so pretty," Ella coos. "You have that purple and black handbag, and I could paint your nails– tootsies too!"

"I find it bizarre how my daughter wants me to go out." I glance at Ella over my shoulder, only to find her tugging a dress over her head. "Why is that? Sick of me making you do your homework?"

"Nah– just want you to have some fun." Ella is draped in a little black dress that is two feet too long on her child body. "I can't wait to grow up and wear pretty woman dresses."

"Don't rush it," I warn. "It's not all it's cracked up to be. Trust me." Looking in the mirror, I decide against the lavender dress. I look like someone threw a curtain on me to cover up my masculine body.

I'll never voice my very private thoughts. Ella will never know this level of insecurity. My body issues belong to me, and I wouldn't wish them on my worst enemy. Just as I know my daughter is considered a *big* girl for her age. I'm hoping once the influx of puberty hormones are exhausted, she'll thin out some. But if Ella doesn't, I don't care, and neither should she.

No one should use the outside as an indicator on the inside.

Some of the most beautiful people are truly vile human beings.

"How about the red?" Ella tosses me another dress, and I quickly remove the lavender one. "I hope I have boobies like yours when I'm older."

Biting back a groan, I don't complain about my appearance, no matter how much I may want to. I'd love to explain how men assume you're a whore and dumb if you have big tits, and cute and sporty if you have tiny nubs. But I don't want Ella to be burdened with the truth about how women are viewed as meat until someone gets to know us personally. Judge. Judge. Judge. But women judge other women worse than a man ever could.

"Some guys like big boobs, but some don't. So don't wish for something because you think someone else will like you because of it. Accept what you get. But, beware, these puppies are heavy, and bra straps dig into my shoulders and back."

I pull a strap away to show Ella how it has left a red mark and a permanent indent, and she mutters, "Ouch!"

"Exactly." I slip into the red dress, fabric swirling around my hips. "If you do get my tits, I'll give you as much advice as I can. If you end up with Auntie Adelaide's, no advice needed– you can run around without a bra."

"Mine are already bigger than Auntie's..." Ella giggles. "Oh, that one is..." My daughter is at a loss for words, because I don't know how this dress made it into the pile. "The girls are um..."

"Yeah, this sends the wrong message." Inwardly flinching, I tear the dress off.

"It didn't look bad, though." Ella snatches up the dress, then stares down at it in her hands. "A guy would probably like it. Aunt Kris–"

"Yeah, don't take fashion advice from Kris." Chuckling, I pick up the black. "Just don't," I whisper. "It's not the type of message a girl of your station should send. There's a difference between sexy and desperate."

"What's the red?" Ella calls me out.

"Sexy," I whisper. "Not ready for that, so out of my league." Daring, I chance a glance into the mirror now that I'm clad in the little black dress Ella was wearing. "Almost perfect."

"Almost?" Ella scurries off my bed to join me at the mirror. "I think it's perfect– but the red..."

"No, on the red," I repeat, still looking at myself. "Ella, piece of advice. I want you to love yourself as you are. No envy and jealousy, because human nature dictates you'll want to be the complete opposite of who you are. But just because you can wear it, doesn't mean you should."

Head cocking to the side, Ella's blonde eyebrows scrunch together in the center of her forehead, and she looks more like Grant than ever. "What do you mean?"

"How to explain this... Okay. Just because you think something is pretty or sexy, or because it fits, that doesn't mean you should wear it. Like the red dress. It fits me, and it's gorgeous, but it's not the right dress for my body. Just because you like you, doesn't mean everyone else will."

"That's so sad." Ella's bottom lip quivers. "I want everyone to like me."

"Love," I breathe, reaching for my daughter. "If someone doesn't like you, they're the one missing out." I brush her beautiful cheek with my palm. "What I mean is that the only person you need to please and to make happy is yourself. You be you– love yourself. But when dealing with others, they may not accept you as you. Fuck 'em, but don't set yourself up for failure around them."

"That's why you don't dress like Aunt Kris?" Ella tries to understand something most women will never learn.

"Exactly, because I'm not Kris. I'm Regina. My body is the opposite of Kristal's, so I'll look desperate flaunting my body, whereas she looks amazing. But on the same token, she'd look ridiculous if she wore what flatters me. You be you."

Holding the red dress in her hands again, "This is you, right? You– when you were with my daddy?"

"Jesus," I whisper a hiss, looking away from my daughter. "Yeah, that's something I would have worn for your daddy, but your daddy's no longer with us, so I won't wear something like that again."

"Why not, though?" Ella looks like she's trying to explain color to the blind, both of us confused by the other. "If Daddy's gone, he can't be sad if you wear it for someone else."

"I doubt–" I can't finish that sentence in front of my daughter. I doubt Grant would have minded if I wore it for someone other than him, and he probably appreciated that I tried to sex myself up when there was no hope for me. For the billionth time, I want to cry because Grant's life ended with me instead of the tiny, fragile, gorgeous woman he was in love with. *Gwen*. But I'll never allow my daughter to know her daddy wanted another.

"This is the one." I change the subject back to the little black dress. "It's flattering, minimizing to my breasts and belly and behind." My hands flutter along the lines of my body, then sink into the pockets. "It has pockets."

"Exactly– it has pockets," Ella deadpans, sounding like her oldest brother. "*Pockets*. Wear the red and knock this guy dead."

"How old are you again?" Eyes flicking in Ella's direction, I make a decision. "No more hanging around Kris."

"Ugh!" Ella huffs, throwing every dress on the floor but the red. "Kris says just because you're a mommy doesn't mean you're not a woman. You didn't pick out the red– Kris gave it to me to give to you."

"Seriously, no more Kris," I warn, pointing in Ella's direction.

"She lives here!"

"Traitor," I tease, scooping up all the dresses. "Help me hang these back up."

"Red." Ella has a one-track mind.

"Black, but I'll let you paint my nails red."

"Deal."

After yanking on a pair of yoga pants and a t-shirt, together we get my closet sorted back to rights, with the black dress hanging on my closet door just in case *Master* ever calls. Being that I'm dealing with Ezra, Cortez, and Dexter, this is probably all for naught.

Dexter didn't want to know me when Grant was alive– he sure as fuck doesn't want to know me now.

Lounging on the sofa, Ella is satisfied because she's painting my toenails a whore shade of red. The house is otherwise quiet, because Kris is at Restraint, probably sucking Cort's dick, and Fate is on the phone to one of her many relatives. Boyd, if I'm not mistaken, because she keeps asking about someone named Torian. I know of these people in name only, because Fate never brings them around our house for obvious reasons.

The day Fate brings her mother to my house is the day I burn it to the ground.

"Auntie Adelaide said I'm going to go to Hillbrook with my brothers." Ella's words strike me directly in the heart.

"Has Auntie ever taken you from this house when she babysits?" I ask the single question whose answer would dissolve a lifetime worth of friendship.

"Museum a few times, why?" Brush suspended in the air, I'm thankful Ella paints nails better than she colors. "A couple times to the grocery store when I wanted to make something but was missing ingredients. But usually Aunt Fate's with us, and Auntie goes by herself while Aunt Fate and I try out the recipe."

"Okay." I release a breath I hadn't realized I was holding. "Yes, you'll be going to Hillbrook, but Whitt will have graduated by then. He's a hairsbreadth away from eighteen as it is… wow."

"Oh," Ella pouts. "Auntie said when Whitt was legal, he would find us."

"Huh?" I grunt in surprise, then my heart pitter-patters out of control. Before I can respond, my cellphone beeps an incoming text message, and my heart stalls.

Master?

"Is that from him?" Ella has the luxury of showing her excitement, while I dampen mine down. "Every night we wait, and he never calls."

Reaching for my cellphone, from where it rests on the coffee table, I'm about to hyperventilate. I swipe the screen to unlock, not allowing my cell to give a preview in case impressionable eyes catch things they shouldn't see.

Upgrade your phone today! Visit your local retailer at 321 Porter Avenue. Dominion, New York.

"What's it say?" Ella grabs my cellphone from my limp hand, when normally she's not allowed near it. "Oh… what? It's not from him. Upgrade your phone? Your phone hasn't even been released yet."

"I know," I mutter, disgusted with myself because I keep waiting for something to happen when I know it won't. "I built the dang thing… it's a spam text." I flop back down on the sofa. "I guess I know what I'll be doing tonight."

"Going out tonight in your little black dress and showing off your painted tootsies?" Ella asks, voice hopeful.

"Nope," I pop the P. "Debugging my spam filter."

Chapter Seven

My exercise partner called off tonight. For the past week, Ella and I have either walked or ridden our bikes around town. Tonight, some cooking show is having its finale on the Food Network, and Fate and Ella even whipped up some snacks to eat while watching. So I'm left to my own devices.

In anticipation of my new life at Restraint and training with the elusive Master who never calls, I went out and bought a new wardrobe that was more respectful and less drag queen prostitute. My little black dress in waiting, now has some new friends of other colors and styles. I invested in several bust-minimizing bras in a size too small to shrink my assets. I was so embarrassed by how I looked in my dominatrix outfit, I threw it away, started a diet, and decided exercise was a wise decision after sitting on my ever-expanding ass for the past decade.

I've always been confident about my sexuality– what I want and need in a partner, and my ability to give them what they want and need in return. But my thoughts have veered toward how Grant was coerced into our affair just as much as I was. He was probably making the best of the situation. I know he loved me in his own way, just not with the same passion and desire as Gwen. Grant accepted me as I was, which was a rarity and a blessing, but that doesn't mean anyone else ever will.

In order to protect Ade, I have to enter a lifestyle that has sexual connotations. Examining the situation, now I realize how unattractive I truly am– it fucking hurts. But it's a good hurt.

Reality.

While at Restraint, I drew a few eyes, but not from lust or appreciation of my body. It was lust for my control and domination, or it was an expression of *look at that freak*!

I'm getting closer to thirty every second of every day. Age is but a number. I love myself as I am. Blah… blah… blah… I mean those things, but that doesn't mean anyone else will be attracted to me. If I plan on getting laid ever again, or at least feeling sexy in my own skin, I have to make a positive change.

My body isn't as it was after sitting on my ass for the past decade in front of countless computers. My breasts are now a DDD cup size thanks to breastfeeding and weight gain. I can't even contemplate all the ways childbirth changed my body. Twice. I'm a 6'2", 185 pound scary bitch with untamed hair.

I've never worried over my appearance until I saw how everyone coveted Fate while dismissing me without a backward glance. Or worse, how Dexter looked through me. Then after he realized who I was, he looked disgusted. Cortez? He was leering at me, but not because he wanted me– staring as you would a car wreck.

Night nine of my new exercise regimen, I walk around the neighborhoods, working my way up to jogging. The ninth night without a call from Master. Without ever laying eyes on me, he found me as lacking as Dexter and Cortez did. I have no worries on Ezra, because I lack what he finds attractive.

In reality, I don't want any of them. I want to be wanted. So it's painful that out of four men, none of them are interested. I should have tried dating before I thrust myself into the BDSM scene. I would have more knowledge and skills to draw from. Life just got in the way, and now it's way too late. I doubt I could get a date unless I showed them my bank statements.

My identity is another issue. I've ghosted for almost a decade, and while I was at Whittenhower Estates, I didn't exist.

One more thing I found out about exercise, there is no escaping your thoughts. When I was with Grant, he taught me how to appreciate the silence, and to accept the succor thinking brought. My exercise partner is the same. After Ella exhausts herself chatting, she falls into a restorative silence. But I don't find it soothing in any way to have my private thoughts assault me.

While I work, I am my work. While I read, I live the story. While taking care of Ella, I am Mommy. While I walk, my thoughts spin like a tilt-a-whirl, and it's nauseating.

My path takes me to an older section of the city. Row after row of brownstones line the street. When I was a kid, I wanted to live in this neighborhood. This was the neighborhood Dad promised after his raise– the one that had us searching the real estate section every night after dinner. I wasn't irrational enough to pick one of the more affluent neighborhoods. I chose the one two steps better than the one I grew up in. Little did I know at the time, I would downgrade to the worst in the city before I turned sixteen. Then at eighteen, I moved to the most affluent neighborhood in Dominion.

It's amazing the journey my life has taken me on.

I should be proudly striding down the street, not scuffing my shoes, worrying about men. I don't need no stinking men.

The irritating buzz in my ass-pocket signals someone is pulling my invisible, digital leash. If I wasn't a technology junkie, I'd smash the bitch. Plucking my cell from my pocket, I smile because my newest program worked. I was so sick of *blocked* callers, I formatted a program to *unblock* them, and installed it on all of our phones. Why should some jackass have anonymity, then have the audacity to ask me who I am when I answer their call?

I don't recognize the number calling me. "Who is this?" I bark into the phone. I hate it when people I don't know call me, but the snap of the call disconnecting pisses me off even more.

"Fuck you!" I growl down at my phone. I used to be so calm and patient. Lately, I want to flail people alive for even the smallest grievance.

Another vibration buzzes my palm while I'm glowering daggers at my cell. Same blocked number, this time in text form.

1(607)654-8785: *½ block North on the right. 163. Red door –M.*

I look over my shoulder like a crackhead, trying to spot who's watching me. Who's M? Is this the elusive Master, or some serial killer who managed to figure out my personal cellphone number when I was outside of their home?

Gut instinct says it's Master.

I've graduated from stupid-girl moments to detrimental-woman idiocies. I can see the red door blazing three houses up. How did that asshole know I was out here? I know people are creatures of habit, but is nine days really a routine? Eight of those days I was joined by my daughter. Oh, God– that's worse.

I'm never leaving the house again.

I should sprint home and check on Ella.

I'm texting Fate one-handed before my mind can even check in with my fingertips.

You safe? Ella? Is the security system activated? Where's Kris? Ade? Answer me, dammit!

Number Cruncher: *Jesus Christ, Reg. What is your malfunction?*

Kris? Why are you answering Fate's text messages?

Number Cruncher: *Winner. Winner. Chicken Dinner. Even I want to know who the Next Food Network Star is– so fuck off. Finish your walk. We're all accounted for on your sofa. Only you're missing, but you definitely need some me time.*

Bitch!

Number Cruncher: *Love you too, sweetie.*

So much for that distraction. I didn't plan on meeting Master while wearing exercise clothing. I had a new outfit picked out that emphasized my attributes without making me look desperate– my little black dress. I don't want him to see me wearing ratty jeans, a t-shirt, and dirty sneakers. My hair's pulled into a ponytail and I haven't brushed it since yesterday. What a great first impression I'll make.

I pace back and forth on the same ten-foot stretch of sidewalk, the entire time I feel watchful eyes boring into my back. I just hope it's Master and not a resident ready to call Wintercrest on the lunatic pacing in front of their building.

After several false-starts, I find myself on the sidewalk beneath the red door. I quickly run up the three steps before I can change my mind. Clacking the cheerfully evil gargoyle knocker on the ornate, wooden door, the sound reverberates to my soul.

This moment is life changing.

I'll do anything for Ade, but this is more for me than her. I need this– I think.

The pop of the lock startles me, and I back down a step.

The door slowly creaks open, revealing an imposing man. I back up three steps until I'm at a safe distance on the sidewalk. I can't peel my eyes from the cement to look at him. I don't know what he looks like except for his brown eyes. They're warm and inviting, so why do they scare me so?

The daunting Dexter from Restraint didn't have this effect on me, but he isn't Master.

"Shh... it's alright," a silky smooth voice coos. "I won't hurt you. You've found the right place."

I keep my head down, but my eyes flick up to see him. Shadowed in the doorway is a lean man who's taller than me. His black hair is cropped short, barely showing that it holds a curl. His eyes are warm, a soft shade of brown the color of whiskey. Only half of his face is visible because of the lighting.

He's the figment of my imagination– the man fucking Apathy Regina. The powerful one I want to become.

I draw two steps closer to see him better, and with a gut-wrenching sensation, I know him instantly. I've seen countless pictures of this man when his campaign staff sent me signed headshots as a thank you gift for my contributions. His anonymity is as important as mine.

What the fuck is he doing in a brownstone when he should be beyond the Gates at Shadow Haven Estates?

I should have guessed when it was Dexter, Ezra, and Cortez playing around. They're keeping it in the family. Master is none other than Marcus Zeitler.

Grant's cuddle and tug buddy. The man who took away my scholarship, and then paid my tuition once I moved into Misery Castle.

Marcus is the man who stared at me through the secret panel to the passageways at Whittenhower estates.

Marcus is the man who never contacted me after his best friend's death– the very man who tried and failed to save Grant, gave Daniel the death notice, but then didn't stick around to tell the mother of Grant's children.

There's no fucking way in hell that this asshole doesn't know exactly who I am, and he has to know I know who he is too.

Lungs seizing, my breath catches in my throat. I feel closer to Grant right this instant than I ever have.

Marcus stands patiently in the doorway, as if he could stand there for hours as I inspect him. At only three or four years older than me, the age of knowledge screaming from his eyes is ancient. Marcus Zeitler knows things that will take me a lifetime to learn.

Not looking at me, Marcus is staring through me, as if I'm transparent before him. My breath hitches as he reads my soul. I drop my gaze again, trying to formulate words, but it doesn't feel right.

I wait.

"This will be a pleasure, Regina." My name rolls off Marc's tongue like a caress. I flinch, the sound harming me, and retreat back to the sidewalk.

"I have no idea what you want, what you expect, or why you agreed to see me after so long." I speak to the ground, but my gaze flicks up to meet his. "I have the feeling if I hadn't gone to Restraint, I would've never met you in my lifetime."

Marc's eyes tighten, creating fine lines at the corners. I flinch again, instinctively knowing I somehow broke a rule I haven't learned yet. I apologize underneath my breath, and he must have sonic hearing, because he acknowledges my apology.

"It's fine, Regina," he stresses my name again, like he's shocked I'm standing on his stoop. "We haven't discussed anything yet. Please, come in. It's too cold on the street for this kind of conversation. I'll explain. Follow me."

Expecting to be followed, Marcus opens the door to the brownstone wider, casting a pale-yellow light onto the street, giving me a better view of him. He's beautiful with the pleasant expression on his face. My stomach knots. I've never been so afraid, not even when I started my life over alone with a child growing inside me. Marcus is the representation of all that I have lost, reminding me of Grant.

Tears fill my eyes and my throat constricts. Years later, all it takes is one thought to derail me– almost bringing me to my knees.

Fingers stroke my chin, startling me when I hadn't felt or seen Marcus move. Without hesitation, my eyes connect with his.

"You're so young to have such a tragic, tortured soul– beautiful," Marc marvels. His hand slides to settle between my breasts, not groping but still touching more than he should. "I can almost hold it in my palm– your heart beats so strong, Regina. It will be my greatest pleasure to break you." Voice hypnotic, he purrs.

Woozy, as Marc's eerie words register in my mind, I'm pushed into the brownstone. The lock clicks into place with deafening finality.

My heart flutters the speed of hummingbird wings, beating as if it can feel Marc holding it in the palm of his hand. The soothing threat sped my blood, yet it didn't frighten me– enlivened me with excitement.

Years without a real challenge have left me numb– I want to see Marcus try to break me.

Marc's smile spreads across his face, showcasing perfectly sharp teeth. The expression meets mine head on, and power stirs in my blood in answer.

"Oh, this is going to be fun," Marc drawls, following it with a delighted snicker.

My shoulders relax. Marcus Zeitler is just a man, one who is similar in personality to me. He won't harm me unless I beg for it, and beg he'll make me do.

Allowing me to check out my surroundings, Marcus waits while I take inventory of the brownstone. Everything is wood: floor, wainscoting, the staircase, and an endless sea of molding. The small foyer rests at the bottom of a staircase, and to its left is a closed doorway, and to its right is a long hallway lined with doors, leading to what I can only assume is the kitchen.

"Before we begin." Marc gestures to the first room on the right. I slowly walk down the narrow hallway that borders the staircase, and then turn into the room where he pointed. I don't know what to expect. More like Restraint, which was a surprise because it wasn't as brutal as I thought it would be.

However, Marc's lair isn't anything I expected, thinking it would be more like a private residence, but it's what Restraint should be. From the outside, you wouldn't know what lurks beneath the stone exterior of this building.

A BDSM dungeon.

"Knowing a little about you," I murmur, not wanting to offer any disrespect. "You live at Shadow Haven, and I've only seen pictures of it in Dominion History textbooks in Elementary school. So color me surprised that you live here."

"Live?" Marc purrs, voice trilling down my spine. "No, but I wish. This brownstone belongs to my closest friend and his partner– not the kind Ezra and Cortez are. Jamie and Alex merely allow me to use this as my getaway from real life."

"Ah, I know how that is." I turn, taking in the space. "So BDSM makes Marcus Zeitler tick? Do I call you your majesty? Your honor?"

Laugh throaty and amused, "I'm not a judge *yet*, Regina," Marcus stresses. "While I love how *your majesty* sounds rolling off your tongue… Master would be a far more befitting moniker, don't you think?"

"Mmm…" With a smile playing along my lips, I turn to Marcus, feeling alive for the first time in many years. An equal in mental sports is a rarity. Ade is the only one who even comes close, with Daniel being smarter than me. "I believe Marc is more befitting, don't you?"

"Grant always said you had big balls," Marcus taunts, seemingly pleased that I'm willing to banter with him.

"Ah…" I suck in a pained breath, hearing the utter love and devotion as his voice caressed Grant's name. "Balls?" I quirk an eyebrow in his direction, cupping my hands near my crotch. "Big, fuzzy, low hanging metaphorical balls. Oh, I've got 'em in spades."

"Mmm… ballsy women, my favorite." Marc's eyes travel up and down my body, and I want the floor to swallow me since I'm wearing jeans and a t-shirt with ratty, unwashed hair. "You're in the right place at the right time, Regina. I think you need me."

Ignoring that, I change the subject. "Is every room like this one?"

"Diversion tactics, nice…" Marc drawls. "Yes, every room on this side of the house is similar to this one, while the other half of the house is the kitchen and man cave, the upstairs houses the bedrooms, and the attic is Jamie's hidey hole."

"Hidey hole?"

"Jamie is probably the most introverted person on the planet. He hides on the third floor most of the time. Jamie's partner, Alex, he runs the errands and takes care of business, so to speak." Marcus points behind himself. "That side is off-limits to my students. The staircases are also off-limits to my students, both the one in the foyer and the one in the kitchen. If your foot touches a step without invitation… curiosity will get the cat thrown out on the street, ass landing quick as shit on the sidewalk."

"Understood," I mutter gruffly.

"Alex will always be off-limits to you. He's a busy man who doesn't dabble in BDSM, and he's usually at Transcend, or wherever he runs off to for Jamie. If you get a glimpse of him and follow to speak to him… pavement burns to the ass."

"Transcend?" My voice pitches high, but Marcus ignores me. "No speaking to Alex– got it."

"Don't get so curious you go to Transcend to find Alex, either," Marcus warns, already having my number. "I mean it."

"You're kind of throwing down a challenge, there, Master," I taunt, voice light and teasing. "The gauntlet."

"Good luck with that," Marcus mutters. "Because Alex already knows to avoid you. My business is my business, and Alex's business is his business, and never shall the twain meet. You are a guest in this house, as am I– don't wear out *our* welcome. Stay out of Alex's areas, and all will be fine. Jamie is another issue, but we'll burn that bridge after we cross it."

"Okay?" My eyes flutter around, feeling a stare devouring me but not finding its source.

"This hallway and the rooms lining it are mine to do with as I see fit, thusly for my students. Feel free to wander these rooms, the kitchen, and the bathroom off the kitchen. The rest–"

"Is off-limits," I finish for Marcus, unable to help myself.

A slight tightening around his mouth and eyes is the only indication Marcus doesn't like being interrupted, but he doesn't chastise me. "Each room offers a different type of BDSM instruction." His voice is soft yet piercing. "We will discuss things further, but let's sit first."

There's nowhere to sit– baffled, I stand and look at the floor.

"Regina, you may look me in the eyes as we speak. Since you're training to be a Mistress, I want us to be on an equal footing, unless and until I tell you otherwise. Do you understand?"

I suck in a sharp breath when I hear *that* word slip from Marc's lips– worse is the fact that it's someone who was important to Grant. Heart clenching, tears stream unbidden from my eyes.

Quickly wiping betraying tears with my knuckles, my voice breaks with agony. "Yes, I agree to everything you've said, but the quickest way to get me to leave is to call me mistress. I can't bear to hear that word, preferring to be called Queen when dealing with matters of dominance. My personal life has nothing to do with this, and I know you understand the value of anonymity and privacy."

"My apologies," Marcus whispers, visibly torn and upset. "Being Grant's oldest friend from the cradle, I do know more about you than you probably know about me. I fear there will be many landmines ready to be detonated instead of disarmed gently."

I reach for Marc's hand to comfort him, to connect with someone who loved Grant as much as I did, if not more. But let my hand fall to my side instead. It's been so long since I've touched anyone that wasn't in my household, and even longer with a male. I feel unsure if my touch would be wanted or welcomed.

"You may touch me as long as we aren't doing instruction," Marcus murmurs softly, compassion and understanding glowing from his amber eyes. "I said we're equals– I meant it, Regina. I will not call you that word. However, I will not call you Queen until you earn it."

I croak out, "Earn it?"

"Yes, *earn* it. When your training is complete, I will call you Queen. I do understand the need to keep our private lives separate from this." Marcus gestures around the room. "We will conduct everything here, as I don't go to Restraint during hours of operation for obvious reasons."

Striding over to a large object draped in damask fabric, Marcus dramatically flings off the covering, revealing a purple velvet settee.

Eyes widening. "Oh, that has got to be tuition bitch's sofa," slips out before I can stop it.

Lips twitching, "Tuition bitch? I'm assuming that's not me, even though I did pay for your higher education."

"You're cuddle and tug," I admit before I can stop myself. "Dexter is tuition bitch. That sofa screams velvet whorehouse, eyesore of a nightmare of a house… and I paid you back tenfold in campaign contributions, soon-to-be your honor."

"Cuddle and tug? How apropos." Chuckling richly, Marcus sits on the settee, patting a cushion in invitation. "This was my grandmother's sofa."

Insert foot into mouth mortification.

"The comfort objects in this room I stole from Dexter before they made their way into his version of Serenity." Marcus is getting off on my speechlessness. "Just wait until you get a gander at his private room at Restraint. It's a good thing Grandmother had a perverse sense of humor, or she might be rolling over in her grave because her furniture is being fucked, sucked, and whipped upon."

Another pat on the cushion, and I obey. Settling next to Marcus, I'm confident but not relaxed. He leans back, angling himself so we're facing one another, with his arm resting along the back of the sofa. Touchy-feely, his long, tapered fingers play with the ends of my ratty ponytail.

"What we know of one another is hearsay." Marcus brings out the lawyer speak. "All knowledge was passed from Grant. True?"

"True," I murmur, trying to desensitize myself to Grant's name flowing from those devastating lips. Devastating in a way a category five hurricane is on the coast. "I don't believe he'd lie."

Marc's eyebrow reaches his hairline. "Everyone lies, Regina. It's human nature, or my profession wouldn't exist… and I can see the resentment lurking in the back of your eyes. Ask yourself why you haven't met me until now, and trust that it had nothing to do with me. All humans lie with purpose."

"Touché." Heart fracturing, my mind flits about, lighting on all the times Grant may have lied to me. "Grant and I had a non-judgmental relationship. I accepted Grant as he was, and I hoped he did the same for me. We were also about nondisclosure not being a lie, because he said there were things he could not tell—"

An elegant finger presses against my lips. "All conversations dealing with what Grant did or didn't tell you will commence at a different location, in the bright of day, preferably out of doors."

My whispered, "What?" is eclipsed by a large object landing on the floor above us with a smash.

"Ignore that," Marc tries to soothe me when I startle. "The man of the house is up and about, no doubt throwing himself," is muttered snidely. "Jamie can be difficult, especially in his quest to understand actions have consequences and the world doesn't revolve around his needs."

"Do you even like your friend?" I comment on the bitterness thickly lacing Marc's voice.

"Yes— well, we all had to find a replacement for Grant, didn't we?" Another smash is the explanation to his point. "Grant was a more agreeable sort than Jamie will ever be. Less controllable, more introverted— a downright defiant asshole, who gives good cuddles but refuses to tug with me."

"I—" Marc's cellphone pings with a text message. Looking at it, he chuckles sardonically, then replies at lightning speed.

Waiting for another reply, Marc mutters absentmindedly, "You were saying?"

"No one could ever replace Grant," my voice is filled with utter conviction. "No one. Not your Jamie, even though he's probably upset how you compare him to your former best friend. That would piss anyone off."

"Oh, no doubt." Marcus laughs, returning yet another text message. An answering crash above has him howling with laughter. "Jamie agrees with you, Regina. How sweet."

"Jesus Christ," I hiss, finding this the most bizarre moment of my life. "Quit tormenting your friend while we're in his house."

"Oh…" Marc drawls. "Jamie deserves worse, and more."

"That's not nice," I chastise like a mother trying to get two brothers to stop bullying each other. Above, Jamie begins cleaning up his mess, judging by the sound of sweeping glass. "If speaking of Grant upsets your friend, then you shouldn't. That's like rubbing your ex-wife in your current wife's face. Trust me, being compared to another woman lasts a lifetime."

"Regina, what do you mean?" Marcus leans forward, and silence descends from upstairs.

"It's not fair to Jamie, you comparing him to Grant. They're different people."

"No, I get that. Ironically so." Marc's lips twist into a grimace. "You said something about being compared to another woman. What woman?"

I find myself blurting out, "Gwen," before I can stop myself.

Marc doesn't say anything. He simply looks at me for a few suspended moments in time with a very serious expression on his face. "Stop!" he orders abruptly in a furious voice.

I freeze in terror, scared I cut another thread tying me to Grant.

What the fuck did I do this time?

Hand lashing out, Marc's fingertips latch onto my face so I can't turn, gouging into my cheeks and chin.

"You made this agreement– get out!" Marcus orders in a calm and cold, deadly tone.

I shift to follow Marc's instruction, but his fingers strengthen on my jaw– bruising. Tears spill from the corners of my eyes from the painful strain.

"I'm sorry, Regina. Had I realized the time, I wouldn't have invited you this evening." Marc's expression is friendly, but I can see the worry etched across his face. His mercurial moods are confusing at best, and petrifying at worst.

"The masters of the house are a curious sort, always breaking the very rules they created. But I'm not one to go back on my word, no matter how much they may be pouting. So I think it's for the best if you vacate, but please rejoin me tomorrow evening at eight. After a refresher in honor, I'll make sure we aren't interrupted unless I deem fit." Marcus pointedly looks over my shoulder and glares at someone.

Jamie?

Alex?

Both?

Whoever the hell it is, their stare is burning into my back, with my body blazing to life under their gaze. Eyes dilating, pupils blown, my body flushes with sweat. Gasping, I start to pant in puffs of air.

Jesus, what's wrong with me?

Closing my eyes, I inhale through the potent cocktail traveling through my veins. I have no name for what's happening, but I'm finally wide awake. My body loses its ability to hold me upright, and only Marc's fingers keep me from sprawling on the sofa.

The gaze intoxicates me– drugs me back to life.

Eyes awed, Marcus smiles while worrying his bottom lip between his teeth. Breaking the tension, he chuckles underneath his breath, as if he can read my private thoughts.

"Well, I would've never thought *that* possible. Yoo-hoo... are you still with me, Regina? Are you doing alright?" His voice flows over my skin, eliciting a shiver after being awakened so abruptly. Senses going haywire, the combination of the penetrating gaze and Marc's voice has me quivering.

A creak of the front door sobers me a bit– I thought the door was locked.

"Marc!" Cortez's voice flows from the foyer. "Sorry we're late."

"Is the boy with you?" Marc shouts back. "If there is a God, please tell me he isn't."

"Yeah, why wouldn't he be?" Cortez's voice is suddenly closer, maybe in the doorway. "My punishment is babysitting duty, remember? Are you getting dementia in your old age already? What the–" Cort stammers, sounding at a loss. "Jamie's... have you lost your goddamn mind... he's right behind Regina... and. Shit!" His voice fades, footsteps loudly running away. "Back your ass up to the door, bub."

"Kitchen stairs– now," Marc whispers hurriedly to the person at my back, apparently Jamie. Sensing him within arm's reach, I lean backward, suddenly aching for his touch, but Marc yanks me with the fingers still clutching my face. Jamie's absence leaves me throbbing and aching for him to return.

"What a fucking cluster fuck of shit." Marcus spews out an impressive string of curses I've never heard before, slipping into Hebrew. "Cort, escort the PB to the bathroom, and then come back to me. Son, you better keep your ass in that room until I get you!" Marcus projects his voice down the hallway.

Gently placing me on the sofa, Marc's fingertips leave my jaw. Gasping in pain, blood flows back into my neglected flesh and the bone throbs as if bruised.

"Oh, I'm sorry, Regina." Marc sounds concerned as he massages the pain away. "I couldn't allow you to turn, but I most definitely didn't mean to leave a mark. I didn't know what to do, and this meeting didn't go as planned, so please forgive my negligence. It'll never happen again."

"It's okay," I slur in shock. "Who's with Cortez? Why can't I see Jamie?"

Refusing to answer me, Marc changes the subject. "Cortez will drive you home," he says calmly while smoothing my hair back down. "This was traumatic for you, and I don't want you to walk home in this state.

"I'm okay." I try to stand, but my head swims, and I land back on the sofa.

It's like I've had a hit of a really strong drug and my body burned its fuel in record speed. I've never tried drugs, and I've never had a drop to drink until a few nights ago. This is a euphoric sensation I'd chase to the ends of the earth.

"Well, if it isn't *Queen*." Cort stresses the Queen snidely as he strides into the room, sans hood unlike the last time I saw him. Too bad he grew into his potential– the fuckface is devastatingly handsome, befitting the charm he oozes. Tanned and toned, with black hair and piercing gunmetal eyes, his ruby lips are killer. "Should I bow? May I call you Regina in private?"

"Yeah, sure– I hate the way you say that word. Just don't fuck up in public, asshole." I'm mad as hell for Faith, or whatever name she's going by now since I can't locate her. You don't cheat on your girlfriend with her big sister– it's disgusting.

Cort flashes me a confused yet hurt expression, like I'm the one being the asshole. Then his face transforms to the biggest Cheshire cat grin I've ever seen. "WOW! Marc, you dropped the ball big time." Cort chuckles and wipes his brow exaggeratingly in relief. "That was fucking close. Way too damn close. The resident hermit was down here, and I bet his little friend was too."

"Seeing Regina walk by was too tempting, and we all fucked up. Jamie was a heartbeat from touching Regina… and like a car accident waiting to happen, Alex was ghosting in the doorway." Marcus falls back to the sofa with a thump. He heaves in a heavy sigh. "Jamie gains ridiculous amounts of courage from Alex– so Regina can only visit while he's working."

"No shit." Cort snorts. "Is Jamie going to roam free like he does with PB? Because I think this temptation will be too great for you to contain."

"It's Jamie's call– I think I just had a heart attack of epic proportions." Chest rising and falling rapidly, Marc's breathless. "It will never happen again. Curiosity is a wicked mistress."

"Well, with the PB here, you would've had two very confused people on your hands. I would have paid to see that. Holy shit, Marc!" Cort laughs, joining us on the sofa by wedging his ass between us. "So, you guys up for some fun?"

I growl at Cort, yanking my leg from underneath his thigh, then I try to squish next to the armrest. "Who is PB? Why can't I see Jamie and Alex?" I repeat. Again.

Only to be ignored, yet again, as if I didn't speak. With violent force, Grant filters into my thoughts, how he felt no one ever heard him.

Regina, you're my echo is screaming loudly in my mind, stronger than when Grant said the words aloud, causing my breath to hitch and my heart to clench.

"You test me at every turn," Marc accuses Cort, neither realizing I have warring emotions terrorizing me. "I don't know what to do with you anymore since punishment doesn't work. So please don't test me tonight, because my old ticker can't take it." Marcus practically begs.

It's like Marcus is a different person around Cortez, open and relaxed, and the intimacy is staggering. But then again, Marcus would have gained Cortez as a ward when he did Ezra since his wife was Cortez's legal guardian.

They're family.

Cort leans over and kisses Marcus on the lips sensually. Mouths parted, pink tongues touching lightly. "You love it. Who are you kidding?" Cortez whispers against the other man's lips. "And you love me– admit it."

Marcus kisses the younger man back with equal intensity, a moan lingering in the air while their lips make smacking sounds.

I ignore the stirring in my belly, because they are a very pseudo-incestuous family... I mouth *Whoa* silently in astonishment. I've never seen two men kiss before, and it's kinda hot yet creepy, since Marc was Cort's father figure.

I've just entered a brand new world of *what the fuck.*

"My God, you're such a fucking tease." Lips kiss-swollen and crimson, Marc murmurs in amusement, eyes wide and bright. Releasing a sultry laugh, he palms Cort's chest, and then pushes him away. "Get outta here– take Regina home and behave while you're doing it."

"Oh, goody!" Cort twirls an imaginary mustache like a Vaudeville villain, and my heart beats triple-time as I try to figure out if he's being a smart-ass or sarcastic.

"I give my permission for Regina to kick your ass if you try anything. While you're gone, I'll take PB back to his kingdom."

Confused, I watch their interaction and body language. Marcus stares into Cortez's eyes for a second, and the raw look of utter devotion trips my heart. I want to bawl from its intensity and strength, because I don't have that with anyone, and I doubt I ever did with Grant.

"I'll see you at home, unless you'll be at the apartment?" Words soft, Marc's voice is laced with hope. Fingertips weaving into the back of Cort's hair, Marcus controls him with a yank, and kisses his forehead in goodbye. "Behave," he warns.

Crawling out from beneath Cortez, Marcus leans down to give me the same kiss to the forehead. His lips are hot and moist from Cort's attentions, only my kiss was more parental or platonic versus romantic or lusty.

"Eight o'clock sharp. Tomorrow night," Marcus reminds me. "I promise it won't be as hectic. Welcome to crazyville, Regina– there's no backing out now." He swaggers from the room, captivating both Cort and me.

A billionaire shouldn't wear worn-in denim that molds to his perfect ass– it's downright criminal.

"Is my little shit misbehaving? I hear you and I have something to discuss. Did you honestly think I wouldn't find out? When will you learn that I'm omnipotent?" Marc's cackle flows down the hallway toward his next victim.

Chapter Eight

Standing from the sofa, this time without the dizziness, I ask again. "Who's PB?" I wrack my brain, trying to work out if I know anyone with those initials. I'm surprisingly comfortable around Cortez after all the craziness of the past few minutes.

"If Marcus wanted you to know, he'd tell you." Cortez is the smuggest person I've ever met, and I don't know if I want to punch the look off his face or kiss it off him.

Kiss it off, because that would disgust Cortez while giving me a taste of Marcus.

While my mind takes a vacation, Cortez is still flaunting his knowledge while keeping me in the dark. "PB is Marc's other trainee, and if he wanted you to know who it was, PB wouldn't be locked in the bathroom like a naughty pet."

"Really? I'm shocked." Sarcasm bleeds from my words. "I thought maybe you'd offer up the goods."

"No." Cort closes his eyes, like it physically hurts to look at me. "You just met Marcus, and it takes a long time to make it into his inner circle. Hell, I don't think Ezra's there yet, and Marcus adopted his ass."

I chew over Cortez's words while he escorts me to his car. "Seriously? Yours?" I ask of the artwork saddled up to the curb. I stare in awe at a brand new, shiny black *Aston Martin V12 Vanquish*. "Compensate much? Did Marcus buy this for you?" Gliding my hand down its sleek lines, I want to purr with pleasure. "Sexy beast on four tires."

"I ask, and he gifts– Ezra, not Marc." Smug. Again. "I'm doing pretty well for myself. I married into money, after all." Smile wide, Cortez buffs his nails on his leather jacket. "The wife likes to keep the husband in the style in which he's accustomed."

"Spoiled much? You have Marcus and Ezra hanging all over ya, then you managed to snag little Divina Hastings. What was she thinking?" I dramatically shake my head in disgust.

"Divina was thinking she wanted to keep her legacy in the family, is what she was thinking." Smug disappears on a wave of insult. Good. "As far as my dick, I have no need to compensate."

"Sure." I snort. "I'm sure it's a Vienna sausage."

Completely ignorant, looking as innocent as an altar boy, "Is that bigger than a Polish sausage?"

Annoyed that I once lived off potted meat, Vienna sausages, canned tuna, and Ramen noodles, sometimes mixed together, I shout, "Google it, you rich cocksucker!"

Halted on the sidewalk in front of the brownstone, Cort won't let me get into his car until after he Googles Vienna sausages on his cellphone. The moment his eyes narrow with insult is the moment laughter bubbles up from my chest.

"Ha-ha, bitch," Cort snarls. "Two? Three inches? Not since I was a toddler."

"Men are so easy to bring down to size," I taunt with a grin.

"I'll have you know, my cock is motherfucking H U G E– just ask your roomie. Fate liked what I had to offer, and I was just a young'un," he mutters cockily. "I wasn't at full capacity yet."

Cort's gunmetal eyes complement the car, and I decide they fit each other perfectly, which pisses me off because I don't want to praise the asshole. "How 'bout I ask Marcus if you're compensating, because I bet he knows the answer."

My mind conjures their shared kiss, and I flush red all the way to the roots of my hair, while turning a bit green that no one finds me attractive.

"Marc has seen, but not touched," Cort mutters wistfully. "It's not like that. I mean– fuck, if I can't explain it to myself, how am I supposed to explain it to you?" He opens the passenger door, finally letting me into the dark, cavernous car. Its dark gray interior matches Cortez's eyes and personality.

Maybe I need to upgrade a bit. This car is more of an investment– it wouldn't be a luxury, not really... or so I lie to myself.

"So you're teasing to pleasing?" I chuckle at Cort's tortured expression.

"Regina, are you joking with me?" Cort acts shocked. "I'm beside myself with glee, since I've annoyed you since we met twelve– thirteen years ago?" His voice is serious, but his tone is light. "You took an instant dislike to me, if I remember correctly."

"No, I did *not*!" I defend, thoroughly confused.

"I'm just picking on you," Cort murmurs with a smile in his voice. "I tease Marcus because I have to for some reason– it's an illogical compulsion I can't explain. I don't even know what I'd do if Marc took me up on the offer."

I offer solutions. "Faint? Come on the spot? Thank him?"

"Can I pick all three?" Cort's laughter is infectious. "I bit off more than I could chew once with him, and it's turned into more of a punishment now." He shudders next to me while he traverses through traffic. "A never-ending punishment that's as pleasurable as it's painful."

"What is it?" Man, the expression on Cortez's face is unfathomable. What does Marcus do to him? I watch as the lights of oncoming traffic highlight his features. Cortez did grow up to be a devastatingly handsome sonofabitch.

"Nah– not answering that. Some secrets are meant to be kept, especially when I'm not even sure Ezra knows what little we do. Marc must trust you, or he wouldn't have kissed me back– he would've punched me instead. I was testing him, and he knew it."

"I don't think it was Marcus trusting me, as much as he wanted to see my reaction to him kissing you back. I know *of*, yet hardly know Marcus. I highly doubt he does anything without a reason, and it wasn't trust."

Ignoring my astute commentary, "So... how's my partner's bitch doing?"

"Excuse me?" I know Cortez is speaking of Ade, and I'm instantly pissed.

Like oil and water, Cortez and I just seem to rub each other wrong, or right, which might be the problem. He's a player, and I'm not even in the game. Excuse me if I'm a bit green around the gills.

"Yeah, like I'd forget who your best friend is. After Grant, you may have been hiding out, but we all knew who was with you and what you were doing. Fate, Ade, and Kris were still seen everywhere, but not acting as if their BFF was gone *and* they weren't living at their childhood homes. Except Ade," Cortez snarls. "Didn't take much to put two and two together, especially when Fate was spotted as the public figurehead of Empowerment– a business dealing with software, devices, and websites. Your specialty."

"Please," I groan, getting angry. "I just didn't want Daniel around."

"All Daniel had to do was have Albert follow his own daughter home. It's not rocket science. I get it– everyone left you alone to lick your wounds and grieve in peace, especially Daniel. He told me he couldn't look at you without seeing Grant, so he'd rather not look at you."

Gut clenching, I groan, "Stop!"

"Niel looks nothing like Grant, by the way. Cute bruiser of a kid." Cortez never shuts up, saying things I'd never allow Adelaide to speak. "Light of Daniel's life. Whitt– Daniel has a hard time looking at the poor kid, seeing Grant. You can see the torture in his eyes, but he does love him with every fiber of his being."

"STOP!" I shout louder. "Please, Cortez. I beg of you."

"Okay, then. Next time I ask you about your cunt of a BFF, you best spill," Cort manipulates like a pro. "Or I'll force you to finally grieve your losses so you can move on."

"You don't know me," I hiss, fingertips clutching the door handle, contemplating jumping out.

"God, Whitt... he's gorgeous–"

"Ade is doing fine," I quickly give in. "Not up to no good. Just working and visiting me."

"The cunt is always up to no good. She's been preying on Ez since we were little kids, but I guess she's getting her wish now."

"I wouldn't wish that kind of life on anyone," I murmur in a horror-struck voice.

"*Wish it on me*," Cort breathes. "Sorry, but Adelaide has always rubbed me the wrong way." He doesn't sound sorry at all.

"Maybe you rub Ade the wrong way. Maybe you both rub each other wrong... and you're one to talk. You're married, so why can't Ezra be?"

"Because I love my wife, as does Ezra. We're *family*. I don't fuck my wife as an experiment. I threw up after I found out Ezra had laid with Adelaide."

"I've kept track of you all, too," I remind Cortez. "So you think it's cheating? Ezra having sex with his own fiancée, while you run around town with your cock in every available hole? Better yet, how does your wife feel about this? You sound hypocritical to me... wait a minute, are you really saying you've never slept with your wife, or do you expect Ezra to never touch his?"

"The difference is that I'm not fucking men." Cortez looks at me pointedly, trying to get me to understand. "Ya feel me?"

"Explain," I order, and shockingly, Cortez does.

"I forgave Ezra for cheating on me with a man. He's never had a problem with me sleeping with women, because I have an insatiable sex drive, which he appreciates. Ezra and I… we haven't been together as a couple, not since…"

"Christ," I cry, reaching for the hand wrapped around the gear shift. "Not since your abduction?"

"Not since," Cort murmurs wistfully, remembering better times. "We have rules now, and Ezra has broken them twice. Divina was part of the rules. We married in an arrangement to keep our money in the family."

"That's so sad." My heart clenches, hating that I understand what Cortez is saying.

"Divina is a happy woman." Cort's eyes cut in my direction, with a smile playing along his lips. "As for Ezra, I've never broken our trust. Ezra has. Sorry if Adelaide makes me see fire, sorry if the very mention of her name makes me want to commit murder, but Ezra didn't negotiate for Adelaide. Ezra just did it, and told me afterward, and then did it again while I waited at home."

A growl echoes around the confines of the car, and I have no idea which of us made the animalistic sound.

"Yeah, Ezra and I aren't getting along real well right now. I've been with him since the cradle, and I think that's what fuels my need to tease Marc. I want Marc to have a taste, and then I want to flaunt it in Ezra's face. I want Ezra to feel the deep-seated pain of betrayal. At the same time, I love Ez so much that I can't hurt him that way. Why didn't he love me enough? That's the question I ask myself every damn day. Why wasn't I worthy of him?"

On the verge of crying, Cortez rests his face on the steering wheel, and I realize we're sitting in my driveway.

"How the hell did you know where I live?" I glare at my white house, voice filled with suspicion. My mind conjures up where I will move us to next.

"Marcus was Grant's best friend. Do you honestly believe Marc didn't know every step you've taken since you were eighteen? He kept away because that's what Grant wanted– for you to have a normal life without the restrictive Whittenhower pressure. It's not our fault all you do is work, and seemed to have forgotten how to fuck. Grant was a horny bastard, and you guys got along so well. We waited to see who your first victim would be."

"You're such an asshole… I assumed that was par for the course, actually." I admit for the first time I expected Marc to take a supportive role in my life. "I just assumed Marc didn't want anything to do with me since he never materialized. But that doesn't explain how *you* knew where I lived."

"Marcus trusted me to take you home, don't ya think he told me where you lived first? I know a lot about you, Regina. More than you'd like, I bet. I'm sure he kept some of your secrets to himself." Cort bangs his head on the steering wheel. "I've been naughty, so Marcus is punishing me. I'm his assistant until he tells me otherwise. Basically, I wipe his damn ass on a continual basis."

"What did you do?"

"Of course, it's all my fault." Cort sounds flabbergasted at my accusation. "It's always my fault. It couldn't possibly be Ezra." Animosity is thick in his voice. "Precious Ezra does no wrong." Remorse flashes across his features the instant the words are out for ears to hear and no longer private thoughts.

Cortez turns to me, then makes air-quotes with his fingers while mimicking Marc's voice. "*Cortez, your attitude is atrocious. Until you can keep your venom to yourself and move back home to the apartment with Ezra, you're my bitch.* End-quote."

"Oh, Marcus doesn't like your discord with Ezra?"

"That's an understatement, if I've ever heard one. Don't ever piss Marc off, Regina. You wouldn't like being his bitch." The glint in his eyes says that he may enjoy being Marc's bitch a little bit too much.

"I'm sorry, Cort. I think we've had a misunderstanding. Truce?"

Cortez flashes me a wicked grin of triumph.

"Put that dangerous smile away, Cort– you're thinking nefarious things." I laugh at him, carefree and effortless for once instead of playacting, and it feels damn good.

"I'm sorry. I know that Ade's your friend, and she's probably really nice, maybe even cool, but you have to see it from my point of view. There is nothing on this earth that could possibly make me like that woman. It's Ezra's fault, not hers. Do you understand?"

Gwen instantly pops into my head. I hate that woman, and I've never laid eyes on her. Jealousy because Gwen had Grant's undying love. Envy that she is a tiny, blue-eyed, blonde-haired heiress of a founder's bloodline. Then there is bitter resentment, because Gwen peppered the countryside with children she never raised, all of them I know– most of them I love with all my heart.

"I get you. I understand your pain better than you realize, and it hurts like hell. All you can do is get up and live through the ache.

Put one foot in front of the other and walk forward. I'd love to say it gets better, but that's a lie. You just have to find things to divert your attention. But you do have one thing going for you that I don't."

"Yeah?" Cort's voice is filled with hope. "What's that?"

"Ezra's still alive," I murmur wistfully, only left with hating a woman I've never met because a dead man loved her. "You can fix this after the betrayal fades. Allow Ezra to re-earn your trust… and I get it about Ade. She's an acquired taste, even for me."

With an odd gleam shining in his eyes, Cort looks like I just gave him the greatest gift. Moving slowly, he allows me time to push him away and not accept his thank you. Light-headed, feeling desperate to feel something– *anything* –I allow it.

Cort's lips flutter feather-soft against mine, and then he breathes, "Truce."

Cortez Hunter, aka Cortez Abernathy, is the third person I've ever kissed in nearly thirty years of life. First there was Roman Alexander. My friend immortalized in my memory as my first kiss. Then there was Grant Whittenhower– my first everything: first time, father of my children, and my first and only love.

How the hell did Cort become the third kiss? Ironic. I find it hilariously how the boy who flirted relentlessly with me at his own girlfriend's sweet sixteen party is coaxing me to kiss him back. Amusement isn't what he's going for, I'm sure, but at least I feel *something* other than numb, even if I don't know what to name it.

The taste is subtle, a complete contradiction– smoky and sweet. My eyes bulge when Cort traces my bottom lip with the tip of his tongue. I shock myself, because I give him access. Parting my mouth under his, I slip my tongue between his supple lips. Hungry, Cort groans into my mouth, and I unhinge. My fingers seek his hair to pull him closer. Feeding at his mouth, I use my lips, tongue, and teeth. With a growl, Cortez takes as much abuse as I can give.

My curiosity gets the best of me, and my hand finds its way to the bulge in Cort's jeans, fingers curving around the hardness. Grabbing me forcefully, he pulls me over the stick-shift into his lap. I hit my head on the ceiling, and break out into a giggling fit.

Regina Regal giggling? Has Hell officially frozen over?

Cort allows me to laugh as he bites my neck, then heads south toward my breasts. The entire time as we kiss, I keep repeating in my head *Ade's kiss is a snack– Cort's is a feast.*

The *Godfather* theme song breaks into our private world, and we ignore it while we tear off whatever clothing is in our way. That's until it goes to voicemail, hangs up, and replays. Three more times.

"It's Marc–" Cort mutters breathlessly against the mound of my breast. "He'll keep doing that until I answer."

"Mood killer. Hurry! You should change his ringtone to Marvin Gaye, then it'd just be sexy background music."

Snickering, Cort grabs his cellphone off the dashboard. "You rang?"

Blaring through the cellphone, *Speakerphone! Now!*

Cort flicks a button, then replies, "Yes, sir."

"Let's get it on…" Marcus croons, doing an impressive Marvin Gaye impression, causing me to freeze in terror. "Horny children, you're being naughty. No sex in expensive sports cars while sitting in Regina's driveway. My best friend's pussycat will not be tainted by you of all people, Cortez Julian Hunter. I didn't give permission for you to play, and you're under punishment, which means no Regina as a reward." I can hear Marc's amusement flowing through the phone. "Regina is the biggest reward I could ever give you, don't you think?

Cort mutters in exasperation, "Cock-blocked? Are you fucking kidding me?" Just as I say, "Wait a minute, how do you know what we're up to?"

"I'm sure Marc has the car wired for sound." Cort answers my question. "The price of his trust is that he tests you for a very long time. I just got rid of the last fucking transmitter." Cort sounds more impressed than angry. "When did you replace the bitch?"

"Last night while you were busy breaking my rules. It's one of your punishments. Lovely conversation you've both had– it's so nice how you're bonding. I was patient until I heard fabric rip. I thought I better end it before you reached the point of no return."

"Oh, how thoughtful, Marcus," Cort mutters sarcastically. "Thanks a fucking lot for the massive case of blue balls. I'm sure Regina's gonna have a belly ache, too."

"Regina can rub the ache away with her fingertips. I was saving her from you and herself. I'm positive Regina would regret this destructive behavior sooner rather than later." Marc's smooth voice purrs through the speaker. "Judging by your conversation, I'll see you at home, Cortez. You have fifteen minutes to meet me in the sitting room. Your activities ramped up my need to turn you into my bitch."

The tone in Marc's voice has Cort blazing red in a fraction of a second. With a hasty flick of his finger, Cortez has the phone call disconnected before Marcus says too much.

"So… um-yeah. See ya around, Cort." I crawl from the car on shaky legs, head feeling light and foggy.

"Told ya I wasn't compensating." Cort smirks at me, his eyes glittering with barely contained lust.

"It was the car– it was all the car," I lie to the background of Cortez's smug laughter.

Holy fuck, it wasn't the car.

Knees wobbling, I walk into my house in a daze. After shutting the door behind me, I lean against it while running a fingertip along my smiling, swollen lips.

"Where have you been?" Three pissed off females glare at me.

Shit! I went for a walk, turned off my phone, and was gone for hours.

"Who won The Next Food Network Star?" Glares and silence abound. "I just made out in an *Aston Martin V12 Vanquish* with Cortez, and it wasn't because of the car." I giggle like a school girl high on hallucinogenic drugs. "And I kinda liked it."

Chapter Nine

Running on a high I've never felt, I ignore the looks of outrage on my family. With my head held high and my shoulders back, I stroll through the house to the kitchen, and then pull Kristal's bottle of Jack from the cabinet above the refrigerator. Without thinking twice, I take a draught of it, shuddering at the gag-inducing taste.

"Rough night?" Coming up behind me, Kristal leans around my shoulder, getting into my face until all I see is her saucy smirk.

Fate leans against the countertop since I've invaded her domain. "Honestly, I don't remember Cortez being bad enough to require a drink... or good enough. I've had better and worse. He was forgettable and mediocre at best."

Furious, Adelaide storms into the kitchen, heels clacking on the tile. "Is there anyone here who hasn't fucked that asshole?" She tries and fails to wrench the bottle of Jack out of my grip. Growling, Ade's working up to a tantrum of epic proportions. "You're being destructive, Regina. It's so not like you."

"Let the woman live a little." Kris turns surly. "Jesus Christ, you have no room to talk, Saint Adelaide. Your whole life has been a series of fuck-ups."

Voice tight with incredulity, Ade snarls. "And yours hasn't?"

"Quit making everything about you." With a glare at Ade, Kris turns back to me, eyes flicking to the bottle in my hand. "That's better with ice and Coke– the liquid kind, not the snorting kind," Kris adds when I narrow my gaze.

"Details!" Fate chirps, stopping me before I demand Empowerment's employees be drug-tested. "We want details."

"Nope, I don't think so. That man's got some major sexual mojo. The way I see it, Ade, you've fucked Cortez by default."

Pulling a face like she's about to be sick, Ade whispers, "Eww... gross," underneath her breath. "I always make Ezra wear a condom– no sloppy Cortez seconds."

"Pretty sure it's Cort's cock in Ezra's ass," Kris offers in, making us all shudder. "As domineering as he may be, Ezra's the bottom in that relationship. Topping from the bottom, quite literally."

"They're not having sex," Fate explains, sympathy etched across her pixie-like face. "Word around Dominion is that after their abduction, Cort said no more gay sex."

"That's true," Ade confirms. "Sometimes Ez actually talks to me about stuff– sometimes," she murmurs wistfully. "But usually I get my info from hearsay, so I don't have to worry about Ez contracting an STD from the whore-master himself." Ade grabs my shoulder, bony fingertips sinking into my flesh. "Get tested first thing tomorrow morning, because that dick has seen more action than a porn star."

"Cort and I made out– that's *it*," I stress, jerking away from my best friend. Suddenly, offended, I decide shock-value is the way to go. "I haven't had the pleasure yet, but damn that boy is *hung*." Whistling sharply, I shake my head in awe. "I take it Kristal's had the pleasure since she hasn't denied it."

We turn as one to our partner in crime.

Kris swallows thickly a few times, and then grabs the bottle of Jack from my hand. "Um… yeah– like a whole lot." She trills a nervous laugh. "More than is humanly possible, actually. Cort always wraps it up, no matter what, even for blowjobs, so no STD talk."

"Sure he does," Ade mumbles with narrowed eyes, peering at Kristal through slits of pure loathing. "Sure he does."

Taken aback, Kris looks away from Ade and back to me. "Reg, if you get the chance, take it. Cort does this thing with his tongue– you'd swear he had a vibrator in his mouth. Fan-fucking-tastic."

Laughing at Kristal's visual demonstration, I wrench the bottle out of her hand, and then take another harsh swallow. My girls look at me as if I sprouted an alien from my head when I down a few more.

I explain with a shrug. "Labor Day resolution: loosen up, have some fun, and relax. I want to add *get fucked* to that list. I want to enter oblivion and feel something while I'm there. Destructive and juvenile? Sure. But I'm sick of being numb all the time."

Smirking, I wait for them to go ballistic.

"Where were you?" Fate asks, only curiosity lacing her voice. "I began to worry after our show was over and I had to put Ella to bed."

"How did you meet up with that dickhead, anyway?" Ade wants to know.

"I'm jealous– the passion never got to the point where I got bruised." Kris yanks at the collar of my t-shirt, showing everyone the suck marks Cort left behind. "You have hickeys. Did Cort attack you? That's so unlike him."

"I wouldn't know what Cort is or isn't like," I admit, feeling a bit sick to my stomach that I made out with him. I kissed Roman after years of knowing him, and I was with Grant for almost five years and two kids. After nearly a decade of grieving, I made out with the first dude willing to take one for the team.

High fading into depression, I walk out the French doors, bottle in hand, and then curl up on the chaise lounge. I stare at the pool, wishing it was a roaring ocean– that would be excellent ambiance. I add get piss-roaring drunk to the Labor Day Resolution list. Guzzling the toxic liquid, it's yucky but effective. I want something fruity and blue. I wonder if they make anything like that.

"Hey, Kris?" I call to the ladies hovering in the doorway. "Are there blue drinks in the Bartender's Guide?"

"Yeah, why?" Amused, Kris takes my question as the invitation it was meant, and sits next to me on the chaise.

"I'd like to try one someday. It just sounds good, is all..." Patting the cushion in front of me, I summon Ade and Fate. "Gather around, I have some news."

A throaty laugh escapes my lips at the varying expressions gazing upon me. I'm feeling tipsy from the Jack and a bit high from how the night has played out.

"Well, I had a great walk as usual– channeling Grant for some help at self-reflection." I lean forward, going into storyteller-mode. "But, can you believe that Ella and I have walked and rode our bikes passed the master's den of iniquity for the past nine nights?"

"Jesus Christ, what?" Ade shouts.

"No, really?" Fate seems genuinely surprised.

Feigning ignorance, "No way..." Kris tries and fails.

"Yeah, really." I roll my eyes at Kris. "Girlfriend, I know damn well you know who Master is, as well as where he plays and trains. No way you didn't."

"No– honest." Kris convinces a pissed off Ade and a confused Fate, but I've learned to read her over the past thirteen years.

"Master was right on my path, and he had the balls to call me when I was on the street outside of his playpen, then text me a demand. I would bet my fortune than none of you would guess who he is… besides Kris, obviously, as it's not fair to play with a stacked deck."

"I don't know!" Kris shouts, making her lie even more obvious.

"You met *the* master?" Ade stresses, face glowing with fiendish delight.

"Damn straight, I did." I take another nip off the bottle of Jack, still looking out over the tranquil pool. I'm not sure how much I should tell them, because I feel a sense of obligation to Marcus because of his connection to Grant.

Impatient, "Well, who the fuck is he?" Ade demands.

Alcohol loosening my tongue, it spills before I can stop it. "Marcus Zeitler, but if I get wind that any of you said anything, you'll regret it."

"Ooooohhhh," Kris sounds spooky. "I'm scared. Yeah, I knew it was him, and his little mutt Cort nipping at his heels. Did you meet the masters of the house? The other trainee?"

"Define *meet*," I stress, lips cracking into an estimation of a smile. I contemplate what I should say as I down more Jack, but Kris already knows, and we're doing this for Ade anyway. "Marcus greeted me, explained the rules of the house. How I would never meet Alex, and if I tried to visit Transcend to find him, I wouldn't succeed. Alex and Jamie are the owners of the house, and both were there, and I had an odd reaction to Jamie when I felt him practically breathing down my neck. What's up with that shit?" I ask Kris.

"You might be brave enough to do and say whatever about Marc's private business, but I'm not." A shiver works its way through Kristal's body. "I know all of them, and was told to keep my trap shut. Put it this way, they terrify me more than you do."

"So much for loyalty," Ade and I say in unison, and I notice Fate trying to communicate something to Kris. "All of you are liars," I mutter, then down a huge swallow of whiskey.

Ade looks bewildered, but Kris and Fate keep their liar mouths shut. From now on, I'm on my own, with everything being kept close to the vest, because I can't trust any of them for varying reasons.

"So anyway, Jamie owns the brownstone, and that's how I got this beauty of a bruise." I point to the fingertip bruises lining my jaw. "I wasn't to see Jamie for some reason. Then Cortez shows up with the other trainee, and chaos ensued. Marcus was about to lose his shit, so the bruise got worse. Then the other trainee– they call him the PB, by the way –he was locked in the bathroom so I couldn't see him. We weren't allowed to see each other for some reason, including this Jamie character– he could see us but we weren't allowed to see him."

"Bizarre," Ade breathes, wheels spinning, and Fate suddenly looks terrified that Ade will reason it out. "So let me get this straight. My future father-in-law is shacked up in a brownstone owned by an Alex who works at Transcend, and a Jamie, who is allowed to see you but you not him. Then there is PB, who isn't allowed to see you, or you him, nor is he allowed to see Jamie, who is allowed to see you all. Let's think this through."

Kristal's soft laughter brings us up short.

"What?" Ade and I accuse in unison.

"Oh, it's nothing– go on." I glare at Kristal for telling me I have permission to tell my story. "Wait a fucking minute! The PB is the guy you're playing with, isn't he? Who the hell is he? Tell me!" I grab Kristal's arm, shaking her with desperation.

"I value my life more than I value your friendship," Kris admits without shame. "You really need to know who Marcus is training, and whose house you're in. But I'm not going to tell you who the PB is because you may kill me for playing with him… but, I know you'll castrate Marcus for sure."

"Goddamn you, Kristal!" I bellow, frustrated. Opening my throat, I chug whiskey straight from the bottle. "You should be loyal to me first and foremost."

Tears glinting in her hazel eyes, Kristal leans toward me with contrition etched across her features. "I love you, Regina. I've known you since I was fifteen, and you've allowed me to be a member of your family, for which I can never repay you. But there was fifteen years where my loyalty was secured by others."

"Fuck," I snarl, understanding but not. "Well, on that note. I have a date with XII and the inspirational words of James Atwater."

"Inspirational?" Kris scoffs underneath her breath, voice warping into a disturbing giggle. "Have fun with James Atwater."

"G'night ladies," I sing, waving on my way by.

Chapter Ten

Listing a bit to the side, I have to keep palming the hallway wall to stop myself from face-planting on the floor, as I weave my way to my bedroom. Nursing the bottle of Jack, I wait for the shower to heat up. After I'm scrubbed and buffed and smelling sweetly of almonds, I take another hearty pull of the whiskey. I'm guessing it's a bad sign that I no longer taste it.

Standing before the full-length mirror naked, I assess my body. With long, strong arms and legs, I could never be called delicate. My belly is flat, but when I poke it with a fingertip, it dimples and reveals a webbing of stretch marks. My groomed, fuzzy mound peeks out from between masculine thighs. My hips and ass round out from my waist disproportionately, with my breasts heavy globes with enlarged nipples.

Gazing at myself, my mind is at war with my nature, and my nature is at war with my body. I am inherently female inside my mind– a mother and natural caregiver, who wants a life partner to call her own. But my body looks more masculine than feminine, with a dominant personality that rivals society's standards of women.

Regina Regal acts like a man, looks like a man, so everyone treats her like a man when she is a woman. When sitting in silence, I'm no longer my body but my mind. I no longer think of how tall I am, or how much I weigh, or how much I'm worth. I don't think of having breasts or a vagina, or the fact that I'm a mother of two. I don't war between who I am and how I look. So it's a mind-reeling experience when people treat me as if these things are the sum of my parts, when they are not.

Having reached puberty so early, I know what it's like to have your inside contradict your outside. I was a child in a woman's body, being treated like a woman by all, and not understanding anything that was happening at the time. I just wanted to play with kids my age who were half my size, not be treated as an adult.

Now I'm a feminine woman living inside a masculine body, with a strong personality society says is masculine because women should be soft of heart. I can't wear pretty things because I'd look utterly ridiculous, nor can I have frilly things because it would be laughable to see me sitting in dainty chairs.

With one gaze, people know I'm the one in charge, never realizing that maybe what I want most in life is for someone to treat me softly, tenderly, like a woman instead of a man. I'm the problem-solver– the fixer. Everyone's rock. But even a rock needs a soft place to fall.

Never afraid of me, even if he wasn't the most dominant of men, Grant understood my need to feel girly, even if it was only on the inside. Giving me something I refused to voice, Grant would tease me how men flirt with pretty little things, even if I felt like a foolish idiot at the time.

My closet was filled with utilitarian clothing that matched my outside, and beautiful, lacy underthings that matched my inside. The lingerie was for *my* benefit, even if Grant got to enjoy how they made me feel, more so than how they made me look. I must have looked like a big-breasted tranny, but Grant made me feel beautiful anyway.

God, I miss Grant.

In no way am I the ideal of feminine beauty. Ade and Fate are willowy– one tall to the other's short, but both are model-worthy. Kris is small, curvy, and intoxicating. She's who you'd chase if you wanted an adventurous kick with your sex.

Wanting and craving and needing doesn't change the fact that I'm not who a man would choose. No man wants a woman who is bigger, stronger, taller, smarter, and earns more money than they do. It isn't good for their delicate egos.

Pouring a large amount of smoothing lotion into my palm, I coat my hair to a glossy shine. I'll flat-iron it tomorrow before I meet with Marcus. He won't catch me unawares again. I won't walk around like a streetwalker wannabe, nor will I show up in jeans and a t-shirt. I'll try for respectable attractiveness.

I've lived in jeans and t-shirts since I left Misery Castle. While I was a resident there, I wore what was purchased for me– presentable blouses and slacks that wouldn't embarrass the family. When I was a kid, I wore whatever clothing I could afford, whether I liked it or not. While at Hillbrook, I wore a uniform. I have no clue what my unique style is. Even now, with the money I have, for me, shopping is awkward at best.

Horny and drunk, stark-naked, I sashay from the bathroom. I wanted to be smooth and smelling sweet in preparation for James Atwater, because he deserves nothing less.

Startled, I meep in shock, then cover my mouth with my palm.

Ade is seated at the foot of my bed, eyes feasting on my flesh.

"I'm not going to get any reading done tonight, am I?" Disappointment eclipses my statement. I cover myself with a pair of pajama bottoms and a tank top. Then I sit next to her and wait to be bitched out.

Eyes red-rimmed, Ade looks like she wants to cry, and it breaks my heart.

"Did you like it?" Ade's fingertips flutter over the suck marks Cort left behind on my neck and upper chest. Skin hyper-sensitive, I close my eyes against the pleasure that emanates.

"Did you think I'd act as a widow for the rest of my life?" I close my eyes in defeat, feeling ashamed of myself, because it should have been with someone who mattered. "Nine years is long enough. I don't think you girls understand how lonely I am– how starved for attention and affection. Just a hug that doesn't come at a cost."

"Regina," Ade breathes, leaning against me.

"Grant was my one and only, and I lost him when I was only twenty-two. But even though it felt as if my life ended that day, it didn't. I will forever love Grant–" I clutch my chest at the acute pain, "Ache for him. But I need something more than a hug– I need to feel like a woman."

With tears clouding my vision, I turn to face Adelaide. "I'm still a woman with needs, even if what I did was stupid. Yeah, I loved how Cort touched me with passion, even if it was fake. I felt like a woman for the first time in almost a decade."

"All I ever see is your femininity." Ade's fingertips skate across my arm, causing my flesh to bead with anticipation. "You hate how I look at you, because it's how you want men to look at you."

"I'm straight, Ade– nothing is going to change that fact." Swallowing roughly, I try to put my feelings into emotions. "I felt enlivened for a few moments, instead of a dead person walking amongst the living."

Moving unexpectedly, Ade kisses my temple. But she doesn't stop me from talking, knowing I usually hold it all in and I have to get it all out.

"Do I think I meant anything to Cortez other than a warm hole? No, absolutely not. I'm not that naïve or stupid. Cortez is witty, snarky, and a complete asshole. But when he smiles, I cream my panties. He's devastatingly sexy, and he knows what he's doing."

"If I throw up all over your bedding, please don't yell at me," Ade whispers in a tiny voice while shuddering next to me.

"Ha-ha. Your issues over Ezra aside, Cortez really is a straight girl's and a gay guy's wet dream, and I need that right now. Will I have sex with him? Doubtful. I was just convenient at the time– a way to stick it to Marcus for some reason."

"Their relationship is odd." Ade sighs, slumping forward until her elbows rest on her thighs. "But not as odd as Marc and Ezra's. Ezra can do no wrong. I've actually had Marc get in my face at charity functions because I wouldn't put up with Ezra's creepy, insane bullshit. Oh, Marcus doesn't yell… the rat-bastard has this way of speaking quietly, like he's seething on the inside but refuses to show it."

"It's called control," I remind Ade with a shrug. "Marcus is a dominant, alpha male who has to be in control of his emotions at all times."

"I call it an asshole who thinks the world revolves around him and his *boys*." Ade makes finger-quotes. "Why don't you think Cort wanted you? If he didn't, he's a blind moron."

I ignore Ade shamelessly checking me out. "I'm not delusional. Cort has sex with Kristal on a regular basis, so he won't be calling on me anytime soon. It just felt nice to be reckless, to act my age for five minutes."

"I'm sorry," Ade murmurs while twining her fingers with mine.

"It's okay. While my ladies were clubbing, dating, and getting engaged, I got to live vicariously. Did you know I've never been on a date?" I muse. "Of course you do."

"Grant didn't want your life together to be led as it had been," Ade tries to reassure me, but it falls on deaf ears.

"But it's more than that. I'd never sat at a restaurant with Grant, went shopping, or even took a walk outside of the estate. I was a dirty secret that was kept locked away in a gilded cage deep within Misery Castle's walls. I wasn't worthy enough to have him hold my hand in public and say, '*this is my woman.*' I miss Grant every moment of every day, but I don't miss how worthless I felt because I was his mistress. How worthless I still feel. Every day is another step in proving my worth."

"Oh, I'm so sorry." A cry shakes Adelaide's voice. "You know Grant died trying to change that fact– he wanted to marry you, Regina."

"I know, so let's not remind me that Daniel blamed me for Grant's death."

"Regina, no–"

"No crying. This isn't about you, Ade. I'm going to pull a selfish for once. I want this, and you're not going to fuck it up by outing Marcus to your father. I know Daniel and Diane are as thick as thieves, so I don't need you running home to Daddy to tell on his BFF's husband. I *need* Marcus," my voice warps with desperation. "Do you understand me? I'm dying a little more every damn day, to the point I'm almost entirely lost to the grief and guilt."

"I understand, Reg. But you've got to understand that Marc's going to try to have sex with you. I know it." Her eyes flicker back and forth in a panic.

"Why are you so worried that Marc's going to ravish me, anyway? He's fabulous to look at, I'll give you that. His voice is liquid sex and his eyes hit like a shot of heroine." I shiver in remembrance. "Don't get me started on his ass."

"Regina, Marcus is a married man. He's going to be my father-in-law someday, and I owe a bit of loyalty to Diane, not only because she'll be my mother-in-law, but because she has been Daddy's rock my entire life. So never forget Marcus is married, and he'll want to fuck you… which only means he'll be stealing my brother's mistress as his own."

"Ade," I gasp, heart beating uncontrollably as her words hit home. "No."

"Yes."

"But Marc's a dominant, as am I. I'm not his type. The lifestyle isn't about sexual orientation. It's about having your needs met, and I fulfill none of Marc's. He wants a '*Yes, Master- anything you say, Master,*' submissive robot. I will never be that."

"You just said BDSM transcends orientation, because Marc doesn't have one. But what you're forgetting is the competitive drive a man has when it comes to the toys his friends had, toys they never shared. Envy and jealousy transcends everything, even rational thought."

"Bullshit," I hiss. "If Marc had wanted in my bed, Grant wouldn't have batted an eyelash. He even hinted at it."

"Oh, don't even try to figure out my brother's motivations, Regina. *Ever.* Grant's gone, and now we'll never know. But Marcus is alive and well, a virile force to be reckoned. One who has two boys following him everywhere– adult boys who don't share their toys. Cort choked me over my own fiancé. What do you think Ezra would do to you over Marcus?" Adelaide issues an ominous warning. "Marc isn't just Ezra's adoptive father. He's like… if you fuck Marc, you're insulting Ezra's mother, and he won't allow that."

"It's a moot point, anyway." An involuntary shudder works its way up my spine. "I'm not fucking Marc."

"If you do, don't tell me. I can't know. Call it divided loyalties, because I'd have to tell Diane, no matter what. She'd only be annoyed at the worst. But then I'd have to tell Ezra, and he's who you should be worried about."

"What are you so worried about? I just said it's *not* gonna happen?"

"It's not about me, remember?" Ade laughs, but the light, trailing sound is strained– forced. "Marc gets what he wants, and he'll want to feel closer to Grant, same as you will. *Do it.* Do whatever feels natural, and don't think of the consequences, but don't ever fucking tell me."

"I'll never be another man's mistress, Ade." Insulted, it's unfathomable how little she must think of me… or is it how powerful she perceives Marcus?

"You're right, Reg. It's your time to live, so we'll hold down the fort while you explore." Ade tries to ease my worry, which only worries me more. She is not the reassuring type, kind of like a baseball bat to the nads.

"I'm sure I'll be the worst dominant in the history of BDSM." I imagine myself failing, and how pissed I'll be if that's the case.

"My guess is that Cort already holds that position."

Ade and I share a snort, and I remember how Dexter said he washed his hands of Cortez.

"I don't even know what to expect… no clue."

Reminding me of the silence I once shared with Grant, Ade and I sit for a while, both of us staring down at our clasped hands. I love Fate and Kristal, but the bond between Adelaide and me was forged through emotional torture– nothing can ever top that.

We're family, through and through.

Sisters.

Startling me out of my reverie, Ade's fingertips ghost against my cheeks, collecting tears I didn't realize had fallen. Her crystalline eyes linger on my lips, and my mouth parts under her undivided attention.

"Just one last kiss," Ade whispers, and then a soft, pleading whimper follows. "I'll never ask again. My Regina is moving on to way hotter, masculine lips. *Please*," she begs in desperation.

Without thought of consequences, I lean forward to capture Adelaide's lips in a kiss. But it isn't the same type of kiss as the one I shared with Cort, where I spontaneously burst into flame, but it does feel really good. Comforting, but not arousing. What has always been absent surges upward, since my skin is electrified from my earlier exploits that never reached fruition.

"AH!" I shout when Ade's lips seek out and suck the marks on my neck. My back arches off the bed and my eyes roll back, body alive for the first time in a long while.

"Ade– stop." I moan a protest I mean, but I don't sound very convincing, especially when I lay passive as she nibbles my flesh.

Ignoring me, "Just this once, and we won't have sex. I promise." Ade rolls on top of me, wiggling a thigh between both of mine. "All of our clothing will stay on, and I won't even touch you with my hands. We'll just kiss," she lures me.

Falling into the kiss Ade promised, I loosely hold her in my arms. It's nice to feel wanted, needed, especially by someone who knows me inside and out– by someone who knows all of my inadequacies, yet still wants me despite all of them, or maybe a little because of them.

Rubbing Ade's back in soothing circles, I allow her to take pleasure from me. Becoming her passenger, I lay passive, barely participating yet enjoying the affection. Ade's sundress bunches under my hands until I feel the cool of her skin beneath my roving palms.

"I know you don't like your body, that you think it's too manly. Let me show you how much I love your body, especially your thigh." Ade rotates her hips and rocks against my leg, releasing a throaty moan. Her heat warms me, and her gasps and moans please me.

A small part of me is happy to give Ade this last thing I've kept from her– the pleasure of my body. But the rest of me is not *that* selfless.

"Ade, you're taking advantage of a sleepy, horny, buzzed woman."

I tease Ade and release an uncomfortable chuckle, trying to make light of the situation. "I had a stressful night." Trying to tap-out, I pat her back a few times.

Yet again ignoring me, Ade issues a demand. "Open your thighs and let me make you come," she rasps forcefully into my ear.

Ade isn't in the teasing frame of mind, nor will she be ignored or pushed off any longer.

Hand skimming down to the back of my knee, Ade lifts, opening me to her desire. Her thin thigh presses hard into my aroused, long-ignored flesh, and I ignite with surprising ease.

We transform into a writhing mass of arms, legs, lips, and hands. Passive, my fingers twist into my bedspread as Ade sucks my nipple through my threadbare tank top. It stings from the strength of her pulls, yet I groan in ecstasy.

My pajama pants are paper-thin and fused to my swollen flesh, slit weeping through the fabric to soak her naked thigh. Ade's panties offer no protection as she rides my leg, with my flesh absorbing her heat and moisture.

Confused and unsure how to stop, I lie submissive under the flex of Ade's hips. She's perfected the movement through experience, and I try to ignore the pleasure coursing through my body. Proof positive, this is not Ade's first ride.

The sudden, piercing pain of a sharp bite on my breast unleashes a real orgasm, one that starts at my scalp and crashes to my toes, before finally cresting at the center of my core. The type of orgasm I haven't felt in almost a decade. Years of empty releases brought by my own hand dissolve in an instant. I'll never go back to that loneliness, even if it means trusting a friend and finally admitting that I don't have to be so damn strong all the time. I can rely on someone else for my needs once in a while.

"Fuck," I gulp. "Adela…" Her name is cut off by the force of Ade's mouth crushing mine. I continue to writhe and moan as she sucks the sounds of my release with her kiss.

After we both come down, "Thank you." Adelaide whispers in the dark, the sound more intimate than it should be. "I won't try for it again. It was enough knowing you loved me enough to let go for a few moments, even though you didn't want to. I'll cherish this memory always."

Lying speechless in the wake of my climax, the reverent quality of Ade's words scares the hell out of me. In an instant, I know Ade doesn't see me as I see her, and I don't know how to come to terms with it.

Adelaide doesn't see me as a sister and a trusted friend, but more like a lover or girlfriend. Nauseated, my throat convulses as I swallow repeatedly. Regret and shame war until I'm utterly bereft with guilt.

"Whitt was right by giving you the name Queen." Ade's words murder all pleasure left in my body. "He's very pleased that you're using it again. You should have seen how bright his face glowed when I told him." I can sense the happiness in her voice, and it's pure torture to experience. "Whitt still loves you so much."

"I can't talk about that kind of stuff right now, Adelaide," I warn in a tight voice, one that no doubt is mimicking the one Marcus uses on her. "Not after what we just did."

Scrubbing my hands over my face, I try to rewind twenty minutes into the past, where I'd demand Adelaide acknowledged my *no*. I hold as much responsibility as she does, because I could have used bodily force to make her stop.

"You were meant to be our queen, and I don't mean at Restraint. You were meant to be Misery Castle's Queen of the Whittenhower kingdom. It was supposed to be Grant and yours, then your children's. We would have been proud to have you as head of the Whittenhowers, even Daddy thought so. No one else is worthy."

"Please stop," I whimper, but Ade keeps speaking, and I try to block her out. Is she deliberately trying to kill me? How can Ade not realize how badly her words wound? "It's too late now– almost a decade too late."

"We can always hope that you'll take your throne someday." The creepy quality to Ade's voice is scaring the piss out of me.

"You have a Whittenhower stashed away somewhere I don't know about? Whitt's still a minor for a few months yet– plus I'm not his type, seeing as how I'm twelve years older than him and missing a dick. But you must have forgotten how the heir to the throne is my own son. So fucking snap out of your fantasy and join reality, Adelaide, because you're frightening the hell out of me."

"I love you." Ade's voice rings clear, no longer holding that warped, creepy quality. "I'd kiss you goodbye, but I made you a promise I intend to keep. Good night, Regina."

At a loss, I watch as Adelaide stands, straightens her dress, and then leaves my room in a cloud of her own satisfaction, not caring that she left total devastation in her wake.

Sensations bombard me from every direction. Ade's taste on my lips, the feel of the pillowy mattress beneath me, the sound of the central-air whirling, the compressive nature of darkness, and lastly, the aching pit of despair I've barely kept in check.

In the absence of numbness is pain.

Now I remember why I locked my emotions in a lead-lined box inside my psyche. Pain– never-ending torture, bottomless loneliness, an infinite emptiness… lastly, unadulterated fury.

Grabbing my pillow, fingertips curling into talons, I scream until my throat no longer spills my pain.

I hate Grant for taking all the important parts of my soul with him, leaving me as nothing but an empty shell of grief, with no happiness, no playfulness– no beauty in the silence. No peace. I blame Grant for creating Apathetic Regina.

I resent my parents for leaving me to fend for myself without a family to call my own, leaving me to be the last Regal with no support system.

I hate Ade for watching Niel grow up and for her ability to have unlimited access to Whitt.

I hate Adelaide most of all.

Ade can use all of her senses to touch their soft skin, hear the tone of their voices, see their ever-changing forms, experience their love, and lastly, feel their embrace. My hate is only equal to the force of the love I feel for her.

My heart tears itself from my chest, and the only relief I'll ever find is in death.

Chapter Eleven

Lying face-down, long ago losing the ability to speak, I suffer the consequences of my screaming tantrum. Flashing blue in the darkness, my cellphone keeps illuminating my ceiling in blinking intervals, announcing a text message. Curiosity getting the better of me, I reach blindly for my phone. Anything is better than being in my head at the moment, even if it's a disgruntled client at one a.m.

Rolling onto my back with my screaming tantrum victim cradling my head, what I find comes as a huge surprise. But oddly, a welcome one.

This is Jamie– are you okay?

Before answering, I save Jamie's number into my contacts. Then I just stare down at the words, wondering if this is some cosmic joke. Is it truly Jamie, or is Marcus bleeding me for information? Snorting, I realize how paranoid and pessimistic I sound. Everyone in the world isn't out to get me. There isn't some underlying secret agenda weaving its way through my life.

–Why wouldn't I be okay?

Jamie: *I just… I just know you're not somehow, and I wanted to reach out to let you know you're never alone. Ever.*

Warmth infusing my system, the anonymity combined with the intimacy of texting a complete stranger has words spilling from my fingertips.

–I'd only kissed two men in my entire life until tonight. A few seconds with my childhood friend, then I kissed the father of my children for nearly five years straight. In the decade since, the only affection I've allowed was in moments of weakness with a very determined woman. But tonight, I managed to kiss two different

people, one being the same woman as before, but I don't know how I feel about that, especially kissing the man.

Jamie: *I've never kissed any.*

Laughing aloud, Jamie's teasing answer actually relaxes me, even if he's not offering up advice on something he knows nothing about. Surprisingly, I realized I needed this. Jamie is safe.

—Ha-ha! How many women have you kissed?

Jamie: *Two.*

—Two? Only two?

Jamie: *Yeah, and I don't expect that number to change in my lifetime. Why are you upset that you've only kissed three men? Do you think the number should be higher?*

—Lower.

Jamie: *Lower? Regrets, perhaps?*

—Yes. I've been numb for years. Apathetic. Tonight, everything I did was out of destruction.

Jamie: *But it made you feel alive? That's only human nature, Regina.*

—To be honest, when the high faded, I was more apathetic than ever, only feeling more destructive. I realized I kissed Cortez because I had to prove to myself that someone wanted me. Carnally. I've been lonely, and I thought I wouldn't feel so alone.

Jamie: *Cort, you say? Hmm... I would have imagined Marcus. Not that that matters. The worst type of loneliness is often felt while being suffocated by a crowd. Sometimes the crowd is made up of those closest to you, but they're too close to see how you're suffering. Sometimes being alone, truly alone, is what one needs to self-reflect.*

My eyes widen as I take in how much Jamie manages to say in such a short amount of time. He texts quicker than a teenage girl, but the words sound like they're coming out of a philosopher's mouth.

—And you don't think I haven't been alone for the past decade? Jamie, you don't know me.

Jamie: *Alone in person, but not in spirit. I surmise you have kept yourself so busy you couldn't think. Thinking is the most important part of self-reflection.*

—Jamie. Shut up.

Jamie: *Yes, ma'am.*

—Self-reflecting hurts too much.

Jamie: *That's why it heals.*

—It reminds me of Grant, so it feels like opening a wound to me.

Jamie: *You have to open the wound to drain it, or else it will fester and never heal. You don't strike me as a person who is a coward, or is afraid of pain. Accept it and let it free you.*

—Shut up, Jamie.

Jamie: *Stop replying, Regina.*

—You don't know me. I don't know you. I wasn't even allowed to look at you.

Jamie: *If I thought for a second that a text message could hold emotion, the tone of yours would be pouting. Marcus wouldn't allow you to see me, if you remember correctly. Marc is a man who never self-reflects. He works, he thinks of what he needs from others, while never learning what he needs from himself.*

—Don't diss Marcus. He's the last thread to someone important to me. You didn't know Grant, and you're probably jealous because

Marcus treats you like shit because you're not Grant. Go smash some more shit in your space, Jamie, because I won't use you to replace Grant, either.

Jamie: *Very well. I'm no one's replacement, nor do I wish to be, nor am I jealous. I'm me. But at the same time, I can't turn my back on a person who is obviously hurting.*

–I'm sorry I said that to you, but don't diss Marcus.

Jamie: *I can understand that, and I find your loyalty very admirable. Regina, I love Marcus, but I accept him for who he is. I'm not badmouthing him. You commented on not seeing me, and I was explaining. I'm terrified to allow you to see me, but at the same time, Marcus won't allow it. Visually. But he'll torture me with your presence.*

–If you hate me so much, then why are you texting me?

Jamie: *Hate? <laughing> As you said, I don't know you. How can I hate someone I don't know? As I was lying in bed tonight, self-reflecting, I felt a pull to contact you, somehow knowing you weren't doing okay.*

–You're right.

Jamie: *About what?*

–You don't know me.

Long minutes go by as I wait for a reply I instinctively know isn't coming. I sit against my headboard, wishing I hadn't been mean to Jamie, because this is the most adult conversation I've had with anyone who didn't surround work or my household. Swallowing my pride, I send another text without getting a reply to my previous one.

–I'm not okay.

I begin to wonder if Jamie is punishing me for my bad behavior, or if the lesson is actually his way of setting firm boundaries. Either choice is better than Jamie realizing I suck at communicating after holing myself away for a decade.

–To answer your initial question, I haven't been okay in a very long time. I hate myself– who I've become, who I was, and who I will always be.

Jamie: *Me too. I hate myself. I've made sacrifices no one understands but me, and it's left me feeling alone, even when I'm self-reflecting. We can hate ourselves together if you'd like.*

–Thank you.

Jamie: *Anytime, Regina. Without judgment, I'll be your confessor, as has been decided by fate. I listen, truly listen, instead of how others will be forming a reply while the other person is speaking.*

–Oh, I'm acquainted with a few of those people. I don't know if I can trust you yet. As we've established, we don't know one another.

Jamie: *True. But sometimes it feels good to confess.*

–You're Catholic, aren't you?

Jamie: *Does that somehow come as a surprise?*

–Marcus seems to have a type he likes to fill as a best friend. Grant was highly devout.

Jamie: *So I've heard.*

–Is that jealousy I hear in your text?

Jamie: *Texts hold no emotion, Regina, and I'm incapable of feeling jealousy or envy against Grant. Not that I don't feel those emotions against others.*

–Only human.

Jamie: *Exactly. Goodnight, Regina. Sweet dreams. I shall see you tomorrow evening at eight o'clock sharp...*

—But I won't see you, I suspect.

Jamie: *You suspect correctly.*

—I had to at least try. Goodnight, Jamie.

Chapter Twelve

Hand hovering over the gargoyle knocker, I can't seem to force myself to tap on the red door. My night of despair is evident in my appearance, and here I wanted to make a good second impression with Marcus. Oh, I'll make an impression all right. My eyes look huge with dark shadows beneath from never having a full night's sleep since I was sixteen years old and my life fell to shit. Tonight I resorted to makeup by lining my eyes in kohl to cover the shadows lurking beneath. Trying to be presentable, professional, but classy sexy, I'm wearing a form-fitting, sheer, black dress and flats.

When I went shopping, I stared with great longing at the gorgeous array of heels in every color and design, some dainty, some perfect for a fledgling dominatrix– all ridiculously expensive. Ella and I had fun trying them on, and oohing and ahhing, but I couldn't bring myself to buy a pair. However, Ella broke me down and she ended up with a pair of pink kitten heels to wear with her apron in the kitchen– my daughter is bizarre, what can I say? The shoes came in my larger size, but I didn't think towering over Marcus in heels is a good idea. Especially when he's an alpha male who thinks he should be the strongest, tallest, smartest, and most powerful.

Male's delicate egos and my horrible fashion sense aside, my biggest problem of the night is the fact that I have laryngitis thanks to screaming uncontrollably into my pillow because of Adelaide.

None of this is going to change in the next five minutes, so standing on the stoop is only making me seem even more ridiculous– and late.

Shoring up my nerves, I reach for the gargoyle, and the door magically opens just as I touch the knocker.

"Regina," Marcus purrs in a pleasant voice, face alight with pleasure because I actually showed up. He probably thought I'd pussy out. Noticing my appearance, his face twists with worry. "What happened?"

Forcing words to flow, I try with all my might to rasp, "I'm fine," but it ends up sounding broken. I tap my throat, "Laryngitis."

"Are you ill?" Marc's concern warms me. No one ever thinks about my welfare, as I'm the one taking care of everyone else. "Do you want me to fetch a doctor?"

Lips quirking up at the corners, I fight back a smile. Do people really fetch doctors in this day and age? "Not ill," I push from my lips.

Shuddering, I realize Ezra's probably said doctor– Adelaide never shut up about Ezra's schooling and the differences between a medical doctor and a psychologist or therapist.

"Come in." Marc's fingers curl around my shoulder, tugging me in from off the stoop, then his hand goes straight to the small of my back like a gentleman. "The nights are starting to chill."

"That they are," I murmur with great difficulty, as my eyes flick about, trying to gauge whether we're alone or not.

"Oh, let me grab a bottle of water for your throat." Marcus disappears from sight down the long hallway, feet padding silently on what should be old, squeaky floorboards. Voice echoing back to me, "The sofa is uncovered in the impact room."

Unsure on the protocol, I wager a guess and lock the front door behind me. Marcus seems like the secretive, possessive type, seeing as how we're playing in someone else's house instead of the Gates. Drinking in my surroundings, I walk to the room we sat in last night. Doing as I was told, I get comfortable on the bordello-esque sofa, and then look around.

The impact room, as Marcus called it, is the front-most room on the right-hand side of the brownstone. Red and black damask wallpaper lines the medium-sized space, with dark hardwood molding from floor to ceiling. Wooden frames are attached to the walls, and restraints hang from the ceiling. The rear wall is dedicated to showcasing objects. While I understand the meaning of *impact room,* it looks more like a room to be restrained until my eyes land on the tools of the impact trade. Paddles, floggers, whips, canes, household items, and tools I have no name for hang in groups by type.

Shivering in anticipation, I wish I would've thought to bring a sweater.

The lone Victorian nightmare of a sofa is situated in front of the windows, overlooking the sidewalk and street beyond. No doubt I was viewed from this very space last night, and the eight nights prior, and just minutes ago.

Creepy.

Striding into the room, Marcus hands me a glass bottle of water. "Here you go." Then he joins me on the sofa.

After unscrewing the cap, I take a small sip, wincing when the sparkling bubbles stings my aching throat. "Thank you," I say much stronger. "My voice works as long as it's wet. I'm doing great, considering this morning I couldn't speak at all." I take another sip because I was straining to force the words out.

"You keep shivering– are you cold?" Ever the gentleman, Marcus pulls his suit jacket off and hands it to me. "Here, this will warm you right up."

Hesitant, I don't want to take the jacket since I worry it won't fit me, but I don't want to insult Marcus either. Sending a little prayer above that I don't make a fool of myself, I allow Marc to help me tug the jacket on. Flashing pearly white teeth, Marc smiles at me, like he could hear my private thoughts and is teasing me. "It fits perfectly, and it matches your pretty dress too."

"Thank you." I tug the lapels, closing the jacket around me. Sinking into the warmth, I simultaneously hide my breasts from view. But there is no denying the very heady, masculine scent wafting from the fabric. Marc's cologne must be called Liquid Sex.

"I'm sorry about how last night played out." Marcus squeezes my knee, and then his face clouds over. "Could you switch seats with me, please?" Not a question, but a demand, no matter the use of the *please*.

Not waiting for my agreement, Marcus stands up, then takes my elbow, so I either have to move or fight him. After a few seconds of my confusion, understanding finally dawns. He wants my back to the room, just as he did last night. Anticipation coils in my belly as I wonder if Jamie is going to be joining us shortly. I resettle on the sofa, waiting for more intrigue.

Tilting my face to the side, Marcus inspects the fingertip bruises he laid along my jawline. They're faint, but noticeable. Frowning down at them, he tilts my head farther back and sights in on Cort's suck marks. Smirking, he traces an elegant fingertip from mark to mark, even finding the one hidden beneath the top of my dress I tried so desperately to hide with Marc's suit jacket.

Body beading with goosebumps, I flush with embarrassment, and secretly wish I could turn off my sexuality while I'm in Marcus Zeitler's presence. For all my protestations with Ade last night, I realize she was indeed correct. I'm not sure if I have enough willpower to deny this male anything he asks, which is why he's the master of the Masters of Restraint.

"Hmmm… these are very nice." The subtle vibration of Marc's words caresses my skin just as much as his roving fingertip. "But Cortez didn't show much control, though. I'll make sure he works on that." Stroking my throat soothingly, it appears Marcus is listening to his own thoughts. "Mustn't markup someone without their permission."

"Seems legit," flows from my lips, making me look like a complete and total fucking fool. But I had to say something to distract myself from Marc's never-ending caresses and murmurs of appreciation. There's no way in hell he's getting as much out of this as I am.

Like a goddamn sponge that hasn't seen moisture in a decade, I soak up all the affection Marcus will dole out, and that leaves me in a vulnerable state.

Shit!

"I'm trying to figure out where to begin, Regina. You perplex me, and this situation has been culminating for many years. I finally have you here, and I'm not sure how to proceed. It's not a position I find myself in often."

"Why don't you start at the beginning, Marc?" My voice is barely above a whisper, but he hears it, nonetheless, since his hand surrounds the column of my throat with his fingertips strumming along my flesh.

"Very wise, Regina. The truth is where I shall begin. I'll start with me. I know you know who I am in the community since you donate religiously to my campaign funds. I know you know who my wife and adoptive son are, especially with Adelaide Whittenhower being your closest ally. That is all there is to know of me, so that leads me back to you. I know everything there is to know about you too."

I would seriously love to doubt that, but this is Marcus motherfucking Zeitler, and he no doubt drilled Grant while he was still alive. It wouldn't surprise me if Marcus kept tabs on me all these years, which annoys the piss out of me since he never tried to reach out and get to know me personally. All Marcus knows is what someone else told him.

Bullshit.

Hand moving lightning fast, my chin is gripped by relentless, elegant fingertips. Splaying to the side of my jaw, Marc's fingers gouge into the bruises that formed after last night.

I didn't think these meetings would be hazardous to my health–
I was wrong.

"Don't ever doubt what I say." Voice slurring with anger,
Marcus isn't as controlled as he first appeared. "We've already
established this." Amber fire blazes into my eyes, then ever so
slowly, his features return to softness.

Like dealing with the baser humans in my childhood
neighborhood, Marc's mercurial emotions don't disturb me. It's no
different than a mother dealing with a child throwing themselves,
only this man can hurt me.

"I wasn't doubting your words." Controlling my voice, I try to
keep all emotion from my tone. "But don't underestimate me,
Marcus. You can't read my mind, so don't assume. I was thinking
of what you said, about how you know all there is to know about
me. So color me surprised that I never heard from you in the years
you were paying for my Hillbrook tuition, or the five years I was
with your best friend, or while I grieved for his death as if I was the
one dying. So excuse my skepticism, since it took until last night
for me to meet you when you've known of me since I was fourteen
fucking years old."

Wheels spinning, Marcus stares at me for several long
moments, no doubt balancing my words with his own recollections.
We all view the world through different, warped lenses. Turning
his face from me, he looks far off into a place I cannot see, deep
inside his own mind.

Minutes pass, and I debate leaving.

Scrunching his eyes, Marcus finally notices how his fingertips
are gouging into my bruises. Wincing in pain for me, he tilts my
head backward again, then examines me for a moment.
Apologizing, Marcus flutters butterfly kisses on the bruises, and
then starts to talk as if nothing happened.

"The past is the past," is his only explanation for leaving his
best friend's widow high and dry. "No matter how controlled you
may be, I could still hear the underlying resentment in your voice.
I suggest you let go of the past and move forward into the future.
We both need allies, and Grant would want this for both of us."

Leaning forward, I get into Marc's personal space. "Are you
shitting me?" My eyebrow raises higher than it's ever been before.
"*Now* you want to speak of Grant?"

Coming closer, an amber gaze captures me, and I have to close
my eyes to the naked pain it reveals.

Pressure– a gentle press has me gasping for air as the supplest lips I've ever felt connect with mine. Confused and vulnerable, I find myself yet again passive when I shouldn't be. Coaxing yet demanding, Marc's tongue slowly parts my stunned lips.

Leaving me groaning, Marc's intoxicating taste invades my mouth and blooms with sensuality. Slow and lingering, the kiss isn't fierce, but it holds no less passion. Falling into his embrace with wild abandon and a mix of desperation and destruction, it's been years since I felt the gentle touch of a man– the comfort and the need.

With Cortez, our shared passions in his car held an animalistic edge, like we both had something to prove to ourselves, and it had nothing to do with who we were kissing. With Marcus, he sips at my mouth, speaking words of grief through his kiss.

With reluctance, Marc pulls away, settling his back against the sofa. "Grant was my best friend, and for a very long time, I was the one he came to when he needed someone. I won't lie by saying I wasn't jealous when he began to pull away from me to cleave unto you, but I respected it. That jealousy kept me away from meeting you while you were living at Whittenhower Estates."

"Because you wanted Grant to yourself?" Try as I might, I can't reason that out. "Were you in love with Grant?"

"No, it wasn't like that." Sighing heavily, Marcus stares at the ceiling for a moment. "I like to be in charge–"

"No shit," I cut him off, adding a snort to the insult. Alpha male horseshit.

"As I was saying, I like to be in charge. I could accept it with Jackson and Daniel, and then just Daniel. So it was a bitter pill to swallow when the boy turned young man pulled away from me to listen to a girl four years his junior. So when it was Grant and me time, or Grant, Dexter, and me time, I didn't want you to invade something so private, intimate, and necessary to my mental health."

"I can understand that, I guess." I try to empathize to the best of my ability. "My girls have had other friends and boyfriends over the years, but I will admit I was envious that they were experiencing things I was not."

"Exactly." Marcus shifts on the sofa, eyes darting about the shadows, looking for ghosts I cannot see. "So I was jealous, and I wanted to keep Grant to myself. But at the same time, I was afraid to meet you, because I might have wanted to take something so important from Grant so I could have him all to myself while simultaneously punishing him for finding a new master."

"Excuse me?" I lean forward, shocked at the level of fury emanating from Marc's voice. "Master?"

Speaking as if he never heard me, "But I was also terrified that I would be enamored with this creature who was somehow stronger than me. That, combined with Grant not wishing me to see you–" Our eyes dart to the ceiling when a large crash echoes from upstairs. "Ignore Jamie– sometimes he expresses himself by smashing shit since he can't speak."

"Can't speak?" That explains the text messages.

"Mute, but enough about Jamie," Marcus evades me.

"But if Jamie's smashing shit, as you say, then he's trying to speak to you, right?"

"No, he's throwing himself." Marc shifts on the sofa in reply to a door slamming on the first floor. Animosity so thick, his voice cuts the air, "Jamie can scurry around this house quicker than a rat. One second he's in the room with us, the next he's upstairs, then a second later, he's on Alex's side of the house."

"It's Jamie's house." I remind Marcus, not liking his attitude one bit.

"My apologies, lord and master who is throwing a tantrum!" Marcus shouts. "I miss Grant because he was so agreeable, pleasant, and loving." Amber eyes glare in my direction, obviously calling me out as the blame.

"Are you blaming me like Daniel does? A son for a son?" I turn to the side on the sofa, staring Marc dead-to-rights, and then spit, "Fuck you," directly in his face.

Profanity-proof, Marcus doesn't even flinch. "No, not Grant's death– I was merely observing how Jamie is not an agreeable creature… one who likes to interrupt conversations when he should stay upstairs like he promised."

"I think I better go." Fed up with this shit-show, I rise to leave. Before raising to my full height, the back of my neck warms, and then a pleasant heat radiates down my spine. "Shit!" Knees giving out, I flop back to the sofa.

"My apologies," Marcus murmurs as his hand cups my elbow in support. "Grant was a very sharing person, who wanted us to meet. My jealousy was getting the best of me, and I shouldn't have said he was the reason I never met you until now."

Taking a deep breath, the heat boring into the back of my neck lessens, no doubt Jamie leaving the room.

"Jamie is a very moral person, and he hates it when I lie– hence the breaking glass above when I tried to lie."

"How does Jamie know when you're lying?"

"I speak, Jamie listens– that's the core of our friendship. Jamie writes it all down, and he will hit me in the face with the journal with my lies highlighted in yellow. But we all lie to ourselves sometimes, so it's helpful to have someone remind you of your faults every second of every goddamn day."

"So Jamie doesn't lie?" Leaning back against the sofa, I like the sounds of that. But that's until Marcus begins to laugh so hard the sound vibrates the impact toys hanging from the wall.

Sobering, Marcus rubs a palm through his dark hair. "Grant had said you were a formidable woman who needed to feel in control, especially during sex. I've been following your career, and obviously you're at the top of the very top. After much coaxing, Kristal told me you have been celibate since Grant, and that's not healthy for a woman in her prime with these appetites. So I'll thank Ms. Whittenhower's sneaky plans for drawing you to me."

"Ezra's your adopted son." I get down to the heart of the matter. "I want to train with you, if you promise to stop acting like a lunatic, because I'll admit I've been living a life of complete and total apathy, and that is not living. But I need something from you in return."

"Doesn't everybody," Marcus rumbles, looking annoyed. "Everyone needs something from everyone. It's human nature to act selfishly. So, let me guess– you want me to make sure Ezra and Adelaide marry."

"Yes," I say without hesitation.

"Do you love your friend?"

"Yes, like a sister."

"Then you will agree with me when I say there is nothing you or anyone else could ever do to get me to agree to convince my son to marry Ade. She deserves a woman who loves her unconditionally, just as my son deserves a lifetime with Cortez. As far as the woman you're here to learn about. Katya Waters is someone from Ezra's past, a girl who was harmed during the abduction, and he needs closure. None of this has to do with Adelaide Whittenhower."

"I-I-I–" utterly speechless, there is nothing I can say.

"As far as the Wintercrest threat, that's just bullshit Diane came up with to terrorize Ezra into marriage, having nothing to do with Adelaide. Daniel would never imprison his daughter in an insane asylum unless she was truly insane– you of all people know Daniel better than that. He's the family man from hell." Turning to me, Marc's amber eyes drill a hole into my skull. "Unless you have something to share with the class about your *sister*, Regina."

"Manipulative and freakishly strong," I admit. "But sane as the day is long."

"Very well, then don't fret over Ade's happiness. After all, Adelaide's girlfriend won't allow anything to ever happen to her."

"Girlfriend?" I squeak, remembering Kris mentioning the same thing, but Ade has been totally silent. "But… Jesus Christ, what is up with everyone fucking with me while dating or married to someone else?" I snarl at Marcus, "You included. You fucking kissed me, you douche!"

"My wife is a lesbian, so get your panties out of a wad, if you think I'm cheating on the bitch."

"What?" I yelp.

"Fuck," Marcus exhales. "What is up with me losing my shit around you?" Leaning his head against the sofa backrest, he sighs deeply with his eyes clenched shut. "Just pretend I didn't say that, okay?"

"Say what?" I ask innocently, pretending I didn't hear what I most definitely heard.

"Nice try." Eyes never opening, Marcus actually spills his guts. "My marriage was arranged, completely out of my hands. Which is why no matter how hard Daniel, Diane, and Adelaide try to do the same to Ezra, I will thwart it at every turn. The only difference, I did fall in love with my wife, while falling in love with her son and Cortez. I'd lost so much family, and I wanted nothing more than to enter a readymade one."

"I know how that feels," I admit, hoping my words didn't break the spell, causing Marcus to stop speaking. With one ear, I listen for smashing glass and slamming doors as Marc's personal lie detector test keeps him honest.

"I wanted the white-picket-fence-lifestyle bullshit. But what did I know when I was only seventeen?" Shrugging, Marcus looks defeated. "I wanted it then, but I sure as shit don't want it now, and I expect I won't ever in the future. So long story short, Diane wouldn't consummate the marriage but expected me to stay faithful in a sadistic sort of way– don't ask, because it's beyond disturbing and sickening."

"My tenure at Misery Castle taught me to expect the worst in people."

"The Whittenhowers are domesticated pets compared to the Holdens– trust me on that one." One eyelid pops open, capturing me in its gaze. "Two years into our marriage, I forced Diane to perform her wifely duty after she had her agent steal my virginity."

"Wha… how?" I lean forward, sensing Jamie's calming presence but I don't turn to look at him while Marcus is distracted. "Agent?"

"The who, what, why, when, or how doesn't really matter, but the event sparked something in me, and I sought BDSM to heal… and that's pretty much how I've ended up here. After the boys were abducted and harmed, Dexter inducted Ezra into the lifestyle because I just couldn't force myself to do it. Then Dexter tried with Cortez, but he wasn't receptive to taking orders from anyone but Ezra or me. Then there is Aaron Frost, the young boy who was harmed the worst. He's been coming around, seeking my hand instead of Ezra's."

"Grant was terrified for the boys, completely inconsolable. After they were found, he was so relieved." Breathing laboriously, I suck air in at a heavy rate, almost hyperventilating. "That was the night Grant died." Rubbing my palms on my thighs, I try to wick the perspiration away.

"I–" Croaking, Marc's voice breaks. "The only thing I wanted when I got back to Dominion that night, after seeing how utterly destroyed Ezra, Cortez, Aaron, and Katya Waters were… was Grant. I found him."

"I know." Closing my eyes, I swallow my tears. "That was the one thing Daniel told me."

"No, you don't understand." Reaching out to me, Marc's fingers entwine with mine. "I found Grant, already on the edge of death… I found him." Shuddering with intense emotions, the entire sofa vibrates with his pain. "I found Grant–" Voice hollow, haunted, Marcus points with our clasped hands to the center of the room. "I found Grant… right there."

With a sharp gasp, I collapse to the sofa, lifeless in shock, eyes riveted to the spot where we all lost Grant. Hands tug me until I'm bundled in Marc's lap, and it's almost as if I can feel Grant's ghost trying to comfort me too.

"Grant died in my arms, and an EMT was able to resurrect him. But he died again in the ambulance… Grant died again, and I've never been the same person from that day forth." Squeezing me tightly, Marcus buries his face against the side of my neck. "Don't ever think you've been grieving alone. Daniel grieves for his son more than Priscilla and Grant's sisters ever could. I grieve for the best friend I lost that day, but not as much as I grieve for the loss of my sense of self."

"Shit!" I sob, squeezing Marcus back. So vital– alive. Here. Now. Not some ghost from the past haunting my every thought.

"Let it out, Regina. Show us how much agony and guilt you've lived with for the past nine and a half years. We have to see it– hear it. Experience it with you so we can take our responsibility and repent. Let it pour out, heal yourself, and realize you're not alone in your loss."

Weeping, the agonizing sound I release from deep within my chest echoes around the room. Mournful, a death wail, to the point even Jamie steps forward from the shadows to rest a hand on my back in a desperate need to comfort me.

"Let it out– stop smothering yourself." Marcus croons, while two sets of hands stroke my back in a soothing motion. "Let it out… release Queen."

"Fuck if I know how," I admit. "Queen is me and I am her."

"No, she's not. You need to let her out to play before you bleed her dry." Marcus pulls my face from his chest, with Jamie retreating back to the shadows. "It's why you look like the walking dead."

It takes all of my honor and integrity not to whip around and look at Jamie, but to do so is to lose this last thread to Grant that I'm so desperately clutching for dear life. To do so would ruin whatever we're building here tonight. Curiosity killed the cat, and I'm already dead on the inside, I don't want to be on the outside.

"Regina?" The upward inflection in Marc's voice makes it sound like a question. "You're very controlled, but we need to allow you to open your wings and fly."

Lost, sounding like a child, "I don't know how."

"Well, I do… You need me, and I need you, and it's exactly what Grant wanted. So let me teach you a healthy outlet for your natural urges, and I promise I'll protect Adelaide the best I can. Not only for you, but because she was Grant's baby sister. You don't always have to do everything alone. You have an ally in me, Regina."

Sliding back to the sofa, now that I know Jamie is safely hidden for whatever reasons he may have, I try to lighten the dark mood that has descended. "Secret handshake?" I offer my hand to

Marcus, along with a smirk. "Allies? Partners in crime? BDSM teacher and student? Grant's biggest fans?"

Arching his neck, Marcus releases the most devastating sound I've ever heard. Pure sex rolls out of his throat in the form of a laugh emerging from his lips. The sound strikes my core like a hit of ecstasy. So potent I close my eyes and shudder as the sound reverberates down my spine like a tuning fork.

Reality exists outside of the brownstone's walls, and everything inside is pure fantasy. Not real. A foggy dream world where I behave like someone I never imagined myself to be.

"No, fuck me." Marc issues a guttural demand. "We seal our partnership by exchanging body fluids. Fuck me, Regina."

"What? You can't be serious." My eyes flick around the room, feeling Jamie but not seeing him because he knows how to blend in with the tricks of light shadowing the room. "Jamie's with us. You're married. I won't be another man's mistress!" I shout in outrage, fist clenching the sofa armrest to the point my nails dig into the velvet.

"Queen only erupts in moments of anger and sex." Marcus proves he knows me better than I wished. "Instead of having you beat the ever-loving fuck out of me, I'd rather you just fuck me."

"You're married," I huff, insulted.

"To a lesbian, I've only had a handful of times in my entire adult life." Marc's voice holds a sharp edge of violence. "As far as Jamie watching, everyone in this room has been a goddamn saint for as long as I can remember. Jamie won't even jerk off with me."

"Why should he?" I defend Jamie. "That is the most bizarre request of a best friend."

"Like Ade hasn't tried to fuck you." Voice quiet and cold, Marcus is definitely insulted. Glaring into the shadows, knowing exactly where Jamie is standing sight unseen. "In a weak moment, where I wanted Jamie to get off instead of whining about being lonely, I tried to touch his dick… eight years, Jamie has punished me."

"It's kind of a big deal." My eyes bug out, body slumping with shock. "You're serious? You want to fuck me?"

"Yes," Marcus rasps roughly. "I want, and I *will* fuck you. Tonight."

"Your definition of friendship is warped!"

"Grant said you liked to be in control during sex, and that's when Queen erupted. So as an introductory offer as my new lover,

I'll even let you be on top. Take the offer or leave it, but it will be the only time you'll fuck me."

"Have you lost your goddamn mind?" I exclaim. "I never agreed to be your lover!"

"You said handshake, and I said body fluid exchange. I don't see how you'd be confused by that." Marcus actually stares at me like I'm the one who lost my mind. "Whether you take me up on the offer, we will fuck. We will be lovers. But after tonight, I'll always be the one fucking you."

"You're insane," I whisper in awe, and an odd sound emanates from the shadows, almost as if Jamie is amused by the most bizarre conversation of my life.

Marcus growls, looking more like a feral animal than sounding like one. Brown eyes blazing, mouth opened as his breath saws in and out on a pant, with his body leaning forward, Marc is coiled with tension before he attacks.

Marcus Zeitler is the alpha in the house, more powerful than I could ever be.

Sex with Grant had been about me. If given the opportunity, Grant would have gotten me off over and over without ever getting anything from me. Sex with this man will be all about him.

Grant was the selflessness to Marc's selfishness, and that is the balance of their friendship, and why Grant and I worked so well as a team.

But Marcus and I will annihilate each other– the more destructive the better to make me feel something for once other than the numbing of nothingness.

The sex will be intense, and by the looks of the bulge tenting Marc's pants– painful. In the absence of pain is death, and I want to feel motherfucking alive for once.

Almost frothing at the mouth, Marcus is waiting as a predator waits for prey. Our gazes holding, we're dominants with half of our nature being animalistic– driven solely by primal instinct. Driven by the need to hunt, capture, kill, and eat. But ultimately, we're driven by the need to mate.

Before I can think, let alone blink, I find myself pinning Marcus to the sofa with my aching crotch grinding into his bulge. I growl at the glorious sensation of his body rubbing against mine. Hard. Demanding. Unrelenting. Marc's hands immediately find my ass, yanking my dress out of the way. Fingernails biting into my flesh, thumbs bruising my hips, Marc presses me down as he forcefully thrusts up, a grinding battle of the wills.

I'm sorry Adelaide– but, sister, your thigh couldn't do this to me.

"I'm going to make you scream," Queen purrs out of my mouth before attacking Marc's lips. The kiss is full of nearly a decade of bottled-up yearning and suppressed passions. Fingertips twisting painfully in my hair, Marcus gnaws at my bottom lip in a deliciously painful way that has me close to release.

Jamie's eyes blaze into my back. Without knowing what he's feeling, it somehow brings me into my head. My head is the place to avoid in all sexual matters. If I can think, it's game over.

"I can't do this," I gasp, trying to push away from Marc's chest, but his arms create a steel-cage around me.

"What's wrong?" Marc's sober, assessing, but on the edge of just taking what I'm not willing to give.

"I can't do this again, Marc. I can't be with someone because of the position they're placed under." Voice barely a whisper, it quivers with aching misery.

"I don't understand," Marcus murmurs just as softly. A line forms between his eyebrows, and I realize he really doesn't get it.

"I know I'm not the most attractive person on the planet. I get that– believe me, I do. But I deserve more respect than you fucking me because it's safe, because you can trust me, and because it's convenient."

"Convenient? What do you mean? If this is about Diane, believe me when I say she's probably fucking her girlfriend's brains out right now, if she's not at some charity function or driving Ezra insane."

"Marc, I've only been with Grant," I admit as if it's a huge secret. "Yeah, Ade's tried to take advantage of the situation a few times, and I fucked up by fooling around with Cortez last night. But that doesn't count like actual sex does."

"It all counts," Marc warns me. "All sexual contact *is* sex."

"Just once in my life I'd love to have a guy want me just because he desires me. I'm not an acquisition, or a broodmare, or an ally. I'm a person, dammit! I have feelings and wants and needs."

I try to push off of Marcus again, and he makes me fight for it. Struggling in his hold, I sense Jamie is creeping very close to me, almost as if he's trying to soothe me with his presence.

Jamie's breath flutters the broken hairs on the top of my head, and I struggle to turn around, to get at him– to see him. It's a compulsion I can't deny. Panicking, I want to scream out my frustrations, but my voice is too raw. I want to hit and scratch Marcus, but he captures my wrists in one of his hands– fingers the tightest of restraints.

"Calm yourself, Regina," Marcus commands evenly, and yet I still fight with all my strength. "You're waking the sleeping beast," Marc warns. "And once he comes out to play, all bets are off. No one has come so close to being taken by force, since the night I lost my virginity, and Cort tests my control daily. Voice thick with power with a pleading edge, "Regina, calm yourself, don't move a muscle, and relax."

Marc's panting is equaled to my rapid breathing. I ease air in and out between my lips in a slow rhythm, and he joins my practice until we're both calmer.

"Word of advice, don't ever stop me once we get going." Eyes held wide, Marcus is controlling every response in his body. "I don't understand the word *no* once *yes* has been spoken– verbally or otherwise. It's a contract struck."

"I–"

"Don't speak!" Marcus snaps, and then issues another threat. "This is a short reprieve while I figure out what just happened inside your mind. Your dominant side erupted, and then you strangled her, and that is the opposite of what we're trying to achieve. After we reason that out, we *will* fuck tonight."

"I don't get a choice?"

"You made your choice when you pinned me to my own sofa, and by riding my dick and shoving your tongue down my throat. Now, explain why you panicked," Marcus commands.

Ashamed with how weak and pitiful I sound, I breathe the truth. "You don't want me."

"Why do you say such a ridiculous thing?" Marc's eyebrows furrow in confusion.

Closing my eyes, I admit defeat. "Balance. You're a dominant male, who craves someone submissive, not a freakishly large female."

"That's not how I operate, Regina. I'm the master of all masters. My kink is being strong enough to force *everyone* to submit, not the weak who easily bend to my will."

"Jesus," I hiss in awe.

"You're intelligent, so use words to explain yourself better." Marc's calm demeanor is at odds with the energy thrumming through his body. He's always poised on the edge of attack, with his fingertips biting into my flesh.

"I've spent most of the past decade locked away in my house, or dealing with clients, never going out into the world. So when I went to Restraint, I didn't know what to expect. It was a physical blow to experience how everyone reacted to me, while watching how they looked at Fate. They wanted her badly, while either dismissing me or coveting me because I could kick their asses."

"And what does this have to do with you and me?" Marcus sounds genuinely confused, obviously never doubting his sexual appeal. "You were never self-conscious with Grant. Is it because it's me? What changed?" Marcus shifts underneath me, proving that he's still extremely aroused and ready to fuck.

Mortified, I can't stop the words from tumbling out. "I'm getting older, and I'm not some tiny, giggly plaything. I've had two kids, so things aren't exactly as they used to be."

Face twisted, Marcus sounds perturbed with what I'm saying. "I can't fathom where this is coming from, Regina."

"Fine– I've never had a boyfriend. Grant doesn't count, because Jackson and Daniel coerced us into creating Niel, with Ella as a blessed accident. I loved Grant with every fiber of my being, but that doesn't change how it started. I've never been on a date, or gone to the movies, or even gone to dinner with a guy."

"That's easily resolvable," Marcus mutters. "From what I gather, dating isn't exactly fun. Everyone bitches and moans until they end up using online dating sites, where they just end up getting fucked in every sense of the word. Neither one of us is missing much."

"Marcus," I snarl. "Just listen to me, okay?"

"Fine."

"So, now I'm sitting on the lap of another ridiculously rich, handsome male, whose only option is me, but not because he wants me. It's not flattering. Neither is being looked through like a windowpane. Dexter was all eyes for Fate, and Cort looked at me with disdain at Restraint. He only touched me last night because I was an available wet hole he could enter– one that would piss you off. I'm not an idiot."

"No, not an idiot, but you're severely naive." Sensing I won't bolt, Marcus releases my hands so he can caress my back while we talk. "Dexter wanted Fate because he's a sadist who loves tender flesh and innocence."

"Dexter, as in your cousin? Dexter Hayes is a sadist? Whoa…"

"Dex got all of the kink genes in the family," Marcus teases with a wink. "Cort and I have similar tastes, as does my son. We like a fight because it gets the primal juices flowing. Cort is partial to Kristal because she's an obstinate brat."

"No, shit," I mutter begrudgingly. "You should have to live with her."

"I couldn't handle the responsibility of having a submissive who allows me to do anything I wished. If I said jump from a bridge and kill yourself, they wouldn't hesitate. I'd rather say go jump off a bridge as a test to their loyalty, because they should set me up with an evaluation at Wintercrest if I asked."

"So if you're a dominant, you don't necessarily need a submissive?"

"You have so much to learn, little domme," Marcus purrs. "Those beneath me, it's my job to elevate them, to make them stronger, to be their port in the storm. Their job is to be my checks and balances, to ensure I don't go off the deep end and take all of us with me."

"We aren't talking bedroom games, are we?"

"No– life. Maître du Jeu is a BDSM community we belong to at Restraint. We're not taught the same way as others in the lifestyle, where the dominant forces the submissive to surrender. The point is for all of us to be stronger versions of ourselves, with the smartest and strongest at the top."

"I agree with that way of thinking. It's what I've been doing with my girls all these years– making them reach their potential, because they wouldn't have been able to without me pushing them forward."

"Exactly. So there is no need for your freak-out in the middle of sex. No more self-conscious bullshit. Queen owns her sexuality, and she does whatever the fuck she wants to get what she wants."

"I'm scared." I admit this before I realize I actually feel that way in the first place.

"You ought to be," Marcus murmurs ominously. "I gather that you think I don't find you enticing, which is utterly ridiculous." He scoffs, pressing me firmly against his arousal.

We hold our gazes as we watch thoughts roll over the other's face. The entire time, Marcus softly rubs my back and makes a humming sound in the back of his throat in contentment.

"I'm confused about your comment regarding Cortez—explain," Marcus demands, expecting to be obeyed.

"Cortez made fun of my nickname." I sound petulant, and I don't mean it to be. "I know Queen doesn't fit me, but that was rude."

"Now you're just projecting your insecurities onto Cortez," Marcus chastises. "I believe he was joking because he knew who you were, which means that the name Queen would have been humorous to him because it was given to you by our second Daniel. Diane's and my life are tightly connected to the Whittenhowers, so don't you believe that Cortez and Ezra would've had two Daniel shadows following them around like pesky little brothers?"

Heart clenching, I can barely stand to listen to Marcus, just as I can never do with Adelaide. But I force myself this time while breathing through the fear and pain.

"I was at Whittenhower Estates several times while you were sequestered in your rooms during functions. I know you remember the one time we came face to face, as I saw it in your eyes when you were on the sidewalk outside my front door last night."

"I won't deny any of that."

Mercurial moods switching in a heartbeat, "Your reprieve has concluded," Marcus says with finality.

"Hey!" I cry, trying to push his hands away as they pull at the hem of my dress and try to lift. I fight to keep my dress on my body, while Marcus seems to gain more than two hands. "Jesus, is Jamie helping you? What the fuck?"

"I said–"Marcus slowly enunciates each word, like I'm hard of hearing or stupid. "Your. Reprieve. Has. Concluded."

Eyes blazing with a terrifying amber fire, Marc's voice is deeper than I've heard it drop. "I explained that your right to say 'no' no longer exists. You can fight me, and I'll unleash my true nature, and it will turn violent, or you can flow with me, and we can have a pleasant time. It's your choice, Regina, make it quickly."

Choice already made when I jumped Marcus on the sofa, I take off his suit jacket and hand it to him. Smiling to himself, he gently places the jacket on the couch cushion.

I wait.

"Good, Regina," Marcus praises me, and I try my damnedest not to allow it to affect me. "You learn swiftly."

"I only have to be told once," I mutter belligerently, and he just smirks in response, knowing I'm testing him.

The demanding fingers return by tugging at the hem of my dress again, and I close my eyes in defeat. Oddly passive beneath Marc's demands, I allow him to remove my dress. It's freeing to not be in control, to not have the burden of the blame if this goes tragically wrong.

The moment cool air touches my skin, my hands seek refuge against my breasts. Deft fingers unhook my bra while knowing eyes hold my gaze. Just to torture me, Marcus slides the straps down my arms at an excruciatingly slow rate.

Coaxing, "Why so shy?" Marcus asks me, voice gentle and kind.

"They're never uncovered. I'm always in a bra, unless I'm in the shower or sleeping, and I never sleep." Grumbling, I admit, "It feels strange to be so—"

"Free?" A wry eyebrow raises in challenge. "Get used to it." Marc's tone implies it won't matter if I do or don't get used to it, because if he doesn't want me in a bra, I'm not wearing one.

Shoring up my courage, I close my eyes in shame, and then drop my arms to my lap, allowing Marcus an unimpeded view of my large breasts.

A soft intake of breath has my eyes flicking open, only to discover Marcus gazing straight ahead instead of at my tits– eyes locked with the man standing less than a foot from my back. Marc's lips curve, as if he's holding a silent conversation with Jamie and his smile speaks for itself.

Smug, Marc looks me dead in the eyes, and then he homes in on my tits, challenging me to protest. Wishing I was numb again, because I can't handle the barrage of emotions battering my psyche, I stare straight ahead and memorize the pattern on the wallpaper.

Swaying, I bask in the warmth of Jamie's body at my back. He's close enough that if I were to breathe deeply, we'd make contact. But if I were to turn my head enough to get a glimpse of him in my peripheral, I'd never see, nor hear from him again. It's a Pandora's Box I'm intelligent enough to know not to open.

"This is not Cortez's work. It's too precise and controlled." Voice rough with lust, Marcus proves he is the possessive bastard I expected him to be. "Someone marked you recently."

Swirling his finger around the tip of my left breast, Marcus follows the path of Adelaide's teeth marks. Seemingly intrigued with my body, both of his hands cup one of my breasts, and I flush with embarrassment since my flesh still overflows his hands.

After softly kneading to calm me, Marcus then digs his nails in deep. He repeats this until my head falls backward in pleasure. The warmth at my back disappears instantly. Frowning in disappointment, I wanted to lean against Jamie while Marcus touched me.

"Who marked you?" Marc's curiosity is laced with anger.

"I'd rather not answer that." I blush from the tips of my toes to the roots of my hair.

"I didn't ask if you if you wanted to answer the question. I asked for an answer." Marcus enunciates each word again, like I'm a goddamn moron.

"I'm aware of that, Marcus. This is me not answering you," I mutter defiantly. "You're very literal."

"Yes, I am, because I train the future Masters of Restraint, as I was trained by the head master of Maître de Jeu."

"Do you realize how redundant that sounds?" I muse, then softly huff a laugh underneath my breath. "I sucked at French while in school, but a wily little boy loathed his French lessons. So blame Whitt for what I'm about to say. Saying *master* twice, even if it's in both English and French, should be like a double negative, completely cancelling itself out."

"Shoot me," Marcus mutters, while that hollow rasping echoes behind me, no doubt Jamie's version of a laugh.

"You're all a crafty sort, so I have to be extremely literal, or I have to ask ten questions to get my initial question answered. My other trainee is an expert in evasion, more so than you are, Regina. So let's try this again. Who. Marked. You. On. Your. Left. Breast?"

"NO." I cross my arms over my tits, trapping Marc's hands beneath, and I refuse to answer.

"Don't test me, Regina. I'm this close to snapping." Marc's hands pulse on my tit, and I grimace in pain. "If I didn't know your lineage, I'd swear you fell off a branch of Cort's family tree. Thank God, I'm not training the pair of you– I'd shoot myself."

Sighing audibly, I roll my eyes, enjoying the pain Marcus causes in retaliation. "Just so you know, you don't scare me, and neither does pain. I already hurt enough on the inside." I simply add, "Ade," to answer Marc's question, knowing he'll never give up.

"Well, I didn't see *that* coming," Marc murmurs in surprise, eyes locked on Jamie again. "You had sex with Adelaide? Really?"

"I don't know if you'd call it sex. I'm not actually up on the whole lesbian thing." I try to sound worldly and experienced, but I end up blushing when my voice breaks. Marcus smiles at me like he thought I was being cute.

"You'll learn. You must be properly educated, or they'll eat you alive at Restraint. I don't want to get into pissing contests over you all of the time... so, was it oral sex?"

Eager, the bulge beneath me pulses at the thought.

"No way!" I inwardly cringe.

"You don't like oral sex?" Marcus asks in surprise, eyes yet again seeking Jamie's instead of mine. Somehow Jamie has become both of our lie detectors.

"Not with Adelaide, I don't." I shudder at the thought. "With Grant? Oral was one of my favorite activities."

"Thank God," Marcus growls, cock going into a frenzy beneath my ass cheek. "Why Ade, then?"

"It just happened, and it will *never* happen again. Ade caught me at a vulnerable point. I was tired, horny, and slightly drunk, and she wasn't taking my nos for an answer. Then Ade was creepy afterward, and I had a bit of a breakdown. My laryngitis was self-inflicted by the screaming fit I had into my pillow."

"How soon after?" Marcus circles his finger in the air, coming up with an appropriate word. "How soon after your '*not*' sex did Adelaide leave?"

"Ade started spewing stuff I made her promise never to speak about, and then left a minute or so after decimating me."

"Adelaide can be such a cunt," Marcus utters vehemently of his future daughter-in-law.

"Hey!"

"Sorry... actually, I'm not, no matter who gets offended by my estimation of Adelaide. I understand her. I even respect her. But I don't like Adelaide as a person– deal with it." Marcus looks a challenge at me, waiting for a protest that doesn't come. "Adelaide knows better than the shit she pulled with you. It's no wonder you dropped. Your first experience in years, and she hits you with words you forbid, and then leaves you to fend for yourself. It's unacceptable, and not unexpected behavior on her part. Adelaide probably got what she was after, and then selfishly left. Am I right?"

"Yeah, you have Ade's number," I mumble. "I love and hate her with equal measure."

"Jamie is most eager for a frontal view of you." Marcus switches topics of conversation so fast I can barely keep up. It's dizzying. I get excited thinking that soon I will see Jamie, and then I notice the tie that materialized in Marc's hand.

"You truly are insane, aren't you?" I groan in a mix of disappointment and anticipation.

Sensing my surrender, Marcus smiles while raising the tie near my face. "Good, Regina. You're a fast learner."

"That you're insane?" I tease while interrupting Marcus because I'm scared shitless. "Yeah, it took about ten seconds into meeting you to figure out you're certifiably insane."

"Nice," Marcus drawls to the soundtrack of Jamie's ghastly laughter. "I'm going to fasten this around your eyes, and then I will place you in the center of the room for viewing." Marcus issues a vehement warning. "Do. Not. Move. To. Touch. Jamie."

"Is Jamie as fragile as the glass he smashes when you tell fibs?"

"Yes, exactly *that*." Marcus plays along while wrapping the tie around my head several times to cover my eyes. I blink, trying to dislodge the fabric, but to no avail. Movement flutters in front of my face, and I grin.

"I can't see you, but I wonder if you're swatting at invisible flies," I mutter snarkily.

"Smart-ass." Marcus chuckles, then gets his revenge by placing me where he wants me.

Standing in the center of the impact room in a pair of black lace panties and flats. I feel overexposed, uncomfortable, and self-conscious. I want to cover my breasts with my arms and run screaming from the room.

But I'm Regina Regal, and Queen does not flee.

With two sets of eyes blazing into my skin, my body beads with sweat under their examination– as if I didn't already have enough to be embarrassed about. Let's hope they find a glossy shine sexy.

My sense of hearing intensifies now that I don't have my sight to rely on. A rasping sound, I identify as Jamie, rumbles in front of me. Soft puffs of breath hit the side of my neck, then the tip of a nose gently glides down the column of my throat. Huffing, Jamie is either scent-marking me, or inhaling my natural scent. Whimpering, I press closer to Jamie, only to have him disappear.

Yet again, I groan in disappointment. "Does Jamie not like me, or something? Every time I try to just feel him on my skin, he runs off."

"He loves the way you smell, Regina." Marc's voice softly calls from across the room, no doubt where he retook his seat on the sofa.

It's just me and Jamie.

Leaning forward, I search Jamie out by using his body heat and the sound of his labored breathing as a guide. My solace– I don't know what Jamie looks like, or what he sounds like, but I love the intensity I feel from his gaze and the openness during our text messages.

Jamie makes me feel beautiful.

I know I'm crazy, but it's how I feel.

"Jamie?" I call out to him, aching to hear him call back but knowing he never will. His body is drawn back to me like a magnet seeking its polar opposite. The heat radiating off him is like a blast furnace, and I suffer from a disturbing craving to crawl all over him and make him mine.

"I believe Jamie is eternally grateful that I finally have a female trainee, especially you. I've only trained Dexter, the PB, and now you. Jamie hasn't had much fun watching, nor will he participate with a male."

Feeling oddly possessive over Jamie already, I don't like how Marcus treats him. "Just because Jamie's straight doesn't make him a homophobe, Marcus, or should I say… just because he won't let you do him."

"Ouch– touché."

"I'm just calling you out on your bullshit since you're acting like Ade." The breath is back and hotter than ever before. I sway as it moves closer to my face, then the lightest of kisses is pressed on the corner of my lips.

I wonder if Jamie is thinking of how many men I've kissed now, or of how many women he has. The thought dissolves in an instant when Jamie shifts slightly, brushing his lips directly across mine.

Whining, it takes all of my self-control not to crash our mouths together, but I know that would be the end instead of the beginning.

Hot breath skates from my mouth, along the column of my neck, and then down my chest, leaving a cooling, moist trail in its wake.

"Use caution, Jamie." Marcus speaks as if I'm a wild animal that's going to harm his best friend. "Don't move, Regina– not a single muscle."

I shout when something hot and damp flicks my nipple. My fingertips bite into my thighs and my spine bows when Jamie's mouth engulfs my breast. There's no gently sucking at the tip. No, Jamie pulls as much of my tit into his mouth that will fit, close to unhinging his jaw in the process. With hearty pulls, Jamie suckles rhythmically, yet he doesn't touch me anywhere else.

A fevered sweat erupting from every pore, with my nerves sparking pure pleasure throughout my system, I weave on my feet. Squeezing my thighs together against the building pressure, with a tongue flick against my tit, I nearly come… but Jamie isn't so lucky.

That strange, raspy sound flows from Jamie's mouth to vibrate against my flesh as he swallows as much of my tit as humanly possible. Scalding hot drops of fluid hit my knee as Jamie makes a strangled noise. Freaking out, he backs away, only to return with a piece of fabric to clean his spendings off my skin.

"It's okay. Shh… you did nothing wrong. It happens to the best of us. You remember it happened to me just last week." Marc's tone is calm and soothing as he reassures Jamie.

It's a weird dynamic, and I don't know what to make of it. Most of the time, Marcus sounds angry with Jamie, almost punishing. But now, Marc takes on a tone you use when speaking to a child. But clearly Jamie is no child. No, talking down a scared animal better describes the tone of voice he uses.

"Actually, I'm flattered, Jamie. I haven't felt very good about my body lately, and that was a high compliment you just paid me." I don't alter my tone of voice as Marc does. "Thank you… and um– your mouth was hot and velvety soft, and I was close to getting off myself."

I know I need reassurance right now, and Jamie seems like an extremely submissive person. I have the feeling he needs constant reassurance.

Out of nowhere, I'm kissed full on the lips– it only lasts a split-second, but a trail of saliva strings as Jamie pulls away. Licking my lips, I try to get a taste of him, but it's not enough.

"Thank you, Regina." Marcus escorts me from the center of the room, and I do feel free walking around in just a pair of panties, like a real woman again. "That was very sweet of you, and I'm surprised Jamie kissed you like that."

"Why is he so shy?"

"We all have our insecurities," Marcus mutters, almost sounding distracted, like he's speaking to me yet somehow communicating with Jamie instead. "Do you still want to be on top? This will be the only time you'll be offered."

I'm floored. No interlude, just straight into the sex.

"Romance is dead– top," blurts out while I examine whether or not Marcus had Jamie '*prep*' me for him with the tit suckling. I know I'm wet enough now. If Jamie's kink is mommy fantasies, I'll gladly take one for the team with my huge tits.

Still blindfolded by the tie, I sense Marcus sitting down on the sofa again. My equilibrium pitches when he pulls me to straddle his hips. Adjusting to moving so fast, I sit astride his thighs, slowly lowering myself. A squeak of shock escapes my lips when I come in direct contact with Marc's naked body.

"We need protection," I protest, trying to distance myself from the forearm-sized cock pulsing against my slit.

"Not between us, we don't." Being an asshole, Marcus rolls his hips until his naked cock slips between my nether lips. I'm ashamed to admit, my body writhes from the exquisite contact. "I'm clean, and other than one mouth I take on a regular basis, I'm celibate. According to your medical records, you're clean and on the shot. I know you've been a good girl," he says with wry amusement.

"I can't believe you hacked into my medical records!" Struggling, I try to stand up, but all I succeed in doing is jabbing myself in the pussy with a very determined dick.

"Really?" Marcus mutters sarcastically, evidently getting off on my struggles, because precum is gushing out and making me sticky. "Out of everything we've talked of tonight, *that* is what you're shocked over." Chuckling, Marcus unravels the tie from around my head, gifting me with my vision.

Feeling ridiculous, I grumble, "Well, hacking is my forte, that's why."

Jamie's still here since I can sense him, but he's to my back, and I wonder if Marcus didn't want me on top after all, just to keep Jamie out of my line of sight.

"How do I know that the mouth you fuck is clean? You may be, but the mouth's owner may be a nasty fucker."

"Hmmm… I think you did a thorough examination of that mouth last night. I think your tongue found him perfectly acceptable."

My eyes bulge. I didn't see that one coming.

"Yes, Cortez's punishment for being a cock-tease is being skull-fucked. I believe Cort said it was as pleasurable as it was painful. A friendly warning: I taught Cort how to provide oral sex, and he learned from example. If you go down on him, expect to be skull-fucked, and then expect me to be livid."

"Is pseudo-incest a kink?" I taunt, finding satisfaction by highlighting Marc's naughtier faults. "You don't like sharing Cort, I take it?"

"No, I don't like sharing *you*." Marcus stresses, and to hammer home his point, he grinds against me, clearly annoyed by the flimsy panties in the way– not that they're a deterrent, seeing as how the seat has slid to the side.

"Ah, you just let Jamie suck my tit and kiss me," I point out. "I feel like I should be thanking you for that."

"Jamie doesn't count," Marcus growls. "I assume you aren't on any antibiotics. I don't think I could explain to my wife a second *oops*." He rumbles a deep laugh. "If you have another accident like Ella, I'll have a line forming around the block by people who'll want to murder me after they hack off my cock and balls with a tarnished meth spoon."

"How very specific," I deadpan. "Castration is so sexy." Trying to follow Marcus in conversation is like absorbing all the information on the ticker-tape on the bottom of a news broadcast. Marcus makes me dizzy, and I'm not entirely sure he's sane.

One second I'm trying to decipher Marc's speech, and the next my panties are torn from my body. Throat opening up on a scream, I find myself impaled on a cock as thick as a Coke can.

"Holy fuck, batman!" Back arching, I come before my body has a chance to register in with my brain. Eyes rolling back into my skull, skin shrinking, every nerve ending in my body quivers in ecstasy.

Poor Jamie's making strange grumbling noises behind me as he struggles to mute his climax. That guy has some weird kinks, but the funny thing is, knowing he's coming makes me come harder.

"Holy fuck is right!" Marcus shouts, followed by a guttural grunt. "If it wasn't for the fact that I've seen your children, I'd think you were a goddamn virgin. I'm going to fuck this pussy for the first time in your life."

Marcus slams my hips down with shocking brutality, to the soundtrack of Jamie breaking glass in the background.

"Ignore Jamie–" Marcus gets cut off by the simple fact that Jamie will not be ignored. Foregoing breaking glass like a furious bride, Jamie decides caressing my back and kissing my shoulders is more antagonizing.

Warring, Marc is brutal to Jamie's gentle. Unable to concentrate on either, I'm consumed with lust.

With Jamie's help, I hang on for dear life as Marcus pile-drives into me from beneath. I thought being on top meant I was in control, but I was a fool. It was all an illusion. Marcus is Master, and he will never relinquish control.

Ever.

Here I'd thought what Grant and I had done in the past was hardcore– wrong again.

Pistoning into me, Marcus growls like a rabid animal. His eyes glow with amber fire, and his bronze skin shines with sweat. He holds my gaze, trying his damnedest to control my mind until I ignore Jamie.

I can't do that.

As punishment, Marcus forces me to submit to his pleasure. He brands me with the biological version of a *mine* tattoo. Unable to stop myself, I join Marcus as he shoots fiery, molten liquid inside of my pussy like it actually belongs there.

I've just been owned by Master.

A soft kiss is placed at the nape of my neck, then Jamie's presence recedes.

Collapsing backward to the sofa, Marcus pulls me with him. I struggle to get up, but his arms engulf me. Not as a cage as before, more like he's cradling me.

The juxtaposition of Marcus going from sexual brutality to gentle affection is the biggest mind fuck of my life.

"Is it because you don't want me to see Jamie?" I ask why Marcus won't let me up, because his tender routine is confusing me. After never having a one-night-stand, I don't know the procedure.

"No, we're alone, but Jamie will fade in and out at will. Right now, I just want to hold you." Marc's voice is so faint I'm not sure I hear him correctly. But I burrow against his chest anyway. "Relax. Hold me back, please."

The childlike quality in Marc's voice has me complying faster than if he'd demanded it. Showing me yet another facet of his complex personality, I try to fit the pieces together to form Marcus as a complete person, and fail. I don't get Marcus, and I'm not sure I ever will. Sad to imagine, but I doubt anyone possibly could.

"That was impressive," he murmurs breathlessly. "You worry about not being a fragile beauty, but I couldn't fuck one like that because I'd break her. Regina, your strength *is* your beauty. You have to accept who you are, because there are no guarantees anyone else will.

"You may find a friend or family member who loves you as you are, but it's a rarity to find someone who truly gets you. I never want to see you doubt yourself again. That isn't the Regina I know… and before you say I don't know you, you have no idea what I do or don't know. You need to have faith in me and in yourself, and let Queen free."

"Easier said than done," I mutter, contemplating if it's healthy or destructive to allow the beyond dominant side of my nature to erupt.

"Ah!" Marc shouts as he tries to regain his breath during an aftershock. Gripping my hips, he flexes into me while another batch of cum is released. Marcus smiles at me so brilliantly that I blush.

"I haven't been inside a woman since my daughter was conceived." Marcus drops as a bombshell when I didn't even know he had a child. "It's been almost thirteen years, so I apologize for being so brutal, but I couldn't help myself."

"We really are similar in some ways, aren't we?" I muse more so to myself than to Marcus.

"Most definitely. I'm sure you'll agree if you gauge what I'm about to say against masturbating to the works of James Atwater. Having my cock sucked by a man isn't the same as being buried deep inside a hot, tight pussy. It's hollow by comparison."

"I feel you on that front– do I ever… now actually being fucked by James Atwater," I muse to get a rise out of Marcus, but his reaction is the opposite of what I expected. Shuddering beneath me, he grunts.

"I swear to God, my cock's spurting for the hell of it. I'm not even coming, but it just keeps pumping out." Marc's laughter is infectious, but then his face clouds with an unfathomable expression. "Thank you for allowing me to be inside of you, cum inside of you. I know how difficult that had to be for you, because I know how much you loved Grant– how much you still do. I won't lie, I feel like an interloper trespassing on someone else's womb."

The never-ending guilt, sorrow, and pain in Marc's voice is so raw and deep that tears spill out the corners of my eyes. "Some days I don't know how I put one foot in front of the other. If it wasn't for my daughter…"

Marc's chest quivers underneath my cheek as emotions finally explode. "Oh, God, Regina!" he cries out, crushing me in his arms.

Then the biggest shock of my life occurs. The strongest man I've ever met sobs in my arms, and I am humbled.

In the shadows, I know Jamie is watching, and I wonder how he feels in this moment.

Chapter Thirteen

Having no idea how long we've slept in each other's arms on the sofa, the sound of the locked front door creaking open wakes us with a jolt.

Stretching his arms above his head, "What time is it?" Marc's voice is rough from disuse.

Straining to reach, I pull my dress closer to me from where it rests on the sofa cushion. Pockets are a girl's best friend. I snag my cell from a hidden pocket on the dress seam.

"Quarter past midnight," I answer, voice also dry as hell. "We must have napped for an hour or more. It's so quiet here without so many girls chattering constantly."

"That would be why I hide out in a mute's house," Marcus mutters wryly. "Ezra's the only male in the Holden family– Shadow Haven has too much estrogen, too."

"Who's here?"

"It's just Cort checking in. The PB should be tucked in his bed, no doubt dreaming of blowjobs and ropes." Marc sounds so exhausted that I don't bother to razz him about what PB stands for. I know he's the other trainee, but that's it.

I pull my dress over my ass so I'm not flashing the room– or Cortez.

"Are you cold?" Marcus sounds concerned as his hands run up and down my arms, trying to warm me with friction.

"Nah, I'm good." I pull the dress to cover my ass and part of my back.

Eyebrows knitting together, Marcus is confused. "Then why are you covering up?"

"I just didn't want Cortez seeing me like this, is all," I mutter bashfully.

"Why?" Marcus tries to get a read on my facial expression, so I turn it off like one does with a light switch. I learned that handy trick at Hillbrook for people exactly like Marcus Zeitler.

Turning defensive, "I don't want to talk about it, okay?"

"You still have misgivings about how Cortez thinks of you?" Lips curling into an amused smirk, Marcus looks at me like he thinks I'm being cute.

No one has ever thought Regina Regal was cute until this man.

"Drop this conversation," I demand.

"Regina. Regina. Regina. What am I going to do with you?" Marc tsk-tsks me, and tosses my dress across the room to land in a flutter of fabric to the floor.

"I'm training you to work at Restraint. You'll manage to keep private for the most part, but some things are par for the course, nudity being one of them. You know Cort– not real well, but you saw him when he was an awkward teenager, and no doubt Adelaide's been keeping tabs on him. You made out with him just last night. So if Cort can't see you in the nude, how are you going to manage with a dungeon full of strangers?"

"It's because he's *not* a stranger" I stress my insane hang up. "Now that I'm committed to this, and not just as Ade's minion, I want to forge a connection with all of you, especially the Masters of Restraint, and showing my ass like a cheap whore isn't going to garner respect. I wish you would have seen how Cortez looked at me at Restraint– it was humiliating."

"There you are." Cort sounds out of breath. "I thought maybe you were upstairs. I just checked in with Jamie, and he told me where you were."

Cortez stops short when he registers Marcus isn't alone. Straddling Marc's hips, cuddled against his chest, he's still inside of me.

"Well, that is something I've never seen before." Cort whistles sharply in amazement, while gawking at us without shame.

"You probably just finished doing this with some desperate woman," Marc retorts while wearing the smuggest grin imaginable.

"No, I meant that I've never seen you have sex– like ever." Cortez swaggers over to sit next to us on the sofa like we're just chatting and not at all connected at the crotch.

"I had to attend some lame-ass charity function with the family. Mothers against children being children? Taking candy from a baby and giving it to a Kardashian? Raising money to buy needy obese pets food? Preserving the moss growing on an old oak tree? Fuck if I know what it was for." Sighing, Cort's head falls to rest on the back of the sofa. "I had to play dutiful husband and son-in-law while I watched the cunt hang all over Ez."

"Par for the course," Marcus murmurs, eyes flicking to mine. "Welcome to our life, Regina. It's boring as fuck... until it isn't."

"Yeah, well... your wife wanted to know where you were, by the way. I made up something about business, not that Diane really gives a shit. She just wanted you to candy her arm during the photo-ops." Sitting up abruptly, "Oh! Tonight we were raising funds to send Hillbrook's French group students to Paris."

Marcus chuckles sardonically. "What? Did they need some cash to put fuel in their private jets for the trip? Or did they want to rent the Eiffel tower for the duration of their trip?"

"Some bullshit your wife and my mother-in-law came up with, no doubt." Cort sighs heavily, then snuggles deeper onto the sofa.

Well, on that note. As if I'm not humiliated enough having Cortez see me like this, he brings up spouses. Regina cheats on her fellow women left and right– I sicken myself.

I try to wiggle away from Marc with some decorum, but it's next to impossible.

Head turning in my direction, the naughtiest gray eyes on the planet check out my tits and linger on my nipples. "Don't get up on my account. Hell, have a rematch– I'll watch." Cort's hand moves to smack my ass, but he gets a palm to the face instead– and it wasn't by me.

"I didn't invite you," Marcus murmurs in a cold voice. "Have you learned nothing under Dexter's tutelage? I'm going to have a serious talk with my cousin." Marc sounds more pleased by how Cortez misbehaves than put out.

"Dexter washed his hands with me because La Petite Sadist is wearing him out." Cort leans back on the sofa and stretches. "Sadism is so much more difficult to teach than charisma and sexual appeal, not that Dex had anything to teach me on that front."

"Ha-ha," Marc mock laughs. "No, it was the cat-fighting between the two of you. Syn gave you a black eye, and that was the end of your training." The look Marc tosses Cort's way implies there's way more to the story.

"I can't imagine why a female would want to give you a black eye," I deadpan.

"Oh, how your words wound me, Regina." Cort clasps his hand to his chest, feigning insult.

"Syn wanted to restrain Cort and work her painful magic. It frightened Dexter enough that he wouldn't allow them in the same building without an escort."

"What did you do?" I accuse.

"There you go, again, always assuming it's my fault. If something goes wrong, who do you all blame? Me!" Aghast, Cortez sits up, pointing at his chest with a furious fingertip.

"So it wasn't your fault?" I ask with genuine curiosity.

"Of course it was… You're not *that* stupid, Regina. The sinful sadist and I have a complicated history. I should have figured out what she'd become, since she made me eat my balls on a daily basis by literally punting me in the crotch– sometimes it was a knee."

"And Syn kicking your nuts wasn't your fault either?" I tease Cortez with a smile in my voice.

"Usually… but not always. Syn has a tendency to overreact, and I worried when I started to enjoy it." Cortez's eyes glint deviously, and I smirk while visualizing Marcus skull-fucking the bad behavior out of Cort.

Turning into a destructive idiot, a giggle slips past my lips.

"What's so funny?" Cort scowls at me, not appreciating being the brunt of a private joke.

"Oh, fuck!" I moan as Marc stirs to life inside me.

"Keep giggling, woman– I won't last long." Marcus roughly grips my hips, thrusting upward, and I freeze in mortification.

Palms splayed against Marc's chest, I warn, "I'm not having sex with you with witnesses."

Lips curling with smug satisfaction, "I think you earned more than a participation award earlier."

"So… um– have you told Regina the mute's name yet?" Cort asks out of left field.

"Yes, they met formally." If you can call meeting formally, breast-to-mouth resuscitation. "Just as Jamie, because Regina doesn't need to know any more than that."

"How did Jamie react to this?" Cortez gestures to where Marc's slowly thickening cock is hidden inside me.

"Jamie did receive a participation award for his valiant efforts." The smirk amplifies in wattage. "An inch from your toe is Jamie's reaction, as well as in the middle of the floor, and one to your right. He also had to clean Regina's knee free of his spontaneous *cum*bustion."

"Very punny, Marc. You make my inner word weaver proud." Cort leans forward and examines the glistening spots. "Jamie is a serial climaxer… wish I was. Big puddles, too. Not the reaction I thought Jamie would have. But then again, I didn't miss the broken glass in the corner."

"I told another fib," Marcus mutters without shame.

"It's a good thing Jamie only takes issue with your fibs when Regina is around, or else the brownstone would be in shambles from your pathological lying."

"Seriously?" My eyes flick between Marcus and Cortez. "So Jamie isn't always behaving like an over-reactive, nagging wife in the midst of a raging tantrum?"

"Fuck, no. Jamie's great to have around." Cort looks at Marc for a split-second before gazing at me again. "We spend a shitload of time together– he's my bud."

"Jamie touched Regina," Marc whispers in awe.

"Willingly?" Cort's jaw drops.

"I swear– he was always twisted, more so now than before, I think," Marc muses.

I try to extract myself again, since this cryptic conversation is extremely uncomfortable.

"I like where you are. My cock is very, very warm and cozy. Snug as a bug in a rug." Marc teases, and then drops his hands. "Why do you keep trying to get away?"

"This is a bit weird, even by my standards." I try again, and Marc lets me go this time. Shuddering, I ignore the glorious sensation of Marc's cock sliding free of my body, and the resulting mess dripping down my inner thighs.

"Weird by your standards?" Cort deadpans, "Said the nun."

"I have to get home before I turn into a pumpkin." I pull my dress on without undergarments. I just want to be covered. While I'm getting decent, Marc climbs to his feet to get dressed, too.

"It's past midnight. You *are* looking a little bit orange," Cort teases me. Shifting on the sofa, he pulls a few scraps of black lace from between the cushions. "Looking for these? Sorry, your panties are in pieces now."

Grinning like a villain, Cort flaunts my underwear, waving the pieces about in his fingertips. Taunting words on the tip of his tongue, Cort's rendered speechless with a gobsmacked look on his face.

I turn to see what has Cortez crazed, and the same damn thing happens to me– gobsmacked!

I can't believe I just had sex with that man. Buck-ass naked, Marcus stretches his six-foot-plus body for our viewing pleasure. Lean and toned, he soaks up our awed expressions with a curve of his lips.

Cort and I watch with our eyes glued to Marc's movements as he redresses in a three-piece business suit. His taut, bronze skin glistens in the light, drawing attention to the perfect deep V on his lower abdomen.

I watch Cort as he lusts after the mouth-watering landscape, and I sympathize with his pain. Marc's partially erect and shiny from our combined juices, and I can't believe he fit inside of me. He's long, but that isn't what makes an impression. Thick doesn't adequately describe Marc's cock.

When Marcus bends to pull up his boxer briefs, we get the view of a lifetime– the perfect curve of his bitable ass. I want to rewind two minutes, and giggle hysterically until he comes again.

Smug, Marcus chuckles as he knots the tie he blindfolded me with around his neck. Then Marc finger-combs his hair, turning to Cort with a shit-eating grin plastered across his face.

"You're looking business-trip-worthy, Marc." Cort leans forward on the sofa to get a better view. "You don't look like a man who was just fucking Regina, not at all... But then again, I like to lie." Cort snickers. "It's the satisfied smirk that's the dead giveaway."

Cort swaggers over to Marcus to adjusts the tie and give his curly hair a pat down.

Marc's grin spreads to an apple-cheeked, brilliant smile, and yet again I'm gobsmacked.

"No toning down the wattage on that smile, huh? At least attempt while Diane chews you out for missing an event. It's the only thing she asks of you." Cort schools the older man on the inner-workings of a happy wife.

"Fuck her– I didn't want to go in the first place." Marcus suddenly turns belligerent. "If Diane wants me as a piece of meat, she should treat me like one instead of ignoring my needs."

"Hey, now… you just crossed ten lines there, Marc. Diane was my guardian, and is my aunt-in-law, pseudo-mother-in-law, and my mom loved her." Cort's face is serious. But when he turns to face me, he grins. "And I wholeheartedly agree, Marc. Fuck her."

"Blood-thirsty little shit, aren't you?" I murmur underneath my breath, as I locate my bra hanging on a wooden structure.

"No one can hurt you as much as a loved one. Straight to the heart." Cort dramatically mimics the action. "May I escort the lovely Regina home for you, sir?"

"That won't be necessary." Marcus straightens his tie. "You're still on punishment, and I don't have the energy to police your car ride since you removed the device this morning. By the way, I had Aaron hide another in its place."

"Ah… fuck," Cort pouts.

"Nice try– go home."

"Yes, Daddy," Cort teases while batting his impossibly long eyelashes.

"You know I hate it when you call me *that*," Marc growls, clearly realizing the implications of fooling around with someone who is legally related to you. "I'll see you at home– I won't be long."

"No rush." Cort pockets my panties, the pervert. "Diane is either still at Misery Castle watching Fox News with Daniel, or tucked in bed after eating expensive pussy."

"Gross." Marc shudders. "It's nice that Regina lives so close to the entrance to Crestview– it cuts down on the commute time." Marc turns to Cortez, voice hopeful. "Are you going to your apartment at Edge?"

"Nice try. Charity event. Ade. No fucking way." Cort's demeanor completely changes. "I'll be pissed for a week, and it'll wear off just in time for the next shindig."

Cort stalks over to me, then tips my chin back. Startled into compliance, he kisses me firmly on the mouth, sucking my bottom lip, and then he quickly pulls away.

"Mmm… Yummy. You taste like sex and Marcus." Cort gives me a quick peck, and then walks to the door, his laughter flowing in his wake.

Tagging behind Marcus, I follow him to the garage hidden in the alley behind the row of brownstones.

"You're in love with Cortez." It's a statement, not a question.

"No, it's not like that," Marcus poorly denies.

"You're so fucking screwed, Marc." I laugh without humor, emotions conflicting.

"I was in love once, or at least I thought I was," Marcus muses, but doesn't elaborate. I have a feeling he's speaking of Diane, and that would explain the '*straight to the heart*' comment Cort made earlier.

"Whoa. That is… I'm speechless. This is yours?" I fondle the rear bumper of a Porsche 550 Spyder. "James Dean, much?"

"How do you know so much about cars?" Marc's eyes twinkle with mirth as he opens my door like a good gentleman should. "I heard you lusting after Cort's Aston Martin."

"Like a good scholar, I like to know a little bit about everything." I slide into the passenger seat. "Some subjects are more interesting than others." The Spyder isn't as comfy as the Vanquish, but it makes up for it in style. "I'm going to have to keep accepting rides just to enjoy the vast array of cars you guys own."

"Sorry to disappoint, but Ezra only owns a black Escalade."

"*Only*," I whisper. "Marcus says only... But I guess in comparison to Whitt's Roadster, an Escalade is like a Kia Rio."

"Ezra's practical." Marcus finds himself hilarious, as if he just told a joke. "This Spyder trumps everyone's vehicles in Dominion."

"No shit– ego much?"

"My family was the original purchaser of this car in 1955 for pocket-change. It's now worth nearly four million bucks. Ego? No. Truth? Absolutely."

"Jesus," I hiss in awe. "I couldn't imagine owning something worth so much. I'd rather give my money away than worry about investing in the wrong people who will line their pockets with my hard work."

"Oh, Fate is the perfect financial analyst to have on your team, seeing as how her father stole every dollar to the Simpson name."

"Lost some money to Thomas Simpson, eh?"

"My father and Dexter's mother were the best of friends with Thomas." Marcus navigates through traffic without a care, when I'd be terrified the Spyder would get a scratch. "Thick as thieves as the saying goes."

"Everyone at Hillbrook is connected," I reason out, not voicing the rest of my thoughts. I've had almost a decade to dwell on a few theories, to the point I don't trust my girls.

"The Zeitlers are known for their shrewd investments. This car was my grandfather's, then my father's, and now it's mine." Marc's voice is filled with pride as he fondles the steering wheel like you would a lover.

"Primogeniture at its finest. One day, Whitt, Niel, and Ella will have to battle with Whitney, whatever Katie named her other kid, and any of Ade's future offspring if she has any."

"Technically, the Whittenhowers are the epitome of primogeniture, so it all belongs to Whitt." Marcus proves he knew all of Grant's dirty secrets. "The Zeitlers aren't like that. When our parents died, my grandmother split everything equally between Dexter and me." Marc gives me a wink, smirking. "Dexter was terrified of hurting the car, that's how I got it."

"Well, I guess I lucked out. No family. No fortune. No complications. It'll be a clusterfuck for my kids, though, between the Whittenhower legacy and my fortune." I sigh heavily, resting my head against the backrest while streetlights play with the shadows in the car.

"Speaking of kids, I named my daughter after this car– Spyder. She's twelve going on thirteen. She has huge, hypnotic emerald-green eyes and the pale coloring of her mother. But she has my black curly hair. Spyder's stunning, and she has no idea I exist. I've met with her a handful of times as a stranger."

"Yet another thing where you and I can relate." My heart throbs with the need to have Marcus drive me to Misery Castle to get me past all the gates.

Somehow hearing my unspoken thoughts, "I'm sorry you haven't had Niel in your life. He's an amazing kid. He has a fire under his ass that Grant lacked, but he's a naughty little bastard like his dad." Marc's voice holds amused fondness, and hearing him speak of my son doesn't hurt as much as when Ade does it.

Maybe after the past few nights of being around Marcus and hearing him speak of Grant as if he's still living amongst us has desensitized me.

We sit in silence the rest of the ride home, both of us missing our absent children. With so many parallels, getting to know Marcus is like getting to know myself. But Marcus is a better looking, male version of me.

We sit in my driveway for a few minutes, neither of us moving or speaking. I'm not sure where to begin or end, but it's like he's shoring up his nerve for something. Stronger than me, more assured, Marc breaks the silence first.

"I have a few weird requests." Marcus hesitates, as if unsure. "First, if you have anything you want to share with me about Grant, do so outside of the brownstone."

"Why?" I glance sideways at Marcus instead of turning my head as it rests on the seatback. "Are you afraid the sound of smashing glass will be a huge motherfucking hint that you're lying? Maybe you shouldn't have told Jamie all of yours and Grant's secrets."

"No." Marcus breathes so quietly, I know I've hit the nail on the head. "Jamie is like a goddamn ferret, stealing secrets he refuses to share, with Alex as his backup. That's a point of contention in our relationship. I'd be an open book to him if only he'd let me in.

So call me selfish if you will, but I want some of our conversations to just be between you and me. Call me jealous, because I want a part of you that he doesn't get to touch."

"It's hard for me to talk about Grant," I admit. "But I do have some things that have plagued me over the past decade that I'd like to share… but not tonight." Before Marcus can pry, I cut him off at the pass. "You said a *few* weird requests."

"Yeah–" There's a blush riding Marc's voice, and it makes me beyond curious. "Could I have a picture of Ella? I'll give you one of Spyder if you'd like. I just know Niel so well, and I want to put a face with the stories I hope you'll share with me."

Like a strike to the heart, rage and agony boil in my blood. "It bothers me how someone, who was a complete stranger to me until last week, knows my son better than I do. Last night, I was cursing Ade for getting to see Whitt and Niel grow up." I heave a heavy sigh, realizing that is *not* Marc's problem. "Sure, I'll bring a picture next time. Name the time and place?"

"Next Thursday, say eight o'clock. My week's booked up because I'm flying to DC in the morning for business– I have to gain some political supporters in order to win the judge's seat. So I won't be back until Wednesday night."

Marcus scrubs both of his hands over his face in a gesture of exhaustion, and I figure it's my cue to leave.

"It's whatever's good for you, since I work from home. If Thursday's too soon, I'll understand," I try to sound nonchalant as I pop the door open to get out, but Marc's hand on the nape of my neck stops me in my tracks.

"Thursday isn't soon enough," Marcus growls, and then kisses me fiercely.

This kiss is like the sex. Brutal, near violence. Intense and powerful. I grip the edge of the seat and hold on for dear life, wishing Jamie was here to anchor me through the storm. I bet on the open road, Marcus drives this car like he kisses and fucks. Fast and hard. Total destruction.

"Go– before I pull you back into this car, drive away, and lock you in the brownstone. I don't think you'd like being kept as a pet." Marc's amused smirk wilts around the edges. "Regina, I want to thank you for not questioning me after I broke down, and for simply knowing why I needed you in the moment."

"Anytime, Marcus." I'm not flippant, and I don't discount his words. "You don't want to know the countless times I've done that in private. But I think it would have been easier sharing the grief with someone who truly lost as much as I did." I whisper in the dark car. "So thank you, too."

In thanks, your welcome, and goodbye, I kiss Marcus softly– my way –and he stills beneath me. Roiling beneath the surface, I can feel his barely leashed need to take over and dominate me. I know Marcus is rewarding me right now by gifting me with *my* kiss.

Chapter Fourteen

Staggering from the car, I do the walk of shame to my miniature, limestone castle. If you can call a gray stone, sprawling one-story with rustic, white shutters and flower boxes a castle.

My home is as modest as I am.

This evening I'm not being very modest, nor am I acting like my usual, numb self. I'm being destructive, and loving every fucking second of it.

Queen is a goddamn empowered woman who owns it.

Flinging off my soiled dress, stinking like sex and two different men, I walk naked down the hallway to my bedroom on wobbly legs with sticky thighs.

The house is silent for once. Peaceful. Ade is probably convincing Ezra to screw her at his apartment, hence Cort's need not to be there. Fate's door is cracked open and I can hear her softly snoring. Ella is whimpering in her sleep. The guesthouse is quiet, so I guess that means Kris is still painting the town red with victims she selected from Restraint.

Entering my room without turning on the light, I slide into home base. "Oh, how much I've missed thee," I sing to my pillowy cloud.

"I've missed you too, sugar dumpling," a smoky voice purrs next to me on the bed.

"Ah!" I cry in the dark, automatically reaching to switch on the lamp. "What the fuck, Kris?" I turn surly, my reality meeting the fantasy I'd built over the past few hours. "I swear I'm moving the next time this happens."

The light illuminates Kristal, and she's staring at me with a shit-eating grin plastered across her face. I'm happy to see she's at least dressed– I've seen stranger things in the past few days.

"You fucked Master. I bow down to you in awe." Kris bows down and presses her forehead to the mattress with her arms splayed out in front. "You truly are Queen."

"How do you know it was Marcus I fucked tonight?" I stop myself before I stick my tongue out at Kristal like a dipshit.

"You just admitted you had sex!" Kris smirks at me because I took her bait. "YAY!" She claps excitedly, bouncing on my bed, her tits almost bopping her in the chin. "My girl's acting her age for once."

"I admitted nothing," I mutter obstinately.

"You don't have to say anything, Regina. Unless you managed to swoosh on your first time out of the marina in a nearly a decade, I'd say that's cum on your thighs. I give you bonus points for riding bareback with Master." She claps again. "Bravo!"

"How do you know I didn't fuck Jamie?" Jamie's name has Kristal's gorgeous tan skin going whiter than a sheet. "Or maybe it was Cortez. You know he'll fuck anything with a heartbeat."

"I'm not sure if you're insulting yourself, or me, or Cortez with that statement." Kristal sits cross-legged on my bed with her eyebrow hitched all the way to her hairline. "How do I know it was Master? Because I saw you pull up in that James Dean car, then I watched as Marcus Zeitler inhaled your face."

"You got me there." I bite back a giggle, because Regina Regal does *not* giggle, even with Queen riding her hard.

"I'm surprised at you, and I'm so fucking happy to see that you're evolving. I'm proud, Regina, and I don't say that lightly."

"Thank you, I think." This time I can't stop the awkward laugh from erupting. "You just praised me for fucking a married guy, while another guy participated. Then while Marcus was still inside me, yet another guy had a conversation with us as if it wasn't odd to be looking at my tits and where my crotch was attached to Marc's… bi-fucking-zarre."

"When you decide to change, you make a *change*," Kristal stresses.

"Nothing's ever halfway for me. But nothing I did tonight would shock you since it's an ordinary occurrence for you." I roll over onto my stomach, not giving a shit that I'm naked in front of Kristal, not after tonight. "I'm sure once the high fades, the guilt and shame will pour in."

In the absence of numb is the eruption of Queen, and with her resurfacing is the truth.

I could close my eyes to the truth, but I'm not a goddamn moron. I was raised in the hood, where every breath I took was for survival, while suffering through a four-year hellish Hillbrook experience. Jackson and Daniel taught me more lessons than I could ever count or repay. I may have been blind with grief for the past decade, but I didn't atrophy into ignorance is bliss.

Something is going on, and I'm willing to play with everyone to find out. Cortez is right about one thing, Marcus is a pathological liar. Jamie is a liar according to Marcus. Jamie said Marcus is narrow-sighted when it comes to what he wants. Then Marcus told me not to speak of Grant's secrets in front of Jamie, which means there is more to all of this than I could ever imagine.

I already know Kristal's a liar.

I trust no one, and I can no longer chalk this all up to paranoia. No way, no how. I need to talk to Marcus come Thursday, no sex and BDSM to act as a buffer. I also need to talk to Jamie, then balance what I hear from the both of them against what Kristal and Ade throw my way.

It all connects, and my instincts are screaming it all connects to one thing.

Me.

"Tell me about the PB," I demand, never looking back at Kristal but expecting her to obey.

"Reg." Kris sighs, then flops down next to me on the mattress. "I told you– I'm the submissive Master is using to train PB."

"Why did Marcus pick you?"

"I was already at Restraint. I fibbed to you a bit." No shocker, that. "I went there on its opening night because it was exactly what I was looking for in my life. I was already working at Restraint when Ade came to me with her conspiracy theory bullshit."

"Maybe it's not a theory," I muse.

"Sure it is, Reg. You may have left our life behind, but I'm still my parents' daughter. I'm still a part of their world, even if it's from the shadows as I serve. That need is bred into my DNA, and Restraint was a way I could both work for Ezra while getting my every sexual need met."

"So tending bar at Restraint was your way of going back to the very life I yanked you out of by educating you and teaching you your true value. You're one of the richest women in Dominion, yet you'd rather serve those motherfuckers a drink?"

"Regina," Kristal chastises me sharply. "I can't help my nature any more than you can. We're all not meant to be leaders– some of us find pleasure and purpose in serving the leaders, helping them be stronger for the welfare of us all."

"You sound just like Albert right now," I grumble into my pillow.

"Well, he is my dad, Reg."

A niggling suspicion in the back of my psyche won't allow me to let it go. "Quit distracting me and get your ass back to explaining the PB."

"Fine. You're the only trainee who hasn't been allowed to troll Restraint– I don't know if it's because you're a woman, or if Marcus is possessive of you. Maybe it's because PB is a charismatic man who gets exactly what he wants, and he wanted to be in the thick of it at Restraint. PB singled me out because he trusts me and is comfortable around me, and Master understood. In this, it's about loyalty, and I hope you understand I can't break my vow."

"A lot of the things Marcus knew of me were straight from you, weren't they?" I accuse. "So much for loyalty."

"I've said this in the past. My loyalties are divided. I lived fifteen years before I met you– fifteen years where unbreakable loyalties were forged. Added to that is the fact that my family has been in service to the Whittenhowers since Dominion was founded. Generation after generation, and I won't break the vow my ancestors made to protect the Whittenhowers from themselves. Regina, sometimes you don't get to come first, and neither does Marcus."

Mulling that information over, I realize Marcus is on the outside looking in, just as I am.

Grant's words from a very, very long time ago flow into my mind. Kristal was to protect the Whittenhower heirs, one of which lives in this very house. Kristal isn't living with me because she's one of my best friends. She's my business partner living in my home to be close to my daughter, all because some ancestral force commands it.

Kristal's parents are undoubtedly looking after Whitt, Niel, and Kate's children.

Understanding but not accepting, I go in for the kill. "At least tell me what PB stands for."

"No, I can't."

"So much for submissive."

"Oh, Regina… I'm the rock in a hard place on this one. My loyalty is forever with PB, but added on top of that, Master made me swear never to tell you. No doubt you've learned how intimidating Marcus can be."

In not so many words, Kristal just told me not to trust Marcus, while telling me I can never trust her to put me first.

"Do you call him the PB to his face?" I try to drag some more information out of her– anything, no matter how big or small, may be important for later.

"No, we call him that just for you."

"Which means Cortez is pulling the wool over my eyes, too," I surmise.

"Don't think like that, Regina." Kristal curls over my back, genuinely trying to comfort and calm me. After brushing the hair away from my ear, Kris breathes words that break my heart. "If I could tell you, I would. It kills me, day after day, watching you die slowly of grief, shame, and pain. I'd take it all away in a heartbeat if it didn't mean mine would cease to beat."

Alarmed, I roll over. "Kristal?" I grab her shoulders, but she pulls away instantly.

"You heard me wrong just now, so let it go." Fluffing her hair, Kristal puts on her seduction disguise. Voice changing back to a rolling purr, "I basically avoid all conversation pertaining to PB, so I don't fuck up and spill it. It's not his name. It's a nickname Cort gave him a long time ago when he was a little kid. I personally think the P needs to be upgraded to a G and the B to an M."

Knowing I've hit a dead-end, I go another route. "Peanut butter?"

"No." Kristal chuckles at my poor attempt of a guess.

"Lead," I try again.

"No, smarty pants." Hazel eyes squinting, she looks at me weird until she figures out I meant the periodic table abbreviation for lead.

"Pottery Barn?"

"Oh, my God! No." Giggling, Kristal slaps my chest, fingers trailing down my breasts like she can't turn off the seductive routine once it's been activated. "That's too funny."

"The PedoBear?"

Kristal's howls of laughter fill the room. She rolls around the mattress, managing to fall off the bed. Her face pops up from the side of the bed like a woodchuck coming out of its hole. Rosy-cheeked with tears dampening her face, I smile down at Kristal because I love her no matter what.

"I think I just wet myself." Kristal's face pales, and then a second later she laughs. "I have to go clean up. You have no idea how appropriate PedoBear is for about another month." Laughing, she holds her side, disappearing into my bathroom.

I don't judge Kristal for wetting herself while laughing. Once you have kids, a laugh or sneeze will have you dampening your underwear with embarrassing results. Maybe all that sex weakened her muscles.

While Kris is locked in my bathroom, I spend the next few minutes rolling P and B words through my head, trying to decipher the coding.

Kristal must have actually wet her pants since she's just in her t-shirt when she returns. "Sometimes I think I love you– I've never laughed so hard in my life."

Staring up at the ceiling, I wear a smile on my face while hiding many other emotions beneath the surface. "I live to amuse."

"I can't wait for you to learn who PB is so we can laugh again." Snickering, she breathes, "PedoBear," over and over again.

"How was Master? Rumor has it Marc's been celibate for years." Kristal changes the subject almost as fast as Marcus does, which means she's been around him long enough to pick up his annoying habits.

"This doesn't leave this room," I demand. "Since your loyalties lie elsewhere, I hope this isn't information you leak."

"If anything, I'll have to relay the fact you finally got laid, and it has nothing to do with Marcus Zeitler. My loyalties lie with the Whittenhowers, and whether you believe it or not, you were one of us, and always will be… and no, Daniel is not who I report to."

"Fine." I roll over to face Kristal. "Whoever the hell you're narking to can get their jollies with my exploits."

"There's the Queen I've been waiting for." Kris grins at me, genuinely thrilled, not just pumping me for information. This is a best friend conversation, one I can never tell Ade.

"It was raw, hardcore, and without foreplay. Marcus said I couldn't say no, and he wasn't kidding. One second, we were talking. The next, my panties disintegrated and I was impaled by a cock the size of a fist. I came instantly, and again while Marcus did. He said he wouldn't wear protection with me, and that part skeeved my ass out... Jamie had to watch. Have you seen him?"

"Whoa… that's why I love the dominant types. Cort can go really hardcore while the PB's a total gentleman. We haven't had sex. I'm used for instruction on the equipment, and that's it. PB is extremely controlled at all times, and that's what gets him off. While Cort doesn't follow any rules, and I think he's learned that from Master."

"Yeah, I caught on that Cortez is more like a naughty brat of a submissive that Marcus wants to break than an actual dominant he trains."

"That's the whispered rumor down at Restraint, too. We all think Cortez isn't dominant at all." Kristal snuggles closer, looking bright-eyed like we're having a slumber party. "I can't believe Jamie came out. He sticks to the shadows while PB trains, and then runs off to his attic or wherever he goes when no one is watching."

Unable to let this go, when I don't even know why I care in the first place, I need Kris to reassure me. "Are you lying when you say you've never had sex with PB? You lie perfectly, and I never know if you're telling the truth," I admit. "So I always assume you're lying.

When I first met Kristal, she was my fifteen-year-old personal maid. I was sickened by the fact that anyone would have to live a life of servitude, so I never allowed her to serve me. Afterward, I made Kristal meet her potential by getting her the best education money could buy, then I gave her a job. After Grant died, I took Kristal with me and gave her a home, a family, and a life.

Now I realize Kristal didn't follow me, because she was protecting me from myself. In those first dark days, the only thing that kept me from suicide was the fact that my body sustained Ella's. After my daughter's birth, Kristal forced me to breastfeed, saying it was the best nutrition for my child, yet again tying me to the land of the living. Every step of the way, Kristal played on my selflessness by forcing me to see someone or something needed me in order to survive.

While at work, Kristal is highly professional. But as soon as work's through and it's time to play, an entirely different Kristal emerges. If she wants something, she will do anything to get it– lie, cheat, and manipulate. She doesn't care about the ramifications. Kristal only sees what she wants, and she grabs onto it with both hands.

In a way, Kristal is worse than Adelaide when it comes to acquisitions. I trust Kris enough to know I can't trust her at all. I know she loves and respects me, and that she loves Ella unconditionally. But that's where it ends.

If Kristal wants to have sex with PB, she will– Marc's punishments be damned.

"We've done everything, except have sex. PB's comfortable with me. He isn't my type, but he'll grow into that type someday."

"So you're grooming him for later?"

"No, Regina– I'm grooming the PB for someone else."

"What?" I protest. "Explain yourself."

"I'm not as I was a few months ago, Regina. I've slowed down some. I had a pregnancy scare, and it shocked me to my core. Right now, I'm only having sex with Cort, and helping train PB. That's all."

"I've never slut-shamed you, Kristal."

"I know… I met a guy a few weeks ago. I want to do it right, so it isn't physical yet. Believe me, I want it to be, but I want him to respect me more." I can see that Kristal is being genuine when she speaks of this man, but she was lying about slowing down– lying to herself.

If anything, Kristal is worse than before. She forgets that we share homes on the same property. Last night, it was like a revolving door at the guesthouse. Fate moved in here last month because she couldn't take it anymore, after waking up to find a stranger in her bedroom staring at her while she slept.

All of my doors and windows are hooked to a security system, and it's not coded but fingerprint scanned. No keys necessary, and no fear of being hacked. If I ever find a stranger in my home, Kristal's prints will be removed from the system.

"Wow. I'm sorry I've been such a shitty friend, to the point you couldn't come to me with your pregnancy scare. I hope you talked to one of the girls about this."

"It's okay– I dealt with it." Kristal cuddles up to my side.

Being a good friend instead of a train wreck, I ask all the right questions. "So, who is he, where did you meet him, and when do I get to meet him?"

Addictive, delighted laughter flows from Kristal's throat. "I spoke with Fate about how I didn't want to live this way anymore. I didn't like who I'd become, and I didn't like the shame I felt when I looked in the mirror after coming home from being with a bunch of guys when I didn't even know their names. Restraint was perfect for me. It's a controlled environment, and I only play with those I trust."

Kristal falls quiet for a moment. She was awful trusting last night, and none of the men were Cortez, and there is no way PB has clones. Her behavior is reminiscent of the junkies and alcoholics zigzagging down the neighborhood sidewalks, speaking of how they're changing after this next hit. Just one more taste and they'll change, when all they do is spiral further and further toward rock bottom.

Sex is Kristal's addiction, and she's being delusional by lying to herself.

"I don't know if I'm ready to talk about him yet. I don't want to jinx it. His name is Alex, and I met him at Transcend when you sent me to deliver the donation check. He's one of the counselors. He's really smart, and funny, and did I mention smoking hot. His personality and mine are almost the same. His style is wicked. I guess I should thank you for sending me that day. My life changed for the better."

I remember that day. In a hurry, I cut a check for three million dollars. I was about to deliver it myself when Ella got sick. I passed the job off to Kris because a sick baby girl comes first.

I wonder if my life would have changed if I'd gone to Transcend instead of Kristal. I wonder if I would have ended up on the sidewalk in front of 163 Covington, debating whether or not I should clack the gargoyle knocker on the scary red door.

Of course I would, because I'm not a fucking moron. Kristal is living in a fantasy world of her own creation, with me as a character in her story. The rich, lonely widow who is too stupid to realize Alex from Transcend, the man who made Kristal want a better life by not fucking a swath through Dominion when she still is, is none other than the owner of 163 Covington, hiding behind that red door with the gargoyle as sentry.

Chapter Fifteen

After Kristal leaves, all I can do is stare at the light being cast against my ceiling. After all this time, when I truly wanted to feel alive, now I want to go back to being numb. There is no shame, or pain, or grief, or betrayal if you're numb. It's the perfect defense mechanism. But I can't unlearn things, just as I can't unsee the truth. Once Pandora's Box has been opened, there is no closing it, which is why I have to be certain I can live with what I may find out.

Marcus is leaving in the morning for a business trip, and I have his number saved from when he called me in from the sidewalk. I could call him, actually lean on someone for once. Marcus is strong enough, but is he honest enough? How can I know if he's working with me, against me, or with them?

Acting on instinct, I grab my cellphone off the nightstand, only to startle when it vibrates in my hand.

Jamie: *Are you okay?*

Chuckling to myself, I quickly type out a reply. *—Is this how our every conversation is going to begin?*

Jamie: *It is when the last I saw you, you were getting pounded by my best friend.*

—Well, that's not at all embarrassing, now is it? Do I detect anger in your text voice, Jamie?

Jamie: *Texts do not hold emotion, Regina, as we already discussed last night.*

—Touché.

Jamie: *Are you okay?*

—Peachy. Hmm... I could be wrong, but from a mile away, I think I just heard that odd growly noise you make.

Jamie: *Really? Because I just heard it as well. Imagine that.*

—Yes, imagine that.

Jamie: *Let's try for the last time, shall we? Are you okay?*

—No, not really. Destructive Regina rears her ugly head, totally squashing Apathy Regina. Sometimes I wish I didn't feel.

Jamie: *Lay it on me.*

—As we've discussed— I don't know you, Jamie, so I can't trust you yet.

Jamie: *I think we were formally introduced when I sucked your tit and came like a moron on your knee. Just saying.*

Shaking with remembrance, as embarrassing as it is to admit, I do so anyway. *—That will be a fond memory of mine. You made me feel beautiful for the first time in a long while.*

Jamie: *You are beautiful.*

—To you, maybe... I'm acting out of the ordinary, and I don't recognize myself.

Jamie: *We all have to live a little now and then. Do stupid shit. Grow as human beings. Perfect is utterly boring.*

—And you know this how?

Jamie: *I have a degree in fucking up and doing stupid shit. I've grown a lot since I've been on my own, made a lot of sacrifices along the way too. But, also, I'm the watcher, remember? You're not the first Marcus brought into my home— first to fuck, sure —but not the first to enter. I watch, examine human nature. It's an art form.*

—And you're the artist? Why is it so easy to banter with Jamie? It's effortless, without a struggle to keep the conversation going. It's been so long since I felt that way, and it terrifies me.

Jamie: *Obviously*

—Smug much? Anyway, it wasn't like me to do what I did. I wanted to connect with someone, to feel something– anything – but especially to Marcus.

Jamie: *Why?*

—He's one of the last connections I have to Grant, as sick as that sounds. I can look at my daughter, look at his sister, and see him reflected. But they didn't know him like Marcus did.

Jamie: *Understandable. If you haven't figured it out yet, I think Marcus loved Grant more than he's loved anyone else– sometimes too much so.*

Explaining myself shouldn't be as effortless as breathing. But maybe it's because Jamie is a stranger, a man without a face or voice, and that's why I don't feel judged. Tapping wildly, my fingers fly against my touchscreen.

—I could feel their connection, and that's why I wanted to connect with Marcus. But now, I feel guilty and slightly ashamed of myself, like I just betrayed Grant.

Jamie: *You didn't betray Grant– trust me.*

—As you've established, you don't know me, so how can you tell me whether or not I betrayed Grant? Maybe I feel like I've betrayed myself.

Jamie: *From what I do know and have learned, I can understand why you feel as you do, Regina. You mustn't beat yourself up about things. Sometimes sex is just sex.*

—But it should be about connecting.

Jamie: *Agreed– but weren't you connecting to Grant via Marcus? Is that maybe why you feel guilty? Or was it how he took you, made you submit? The sex wasn't what you're accustomed to, was it? Do you like it softer, Regina? Do you like to be the one in control at all times? Finding out Marcus was more than you bargained for, was that a good thing, or a bad thing? Was it freeing, or suffocating?*

–Get outta my head, Jamie!

Jamie: *Yes, ma'am.*

–You know you're right, right?

Jamie: *Yes, but I thought it would be best to voice it, because maybe you didn't know how to voice how you're feeling.*

–Are you a therapist by trade?

Jamie: *No, but my housemate is. Alex is a drug and alcohol counselor, as well as a life-coach. Living with a therapist has its advantages and pitfalls. Sometimes it's insufferable, because he makes sure I deal with my shit. I didn't used to, you know? There was a very dark period in my life where I contemplated ending everything. I know many will see that as weak, but with Alex's help, I was able to find the light.*

The infamous Alex, eh? The one Marcus said would avoid me at all costs, even if I went down to Transcend to snoop around. Kristal's new boyfriend. No way in hell would a therapist want to be with that train wreck of a sex addict.

Nevertheless, I've been in a dark place before, and Kristal helped me see the light. I never want anyone to feel the suffocating darkness I felt, especially Jamie.

–Shit, Jamie. I don't know you very well, but I think the world would be a darker place without you in it.

Jamie: *Thank you– that is kind of you to say, and it means a lot to me to read it, Regina.*

–Why can't I see you?

Jamie: *That's a conversation best left for a later date. I already trust you. But as you said, you don't know me enough to trust me. It's a deep conversation, and I can't have it with someone who is unsure of me.*

–Are you okay?

Jamie: *Thank you for asking, Regina. No one besides Alex ever seems to care. Marcus is always so busy resenting and punishing me to stop and listen. He has me make him feel better, never once noticing that maybe I'm not okay. Regina, you're a beautiful person, inside and out, because even when you're down, you still think of others.*

If I had to say this to someone's face, I couldn't do it. But the anonymity of text messaging with a faceless man is invigorating, freeing any inhibitions I may have.

–That's just the few orgasms you had while looking at me, or was it from looking at Marc?

Jamie: *Ha-ha! I'm about as straight as straight can get, which is a point of contention between Marcus and me. I'm sure you caught on tonight about our tiff from years ago when he tried to touch my dick, and I'm sure Grant told you of their relationship.*

–Yeah, I called Marcus Snuggle & Tug for a long time, or was it Cuddle & Tug… I can't remember which.

Jamie: *That's adorable, and that's the emotion which should be placed on that action. Intimacy is amazing with someone you love and cherish, unless one of you feels a different type of love. Then what once used to be a comfort, now turns into a tainted, destructive act.*

–Choir. Preach. I've got my own BFF with a crush on me. She fancies herself in love with me, and manipulated me into… stuff. Never again.

Jamie: *I see you do understand perfectly, Regina. Because if I allowed it, Marcus would be fucking me like he was fucking you tonight, or maybe he'd want the softness with me making love to him. I don't know– I'll never find out. But what I do know, the man doesn't understand the distinction between intimacy and sex, getting it all mixed up. Marcus loves me as much as I love him, so he thinks sex is the only way to show it, when a hug and a connecting conversation is enough. Marcus got to Alex once, but I stepped in to make sure it didn't progress further than foreplay. Being the loyal type who is a one-woman man, Alex isn't wired like that, but he also didn't dare say no.*

–My girl is like that. Kristal. All of her validation comes from sex, no matter how much I praise her hard work. I'm sure she's been roaming around your home.

Jamie: *Yes, I know Kristal well, but not in the biblical sense. & I won't lie, Kris is a thorn in Alex's side. Bit of a predator-prey situation between them, when they should have left well enough alone. A word of warning, Regina, because I don't want your heart to get crushed should you become invested. Marcus isn't straight. He isn't gay. He isn't bisexual. Marcus doesn't know what the fuck he is, and he never stops long enough to figure it out.*

–Fucking lovely.

Jamie: *Exactly. I see we understand one another. Marcus is an amazing person– on his own terms. I have to go, Regina. I'm only good for a few minutes of intense conversation until it gets to be too much for me. So I apologize in advance for my behavior.*

–I understand. Truly. Go recharge your introvert batteries.

Jamie: *Regina, you do understand. Thank you. Same time, same place tomorrow night?*

–It's a date! Goodnight.

Jamie: *Sweet dreams.*

Chapter Sixteen

Jamie has a way of comforting me while soothing me to sleep, but at the same time, he has me thinking clearer than I have in a decade.

Jamie takes the grief away, and I don't want to examine that too closely.

Mind whirling with a plan, I scrubbed my body of the contaminants. The more I think of the situation, the more I feel Marcus is in the same boat as I am, but that doesn't give him the right to have his DNA hitching a ride in my vagina.

After donning a pair of black yoga pants and a hoodie, I stalk around my room, waiting Kristal out. Cellphone in hand, I contemplate if I'm making the world's worst decision of my life—either way, it will be life-changing.

My thumb hits the call button with no command from my mind. No way to back out now, I wait for my call to be answered.

"Regina?" Marc's voice reverberates with concern. "What's going on? Are you okay?"

"Are you alone?" I whisper, as if someone could be listening in and I don't want them to overhear.

"Yes, why?"

"Where are you?"

"I'm in bed watching Netflix." Marcus sounds taken aback and slightly annoyed. "Explain yourself. I can't help if you don't let me."

"I'm going to sound fucking paranoid," I warn. "But you have to listen to me. We can't speak on the phone, or inside anywhere because I don't know who to trust."

"What's going on?" Fabric rustles as Marcus moves in his sheets.

"Grant told me some things long before he died, and I think it's time I shared them with you, even if it bites me in the ass."

"Shit!" A thud echoes from Marc's end of the line, then feet are padding across a wooden floor. "I'll meet you at your house—this I have to hear."

"No, my house isn't safe, either."

"What the fuck, Regina?"

"Meet me at the pull-off just before the main gate." I lean forward, looking out the French doors to the guesthouse. "I'll be on foot. I can't chance anyone seeing me leave. I'll meet you there in ten minutes."

I pocket my cellphone before Marcus can even reply. With one last glance, I make sure Kristal is preoccupied with the four men haunting the guesthouse. Through the windows, light casts on Kristal, showcasing her giving one guy a blowjob with the others fighting for her available holes. So much for only doing Cortez and playing with PB, all because she's turning over a new leaf for Alex from Transcend.

I smell bullshit.

Slipping through the cracked door, I pad over to my daughter's sleeping form. Ella's curled around her pillow, breathing softly while she dreams little girl dreams.

"I love you, baby," I whisper against the top of her fine hair.

Stirring slightly but not enough to waken, Ella mutters in her sleep. "Daddy?"

Heart clenching, I realize the little girl dreams will never be realized, and nothing could possibly hurt as much as that. After one more kiss, I slip out of the room. Ghosting down the hallway, every window I pass overlooks the guesthouse, and I make sure Kristal is still engaging in her addiction.

It takes all of thirty seconds to reroute the security system so it no longer alerts the guesthouse when the front doors are opened or closed. I'll reengage it when I return. The precaution I took was for Ella, or so I told myself. Now I realize it was a way for Kristal to keep tabs on all of our comings and goings.

I hit the driveway running, without a backward glance, fearing any pause would be visible from the guesthouse. In less than a minute, I leave my neighborhood behind, because my house is situated on the outskirts of Dominion, closest to the Gates. Subconsciously, I think I was punishing myself for setting up residence at the wall, as if I was on the outside looking in to the one place I didn't want to be but belong.

Towering high with menace, the wall protecting Dominion's founding families rises before me. Sprinting across the pavement, I enter the tree line to the left of the main gate and the security booth. No doubt the area is wired to a security feed, but our conversation will not take place in view of the gate.

Waiting long enough, I have the urge to check my cellphone, but then I realize I have no idea how long Shadow Haven's driveway is. I should have factored that in, because it takes seven minutes going at dizzying speeds to traverse the winding drive to Misery Castle, then another five to drive through the Gates.

The mechanized sound of the main gate opening draws my attention to where a black SUV is rolling through without stopping to chat with the fellow manning the security booth. I recognize the grill of the Escalade, and realize Marcus must have nabbed Ezra's vehicle from their garage.

Readying to step forward, the SUV picks up speed. Darting behind a tree, I watch as Ezra rides by in the passenger seat with a burly man driving– he looks suspiciously like the guy at Restraint. Not Aaron from the front door, but his doppelganger who haunts the inside of Restraint.

Mulling over the oddness, it's two minutes later before the gate is opening again, revealing the low purr of Marc's Spyder. This time I do step from the darkness and into view.

"Get in," Marcus orders, rolling up alongside me.

For once, I'm in charge. "No– park and get out."

Eyebrows knitting together, Marc doesn't like my suggestion, nor does he like being bossed around. Wearing a sour puss expression, he does as I asked.

I don't wait around to argue, being I know that's where this is headed because I had the audacity to order Marcus fucking Zeitler about. Ghosting back into the trees, I keep looking over my shoulder to make sure Marcus doesn't lose sight of me.

Bitching underneath his breath the whole time, Marcus follows me a quarter mile into the woods surrounding Crestview. Deciding I've wandered far enough, I lean against an oak tree with my arms crossed defensively over my chest.

"Well, I have to catch a plane in exactly four hours," Marcus is grumbling when he comes to a stop in front of me. Looking seriously put out, he glares me down. "If I knew you wanted to go exploring in the woods, I would have given you the code to my driveway gate and we could have ventured to Ezra's tent in the woods… or, ya know, you could have gotten in my goddamn car like I asked."

Oh, Marc's pissed. I bite back a laugh. "I've seen firsthand how cars can be bugged." I uncross, and then re-cross my arms. "Even if you think you're the one doing the bugging, that doesn't mean someone else isn't retaliating."

Biting his bottom lip, Marcus contemplates that for about thirty seconds before admitting defeat. "True. So it's safe to assume you made us wander in the woods because it was unexpected and no one would follow us." Tugging at his pajama pants, he reveals his house slippers. "Wish someone would have told me to dress for rugged terrain."

Pussy.

"What was Ezra up to at this hour? Who was driving Miss Daisy?"

"Nice segue." Marcus mirrors my stance. "What's it matter, anyway? Shadow Haven is Ezra's house, and he can visit whenever the fuck he wants."

"Defensive much?" I raise an eyebrow in challenge. "Who was the dude?"

"Roarke Walden– he's a cop. His parents work for us, and he was raised at Shadow Haven. He follows Ezra around. Roarke's family."

"Do you ever question why, or do you know why? Or are you so used to seeing it, you don't see the fact that a psychiatrist shouldn't need a 24/7 bodyguard."

"Ezra misbehaves," Marcus mutters sheepishly, slumping against an opposing tree. "He has mental problems, so I prefer he's not alone. Why was Ez driving around at nearly three in the morning? Because he can't sleep until he's checked on each and every single one of us. Cort is in their childhood bedroom, and I'm down the hall, with Diane at the other end of the corridor. Ezra checks because he was stolen from his bed, as was Aaron and Cortez… and Roarke makes him feel safe."

"Shit!" I hiss with feeling. "I'm not paranoid, Marcus."

"Spit it out, Regina." Marc steps forward, arms crossed over his chest, with his eyebrows angry slashes across his forehead. "What the fuck is going on?"

"I don't know," I whine. "But I'm thinking clearly and seeing shit I shouldn't."

"As you said to me on the night we met, start from the beginning."

"Beginning?" I huff a humorless laugh. "Everyone in my life is connected. I was already going to Hillbrook when my father died and my mother was diagnosed with cancer. It can't be a coincidence that we moved into the building across from Stanton Green."

"You know Stanton Green?" The amazed yet horrified tone in Marc's voice alerts me to the fact he has no idea what the fuck is going on either. "When we went to Hillbrook together, he was just a normal kid. But then he took over the family business– I can't nail that asshole down with an indictment for nothing."

"Good luck with that." I trail a laugh. "Do I know Stan? Yeah, I do. For more than two years, he was my neighbor, his enforcer was my friend, and I babysat his daughter."

"Why is this so odd?" Marc mutters, hella confused.

"Bianca Green? Dominion's mafia princess is Whitt's little sister."

"What?" Marc barks, stepping forward like he wants to shake the piss out of me.

"You said beginning, so we have to back up some. I've come to the conclusion that nothing is a coincidence. When I first met Grant, and even before, it was like I was being vetted for something. The education. The fact that I was protected by the lord of the underworld. Albert drove me through Dominion, through the Gates, explaining everything, and my reactions pleased him."

"Maybe Albert was making sure you would be the right woman to carry the Whittenhower heir."

"Maybe, but doubtful." Pacing back and forth, I let it all out. "Grant explained some shit too. It all connects to the founders. Whittenhower. Holden. Zeitler–"

"Meyers," Marcus interrupts, knowing more than I do. "Spencer. Fontaine. The Simpsons were added when I was a small child with my family's influences. Their bloodline went back to the conception of Dominion. So what?"

"The servants aren't servants. They're like mafia enforcers, but why?" I spit out. "Albert, Martha– Kristal… they protect the Whittenhowers. Julian Ramirez protects Stanton Green."

"Kris?" Marcus growls, getting the hint. "But I don't understand. I'm the only Zeitler, so shouldn't I be in the know?"

"I don't know what's up, Marcus." I continue pacing while throwing out theories. "It's probably some fucked up group of men and women who get together and negotiate who marries whom to keep the bloodlines pure yet prevents incest. A way to keep all of Dominion's power, influence, and money with the founders. Grant was forced to marry Cora because she was a Spencer."

"You think?" Marcus snarls, chest puffing up. Then he bellows so loudly I cower. "MY FUCKING FATHER SOLD ME TO THE

HOLDENS! It was out of my grandmother's hands, even after my father died. I was dropped off at Shadow Haven when I was still a kid, going to Hillbrook at the same time as my adopted *son*. You have no idea what it was like being a Jew in a Catholic school– Judas ring any bells? Then I was married to a controlling, frigid lesbian who was almost fifteen years my senior. So, yeah, Regina. I FUCKING GET *THAT*!"

"Calm yourself," I caution, holding my hands out, hoping my steadiness is infectious. "Grant always acted like this shadow was hanging over his head, and I thought it was Jackson's death."

"It wasn't," Marcus whispers, voice hoarse from screaming. "My best friend changed, and at first I blamed *you*." He gets into my face, but then backs off. "Grant was never the same after Jack died."

"I know," I breathe back, tears thick in my voice. "Believe me– *I know*. I was with them when Jackson died. He spoke to Grant in code, then did this ritualistic thing with Albert. Daniel was as in the dark as I was, I can tell you that. Then Jackson took my son, and said he was their future. Jackson died holding Niel, and it comforted him."

Sniffling, Marcus falls backward, allowing a tree to prop him up.

"Within seconds of Jackson's death, Albert had a body bag. No coroner– nothing. I've seen enough death to know the procedure." Voice low, I relive the moment as if it's happening in real time. "Grant was so cold, refusing to look me in the eye. Daniel was in a defensive position over his brother, screaming, fingernails turning to claws to protect Jackson… and do you know what they did?"

"What?" Marcus barely makes a breath of a sound.

"Grant and Albert took Jackson's body, saying the founders had to say their goodbyes. Gentle Grant– they just took Jackson away from Daniel, leaving us more confused than ever… then Grant was never the same, never could look me in the eye. He would disappear, and when he came back, he was distraught, almost suicidal."

"GRANT DID NOT COMMIT SUICIDE!" Marcus bellows, more possessive of Grant's memory than I am, and I'm the mother of his children. "I was with Grant when he died, Regina. Nothing was self-inflicted. He took Cora to the house that was to be yours. *Yours*– with Grant, Whitt, Niel, and Ella as a family. He was going to marry you."

"Jesus Christ, Marcus!" I step away, on the verge of sobbing. "Are you trying to kill me?"

"No, I'm telling you the truth. Grant was meeting with Cora to ask for a divorce, but she brought her father with her. It was obvious Henry died from a heart attack, and the rest was a murder-suicide."

"So the brownstone was meant to be my house?" I croak out. "It was the neighborhood my dad promised me, and I told this to Grant."

"Grant loved you more than anyone." Marcus looks away quickly to hide the wash of jealousy flashing over his face. "More than he loved me. He never forgot a single word you said... but–" his voice pitches high. "But there was some weird shit that went down. I was so distraught over Grant, over the boys being abducted and their going fucking insane when they returned, that I never examined what happened when I had Grant dying in my arms."

"What happened?"

"Grant had called me, checking in and asking when I'd be home from Pennsylvania. He wanted me to meet him at the brownstone to show it off. I found a very different scenario when I arrived. I didn't call an ambulance– the EMT just ran in seconds after I did. While he was working on Grant, others came and took care of Henry and Cora, just as you had said with Jackson. I never thought twice about it, and I'm the fucking District Attorney, for Christ's sake."

Mirroring each other, Marcus and I pace in a small space between trees, deep in contemplation. My mind spins, wondering if this is important, or nothing at all. Maybe I'm being paranoid and this is just a coincidence, or maybe it truly is a conspiracy. Either way, I have to find out.

Stopping before me, Marc's arms fall to his sides. In the moonlight I watch his throat work as he swallows thickly. "Diane wouldn't have sex with me, so she sent Ezra my way thinking to satisfy me in case I liked boys, when I just wanted my wife. I woke in the night to find him... never mind what happened after that. But I snapped, and I lost my goddamn mind. Diane sent me to her friend, and I went... and I didn't come back for an entire year."

Yet again, Marcus confuses me how his mind works, and I'm left at a loss with nothing to say.

"I don't know what's going on, because Grant would never tell me." Tears no longer a threat, Marcus looks utterly betrayed. "We were best friends, closer than brothers, so much closer than Dexter and I could ever be, and I loved him with every fiber of my being." Punching himself in the chest, spittle hits me in the face from the vehemence of his words. "And I hate his fucking guts!"

Breaking our gaze, Marcus stalks fifty feet away, only to return a minute later. "Grant kept secret after secret like a fucking rat, and I would have helped him, but he didn't trust me. But he trusted *you*." Breathing heavily, almost on the edge of hyperventilating, what Marc says next leaves me speechless. "My daughter... I never once had sex with her mother– she tried, and I couldn't finish, so she thought just like Diane. That I liked boys. So my punishment was being locked in a room and milked like a goddamn cow... by the same EMT who saved Grant's life, and then let him die."

Eyebrows knitted together, I gasp, "What?" My mind reels, remembering the joke Grant and I shared about billion dollar sperm and how he knew of a man who had his stolen.

"Everyone is a liar, and they're going to start telling the truth," Marcus seethes. "Starting with that silent motherfucker, then I'm going after Leviticus Wilson."

"Marcus," I caution. "Think clearly. Be rational. We need to act as if nothing is going on, while being observant. We'll learn more this way than demanding truths no one is willing to admit. What do you think sparked this conversation in the first place? Kristal all but admitted she's stuck with me for the past decade out of loyalty to my Whittenhower daughter. She told me some bullshit lie about dating a guy named Alex from Transcend."

"Oh, that's fucking rich." Marcus laughs without humor, taking on a manic edge. "Fucking Jamie!"

"What does Jamie have to do with this?"

"My daughter is a Fontaine," Marcus spits out, changing directions yet again. "Another goddamn founding family– so, yeah... this shit connects. Including you." Stalking away, he snaps a limb off a tree and begins to beat the trunk with it. "My wife wouldn't give me a child, wouldn't sleep with me, saying Ezra was enough. So when I snapped, she shipped me off to her childhood friend, promising BDSM as a tool to control my *unnatural* urges. It was a trap, probably commissioned at those meetings you suspect."

"Probably," I mutter. "Hell, I think I was targeted when I was thirteen at Transcend, and they've been nudging my path ever since. When I get out of line, someone intervenes."

"Tell me who you think is involved," Marcus demands, calming some but still seething.

"What I know as a positive: Jackson handed the throne to Grant, and neither thought Grant was strong enough to shoulder the burden, nor Whitt. So that is why my son was created. Grant always talked about the legacy like it was separate from their business holdings and properties, which Daniel is in charge of. Whittenhower enforcers: Albert, Martha, and Kristal. But there are a lot of Whittenhowers, and Jackson had asked Albert to watch over Grant until he picked his own enforcer. But who?"

"Alex," Marcus spits.

"What?"

"How do you think Grant's brownstone is still in our possession? Alex owns it– Grant put it in his name so Daniel wouldn't find out. Alex was shoved up Grant's ass for a good year before his death. No doubt Alex and Kristal are tag-teaming us."

"Shit!" I hiss, suddenly furious. "I hate feeling powerless, like they think me a fool."

"Really, Regina?" Marcus glowers at me. "How do you think *I* feel right now?"

"You're such a narcissist fuckface, Marc," I snap. "My *I* was the collective *I* of you and I, dumbass. I was saying I know how we both feel."

"Should've just said *we*." Marc points out like an asshole.

"Fuck you," I mutter dismissively. "Whittenhowers are done. I assume they're waiting for my son to grow up and take over for Grant in their shenanigans with Dominion's denizens."

Marc's insane laughter draws me up short. "Yeah, I'll handle who's in charge of the Whittenhowers," he warns with violence riding his voice. "I'll watch and never question, but eventually I'll get retribution over the betrayal."

"Okay…" I draw out, finding Marcus a bit too blood-thirsty for my liking. "Spencer: Boyd with his wife and son, even though technically they're Simpsons."

"What?" Marc squawks. "What do you mean Boyd is a Simpson?"

"Your question brings me to the Meyers. Gwen. The biggest whore in all of Dominion, rival with Cora for the mother of the year award," I mutter sarcastically. "Gwen had three kids with Thomas Simpson: Fate, Boyd, and Faith. Then the Whittenhowers needed an heir with Jackson's impending death, so the old cunt molested Grant and made Whitt. Then she preyed upon another young man– Stanton, creating Bianca."

"Fuck, Regina." Marcus strides up to me, looks me dead in the eyes with a smile curling his lips. "You know a lot– you're an untapped source of information I never thought in a million years knew anything. I honestly didn't think Grant trusted you at all."

"Thanks," I mutter dryly. "Thanks for the backhanded compliment, Marcus."

"It's true," Marcus replies with a shrug. "Okay, so who are the meddling founders, hell-bent on keeping their position of power? Whittenhower. Meyers is that Gwen bitch– I seriously need to get at the whore for touching Grant. Spencer is Boyd– he's such a nice man. What the fuck is wrong with this picture? Fontaine is Spyder's black widow of a mother– Olivia." Raising an eyebrow in challenge. "Simpson?"

"Goddamn it!" Charging across the woods, I grab a limb off the forest floor and slam it into a tree trunk with satisfying violence. "FATE!"

"Bingo!" Marcus chirps, like he's enjoying my sense of betrayal because it's feeding into his own.

"Your son!" I scream to hurt him back. "Ezra is the Holden."

Smirk replaced with a frown, Marcus looks like he wants to cry.

"It's true. Grant was explaining enforcers to me, and I heard this from Albert in the past and Kristal tonight. Enforcers are to protect us from ourselves. Grant said all of the non-legacy kids at Hillbrook were enforcers– except for me. He said Ezra had three, but he never explained it to Cortez because he wanted him as his lover instead."

"Cort doesn't know?" Marc's head hitches to the side, almost as if he's gazing at Shadow Haven in the distance through the trees, and viewing Cort asleep in his bed. "Aaron Frost and Roarke Walden. My son is a member of whatever the fuck is going on. I'd love to deny it, but his mental illness would get off on this shit."

"Okay." I take a deep breath, and then say a little prayer Marcus won't kill the messenger. "There's one family left."

"No there isn't," Marcus mumbles, beyond confused.

A heartbeat passes.

Then another.

And another. An owl hoots in the distance, seeking out its prey.

"Primogeniture," I remind Marcus because I can't stand the silence. "Absolute primogeniture. You're the youngest of the youngest, even if you were born a son to the son. The Whittenhowers were Jackson, Grant, and it should have been Whitt, not Niel. I don't know what happened in the Holdens to change the line of succession because it should have been Divina. Fate is the oldest of both the Meyers and Simpson children. Stan, bypassing Caleb, then Bianca. Boyd has the Spencer name. I don't know Olivia Fontaine, so I have no idea who her first born was."

"Leviticus Wilson," Marcus repeats again, and I shudder to think the woman used her own son to do that to Marcus, but then again, it sounded like Diane did the same with Ezra.

Evil doesn't bypass motherhood, it seems.

"I don't know what you're trying to say, Regina." Marc leans against a tree, crossing his arms, purposefully being obtuse. "Divina has lupus. We married her to Cortez to keep the Holden legacy in Ezra's hands, knowing they would share. Shadow Haven and all of its monies have belonged to Ezra since his birth. We already established my own son is fucking with me, so why twist the knife deeper."

"I'm not talking about Ezra any longer, Marcus." Holding his eyes, I try not to show an ounce of pity. Then I remember Marcus is more like me than humanly possible, so I walk back to the car to the soundtrack of his bellows of rage and the splintering of wood against wood. Then, finally, a sound that can only be described as the ultimate death wail of betrayal.

Dexter.

Chapter Seventeen

Sitting in the Spyder, being a good girl by not putting my sneakers on the dashboard, I lean back and stare at the stars glittering overhead. It's peaceful now that Marcus has stopped beating the shit out of innocent trees. For a man who loves to teach others how to control themselves, he sure does suck at it.

Not to sound narcissistic, but I've had a shitty night too, but you don't see me turning into a billionaire lumberjack. Allowing my mind to wander in any direction it pleases, I wonder what else these founders do besides arrange marriages and choose when children are born. Anything malicious?

Pretty sure calling in my mother's debts, having me fired from not one but two jobs, and revoking my scholarship counts as evil deeds.

I bet it was Dexter who revoked my scholarship, because Marc's betrayal can't be feigned.

Grant couldn't look me in the eyes once he was one of their ranks, whatever they call themselves. Now I realize it's because he was forced to do things I wouldn't find ethical. He knew I'd never judge him, but he probably judged himself, or feared I'd think less of him if I knew the truth.

With death, the living are only left with unanswered questions.

"He's not involved," Marcus rasps from the darkness, voice rough from screaming.

My eyes flick in his direction, and I wish I hadn't looked. Eyes haunted, face streaked with tear-tracks, Marcus doesn't look like the same man I've come to know.

Broken.

"He's not involved... He's too–" leaning against the side of the car, Marcus pleads with me to agree with him. "He's too ethical. He probably knows about it, and knowing him, he's protecting me from the truth. You didn't see his face when I returned from my one-year tour in Vegas. He was destroyed. He knows, but he's not involved."

Turning my head, I face Marcus. "Why are we only using pronouns?"

"Get out of the car," Marc growls, grabbing my shoulder with one hand while the other reaches in the car to grip the door handle. Not waiting for me to comply, I'm manhandled from the car.

Dragging me while I'm still stunned into passiveness, a seething Marcus bends me over the hood of the Spyder. Cupping his body along my back, he presses his lips to my ear. "My son probably has my car bugged, that's why."

"Shit!" I hiss, body jerking as my yoga pants are yanked down my ass, barely making it past my hips. "Marcus, what the fuck? Stop it!"

"We came out here in the middle of the night for a rendezvous– a rendezvous we will have." Frozen in shock, all I can do is stare at the windshield as Marcus yanks the front of his pajama pants down, freeing his erection.

"Marcus," I warn, shock melting. At the first touch of his cock against my ass cheek, I freak the fuck out. "Don't!"

Arms flailing to gain leverage, my legs are kicked apart, then a heavy body fills the void so I can't move. "You called me because you wanted a rough fuck, so a rough fuck is what you're going to get."

Head whipping back, I glare over my shoulder at Marcus. "Goddamn you," I snarl into his face. "Why are you acting this way? I get that you're upset, but hell if I'm going to let you take it out on me."

"It looks like you have no choice in the matter, Regina." Manic amber eyes stare right through me as he jerks his hips, hammering his cock home.

Jerking in pain, I gasp through the sensation of his flesh conquering mine. "You just burnt a bridge you needed, asswipe." Fingers clenching and unclenching, a threat is realized. "I'll scratch the fuck outta this car, Marcus. Don't think I won't. Every thrust will cost a scratch. What'll that cost you?"

Growling deep from his chest, I feel it more than hear it. "The Spyder is priceless."

"So am I." I jab my elbow backward and hit him square in the sternum. Marcus begins gasping for breath because his lungs fail to fill. "So get your dick outta me, and back the fuck off."

"I-I-I–" Sputtering while blinking, Marcus tries to clear the red of fury from his vision. Slumping forward, he curls around my back, with the side of his face resting between my shoulder blades. "I'm sorry."

Losing all strength, every muscle gives way in my body at once. Tugging on my hood, I use it to pillow my face from the cold metal, with my arm supporting it. The only part of my body that is chilling in the night air is a few inches of my belly and my ass cheeks, with Marc's cock keeping my yoga pants from falling back into place.

I think about it– I really do. Scratching the Spyder, at least once for the single thrust, but I can't bring myself to destroy something that is truly priceless. Hating that I understand how Marcus is feeling, I try to hang onto my anger, but I can't.

"You're sorry?" I murmur against the side of my arm. "You tried to scare me, then attacked me, and violated me. I'm sorry really doesn't cut it, Marcus. I came to you because you said we could be allies, and with one temper tantrum, you broke the tentative trust we had built."

"I snapped." Marc's words flutter against my spine as he speaks. "Sometimes, even to this day, I lose control. It's why I skull-fuck, Cortez. I take all of my aggression out on his mouth so I don't hurt anybody else. He understands."

"I'm not Cort," I remind Marcus. "And my vagina is not for rent."

Moving closer, Marcus snuggles against my back, and I remember Jamie's words from earlier. Jamie said Marcus couldn't distinguish between sex and affection. Maybe Marcus can't distinguish between sex and violence, either.

Invading my hoodie, arms come around my sides, hands splaying along my belly, thumbs brushing the bottoms of my breasts. "I am sorry," Marcus whispers. "Everything you said hit me so hard, I snapped. I learned thirty-four years of my life have been orchestrated. My aunt must have been in the Zeitler position, with my father by her side. When they died, it would have fallen to Dexter *and* me. Because each founder needs an heir, right?"

More than trying to comfort Marcus, I truly believe what I'm about to say. "You're probably right, actually. Dexter knows, but he's too ethical to participate, which meant you were out of the game too."

"Thank you." Marcus snuggles closer, burying his cock deeper.

"You have no plans of taking that monstrous thing outta me any time soon, do you?"

"No," flutters against the side of my neck. "The only person I've ever fallen in love with betrayed me more than anyone else."

I'm applauding myself for being so calm and rational. Later, I'll freak the fuck out if I allow myself. Marcus needs to learn my level of control. "What does that have to do with this rape routine?"

Voice stiff with rage, "Grant betrayed me, so I had to fuck his wife– why can't you understand that?"

"Jesus Christ," I hiss, trying to move forward to get away from Marc, but he presses me harder into the hood. "You were *in* love with Grant?"

"Still am," Marcus confesses. "It's not like it ever goes away. I hated you, by the way." Moving slightly, his flesh parts mine. "Grant wanted me to meet you, wanted us to do stuff together like normal friends, but I was jealous. I knew if I looked at you, I'd do something rash."

"What could be rasher than this?" I comment on the fact that Marcus is now rocking back and forth ever so slowly, while adding a low moan for effect.

"Doing this when you weren't on birth control would have been far worse," Marcus murmurs against the shell of my ear. "We were both in love with Grant, and he betrayed us both, so just relax and connect with me."

"You're fucking insane." Slumping forward, I admit defeat. "And Grant never betrayed me."

"Keep lying to yourself, Regina, if it helps you sleep at night." Hands rising, Marcus cups my tits, fingernails pressing in with bruising intensity. Biting back a moan, I try to ignore how his body feels slicing through mine.

"Just don't leave your cum in me this time," I warn. "Because I'll just douche it back out again."

"Of course, *Mistress*," Marcus twists the one word I demanded he never use, just to gut me. "Only precious Grant is allowed that special treat."

Head whipping to the side, I glare at the asshole fucking me. "You're the one who was in love with Grant, so quit acting like you hated his guts."

"I *loathe* him." Marcus shudders with the potency of his emotions. "You should hate him, too. It drives me to the brink of insanity how you grieve for him, how I grieve for him, and Grant doesn't deserve it."

"The *brink* of insanity?" Reaching back, I slap Marc's ass as he begins to thrust harder inside of me. "What the fuck does actual insanity look like?"

"My son," Marcus admits in a grave tone. "Shut up– if you get off before I do, I'll pull out. If you don't, I won't. That's how it will be from now on. The two people who are in love with Grant will fuck each other for the rest of our lives since I can't have him."

Rolling my eyes, I stay silent, refusing to comment on how every time Marcus speaks of Grant, it's always in the present tense. Rocking back and forth, my fingertips try to find purchase on the hood of the car without scratching its precious surface.

"Don't be stingy," I grumble to the man fucking me like he has something to prove. "You seem to have an aversion to foreplay, so how about some attention to my clit, 'cuz your dick ain't doing shit for me."

"Keep talking like you came straight out of the gutter," Marcus murmurs wryly against the shell of my ear. "I like it."

"I *did* come out of the gutter, fuckface," I remind him.

Not wanting Marc's jizz inside of me, I reach down to take care of business, but my wrist is caught in an angry grip. Smacking my palm on the hood of the car in a silent order, he expects it to stay there. Marcus grips my tit in one hand and the other is shoved down the front of my yoga pants.

"I hate foreplay," Marcus growls, fingertip touching my clit with surprising gentleness. "But for you, anything, snuggums."

Laughing unexpectedly, I gasp out, "You're such an asshole," and Marcus joins in with his infectious laughter.

"Seriously, though," he whispers in my ear, voice breathless. "I want you to get off with me. Every time."

"Okay," I whisper against the hood, breath clouding the metal with condensation. "I'm down with that."

"Good." Marc's nose nuzzles my ear affectionately, then his lips flutter out a word spoken like a vow. "Partner."

"Ugh!" is torn from my throat when Marcus thrusts so harshly my hips meet the front of the Spyder, causing the car to rock on its suspension. "Ugh!" mouth hanging wide open, cheek pressed against the cold metal, my breath makes the hood damp. "Ugh!" Every thrust harder than the last, cock branding me from the inside out.

Violence turning to softness, Marcus curls around my back, mouth fluttering kisses along the nape of my neck. "I'm sorry. I promise to seduce you next time instead of taking without asking."

Fingers leaving my clit, Marcus shoves them into my mouth. "Suck," he commands. "Get them wet." Obeying, my mouth works to suck my own taste off Marc, tongue rolling between his fingers. Pulling free of my body, "Spit," he orders, holding out his bent fingertips in front of my face, and I obey that order too.

"Argh!" I gasp in shock as Marc takes my clit between his fingertips and starts to jack it off like a cock, rolling and tugging my flesh. "Jesus Christ," grunts against the hood as I writhe around like a fucking idiot. Rocking against his hand, I shove my ass out, trying to work his cock as he works my clit.

Marcus doesn't move anything but his fingers, allowing me to do all the work. Every muscle in my body seizes, neck hitching backward. "Oh, my God! Oh, my god. Ohmygod.... Ohmygod."

Orgasming from the tips of my toes to the roots of my hair, a guttural grunt of victory is pulled from my chest, but I celebrate too soon. Enlarging, Marcus joins me. Neither the victor, nor defeated, we come at the same fucking time.

"Goddamn it!" I snarl against the hood as Marcus pulls out. Knees weak, pushing off with my palms, I turn until my bare ass is resting on metal. Then I lean backward, legs still shaking uncontrollably, pussy still pulsing and clenching every few seconds. "That thing should be registered as a weapon."

Smug laughter flows from Marc's lips, amber eyes drinking me in. "This?" Marc palms his cock, slick with a combination of my cum and his, then he flicks it until a stream of jizz hits my thigh, soaking into my yoga pants. "I love a good challenge."

"No shit." Using all of my strength, I tug my pants back over my ass.

"I wonder what the percentage will be that I get to soak Grant's pussy versus spilling my seed upon the earth."

Rolling my eyes, I don't answer that. Marcus is already smug enough, I don't need to add to his ego. Something tells me I'm going to be coming a whole lot. I better buy stock in Summer's Eve.

"Get in," Marcus orders, opening the passenger door. "I'll drop you off a few houses down so Kristal and Fate don't catch wind."

Refusing Marc's order, I do it only because it feels like a minor victory. "Nah, I'll walk." Jogging backward, I taunt Marcus with my disobedience. "If you ever force your way into my body again, you'll be short one dick. Got it?"

"Understood," Marcus murmurs so quietly I don't hear the word, but contrition is etched across his face. "Text me as soon as you get home safely."

"Will do!" I take off through the woods, noticing the purr of the Spyder is flying like a bat out of hell in the wrong direction.

With a sudden need to protect, I find myself tugging my cellphone free from my marsupial pouch and dialing a number before it even registers.

Obviously Jamie doesn't speak, but I can tell he answered.

"Marc's on his way to beat the fuck out of you– just a heads up," I mutter quickly, then hang up.

Three seconds later…

Jamie: *Ah, I take it Marcus convinced you to speak about private things outside of this house?*

–That would be the all of it, yes. Probably so you wouldn't break everything in the house.

Jamie: *Thanks for the heads up. I hope he didn't harm you.*

–Only emotionally.

Jamie: *Oh, Regina. Are you okay?*

–Why do we keep meeting like this, Jamie? <laughing> I'm okay. I'll always be okay.

Jamie: *Because you're a survivor. Marc's here already. He must be pissed.*

–Protect yourself.

Jamie: *I always do. No matter how badly he may want to, Marcus will never harm me.*

–Yeah, he'll just take it out on me instead.

Jamie: *That's my greatest fear. Stay safe.*

–You too. Text me when he leaves.

Jamie: *That won't be until he has to catch his flight, but I will do just that. Thank you.*

Pocketing my cellphone, I jog the rest of the way home. Less than five minutes later, I'm sneaking into my own house. Then I reprogram the security system. On my way down the hallway of windows, I notice Kris is still entertaining her orgy, and I take a deep breath.

After checking on both Fate and Ella, ignoring the pain of knowing Fate has been keeping many secrets, I hop in the shower.

It isn't until I slip between my sheets that I realized I never texted Marcus back to say I made it home safely.

–I'm home.

Marcus: *No shit. I'm guessing you've already showered me down the drain.*

–Jamie says emotion can't be conveyed through text messages– I'd say he's wrong.

Marcus: *Your statement, combined with the fact that Jamie was waiting for me, means you're a goddamn traitor.*

–Still mad at the world at large, I see.

Marcus: *I would never harm Jamie, Regina. NEVER. I wasn't coming here for violence.*

–Then why?

Marcus: *Comfort. Absolution. Confession. Pick any of those and you'd be right.*

–It wasn't a chance I was willing to take, Marcus. Not after what you did to me on the car hood. Call me a traitor if you will, but it's not in my nature to turn my back on someone who is in danger.

Marcus: *I hate that I like you.*

–Nice.

Marcus: *I thought we were to be truthful with each other. So I was being honest. I truly hate that I can't hate you, even if I want to. For some reason, I see every damn thing in you that Grant loves about you– things he should have loved about me.*

–This is coming from someone who's BFF is in love with her… Marcus, you can't make someone love you. There are many factors. Grant loved you, but he was incapable of being in love with you. You're in pain from the rejection, but there is a great deal of guilt associated with people on my end. Every time I look at Ade, it's something that infects our friendship, making it easier for us if we don't see each other. Deal with it and move on.

Marcus: *I am… to you. Congrats!*

–I'm sick to death of always being someone's second choice. Fuck you!

Marcus: *You liked it– don't lie. You've got some bad kinks– the worst to have, and I'll make sure to keep them in check. I promise. Good night, Regina. Jamie is fine. He's actually asleep, and I'm lying next to him while texting you.*

–You confuse the piss out of me.

Marcus: *Imagine 'being' me, eh? I'll keep in touch. The next time we see one another will be your first lesson in BDSM. Sleep well.*

Who the hell could sleep after this night? Admitting defeat, I crawl out of bed and slip into my daughter's. Curling around Ella's sleeping form, I drink in her strawberry scent, and allow her innocence to purify me.

Chapter Eighteen

I don't know which is more difficult, living and working with Fate and Kristal while not trusting them, or entering the brownstone after how Marcus and I left things. But since I've soldiered on an entire week of acting as if nothing is out of the ordinary with my girls, I think I can handle Marcus Zeitler. Plus, for all I know, the founders group gets together for a quilting bee, drinks tea, and then trades their relatives to prevent inbreeding their lineages– a fun activity as old as time itself.

Peering into the front door of the brownstone, I'm shocked no one is ambling around. "Yo!" I project down the main hallway. Pandora's Box is calling me, telling me to either open the door to my left, or run up the staircase. But knowing I can't unsee, I go to the right, straight down the hallway, and begin peering in doorways. "Regina is reporting for Queen duty."

"Then get your ass in the impact room!" Cort shouts from what I can only assume is the kitchen. "We'll be right out."

Grumbling, "Such a warm reception," underneath my breath, I earn three distinct laughs in reply. The impact room looks as it had on the past two visits. The sofa is uncovered again, and on top of the end table is a folded newspaper, a Coke can, and a notebook.

Curiosity getting the better of me, my fingertip nudges the cover of the notebook open, finding perfectly slanted masculine handwriting. "Hey!" is shouted at the same time the cover snaps shut on my fingertip. "Privacy!" Cortez chastises me. "That's my plotter book."

Backing away while raising my hands out in front of me, "Sorry, so sorry!"

"Yeah," Cort mutters while staring me down, then the ass bites into a piece of pizza. Flopping down on the sofa, he eats his snack while keeping one eye on his notebook and the other trained on me, like I'm going to fight him for the book.

"Cortez is possessive of that notebook," Marcus purrs as he glides into the room, sans pizza slice. Brushing a kiss over my cheek, I can smell tomato and oregano on his breath. "Again, I apologize for my asinine behavior."

"As you've done all week on the phone," I remind Marcus, kissing his cheek back.

"Well, when one does something that could land one in prison–"

With an eyebrow raise, I interrupt the same spiel I've heard all week. "–Especially when one is Dominion's District Attorney."

"Yeah, there is *that*." Marcus walks over to the end table and picks up Cortez's notebook, earning a shout of protest.

"Put that down!" Cort coughs, nearly choking on his pizza.

"Relax." Marcus pulls a face. "You're not going to relax as long as Regina and I are in the same room with this book." Striding to the hallway with the book in his hand, Marc returns a second later without it. "Your fellow word weaver is taking it up to his cave."

"Uh, okay." Cort leans back on the sofa, and begins chewing again. "Good thinking. Jamie respects my privacy."

"Of course he does," Marcus murmurs, then whispers something underneath his breath I can't hear. Reaching for the paper, he snaps it open and begins to read.

Okay...

With Cort snacking and Marcus reading, and Jamie ghosting, I decide to look around the toys since no one is paying me any attention. At first this annoys me, because tonight was to be my first BDSM lesson, but then I realize they're gifting me with a snapshot of their everyday lives, showing me who they are in essence.

"Do you spend a lot of time here?" I direct to Cortez as I inspect a wooden frame meant to restrain a person– it was moved slightly from the wall, catching my eye. *Shiny!* I don't bother engaging Marcus, because he's devouring the news.

"Jamie's my crit partner." Cortez takes a heavy swallow of Coke.

"A what?" Noticing a hinge, I pull the frame, and the entire structure swings out from the wall.

"Jamie's my writing critique partner– that's why he's welcome to my notebook." Popping the pizza crust in his mouth, Cort jumps up from the sofa. "That bolts to the floor." Striding over to me, he takes the wooden structure from my hand. "Let me show you how it works."

Reminiscent of a giant picture frame with no picture, Cortez swings it out from the wall, and then bolts it to the floor. "There are two pegs at the top– here and here." He points them out at the upper corners. "This only works with tall people." Stepping away, he offers, "Try it out."

"Why the hell not?" I murmur, and I swear I hear Jamie's bizarre laughter flow down the staircase. "Does he have sonic hearing?" I place my hands on the pegs, finding it not too uncomfortable, since I am very tall for a woman.

"It's an old house." Cortez struggles to reach as he buckles lengths of leather around my wrists to secure me to the frame. "Everything we say on this side of the house flows up the front and back staircases, directly into Jamie's ears. He has a comfy chair and a notebook at the landing, and he listens like an old biddy."

"How very Jamie-esque," I murmur, the first stirrings of unease entering my veins. Cortez crouches, tugging my feet where he wants them.

"Divina is hosting a fundraiser for lupus research." With the flick of his fingers, the newspaper bends so Marcus can gaze at us. "Did you know your wife was doing this?"

"Yeah. I know Divina usually keeps to herself, but after last month's relapse, it became priority number one." After strapping my ankles to the corners of the frame, Cortez comes to his feet while chuckling, and I swear Jamie mirrors the sound. "Marcus, your attention span is shit. I wrote the article for Divina, and I read it at breakfast yesterday morning."

"Oh…" The newspaper is snapped back up, hiding Marcus from view. "I must have had jetlag."

"That excuse only works when you change time zones. It was a twenty minute flight south to north." Surprisingly, Marcus ignores Cortez's dig.

"Remind me to cut your wife a check," I say to regain Cortez's attention, and he looks touched from the gesture. "So what's this frame supposed to be for, anyway?" Tugging, I try to dislodge my hands, then my ankles, and that unease blooms to full-on panic.

"Did Regina seriously just ask that?" Cortez snickers while looking Marc's way.

The newspaper dips again, and all I can see is amber fire and the upper curve of a wicked grin. "I can't believe you coaxed her into the position she's in. I thought Regina knew better, especially around you."

"I know, right?" Laughing, Cortez rubs his hands together like a villain. "Awesome!"

"What?" I squeak, and renew my efforts to free myself. But I'm not Houdini. The frame barely moves because it's bolted to the floor.

After gently folding the paper, Marcus rises to his feet. "Lesson number one: never trust Cortez." Hips rolling like a feline predator, Marcus stalks around me. "Lesson number two: this frame is meant to restrain your victim, giving the dominant access to three hundred and sixty degrees of flesh."

"Shit," I hiss with feeling. "I'm so fucking stupid."

"Highly educated and abnormally intelligent, I'd say." Marcus brushes a single fingertip down my cheek when he comes to a stop to face me. "Short-sighted when it comes to how sneaky and conniving Cort can be."

"Yeah, I get that now. Cortez made this look like it was my idea, when he had purposefully turned the frame out so it would catch my attention."

"Yes and no," Marcus purrs. Leaning forward, he runs the tip of his nose along my jawline, then he whispers in my ear. "Cortez did make it look like it was your idea. *But*, I'm the one who made sure this of all things caught your eye."

"Motherfuck," I grumble in defeat.

After a quick kiss to the corner of my mouth, Marcus steps away abruptly. "What should we teach Regina first? I think while we have her undivided attention, I should explain what Bondage, Discipline, Dominance, Submission, Sadism, and Masochism means."

"Oh, for the love of all that is holy!" Cortez shouts dramatically while falling to land on his ass on the sofa. "NO! No Dexter shit."

Flipping around to look at Cort, Marcus sounds utterly lost. "This is the most important part, don't you think? Actually explaining what BDSM means."

"Marc, Regina is on XII– she needs no explanation." Cort glares at Marcus, begging him with defiance not to do technical lectures. "If I have to hear this shit one more time, I'll gouge my eardrums out. Then you'll have a deaf and a mute on your hands."

"How did you train the PB?" I inquire, wondering if it was such a clusterfuck.

"Marcus sat him down in a chair and taught him like it was elementary school," Cortez mutters in disgust. "It was boring, and Marcus made me sit through it." Pouting, he mutters, "You promised."

"Fine, I'll concede." Marcus levels me with his stare, trying to see *inside* me. "The PB didn't know any of this, but Regina must have a general idea after reading twelve very detailed and highly accurate books. Okay."

"Okay?" I mutter to Cortez's cheering and Jamie's bizarre laughter flowing down the staircase.

"First things first, Regina has self-confidence issues." Marcus tugs on my dress and I flip the fuck out.

"Goddamn you, Marcus!" Heart beating out of control, I'm simultaneously lightheaded and invigorated. "Didn't we already settle this shit? You promised to never take what I'm not freely offering."

"Regina," Marcus murmurs gently, expression tender with no hint of violence or need to ruin me. "As we discussed in countless conversations this week, I'm sorry. I will not have sex with you again unless you ask me. I don't begrudgingly like you anymore– I genuinely enjoy your company."

"What the fuck did you do to Regina?" Cortez is on his feet in a heartbeat, charging across the room to intervene.

"You're no one's white knight," Marcus snarls at Cortez. "If I wanted you to know one of my more shameful moments, I would have told you already. Besides, after I told Jamie, he wouldn't text me back until Regina and I had made peace."

"Oh, so *that's* why?" Eyes narrowed, I glare at Marcus. "Nice, and here I thought we had come to an understanding."

"We did," Marcus protests. "We're good, aren't we?"

"Yeah, until you tried to take my dress off me." Tugging, because I can't help myself, the leather bites into my wrists and ankles. "Explain why this is necessary. This isn't *me*."

Cocking his head to the side, Marcus contemplates my words. "What do you mean?"

I try to put my thoughts into words, but I don't know if it will make much sense. "I'm the D of BDSM, both of them. Dominance and Discipline. I don't need the trappings of the rest of it. It's a given that I want to be in charge, but not because I get off on it. If someone knows more than me, I agree with them. If someone asks something of me and I don't know how to do it, the first thing I do is seek out a way to educate myself. I *am* in charge of my life and those around me. Dominance. I am nothing if not disciplined. Contrary to what most think, that doesn't mean punishment, but the very definition of the word. Self-control."

"See!" Cort shouts, excitement warbling his voice. "There was no need to give Dexter's lectures."

"I see," Marcus drawls, looking seriously put out, like I'm a bitter disappointment. "So you don't want to play with the toys? With me?"

"Actually, no," I admit for the first time, realizing the truth of my words. "I know who I am and what I want. I'm almost thirty, not someone who has no life experience. If you want to make me happy, let me run Restraint, inside and out of the dungeon." Smiling to myself, "I like the sounds of that. Yes, that sounds amazing."

Cortez curls around my back, resting his chin on my shoulder, staring at Marcus who is standing before me. "Reg is a workaholic, we all know this, and it would give me more time with Ezra."

"Be that as it may." Marcus shows he does know the very definition of discipline– his voice holds no inflection. "The last thing Ezra needs is idle time on his hands. But I'll mull the suggestion over, because it is a good fit. Regina would keep everyone in line in the dungeon. Regardless, she must train on everything."

Parroting Dexter, or maybe Marcus, Cort chants near my ear. "A dominant must experience everything they plan on doling out." He nips my earlobe with his front teeth– his snicker vibrating my flesh. "In other words, Regina has to play with all the toys. Both dishing it out and taking it."

"Motherfucking lovely." Groaning, my eyelids slip shut as I come to terms with my fate.

"Dress. Off." Marcus orders, tugging at my hem. "No helping, Cortez. Go sit on the sofa. Your job is to make Regina so uncomfortable, she'll eventually get over this pathetic insecurity of hers."

"If uncomfortable is the game plan, then I'm your man." Stepping away, Cortez slaps my ass, and then swaggers over to the sofa. Leering, he leans forward while licking his lips salaciously. "Mmm… let's see those luscious tits!"

"Jesus Christ," I groan in mortification, head sloping forward on my neck. "Let's get this over with."

"Cortez," Marc calls over his shoulder. "Would you believe it if I said Regina thinks you're making fun of her right now, and not at all commenting on the best set of tits you've ever seen?"

"You're shitting me, right?" Cort tilts his head, regarding me intently. "I was breastfed as a child, I'm sure."

Laughing from deep within his chest, Marcus reaches up to unhook one of my wrists. I immediately draw my arm down, shaking out my hand to wake it back up, then I reach to unlatch my other wrist.

"Tsk-tsk..." Marcus croons, capturing my wrist in his unrelenting grip. Treating me like an inanimate object, he tugs my arm out of my dress, then unhooks my bra. My tits spill forward to rest against his chest. "Mmm... I wasn't breastfed, maybe that's my fascination. My mother was like a pit viper. Irony, so is my wife and the mother of my daughter."

Swirling his chest against mine more than necessary, Marcus reattaches the leather strap around my wrist, then repeats the procedure with my other arm. Then he leans down to unhook both of my ankles, and I'm tempted to fight.

Laughter trickles past my lips when I envision kicking Marcus in the face, and the varying looks of horror that would cross Cort's and Marc's faces.

"Don't even think about it," Marcus warns, capturing my foot, thumb tickling my arch.

"Too late," I sing, voice light and airy with a smug smile plastered across my face.

"Hurry up, Marc," Cort whines impatiently from the sofa. "I want a good look at all the assets. Let's see that pussy. Unleash the cunt!"

"Oh... my... God..." I cry, so badly wanting to cover my face with my palms. "This is so humiliating."

"Cortez was either a heckler or a court jester in a past life," Marcus murmurs wryly as he tugs my panties down my thighs. Leaning forward, he nips my hip. "You shaved." He sounds surprised.

"Hair-free!" Cort shouts from the sidelines. "Reg wants some tongue-to-pussy action! Prove your worth as a cunt-licker, Marc."

"Says the cocksucker." Eyes rolling downward, I look straight at Marcus as he kneels by my feet. "It was easier to clean unwanted cum from my snatch," I deadpan.

Instead of getting offended, as I hoped, Marcus grins up at me, and my resolve cracks. "The feeling is mutual now," I admit. "I don't want to like you, to lust after you, but I'm warming to you, you bastard."

Impossibly long eyelashes shuttering his eye, Marc winks at me. "That's the plan." He rises to his feet. "You're not embarrassing Regina enough, Cortez." Then my underwear sails across the room to land in Cort's outstretched palm.

Palming my panties, Cort shoves them against his nose and mouth, and inhales deeply. "Mmm... nothing smells better than expensive pussy, especially when it has low mileage."

"Kill me." I groan in mortification.

"Regina," Marcus purrs, hands rising slowly to cup my breasts, slow enough for me to protest but I don't. "You'll see all kinds of depravity at Restraint, and we can't have the dungeon's ruler blushing, now can we?"

"Holy shit!" Cort and I shout at the same time, with me adding, "Really? I can run the dungeon?"

"In due time," Marcus murmurs noncommittally. Holding a tit in each palm, my flesh spilling over the sides of his hands, Marcus seems utterly fascinated. "Cortez, you can do better than that."

My eyes flick up to catch Cort jamming my underwear down his pants... and he begins to jerk off with them. "God, nothing like silk wrapped around my exquisite cock."

"Not that shit again," I grumble, sounding annoyed. But I can't stop my laughter from spilling when Cort actually gets into it, masturbating with my dirty underwear.

Smirking like the Devil himself, Marcus whispers so only I can hear. "Never fear– you'll get your revenge on Cortez. I'm letting him have his fun now, because he'll be your bitch during training. You'll receive from me, and you'll give to him."

For a split-second I feel bad, but then Cortez actually ejaculates into my underwear, screaming, "Liftoff!" as he comes. Then he wrenches my underwear from his pants, with strings of cum landing all over the sofa.

"Regina," Marcus whispers my name as he leans in for a kiss. Lingering for a few seconds, he smiles. "Cort deserves whatever you give him and so much more."

Sprawled across the sofa while wearing a satisfied grin, Cort holds my nasty panties up to me, dangling them from his fingertip by the waistband. "Want these back?"

"They're yours now, buddy." I shudder with revulsion, not finding cum particularly pleasant in the least.

"Well, now that the embarrassing portion of the evening has concluded, let's actually make Regina feel beautiful, shall we?"

"Erm... What?"

Fingertips brushing the hair away from my ear, Marcus stares at me intently. "You are beautiful, you know? And before you protest, remember you and I promised to be honest with each other."

"I'm really not, though." Eyes slipping shut, I mutter the truth. "I look like a drag queen, only I have real tits and I don't have to tuck. Just call me Post-Op Regina."

"Beauty is in the eye of the beholder." Marcus kisses the corner of my mouth tenderly, at odds with the intense expression on his face. "We all hate ourselves, but you need to stop letting everyone else know it."

"Why?" I gasp.

Hitching a finger in Cortez's direction, Marcus gives me the best lesson of all. "Because it's exploitable."

Lazy like a cat lying in the sun, Cort slurs his words. "If you love yourself enough, other people may buy into it. Look at me." He parts his hands, showing off his tall, tan, and lean physique. "In my head, I'm still that chubby, mixed bastard without a father, but no one would know that…"

"Cort," Marcus breathes, looking ready to cry.

"I know– I know. You love me." Cort sits upright on the sofa. "Won't touch me, but I know you love me."

"Jesus Christ, enough pity partying," Marcus barks, no doubt spiraling down the same rabbit hole. "Cortez, you're hot as fuck, and I don't touch you because it's like incest."

"He sucks your dick!" I interject. "How is *that* not pseudo-incest?"

Jamie's ghastly laughter flowing down from upstairs is the exclamation point to my comment.

"This isn't about me." Marcus is clearly flustered, which is like a gift unto itself. "My point being, Cort is awesome just as he is, as are you, Regina. You have many people who love you for who you are, and several who lust after your body– including me. So no more tiny violins playing the world's saddest songs."

Cort and I laugh, with Jamie as our backup. Fed up, Marc stalks behind me to parts unknown. My laughter is abruptly cut off when a blindfold is fitted across my eyes.

"Dun… dun… dun…" Cortez sings ominously. "Hey, Jamie? Batter up!"

"Um– what's going on?" Wiggling my nose, I try to dislodge the blindfold.

"This is so sweet," Cort croons. "If I cry, will somebody hold me?"

"Grow a pair," Marcus grumbles, voice getting farther away, no doubt joining Cortez on the sofa. "This is the '*Regina is beautiful*' portion of tonight's training, so she'll have the confidence to walk around in jeans and a t-shirt, or a ball gown at a charity function– which she *should* be attending, instead of hiding like a coward –or naked in the middle of Restraint's dungeon, commanding obedience while making cunts drip and cocks throb."

No doubt my blush is visible. "I have to say, that was more embarrassing than Cort's attempts."

"Because you know what I'm saying is true," Marcus states with confidence. "You know that you're strong enough to command an army in the buff, and still be respected. So stop worrying about this shit, because it weakens you. Understood?"

"Yes, sir."

"Did Regina just call me sir?" Voice shocked, Marcus teases me. "I suddenly feel faint."

A heated gaze warms me, and I can feel its path of travel going from my face to concentrating on my tits, even as it takes a detour to the apex of my thighs. Shivering, my body beads with a feverish sweat.

Legs weakening, "Oh, shit," slips past my lips.

"Jamie gives the best hugs," Cortez whispers. "He is going to hug Regina?"

"Shut up," Marcus whisper-shouts.

"Yes, Master."

Sweat breath whispers across my cheek, and I do feel beautiful– it's inexplicable.

"Hi," I whisper to Jamie, knowing he can't say anything back. For the past week, we've spent one a.m. until two a.m. text messaging back and forth. He's a calming influence, to the point I actually sleep now, getting five uninterrupted hours in a row.

At the same time, Marcus pesters me at Midnight, because he has to come first in all things. Only he has to actually talk on the phone, saying he has to hear the emotion in my voice.

The juxtaposition between Marcus and Jamie is dizzying.

Slim fingertips pluck at the buckle securing first my ankles, then my wrists. Rubbing soothingly, Jamie massages to get the blood flowing. An odd noise rumbles from his chest, some foreign communication attempt I can't decipher.

"Jamie's chastising me for leaving you strung up for so long, Regina," Marcus plays interpreter.

"Do you engage in BDSM?" Curiosity is thick in my voice. "Is that why you allow Marcus to take over your house?"

Dropping my hand abruptly, I fear I've frightened him away, but I'd forgotten Jamie speaks with his hands. A fingertip smooths across my belly, tickling me in the process.

W A T C H.

"Sorry, I forgot. You already told me you observe everything."

A low moan pours out my throat as two hands begin massaging everything in reach, including my breasts. Swaying on my feet, I feel woozy from a barrage of emotions striking me all at once.

The silence should be uncomfortable, but it's soothing. The rhythm of Jamie's strokes against my skin is electrifying yet frustrating. He comes so close to hitting where I want his fingers to seek, but he never makes contact, including teasing my nipples by skirting around the edges.

Visibly trembling, Marcus takes pity on me. "Cort, leave the room and shut the door behind you, please."

"Uh," Cort huffs, not in disappointment but hurt. "I get it. Okay."

Literally operating on blind faith alone, I'm led across the room to the sofa, and deposited on Marc's lap. I worry about him taking advantage, but all he does is maneuver me about until I'm sitting in his lap with my back to his chest and my feet trailing to the floor. The sofa cushions sink as Jamie joins us.

Back arching, a low moan pours out my throat as two sets of hands massage me in tandem, neither venturing to the sexual locations. I thought I'd been embarrassed before, but I was wrong. Scissoring my legs open and closed, I wiggle around in Marc's lap, involuntarily looking for some relief to the pressure. Rocking my ass back and forth, I can't shift my hips enough to grind my aching pussy against the bulge I'm trying to ride.

Marc's throaty laughter increases the more I writhe. "Do you feel beautiful yet, Regina? Or do you need more?"

"More," rolls out between my parted lips.

"More what?" Marcus breathes the taunt in my ear. "Hmm… tell us what you need."

Spreading my legs wide, "Please," I draw out, begging shamelessly.

"You're a wanton creature, aren't you, Regina?" Marcus purrs against the side of my face, and I strain to open my legs farther in silent invitation. "Spectacular. The more I get to know you, the more likely I'll never let you go."

"Ungh," I grunt when two slim fingertips slip right inside me, curling expertly, and then they begin to thrust. Not too fast, or too slow. Not too hard, or too soft. Just right. Coordinated, a thumb presses against my clit with every pass.

Jamie.

"Wow… she's so wet, I can hear it– gorgeous how it glistens on your fingers."

"Please." I'm not too proud to beg anymore. Foggy-headed, every single nerve in my body is throbbing for one thing, and I can't think of anything else. "God, please."

"Which one of us is God?" Marcus chuckles deviously. "I like the sounds of it. What are you begging for?"

"I feel empty." Neck arching, I roll my hips, fucking Jamie's hand with abandon.

"Cock? Do you need cock, Regina?" Marcus is toying with me, but I don't even care. "Jamie isn't ready to be inside you yet, not that he doesn't want to… if only you could see the wet spot growing on the front of his jeans, and his gorgeous bulge."

"Please," I beg again, voice breathy. "I ache everywhere."

Wet and scorching hot, Jamie's mouth sucks my nipple in. Just as last time, he practically unhinges his jaw, trying to fit as much of my tit in as possible. But then he bites, and the pressure building in my lower belly becomes too much to bear, but it won't release.

Voice taking on a serious edge, Marcus tries to get me to think straight. "As we agreed, after my misfortunate indiscretion, you have to ask me to fuck you this time, Regina. That was our agreement."

But I'm too far gone to think rationally. "I need a cock in me, and I don't care whose."

"I volunteer!" is shouted from the other side of the door.

"One day…" Marcus murmurs, followed by a few words that are too low for me to understand. "As you wish, Regina. But don't pull a Cortez and blame me later."

It's a struggle, because Jamie is now sucking and biting my tits while palming them greedily, all the while making ghastly noises from deep in his chest. The sound should frighten, but it has me beyond aroused, enough so that Marc's cock isn't going to hurt going in this time.

Jamie's fingers slip free of my body as Marc tips my hips backward. Fumbling, after accidently skimming along my clit with his cockhead, which elicited a sharp grunt from all three of us, Marcus manages to get his dick in me.

Groaning in relief, all I can do is take it. Marcus isn't brutal, either because Jamie is with us, or because he can't be with Jamie's mouth and hands attacking my tits– his odd sandpaper tongue is a blessing and a curse, because while I wonder what it would feel like curved around my clit, I *know* how amazing it feels rasping against my engorged nipples.

The combination of the way they both touch me, the sounds they're making just for me, and their scents, I truly feel beautiful and wanted, and I hold no shame over what I'm doing.

The orgasm slowly weaves its magic over me, and everything is just muted background noise. Marcus is surrounding me, inside me, but it's all about my pleasure. Jamie's wrist brushes against my calf as he takes himself in hand, spilling a hot wash of cum on the top of my foot.

Respecting me, Marcus actually pulls out at the last second, only to splatter my neither lips with his seed.

Curled up in Marc's lap, I drift in and out of a pleasure-induced coma, more satisfied than I had been in the past decade.

"Regina wants you to make love to her," Marcus murmurs so quietly I almost can't decipher the words. "We should just take the mask off her and let nature take its course."

Jamie kisses the inside of my thigh, eliciting a shiver to work its way along my spine.

Voice steady, like he's afraid to push Jamie, Marcus treads carefully. "I know you're terrified you'll lose her, so you'll take whatever you can get. But you'll have to tell her eventually."

A brush of hair tickles the inside of my leg, and the movement of Jamie's arm speaks to him using his fingers to communicate with Marcus.

"I'll give you a year, or I'll do it myself," Marcus warns. "Regina and I made a pact to tell each other the truth and keep no secrets. Don't do this to me, Jamie, because I know I'm more on borrowed time than you are. It would be very easy to fall in love with Regina, only to lose her because of you and your secrets."

Chapter Nineteen

Jamie: *You did very well during your first lesson. Very powerful and controlled. I was surprised you were able to keep your good humor while being held powerless. It speaks volumes to how much you trust Marcus, even after what transpired last week.*

–Thank you– I think. I know you say you're an observer, liking to watch. But have you actually participated in the lifestyle, Jamie? I only ask because you've allowed Marcus to take over your home, and your roommate doesn't seem to have anything to do with the lifestyle either.

Jamie: *Alex is scared of BDSM after dealing with Marcus. As you know, Marcus can become intense, and since I always refuse him, he'll try to harm me by hurting those closest to me. Alex has been a target, but not in the physical pain sense. More like Marcus confuses Alex sexually, and he has given in.*

–Marcus forced himself on Alex?

Jamie: *Oh, no. Ha-ha! I know this will be hard to believe after what Marcus pulled with you. But Alex has a unique personality where he wants to please everyone. Not in the sense of a submissive, because he doesn't have a submissive bone in his body. Alex gets off on giving pleasure, but he's also a very conservative soul. Marcus fed into this, even though I forbid it, and it left Alex reeling.*

–You forbid it? I just don't see Marcus listening to you.

Jamie: *Not listen, just respect my wishes is all. It's a 50/50 chance he does, and it's my job to protect Alex from my best friend. Marcus can be highly irresistible when he wants something, and some of us are stronger at denying the pull.*

–No shit!

Jamie: *You asked if I participate in the lifestyle. No, I don't participate. Voyeuristic, I simply enjoy observing and learning. Humans are at their baser form during BDSM.*

–How so? I mean, I guess I don't understand watching and not wanting to participate. But in a way I do, because I think I'd enjoy telling the participants what to do while sitting back and watching the results.

Jamie: *Ah– that's also Marc's predilection. Playing God. A long time ago, I enjoyed the power-exchange in the bedroom. Even then, it was about watching. I gave my power away, freed myself, solely so I could witness a woman bloom with confidence. It was the loveliest thing I've ever laid my eyes upon.*

–She sounds like a lucky woman, Jamie.

Jamie: *I doubt she sees our time together the same as I do. But I felt like the luckiest man alive, and I cherish every moment spent.*

–Memories are tricky. They can be rewritten subconsciously, our emotions and insecurities warping what truly happened until it suits how we feel about ourselves today. Obviously I have some hang-ups now, or else Marcus wouldn't have used Cortez to mortify me. But I keep trying to hang on to what I first felt in the past, versus how I feel about myself now, knowing it's entirely different. But I can't seem to remember that previous version of myself.

Jamie: *Very astute, Regina. This is true, which is why I journal everything, no matter how big or small, because it's all important. When I read my words back from years ago, it transports me to who I used to be, and I learn from it.*

–I wish I would have done that, but you can't describe a sound or a scent in written form, not enough to remember it always. One of my first ideas was a digital camera that captured a sound bite with the image. Not like a video, but just a two second candid moment with sound. Like the laugh as the camera flashed.

Jamie: *And you invented that, didn't you?*

—There's an app for that! <Laughing> Yes, I created a program long before 'apps' were a thing, and a huge digital camera company bought the rights. This was way before just about every cellphone took pics, causing digital cameras to become obsolete. But there is nothing I can do to trap scent for all eternity.

Jamie: *Scent is the killer, isn't it? At the time it's meaningless, until they are gone. Then you catch a whiff, and it literally kills a part of you.*

—Yes. Jesus, yes. I feel horrible admitting this, but I can't remember Grant's smell at all. Never could. I catch a floral note and remember my mother, or the scent of machine oil reminds me of my dad. But Grant… I draw a blank, and it makes me feel like I didn't love him enough if I can't remember.

Jamie: *Maybe you loved him too much?*

—I think I can't remember because it wouldn't be a comfort like it is with my parents. It would hurt too much. My daughter smells like strawberries, and in the future, even after she smells like a woman, strawberries will remind me of Ella as a little girl. My son, though… my son won't smell the same, will he? He won't smell like a little boy.

Jamie: *Guessing by the fact that he's twelve, he probably smells pretty ripe.*

—Jamie!

Jamie: *Adolescent boys STINK. Trust me— I was one once. Boy just pours out of our pores. RIPE.*

—I wouldn't care.

Jamie: *No mother would. But you'd probably drag his ass to the floor, yank his arm over his head, and cake the deodorant on him.*

–This sounds like personal experience…

Jamie: *My father did that to me on occasion. He laughed the entire time, sounding like a growling bear. Deep and resonating. So instead of mortified, like I was at the time, it's probably one of my favorite memories. Thank you for reminding me, Regina.*

–You're very welcome. Goodnight, Jamie.

Jamie: *Sweet dreams, Regina.*

Five years prior to the present...

Chapter Twenty

I have to say, my training hasn't been what I expected. Nowhere in my wildest imaginings did I think being encased in latex with only a hole opening around my mouth and nose would be in the repertoire.

The past year has been a test of my patience and will. It's also been totally unexpected and liberating. Three times a week, I visit the brownstone, where I've been worked over in every room, gaining experience on every piece of equipment and wielded every toy. I've excelled at some, and hideously failed at others. I've found what flips my switch and what turns my stomach.

I've come to the realization that Marcus is a twisted sonofabitch. If I suck at it, I do it until I perfect it, and then do it yet again. If I hate it, I do it until I can tolerate it, and a few dozen times more. If I love it, it becomes my reward. If it makes me physically ill or frightened, it's my punishment.

Kristal has kept Alex to herself, so I never find him home when I'm in residence, nor does she realize I know her supposed boyfriend and the owner of the brownstone are one in the same. However, tonight Kristal is bringing Alex to dinner at my house. I try not to think too much about who Alex truly is, because I fear it will tear my heart out and twist my guts. Which is the same reason I've never interrogated Marcus about that cryptic conversation he had with Jamie a year ago, knowing my patience will eventually pay off and all questions will be answered.

I've been running on pure faith, because this is the only part of my life that evolves the apathetic and the destructive sides of my being into Queen. Only when I'm Queen am I empowered and comfortable in my own skin.

What surprises me the most is how we interact. When I visit, we always eat together before my training. Jamie sits in the shadows, but he does join us. Still not allowing me to look at him, Jamie has continued to text me every single night, and I've slept better because of it.

After my training has concluded for the night, we either sit and talk, or Marcus and I take a walk if we want to discuss things of a sensitive nature. There hasn't been any new information to surface on the founders, so we pretty much brainstorm and sound like insane conspiracy theorists.

A few times, we've gone to the movies or taken turns driving the Spyder at breakneck speeds down the deserted highway at three a.m. It's not always just me and Marcus either— Cort is with us more than not.

Marcus may be a sonofabitch of a master, but he's a loving one. He demands total submission, and gets off on it when we disobey. I've learned the hard way not to say no, because his punishments never fit the crime.

Marcus was obviously lonely in a way that only the wealthy can feel— I know this because it's how I've lived for the past decade. The absence of trust is heart-wrenching, but a very necessary part to survival. These stolen moments of time, the comforting touches, the shoulders to cry on, and the laughs we share, are all a way to bond Marcus to us, and us to each other.

I'm not *in* love with Marcus Zeitler, but there is definitely a reverence that exists in me for him. Grant's ghost won't allow me to fall in love, but also is the knowledge that Marcus will never be a man who can place his partner above all others. Marcus loves us all equally. As the strongest, he sets himself apart. I can't fall in love with a man who is incapable of truly loving me back, not when there is a list of loyalties a mile long keeping a true partnership from forming. I respect Marc's ability to love and care for all of us, but it makes me feel like I'm a dime a dozen. Not unique in our master's eyes.

Replaceable with the next trainee, where I will become a forgotten member of his adoring ranks.

What Marcus has done is create a family he can trust, one that would lay down their lives for him. He's created a shelter in the storm for all of us. I love Marcus with my whole heart, and I'd protect him as I would my own children. I don't love him as you do a man, for he is no ordinary man. Marcus is a god walking among ordinary men… and right now I want to kick his perfect, marble-sculpted ass.

"Stop pelting me with pistachios, asswipe!" I've endured several minutes of Cort's ministrations.

Yes, I love Cort, too. But he pisses me off in equal measure.

The sensory deprivation room is the size of a pantry. Marc led Cort and me in here and said, *"Play nice, children. Don't kill each other. I'd be very angry if you did.*" Where he tapped the corner of his eye and frowned exaggeratedly. "*I may even cry a little.*"

Marcus left me in here for Cortez to terrorize. As if I could harm Cortez while I'm suctioned to the wall by a latex sheet. I can barely breathe, let alone exact my revenge on the asshat tossing nuts at me and laughing when they bounce.

"Why are we doing this again?" It's my fifth time attached to the wall with latex, and I've yet to learn the reason. All I ever come away with from this experience is a case of boredom and chafing from sweating in unbreathable latex.

"Hell if I know." Sightless, I can hear the shrug in Cort's voice. "You should've had Dexter train you. You would've been done months ago and already initiated. Maybe even running the dungeon, and I could have more time alone with Ezra." The animosity is thick in Cortez's voice. "Dexter is wordy and lacks on practical instruction, and he was more interested in hurting me, and I him, but I spent most of my training fighting with Dexter's mini-me."

Cortez isn't using a metaphor– he literally means he fought Dexter's sadist protégée every day for weeks. Like cage-match style, punch to the kidneys, and break your nose knock-down-drag-out fights.

Personally, I've never met the woman, but she scares the piss out of me. Cort also dislikes Dexter. I don't know what the three of them are pissed about, but Cort is the center of the issue. They seem to get along fine without him.

I haven't set foot into Restraint since the first night Ade sent me on my mission over a year ago. Marcus won't let me go until my initiation, stating he wants his trainees to be perfect examples of him. The PB has been training for well over two years.

"Is Jamie here with us?" I ask of the resident recluse who intrigues me to no end.

"Of course." Cortez snickers like a teenage boy. "A couple of those nuts were Jamie's."

"I know I've asked this in our text messages. But why won't you explain how you became mute? Were you born that way? Why won't you allow me to see you so we can communicate like you do with everyone else?" My voice sounds sad yet desperate, even to my latex-covered ears.

"Are you sure you want me to tell her?" Tone surprised, Cortez asks Jamie after a pause. "Very well, I will… Regina, Jamie is obviously mute, but only able to make a few sounds because his vocal cords were injured during his adult life. I'm sure he'd love to talk to you, but he can't, because he speaks with us through sign language."

"I get that, but it wouldn't be an issue if he'd let me see *him*. I'm sorry," mumbles from my lips, the only thing exposed besides the tip of my nose. "I don't want to pressure him."

"Jamie doesn't want your pity, and he says he's glad you finally know a bit more." Cort translates.

"How can I communicate with him in person if he won't let me see him?" I whine.

"Speak to him, Regina. Jamie's right here, for Christ's sake. He's not deaf. I talk to him and he speaks with his hands. We also text and email, or he writes on a tablet."

"I'd love to. I wish you'd let me see you, Jamie. I'd learn sign-language." I try to persuade him. "Why can't I see you?"

"I'll answer this one, even if Jamie gets pissed at me. He's very much a man, who isn't as pretty as he'd like to be. You're a gorgeous woman, Regina, and Jamie doesn't want to see the look on your face when you get sad by his appearance. A man wants to turn a woman on, not frighten her."

"I'm not *that* shallow," I protest.

"We know that. But Jamie's still a guy, and he'd rather you be his friend as you both are now, not out of a sense of pity once you see him. Or worse, refuse him once you do see him."

"Okay," I concede, but not without disappointment. "I'll talk to you in person, Jamie, and I hope my pressuring you won't make you stop texting me. I've come to need it to feel peace in order to fall asleep at night. You're the last person I talk to every night."

"Jamie said your words touched him." Cort's voice is filled with concern. "He just left, probably hiding out in the attic."

Worried, my voice warbles and tears fill my eyes. "I didn't mean to push Jamie away."

"He comes and goes at will. Sometimes I look and he's here, but a second later, he's gone. The next time I look, he's back. It's just how Jamie is."

"How bad is his face?" I want to know, but at the same time I don't.

"Jamie was attacked, both with a knife and poison– a type of acid, I think. The poison scarred part of Jamie's lip, his tongue, the inside of his mouth, his esophagus, and his vocal cords. There's also a slash through his left eyebrow, down to his nose, where it zigzags across his cheek to the corner of his lips. All on his left side.

Jamie's still a devastatingly handsome bastard, but he is entitled to his pride."

"That's so sad," I cry.

"Jamie doesn't want pity." Cortez sighs heavily, then abruptly changes the topic of conversation. "Five more minutes, then I can release you from the wall."

"Explain why I have to do this again."

"I have no idea." Cortez sighs again, sounding emotionally exhausted. "I've personally never encountered most of the shit Marcus makes you do, so I can't help you on the why of it. This is one of those times where I have nary a clue."

"That's such a comfort," I mutter sarcastically. Even muffled by the latex, I can hear better than usual with my vision removed. "Why is there so much traffic in the brownstone tonight? It's usually just us."

"Tonight's the PB's initiation… and you're not invited." Cort announces with a taunting edge to his voice.

"Thanks, assmunch. Since you're being so forthcoming for once, riddle me this. Why do you guys insist on calling the other trainee the PB, anyway?" I ask for the thousandth time, knowing I won't get an answer, but insanity is expecting a different result.

Tenacious, my name is Queen.

"PB stands for Pretty Boy." Cortez answers and I gasp in shock. "It's because he's so goddamn pretty it hurts to look at him."

"I can't believe you told me," I mutter in a mix of shock and awe. "What was the big deal about hiding that name, when it means absolutely nothing to me?

"Just following orders," Cortez replies.

"Oh, and you're so obedient." Laughing at the ridiculousness, Cort joins in with me.

"Your initiation will be coming up soon, because I can't figure out what else Marcus needs to teach you. At the initiation, you'll formally meet the Masters of Restraint one at a time. Pretty Boy will be one of the masters you'll meet, so the wait won't be long."

Alex will be introduced to me tonight. Pretty Boy soon. The year Marcus warned Jamie with has met its conclusion as of last month. I've been waiting for one of them to reveal Jamie to me. My patience is finally paying off.

"Cort, get out!" Marc's voice permeates my covering, and he sounds furious. Manic, on the edge of harming one of us because he's emotionally distraught. Par for the course with Marcus Zeitler, but only Cortez and I are used as his outlets.

I worry Cort's in trouble for telling me the secret of the nickname. I want to defend him for once, but I know better than to face Marcus down when one of his mercurial moods hit.

"Yes, Master," Cort says snidely, evidently annoyed to be singled out yet again as the issue when he's not.

"Don't fuck with me tonight, Cortez," Marcus snarls. "It's initiation night, and I can do whatever I want with anyone I want. Do you want me to do a repeat of yours? I can have Ezra kneel for you again."

"No, sir. I apologize for whatever happened that you're taking out on me." I've never heard that tone in Cort's voice before. Serious and scared when he's usually the court jester.

What exactly happens at initiation?

"Good boy," Marc coos to Cort. "Our newest master had a request on his initiation night, and I've been *forced* to reward him."

"That explains the mood," Cort murmurs softly, trying not to offend Marcus.

Mood stabilizing, Marcus requests like a polite gentleman. "Please join me in the bondage room while they have their privacy."

"Whoa… how the hell did you pull this off, Pretty Boy?" Cort sounds impressed by the man– full of pride. "You are one helluva manipulative ass kisser."

"Out!" Marcus orders again, but this time there is laughter lacing his voice. "Regina can't see you, but she can hear and talk. Don't talk to her, because if you do– no initiation. Understood?"

With bated breath, I wait for Pretty Boy to say yes and fail the test, but he proves he's smarter than that.

"So did Marcus make you do this ridiculous shit too?" Nervous, I begin babbling to Pretty Boy. "You wouldn't happen to know why, would you?" I can feel the intensity of his stare, similar to how Jamie is always eating me alive. "For the life of me, I just don't get the reason behind suctioning me to the wall with a sheet of latex."

Pretty Boy taps me on the lips with a fingertip– the universal gesture of *shut the fuck up*.

The part of me who is Queen doesn't appreciate that from Pretty Boy. "How about we play this as a game. I ask a question, and you tap me once for yes and twice for no." *Tap*. "So did Marcus make you do this ridiculous shit, too?"

Tap.

"Do you have any idea why? Not that you can answer me, which makes the question utterly ridiculous. But I guess I just want to know if I'm as daft as I feel."

Tap. Tap.

"Thank God, I'm not the only one who doesn't get it." I take a deep breath, the nervousness nearly suffocating me. "Are you scared about tonight?"

Tap.

"Me too. Well, for you tonight and for me when I finally get my initiation. Any clue about what Marcus was hinting at with Cortez? The threat about Ezra?"

Tap.

"Shit!" I hiss with feeling, excitement stirring in my belly. "You can't tell me! Remember to tell me in the future, because I'd love to know what scares the shit out of Cort."

A very deep sound rumbles from Pretty Boy's chest, and it's surprisingly comforting. He's struggling not to laugh, so I shut up. I doubt Pretty Boy wants to chat with me, since he can't respond. I'm seriously getting sick of this blind and deaf routine.

Without permission from me, inquisitive hands roam my body where the covering has shrink-wrapped against my curves. Pretty Boy makes a sound of appreciation in the back of his throat as he fondles my breasts.

I'm actually surprised Marcus is allowing this. He has a hands-off policy in effect. Marcus is the only one allowed to touch me sexually, and usually it's as an outlet for his moods. Once in awhile, it's an intimate experience. I miss Jamie joining us during those times– he always runs off the instant Marcus gets the '*I'm going to fuck your brains out*' look in his eye.

This past year has been filled with hurricane-force sexual tension. I haven't been rewarded very often, and Cort can't behave long enough to be rewarded. But when Marcus gets a wild hair up his ass, one of us gets fucked: Cort in the skull and me in the pussy. I'm shoved from the room and locked out while Marcus takes Cortez, and he will never allow me to switch it up and suck him off instead.

No foreplay.

Ever.

It would be quick to assume Pretty Boy must play by the rules, or else Marcus would've never allowed him to touch me so intimately.

The need to bitch and complain about boundaries is eclipsed by the fact that I haven't been touched in nearly three months. My mouth always spews thoughts my mind tells it to not say, and then I'm punished. I've been a bad girl for almost three months, and Marcus has kept his cool around me. No doubt he's using Cortez as an outlet when no one is watching.

Insanity, I never thought I'd be jealous of an act of punishment and emotional torture.

My eyelids slip shut behind the security of my covering as Pretty Boy caresses me. It feels amazing to be touched through the latex– smooth and nerve tingling. My senses are heightened, and the lightest of touches reverberates throughout my entire body.

I get it– this exercise is two-fold. One, the sensual aspect of being touched with the latex amplifying the experience. Two, so I won't freak when I'm fondled at Restraint. There will be times when my body won't belong to me, and I'll have to flip a switch in my brain to survive it.

Every square inch of my body that Pretty Boy has access to, his nimble fingers explore. He's particularly fond of the split between my thighs, rubbing a fingertip between my lips, concentrating on my over-stimulated clit. I worry that Pretty Boy will somehow try to take advantage, but then I realize he's merely exploring, not molesting for sexual gratification.

All of the sudden, Pretty Boy leans against me and embraces me in the only way he can– he covers me with his body and leans all of his weight against me. Exactly the same height, we touch at the forehead, nose, chin, chest, hips and thighs. His rigid arousal presses eagerly into my mound and belly, rubbing in a circle slightly. His sweet breath flows into my mouth as he pants rapidly like he's running a marathon.

Yet Pretty Boy holds himself back from connecting our lips. Very controlled, he has earned his right to be a Master of Restraint.

Asking more out of curiosity than need, "Aren't you allowed to kiss me?"

Pretty Boy makes a noise of desperation from deep inside his chest in answer.

"Not yet, or never?" The same sound of frustration erupts. "Oh, sorry. The questions have to be one at a time. Not yet?"

Pretty Boy taps the tip of his nose against mine once for yes.

"Oh, do you want to?" I receive the growl of frustration again. It must be a sound he makes often– he's perfected it. His fingers grip my hips hard enough to bruise, and he presses against me so firmly that I wonder if he's trying to join his body to mine, or push right through me.

"That's enough," Marc issues softly, treading lightly. "I know you're frustrated right now. You'll get your chance to bare all of your grievances and emotions to Regina at her initiation."

Pretty Boy growls again, but it takes on an edge of aggression.

"I get it– you want to tear my goddamn head off." Marcus doesn't sound angry, only sad, or maybe distraught. "See how you feel right now? Betrayed? That's why I've kept you separated for the past year, even if you hate me now that you've learned the truth. Regina didn't know you were here, and you didn't know she was here– so it was for the best until both of you were ready. Kristal's being properly punished for telling you. So be thankful that I've offered you this boon, because Regina doesn't have the relief."

"What are you talking about?" I demand. "And you can't punish Kristal for anything. She doesn't belong to you– Kristal's ours."

My words affect Pretty Boy. A soft sob is released, causing Marcus to deliver words of comfort underneath his breath. I hear a rhythmic patting, and I know Marcus is hugging his protégé.

"Cortez will take you to Restraint. He's waiting in the foyer, and I'll be there shortly."

"What's going on, Marcus?" I demand. "You said no secrets between us."

"Except for the major secret you and I have been dancing around for over a year?" Voice strained, Marcus doesn't sound like any version of himself I've ever met. "Did you enjoy Pretty Boy's touch?"

"Why do you sound so possessive?" I comment when I know I shouldn't. "What the fuck is going on?"

"Possessive?" Marc's laughter holds no amusement, only irony. "I feel like I'm always at war with those who came before me. Who gets possession of Regina Regal?"

"No one owns me," I snarl. Fed up, I struggle behind the sheet of latex, trying to remove myself from the wall, but I can barely twitch a muscle.

"I was curious to see Pretty Boy's reaction to you. It was a pleasant surprise, but not uncommon that he'd identify with you in such a way. Sexuality develops when you're on the cusp of maturity. It will help him during his initiation, because he looks as crazed as a wild bull. All that anger, sadness, and hunger will be interesting when he unleashes it on the other masters."

"I don't know what you're talking about." Frustrated, my voice cracks. "You get that, right?"

"I know, Regina. Soon all will be revealed. I just hope you won't hate me, which is why this has dragged on for as long as it has." Rough, Marcus squeezes my flesh, and I groan in response like a shameless whore addicted to his validation.

"I see you've figured out the purpose of this exercise. I waited for Cort to figure it out– I thought for sure he'd cop a feel and play with you. Here I anticipated his misbehavior, and he ruined the exercise by behaving." Marcus mocks, "So disappointing."

Marcus bites my breast ruthlessly, and a strangled sound emits from my throat. I hate how this man affects me, how I go straight to lust with a single touch.

"I see Pretty Boy is already rubbing off on you– you're already mimicking him." Teasing, Marcus growls the same sound a few times.

Distracted by his vicious playfulness, I cry out in ecstasy when Marcus bites a new location– one his mouth has never been near. Attacking my cunny with his tongue and teeth, I can't feel anything from the licks except the cooling of the latex and a slight vibration. On the other hand, Marc's bites sizzle to my core. Feasting on me, Marcus has me to the edge of writhing, which is frustrating since I cannot move an inch.

Just before I fall over the precipice into oblivion, Marcus yanks me from the wall, flips me around, and presses my hands to the chair rail, making sure my nails dig in. While I'm acclimating to the position change, he impales me with his cock.

All I can do is hang onto the chair rail, fingernails scoring the wood, as Marcus fucks me from behind like a rabid animal.

Growling, Marcus marks my back, shoulders, and neck with his teeth. He wraps my hair around his fist and anchors me. The echo of pounds, moans, and growls is loud to my uncovered ears.

Marcus is always rough, finding softness the most difficult part of intimacy, but he's never like this. Feral.

'I want you to get off with me. Every time.' is the first promise Marcus breaks. No doubt it's only the first of many to come, and the first I've come to realize has passed.

"Go home– Alex is waiting to reveal himself." Marcus hisses while emptying his body into mine for the first time in over a year.

With rough movements, Marcus disengages, and then flees the room before I can breathe again, let alone rally against him.

I'm left reeling in the aftermath of Marc's onslaught. I heard a note in his voice I never thought I'd hear directed at me. Every other time I've heard the tone it was *against* me because of Grant.

Jealousy.

Tears prickle my eyes as I come to the realization that Marcus has found yet another person he's possessive over, while simultaneously being jealous because he can't have them. Kristal's fictitious boyfriend, the master of this house.

Jamie warned me that Marcus was not straight, nor bi, nor gay, because Marcus doesn't know what the hell he is.

Marcus is lusting after Alex while fucking me.

When will I ever be enough?

Chapter Twenty-One

With very limited resources, I tried to freshen up before I left the brownstone, but it was to no avail. I couldn't look any more jaded unless I tattooed whore across my forehead. I'm wearing a cotton dress that scoops low in the back, almost to the crack of my ass. Marc bought it for me and he commanded that I wear it this evening. I will admit I look like a high-class hooker in the dress, especially since I can't wear a bra.

What makes me look like a wadded up tissue/cum receptacle are the marks all over my body. Purposefully, Marcus didn't use control or finesse. I have at least twenty marks running up my back and neck and none of them are covered by the dress or my hair. Marcus ruined my hair by fisting it, so I had to twist it up or look like a fucking mental patient.

My neck looks like one of the *Lost Boys* ravished me. It's like Marcus knew where the dress wouldn't cover and bit me on purpose.

Tonight I finally meet the man Kristal's in love with– Alex. I have no idea what Kristal and Alex are actually up to, but they made us wait a year, saying he was a nice gentleman and we would corrupt him. I laughed in Kristal's face– she'd be the one doing the corrupting. So here I am looking like I was fucked by an angry tornado as I enter my home to meet the virtuous Alex.

Spinning her tale into a web of lies, everything Kristal says or does contradicts itself, to the point I feel she's purposefully fucking with me. She paints poor Alex as an idiot who believes he and Kris are exclusive. According to Kris, Alex is so deeply in love with her, he's been bringing up marriage. In his uncorrupted glory, Alex is monogamous, while Kris feeds her addiction several times a night by hosting orgies in the guesthouse.

Now I just treat Kristal how I would treat an addict. I humor her and pretend to accept her delusions with Alex. I've often wondered if she's started to believe her own lies. I accept Kristal as she is, as I do everyone else in my life. I'm not normal, so I don't expect anyone else to be. But I don't like being dicked with, strung along, and lied to, especially when the foundation of our friendship was supposed to be mutual respect.

Dressed to the nines, "What the fuck happened to you?" Kristal rushes up to me, eyes held wide in awe. "Are you okay?"

Yeah, I've never came home from the brownstone looking like a train wreck. Kristal's concern for me is a relief, because that must mean Alex isn't here yet.

"What happened to me is a jealous Marcus on his way to the Pretty Boy's initiation. Probably having something to do with you telling Pretty Boy I was training too, but that wasn't explained as Marcus took his frustrations out on my hide."

Hand paused mid-air to cover her mouth, Kristal has the audacity to look horrified.

"Hell if I know what Marcus is jealous about, but he took it out on me anyway. I'm in pain because he didn't appreciate feeling the emotion. He said something about your boyfriend, Alex. I think your master is either a fan of yours or Alex."

Shoring up my emotions, I try not to allow Kristal to hear my sadness and disappointment. I cried the whole way home in a mix of betrayal and humiliation. I'm not in love with Marcus. I have no territorial feelings for him, because I know he's *Master* and special rules apply. But just once I'd like to be the object of someone's affections, at least a small taste.

Annoyed that I have to playact that I have no idea who Alex is and that Kristal isn't betraying me with every lying breath she takes, I have bigger priorities. "Let me shower and cover up this disaster." I point to my neck and back. "I don't want to embarrass you, because I know how important this meeting is for you."

"Too late for that, Regina." Kristal whispers in embarrassment while stepping to the side.

Alex and I lock eyes in shock, and I sway when the connection is met. His face glows with delight and mine pales in shame.

My world crumbles at my feet. I don't know if I want to bawl, scream, beg, die, or faint. I do know I want to dig a hole and bury myself in it– maybe light myself on fire with gasoline, because that has to hurt less than this betrayal feels.

Turquoise gaze locked on my green, several realizations hit me all at once, nearly taking me to my knees.

One: Marcus wasn't jealous because of Alex or Kristal. He was marking his territory, and I'm going to kill him the next time I see him.

No one owns Queen.

Two: Marcus knew– he knew for a whole fucking year and selfishly kept it to himself. Hell, Marcus has known for almost fourteen years, which is where his territorialism and fear sprung from.

Three: Marc's betrayal doesn't cut as deeply as Kristal's. There is a sister-code which should be upheld at all times. I don't give a fuck what Kristal is doing with Dominion's founders, but this…

Four: Alex from Transcend, the Alex who owns the brownstone which was to be my home with Grant… Alex who has been conspiring with Kristal, and most likely fucking her too… He avoided me, didn't want to see me, and he knew where I was all of this time, and didn't cross the foyer to at least say fucking *HI!*

Alex didn't want to see me, and that almost hurts the worst.

Five: I made Grant promise to never tell me what happened, and not only did he keep that promise, he took care of him– for me.

I have never loved Grant more, nor hated everyone else as much as I do this very instant.

"Sweetheart?" My nickname is a caress from his lips, and I sway from the sound after being devoid of it for my entire adult life. I never thought I'd hear his voice again, so the pleasure's compounded by the fact that he used my nickname.

"Sonofabitch." I whimper underneath my breath, heart breaking from a billion little betrayals. "Roman," rolls from my lips while I close my eyes in shame, because he's seeing me for the whore that I am.

Roman Alexander allowed me to get into the Lincoln Town Car with Albert because if I had stayed, I would have had to whore myself out to survive. Every day since, I've been nothing but a whore.

"You two know each other?" Kristal asks, hurt. The consummate actress can't hide the edge to her voice that is noticeable after knowing her all these years.

"I can't have you see me like this, Roman." Mortified, I cover my face with my palms. "I'm going to go crawl into a hole and die now."

The door opens behind me, and Ade and Fate enter, lightly chatting about how excited Ella was to go on an overnight playdate. Yet another trick Ade thinks me too stupid to realize, because the playdate is with Katie's daughters and my son. Ade looked me in the eye, lied, and then took my daughter to Misery Castle to see the Whittenhowers, and it wasn't the first time.

Past and present crashing, I bolt like a startled animal, making a run for my bedroom, but a strong arm snags me around the waist before I even get to the neck of the hallway.

"Shh… It's okay." Roman's promise is a lie. Nothing has *ever* been okay. "Calm down, sweetheart. I've got you."

Dropping to my knees, my sobs echo down the hallway. Roman collapses with me, trying to hold me as I attempt to crawl away. "Let it out, Reggie." Roman murmurs more pretty lies while rocking me back and forth. "I've got you. You're going to be just fine."

"What's going on?" Kristal whisper-shouts in outrage.

Combusting, I let it pour out. "What could possibly be my malfunction, Kristal? Every fucking one of you has been lying to me every goddamn day for years. YEARS!"

Fate and Ade watch the scene play out with horror-struck eyes. "Oh, no," Fate cries for me, always compassionate and empathetic. "No, Kris. How could you do this to Regina? Roman Alexander is your boyfriend?" She gazes at me with pity, and the sight makes me want to curl up and die.

"Oh, Kristal, how could you? There's no way you didn't know." Ade's voice pitches high. Irate, she's never one to hold her tongue. "No fucking way homeboy didn't know. No fucking way. Both of you assholes should get out of Regina's house. Now."

Emotions warring, in this moment, I'd do anything to keep Roman in my house, even if it means playing pretend by ignoring the harsh reality battering against my psyche.

"I have to shower now," I murmur numbly, coming to my knees. "Fate, you can start dinner without me– I've lost my appetite." Taking a cleansing breath, I say the ultimate truth, no matter how badly it may hurt. "No worries, Kristal. You didn't break the sister-code, because Roman was never mine."

Words belying my actions, I run my hands through Roman's inky strands of silk. His hair is as soft as I remembered– softer. He still wears it swinging just under his chiseled jawline.

In wonder, I pull Roman's hair back away from his forehead, and just stare into the face I never thought I'd see outside of my dreams. I look into the blue-green pools of his eyes and smile.

Roman Alexander is alive, healthy, and happy. It doesn't matter that he avoided me for the past year, or that he's purposefully partnering with Kristal for some reason, because he is in my life again. After so much death, I tell myself this isn't about my emotions. A higher power answered my call and spared Roman's life, and that is all that matters. I have my friend back, if he'll have me.

I just can't have Roman seeing me as I am. It kills me to know that he will see me as a whore, has heard the things I've said and done inside his house. I'm utterly mortified.

Kissing Roman's forehead, I allow my lips to linger as I inhale his intoxicating scent– clean, fresh, and exactly as I remembered.

Roman.

Lips still forming a kiss, I breathe, "I've missed you so fucking much," against Roman's forehead, and then I pull away.

In a march as old as time, I suffer through the walk of shame to my bedroom. After grabbing a pillow from my bed, I crank the water in my shower to the gates of Hell scalding. I scream my throat raw into my pillow, muffling the noise, and allowing the flow of the shower to eclipse the mourning sound that escapes around its edges.

Realizing I'm not to blame– I never have been –I stop punishing myself for other's actions. My scream shuts off before it turns to laryngitis. Instead, I attack the two who are partially to blame.

It takes longer than usual to text Jamie, because my fingers won't stop shaking. If it wasn't for autocorrect, Lord knows what my texts would actually say.

–*Did you know?* I figure that even though I'm being ambiguous, if Jamie knows, he'll understand the hidden meaning of my words.

Jamie: *Yes.*

Is this what Marcus was going to tell me if Jamie didn't? Jamie was given a year to tell me Roman Alexander was the owner of the brownstone? I actually contemplate opening Pandora's Box by asking Jamie outright.

Jamie: *Regina? Are you okay? I left the house earlier, but Cortez gave me a rundown on what happened.*

–*No.*

Jamie: *Talk to me.*

–No.

Jamie: *I understand.*

–I don't think you do.

Jamie: *I do.*

–I'll text you at bedtime. I've got a lot of shit to handle right now.

Jamie: *Thank God!*

I'm not so nice to my next victim. I quickly queue up Marc's number, knowing he's at Restraint for Pretty Boy's initiation. Marcus doesn't like texting with me, saying it's because he wants to hear the emotion in my voice as we speak. Yet I've often wondered if he didn't want a digital footprint of the content of our conversations.

Still, even after being betrayed, I follow Marc's directive.

With the patience of a saint, I wait while the phone rings, then goes to voice mail, and then I give Marcus the emotions he seeks.

"Fuck you, Marcus! Fuck. You." I shout into my cellphone so loudly the words reverberate in my eardrums. No doubt Marcus will get the message loud and clear when the emotion in my voice renders him deaf.

I quickly wash and douche, wondering if it's possible to give a man a vasectomy with my teeth without leaving long-lasting harm. Marcus broke three promises tonight. He fucked me for no other reason than to dominate me, with no thought to what I needed, then he came inside me. But all that pales in comparison to keeping Roman a secret.

But Roman Alexander is a big boy, and he could have easily come to me.

Curiosity overwhelming my embarrassment, I want to look at Roman, listen to his voice, and watch him. I need to see how he's aged. I haven't spoken to him in fourteen years, and I haven't looked at him in nearly twelve.

It hurts to think of how Grant helped me grieve the absence of Roman the night I thought I'd lost him to a bullet, and now Roman is the one alive and Grant is dead.

I find everyone chatting on the patio around the pool. A Queen does not sulk, so I pull my shoulders back and raise my head high and join them.

"Hey." I sit next to Ade and across from the phony lovers. "I feel so much better after my shower."

"Good, you're back." Ade bumps my shoulder with her cheek, lingering longer than necessary. "I'm sorry, but I have to run. There's something happening tonight and I have to be there."

"Ade what could possibly be more important than this?" I ask of Ade's selfishness, but I'm not at all surprised. Over the past few months, I realize the life I've built is just a series of smoke and mirrors. I wish it were possible to go back to when I was thirteen and I hadn't met a single person in my life today. It was just my parents, long before Hillbrook, accidents, cancer, and a long string of death and betrayal.

But then there would have been no Grant, or Whitt, or Niel and Ella.

"Daddy's throwing Whitt a party tonight." Ade looks pointedly at me, and I understand the gravity instantly. Whitt has never had a party in his honor. Daniel is conservative when it comes to affection and recognition. He doesn't even realize that skipping birthdays is an issue.

"Why? Whitt's nineteen." I never ask of Whitt, but something in Adelaide's demeanor raises alarms.

Whitt being recognized as a Whittenhower is highly unusual.

"I have to hurry." Ade stands to leave, yet still won't look me in the eye. "The party starts soon."

"Ade, why so late? Those events usually start at seven, not almost midnight."

"Goodnight." Ade ignores my tenacity because she's more bullheaded than I am. "It's nice to finally meet you in person, Roman– or Alex. Which do you prefer?"

"You can call me Roman." He shifts in his chair, looking surprisingly relaxed around a woman who should make him beyond intimidated. "I use Alex at Transcend so no one associates me with who I used to be."

"Roman is a very nice name, but I do understand the distinction. Goodnight," Ade says in parting, then flees before I can stop her.

Kristal flashes me a look of pity, and it kills me– pity because Ade is keeping secrets about Whitt, or pity that she's fucking me over with Roman?

All I feel is hollow emptiness as I realize Adelaide is with both my son and daughter tonight, celebrating a moment in Whitt's life, and I was not a part of it. They are *my* family. Mine.

In my heart of hearts, I know I will never marry and I'm done having kids. I wasn't enough for Grant, and I know I'll never be enough for Marcus, and I never wanted Roman like that in the first place.

I at least want my friend back.

Eyes unable to leave his face, I search for the truth etched across Roman's features. "Wow, I never would've guessed you'd be sitting on my patio right now. I'm glad."

"I know, who would have thought that Kristal donating all that money would bring me back to you someday." Roman smiles at me, and then turns infatuated eyes Kristal's way.

Oh, so that's the game we're going to play?

I'm biting back laughter just as Fate interrupts Roman. "Kristal didn't donate the money to Transcend. Regina did." Infused with betrayal, Fate doesn't realize Kristal, Roman, and I are playing some fucked up game where there are no rules.

Roman gazes back and forth between the three of us, genuinely looking confused, but I don't buy the act.

"Oh, I'm sorry if you thought it was me." Kristal laughs off getting caught in the act. "Regina is Empowerment."

"Oh," Roman looks like he's seeing Kris for the first time, and that confuses me more.

"Kris, will you help me pick up the mess in the kitchen?" Fate stands and holds her hand out to Kristal. "Those who eat it clean it up, that's the rules. I cooked it, Roman is our guest, and Regina didn't eat, so by elimination…"

Girl power is alive and well with Fate Simpson– I'll never forget this moment.

"Sure," Kris mutters snidely as she takes Fate's hand and allows herself to be led back into the house and the kitchen beyond.

Roman and I just stare at each other for several long moments, eyes tracking over each other's features. It's a shock to be in his presence, but it's time I got some goddamn answers.

"Would you like to take a walk with me?" Kristal's jealous gaze is burning a hole into my back from the window over the kitchen sink. "The tension from the kitchen is stifling."

"Yeah, I would." Roman grins at me, tucking his hair behind his ear in a gesture that epitomizes him, reminding me of a time long ago in a different place– another lifetime.

As we walk, we're quiet for a few minutes, and it reminds me of how it was in Grant's presence. But then I remember Alex and Jamie are roommates, and silence must abound when living with a mute.

Turning out of the neighborhood, being drawn closer to the wall surrounding the Gates, I go into interrogation-mode, not allowing myself to show my own hand first. "I want your story, Roman."

It's fall, but the air's warm and moist. We're walking shoulder-to-shoulder, hands grazing once in a while as we swing our arms. It's companionable, like we haven't spent the past decade and a half apart. We'd shared a brief kiss, but he will always be my friend, my protector when I couldn't protect myself, so I'll forgive Roman if he cuts the shit.

"There isn't a real big story to tell." Roman finally answers at length, eyes gazing at the wall as it comes into view. "I was shot by a buyer who wanted my stock. It took months to recover, and then I had to go to a rehab hospital. The blood loss affected the nerves in my right shoulder, leaving a few fingers numb. For a while I couldn't even grasp anything– trying to write sucked."

Roman chuckles at some memory remembered, and then continues on. "On one of my return visits, I met Jamie during his rehab– for his face and voice and whatnot –and we became fast friends."

"Wait– you said Jamie." I cut into Roman's story, because Marcus said Grant had Alex shoved up his ass, which is how '*Alex*' ended up with my house. I hold my breath, hoping I'm wrong, while simultaneously hoping Roman will tell the truth.

I want my friend back, but not if he's a goddamn liar like Kristal.

"Yeah, my Jamie is your Jamie– the brownstone is my house." Roman actually admits it, and it's a shot to my heart.

Flipping around, something vital fractures inside of me. "Just cut the shit and be real with me, Okay? I'm still the Regina you used to know, only older. I may ignore the signs with everyone else, but never you."

"Okay." Roman's voice breaks, causing his stride to falter.

"Good, then. Explain how you knew Grant," I demand. "And don't say it was through me. How did you end up with my house? How?"

Stopping in the middle of the sidewalk, we both forget we're taking a walk. "Shit!" Roman hisses with feeling. "Marc told you, didn't he? He was always so goddamn jealous of me around Grant, and it was Grant for Christ's sake– the man only had eyes for you."

Enraged, my palms land against Roman's firm chest, propelling him back several feet down the sidewalk. "Explain," is gritted out between my clenched teeth. "Explain that shit to me, Roman. How the hell were you buddies with the father of my children, and hanging out with Marcus Zeitler? Explain. Now."

"Okay. Okay." Roman puts his hands up, palms facing out, showing me he surrenders. "Grant kept in touch with me after you went with him. Okay? We talked a few times a month, just the basics. But after I got shot, he and I formed a type of partnership."

"Admit it," I demand. "You were Grant's enforcer– that's the only explanation of how you ended up with the very house Grant died in."

"What?" Roman squawks, taking a step back. Russet face paling, he looks on the verge of sickness. "Don't ever use that word again, Regina," he warns so quietly I can barely hear him. "Never again. Do you understand me? I don't know where you heard it, but shut the fuck up."

Well, that pretty much answers that question, doesn't it?

"I guess I shouldn't ask if Kristal is your partner in crime," I whisper-shout in Roman's direction. "Because she sure as fuck isn't girlfriend material. Jamie has said countless times how you're a one-woman kind of man, and Kristal is *not* your type."

Lashing out quickly, Roman's fingers bracelet my arm, tugging me to his chest. Facing off, we glare each other down. "Unless you have a death wish, shut the fuck up," Roman snarls while his eyes flick about, lighting on the wall near our right. Yanking me down the street, away from Crestview, Roman's fingers shake against my arm.

"Grant was my friend, Regina," Roman says at an audible level. "Since you were my friend, and he was the father of your children, he befriended me, and that's all anyone ever needs to know on that subject. Including why I own the brownstone." Pinning me with his furious gaze, he adds, "Especially *you*. Keep your goddamn nose out of shit Grant wanted to protect you from. Got it?"

"Yeah, your reactions tell me more than your words, Roman."

"You're as stubborn as ever, Reggie." Roman drops my arm like I've burnt him. "As for Kristal. She is a highly intelligent, beautiful woman, who is as seductive as they come."

"No shit– I never said she wasn't." Chin hitching high, I'm all but challenging Roman to an actual fight. I have so much aggression boiling in my blood, and only the truth will dissipate it.

"I work at Transcend, Reg. Don't ever talk down about someone's past." Roman glares at me. "I have a past. You have a past. No one is perfect. We all make mistakes."

"I'm not slut-shaming Kristal," I defend myself. "She can fuck whomever she wants as long as she's not hurting anyone. But there is a difference, Roman. She's still repeating those mistakes, and it's in the present, as in last night and after you leave tonight. I respect you, and I want you to respect yourself. Since you're trying to distract me from the word I'm not allowed to say, I hope to God Kristal truly isn't your girlfriend, because I know for a fact she's a Whittenhower word-I-can't-say."

"Kristal *is* my girlfriend, Regina," Roman bites out. "And no comment on that other shit. I told you to drop it. You don't understand, and Grant didn't want you to understand, okay?"

"Consider it dropped– for now," I tack on. I reach over to tug Roman's arm to get him walking again. "This isn't the reunion I envisioned, I'll admit, and I'll refrain from asking where your self-respect went if you truly are Kristal's boyfriend."

"Refrain, you say?" Roman drawls out. "Seems like you managed to make a statement by saying you wouldn't. Which means I won't make the same statement about you, even as I make it."

"I deserve that, I guess." Taking a deep breath, I get to the heart of the matter. It's the one thing that's making me lash out and perpetually be on the verge of tears. "Why didn't you come to me in the past year? You were behind a shut door, and never once came to me, even if it was a simple hi."

Roman reaches out to graze his fingertips down the back of my hand in a gesture of comfort. "Regina, why do you think?" Roman replies, voice tight with emotion.

"I don't know why you wouldn't," I murmur in shock. "I don't want to think of why, because it would hurt too much– truth be told, it's all I've thought about since I laid eyes on you, Roman."

Hearing the tears in my voice causes Roman to hold my hand, squeezing every second or so. "It's not like that, Regina. A long time ago, you made Grant make a promise, and he's kept it and I kept it for him. I understood why you'd ask that of him, after all the hurt and pain from losing your folks, then Grant."

"In the moment, I was so lost to grief over seeing you lying in that hospital bed, I couldn't handle it. Now I wish I hadn't forced Grant to make that promise."

"It is what it is, Reg. I did try to see you the first night you came into the brownstone. I stayed in the doorway as Marcus gripped your face so you couldn't turn around and see me or Jamie. You know Marc's rule is law, even inside my own house, and I was keeping your wishes."

Mortification punches me in the gut. "How much have you seen?" I can handle Marcus, Jamie, and Cortez, but not Roman seeing me in that manner.

"Honestly, nothing." Roman tries to put me at ease. "I wasn't allowed in the house when you visited. Your training schedule mirrored my work schedule at Transcend– by design, I'm sure. I wanted to see you, but knowing you were okay was enough for me," he murmurs softly. After a gentle squeeze, he drops my hand.

"I only made Grant promise not to tell me if you lived or died, because if you had died, it would have killed me, and if you had lived, I would've been tempted to spend time with you. I've missed you every day, and a day hasn't pass that you weren't on my mind." The hollow ache in my voice surprises me and Roman.

"Mine, too. But I was the lucky one, because I could see you coming and going from Transcend, and I could ask about you. I'm sorry you didn't have the same comfort, but we were abiding by *your* wishes, Regina."

"Okay." I brush off the past, because once it's over, you can do nothing but move on from it. Whether I'm buying a load of shit or not, I feel Roman is being honest with me for the most part. "Tell me your story. How'd you end up at Transcend?"

"Jamie and I, he couldn't talk and was healing, while I was struggling to relearn how to use my right hand. What a pair we made." Roman's laughter holds a wealth of affection and respect.

"At first, Jamie helped me get into Transcend as a mentor and motivational speaker against street violence. Then I used the money I earned to go to school to become a substance abuse counselor and life coach. Now I help the kids who were like us, by finding them scholarships and showing them there are outlets for their creativity and a true future. As for the adults, I help them get back on a healthy path. I never in a million years would have guessed this was where I'd end up, but it's where I was always meant to be– making a difference in many lives to make up for all those I destroyed by selling them drugs. I'm dang good at it, too. It's my actual calling."

Hearing the passion in Roman's voice fills my soul with happiness and contentment. I want Roman to have a fulfilling, happy life. While listening as he continues to speak of the kids at Transcend, how much he loves working there, and how great his coworkers are, his voice is full of hope.

As Roman tells me how he never thought he deserved a normal life, it resonates within me, because I still feel that way to this day, even if it's the only thing I want most out of life.

Roman then explains how he met Kristal at Transcend– he says for real, bypassing over the word enforcer, but it's underlying. Meanwhile, Roman doesn't say *when* he actually met Kristal. For all I know, Grant introduced them, seeing as how Transcend is Priscilla's baby. As he describes how much fun they have together, I truly believe Kristal is Roman's girlfriend. Maybe not in the serious way she made it sound, but he's only fucking her, even if she's fucking everybody else.

Roman's voice charges with adoration as he speaks of Jamie, going as far as to say Jamie saved his life. Roman explains how Jamie inspired him and helped him find his true worth.

I want to know that side of Jamie, when all he offers me are text messages filled with platitudes. Feeling like Marcus over Grant, I'm suddenly jealous of Roman out of nowhere, because he gets to see a private side of someone I've grown to love, which has me reevaluating the dynamic between Marcus and me. Neither one of us allows anyone else in, including the other, even as we call each other partner, which is why Marc hate-fucked me earlier this evening.

Refusing to go in the direction my mind is traveling, I can't help the huge grin that spreads across my face as we walk and I listen to Roman talk. The boy who was holding up the corner of my building, swapping drugs for cash, and giving me the lifelong lesson of not selling my body for money, actually has his shit together.

While I may have too much money and a never-ending supply of work, my actual life is *not* in working order. I just keep trading in one type of high for another to chase the pain, guilt, and grief away. I don't know how to find that life my dad promised my mom and me, but I know my children and I deserve it. Money can't buy that type of simple happiness.

"I really didn't know you were Empowerment, sweetheart, but I should have guessed. Sixty-three of my kids are on scholarships because of the money you donated, just this year alone. They speak of you as a saint down at the program."

Roman sounds awed of my success, and it reminds me of the tone my mom would take on when she spoke of the elite. It was as if they weren't normal men walking the streets, but Gods among men. Now Roman speaks of me this way, and I don't understand the weird emotions the tone elicits. If anyone is more than human, it's the folks at Transcend making a real difference in the world.

"I'm so glad you got out of there." My voice cracks with emotion, and I don't even bother hiding it.

"I know you don't quite believe me, but after Grant's death, I tried to forget about you because it hurt too much. I knew Marcus was keeping tabs on you, and I allowed myself to just live life."

"That's understandable, Roman, and I don't begrudge you that for one second."

"Good." Roman reaches over to squeeze my hand. "Back when I knew you, you were friends with Ade and Fate, and the name Kris was never tossed about. So when Kristal described your lives to me, she called you Regina. Since it's a popular name, I never thought it was you. Obviously since I'm not a moron, I figured it out pretty quickly. But I had to get that out in the open, not wanting you to think I was doing your best friend to spite you."

"Kristal knew who you were, though," I murmur softly. "It's the sister-code. We all have a list of names, and yours is on mine. Has been since I met you. I've known Kristal since she was fifteen, and that's how long she's known who's on the list."

"Well, that makes me feel like shit." Roman sighs. "Like I'm Kristal's spite-fuck because she's jealous of you."

"Sounds pretty accurate, but it also makes me sound like a narcissist. So I'll let you figure out your relationship to the girl who has been in my household her entire adult life."

"Regina, are you alright?" The corners of Roman's eyes wrinkle with concern. "That was the first thing I wanted to ask you, and I didn't get to do it."

It makes me sad that I've missed so much time with Roman. Last time I saw him, he was twenty. Now he's inching closer to his mid-thirties, and his life is etching his face. Last time, I was pleased to see Roman had whiskers as he laid in ICU. Now he has a five o'clock shadow darkening his skin, and I want to be around when it turns white with wisdom.

I've missed so much, and not just of Roman's life, or the boys– I'd been missing out on my own life too.

"I'm doing better than last year." I shrug. "I'm living now, instead of merely existing. I work normal hours, eat and sleep, and have learned to let go and play sometimes. I'm not quite there yet, but I'm on my way."

"About how you looked when you came home tonight– I heard some of what you said…" Roman trails off. "I know how Marcus can be, and it's utterly terrifying. Then there is that BDSM bullshit Marc's into, and Jamie observes for his plot devices."

"I don't know how to explain to you how my life isn't built for a conventional lifestyle. Men don't notice me."

"Someone noticed you," Roman grumbles underneath his breath, and I ignore it. "Marc seems to have noticed you. Violently so. Grant said you liked to be in charge in the bedroom, but the sex was gentle and giving."

Heart clenching, I don't have the strength to explain that I only seem to get through sex with Marcus because he's not soft and gentle. Marcus is the complete and total opposite of Grant in all ways, so that makes it feel as if I'm not betraying Grant's memory.

"I'm not cut out for what most people would call normal. I love my daughter and I provide a stable, loving home for her. But I can't see myself married and only caring for my husband and kids. Grant was the perfect fit because he understood personal boundaries and the need for space. No feelings were hurt when I had to work or he had to write. We just fit."

"God, Reggie," Roman croaks out. "Hearing the tone in your voice is killing me. You have to know that."

"Do I ever." I laugh without humor. "My life's work is too important. It's selfish, but I've given a lot up, and I give even more back to everyone else. I volunteer by donating my time and the majority of my money. The bond between my daughter and me is solid, and I don't allow certain things to influence her or enter our home. My deepest grief belongs to Grant, and my deepest regret belongs to not raising Niel, even if I know he's perfectly content and happy where he is."

"You don't even have to explain that to me, Reg. I can hear it in your voice, and I can't imagine how painful it must be to be without your son. But that doesn't explain what you're doing with Marcus. It's not normal. I know what goes on across the hallway from me, and I can't even contemplate you being in that position."

"What position?"

"I don't know," Roman's voice dips to a whine, and I realize I've gotten used to being around open-minded, nonjudgmental people, even if they are prone to destructive temper tantrums.

"I guess the difference is if you had an actual relationship with Marcus. But this BDSM shit, I just can't see you like that."

"Well, this is me." I spread my arms wide. "This is the girl you picked on. The girl you gave money to. The girl you held hands with while her mother died. This is the girl who gave you her first kiss. She wavers between apathetic and destructive because she's numb inside and out. She does weird shit to get off because she feels powerless and insecure the rest of the time. She's found a unique family when she had none to call her own. Her name is Queen, so take her as she is, or don't take her at all."

I've dumbfounded Roman into silence, and his response to my outburst has my body jolting with an unseen force. My breath rasps out sharply and I quiver with anticipation. I have to flex and relax my hands into a fist to release some of the violent energy teeming in my veins. Roman's silent judgment brings my dominant nature to the fore.

Queen erupts like never before, and I welcome her home at last.

"It's not that," Roman backpedals in the face of my fury. "I just can't see a woman kneeling down and groveling for attention. I don't know why they'd like it."

I want to tell Roman to take a long look at his girlfriend, because I keep giving Kristal a hand-up, and she keeps kneeling back on the floor, no matter what.

"Roman, I don't do that for anyone, not even Marcus. He doesn't want me to grovel and beg, because he likes to see me strong. I'm the woman who stands towering over the cowering submissive. Marcus is training me to be his equal, and I bow to no man."

Lost to whatever force is compelling me, my voice is no longer my own. It's the voice that would erupt from nowhere and speak words I never thought possible. It was the voice I used as I dominated Grant. Throaty, husky, and sultry– Queen's voice.

I back Roman up against a tree with just the sound of my voice and the force of my gaze. His judgment over my lifestyle infuriates me to the point I want to prove him wrong. Queen says there's a part in Roman that has remained untapped, and it's my duty to set it free.

Eyes dilated and glazed over, Roman's nostrils flare as he tries to come to terms with the need I just fired in his belly.

Roman experiences the urge to fall to his knees and beg, but he's battling it with all of his might. A war rages inside him as I press his back into the tree. He wants to fight me back, yet simultaneously, he wants to submit.

I don't know if I want to laugh or cry.

Roman's a switch, and he hadn't realized it until this moment.

The terror over the revelation makes me want to fuck Roman against this tree, right out in the open. I want an audience. I want to mark him as mine. But at the same time, I want Roman to prove his strength- his worth. I want him to fight me for the upper-hand.

I've never felt so close to Marcus as I do now, because I know this overwhelming, discombobulating sensation is something he experiences on a daily basis.

Closing my eyes, I pray if Roman isn't in my sights, I'll be able to remain in control. Queen is Dominance and Discipline. Now of all times, I wish I was in the sensory deprivation room.

Roman's scent is stronger with his arousal. A new sensation is born inside of me, one I thought I'd already welcomed but it was only a slow trickle. Queen erupts from my soul to stay, taking all of my insecurities and pitching them into the fire burning deep in my belly.

Empowered, I can be intelligent, in charge, a mother and a wife, a friend, a compassionate, giving person, and I can be all those things with confidence. I am not a bitch just because I am more than most men. I am Queen.

Marcus hasn't allowed me to play with a submissive yet. Only Roman isn't a submissive, he's a challenge– a challenge I long to accept.

Marcus was jealous because he foresaw this happening. He and I are equal, and we can't give each other what Roman could give me. As sad as it is to think, it's another nail in our coffin, even if we manage to allow the other one in. We're great as each other's snack, but never a life-long meal, and Marcus requires many meals from different tables.

My eyes snap wide open to connect with Roman's, only to find him gripping the tree and leaning away from me as far as he can get. He's utterly terrified. Yet at the same time, he's pissed off because he's painfully aroused.

Whimpering, Roman involuntarily presses his hips to mine, proving that he's starved with arousal. He presses and releases his bulge against me, asking for something he can't handle.

Roman's fighting his needs, and I'm proud of him because he'll make a strong dominant someday. But I'm the one who needs to fight my nature, as I'm the one who's supposed to be in control.

If Roman was a submissive, he would gain his control from me. I thank God that he's a strong switch, and he's fighting me and himself. However, I'm failing miserably.

Backing off, I shake my head to clear the lust fog. This is what Marcus meant about once you say yes, there's no shutting him down. No is a hard concept when the predator sights its prey. We aren't running bunnies– we're tigers hunting lions. The thrill is a better pay off.

"I'm sorry. That's never happened before. I don't know what came over me. I apologize. Please don't be frightened of me," I beg.

I don't dare look at Roman because I feel mortified by my brazen behavior.

I know why Marcus trained me so thoroughly– I'm a menace. Dexter trains the ones who won't harm their prey, while I almost took down a childhood friend on the sidewalk like a wounded antelope.

We walk back in silence, with Roman following me a step behind and to my left, as if he's worried that if he walks next to me, I'll attack.

"Where'd you guys go?" Kristal asks the second I open the front door. She and Fate are seated on the sofa, while she looks beyond guilty, Fate looks worried.

"We just went for a walk to chat about the past. See, I brought Roman home in one piece." I smile sweetly and innocently– I've never been either.

Jaded, my name is Regina Regal, and I've just been Queened.

Oh, how I'd love to tell Kristal the truth, but a liar deserves a lie in return. I want to shout in Kristal's face that I just corrupted her boyfriend on our walk, and I'm pretty sure I just awakened something in Roman that he'll never be able to turn off again.

Once the slumbering beast is awakened, it will never sleep again.

I quickly look at Roman, only to find him staring at me with unadulterated lust. His pants are bulging gloriously. Sensing my attention, he angles his hips toward me like a divining rod pointing to water.

My mouth salivates yet dries up at the same time. Roman's offering, but I can't partake, not when he's drugged with lust. While it may feel exceptional for many reasons, and I'd love to feed Kristal a dose of bitter medicine, I am not that type of woman, no matter what my past may dictate.

I drag my eyes from Roman's crotch to witness Kristal following my gaze.

Covering her mouth like a concerned grandma, "Oh, dear," Fate whispers, and then she runs off to hide in her bedroom.

Fate really is the perfect submissive.

I grow a pair of cojones the size of wrecking balls, and I wreck their sham of a fake romance that lies built. Kristal the innocent– Her jaded makes mine look positively virginal.

"Roman's staying the night," I say for sheer shock-value. The bulge in Roman's pants has an enlarging damp spot, and Kristal looks ready to commit homicide.

"Kris, you can thank me in the morning after Roman *fucks* you like a lunatic. I'm sure he's never really *fucked* you like you're used to. As much as it pains me to say that he'll be inside you, pleasuring you with his body, I'm flattered that I put the steel in Roman's cock tonight."

"Regina," Kristal gasps, appalled because I've never behaved this way.

"Just in case you didn't understand, I was basically saying fuck you over and over again– so either go get fucked, or go fuck yourself, Kristal."

Leaving Kristal and Roman in stunned silence, I walk away. Catching Fate peeking out her cracked bedroom door, I give her a wink, and she grins at me in return.

I feel extremely close to Marcus right now. This must be how he felt earlier this evening when he marked me two dozen times. Who knew– Queen is a territorial creature.

My sister-code list only ever included Roman, Grant, and the boys. Sister-code: do not touch what's mine. With Grant gone, how hard was it to avoid one man, a young man, and a boy? Ade's list is only Ezra. Fate and Kris have no issue with sharing what is theirs because of their submissive natures. There's no need for a feeling of propriety when you're the property.

It's an unspoken understanding that we've always abided by. Until now. We know Ade would kill us if we touched her cellphone, so I can't imagine the fallout if we had the pleasure of Ezra inside our bodies.

Adelaide Whittenhower would kill to keep Ezra Zeitler.

I breathe through the fury, pain, and arousal, because I know Roman's going to fuck my best friend under my own roof, and it's going to be the best sex he's ever had.

I'm under no delusions that Kristal didn't know who *Alex* was. If she touches anyone else on that list, it's going to get personal.

I'm going to go one step further than my Marcus would– I'm going to deny myself the pleasure of hunting Roman. It will solidify my control. One day Roman will see Kristal for who she is, and he may or may not come to me. A good hunter is nothing, if not patient.

Marcus has taught me well. He has been patiently hunting Cortez since they met, and predator and prey don't even realize it.

Chapter Twenty-Two

Curled up in bed, I'm gazing out the French doors, across the lawn, and to the guesthouse beyond. There are no lights on, but I know right now my childhood friend is inside my business partner/lying best friend.

Feeling lonely, I just want to sit with Roman in silence and enjoy his company, but Queen had to rear her dominating head and go and ruin it. I didn't want him to see me like that. Ever. All I wanted from Roman was the truth and friendship, because I genuinely missed the hell out of him.

Not even Jamie's texts this evening could stop my mind from wandering enough to fall asleep. Jamie had apologized for not telling me Alex was actually Roman Alexander, while simultaneously blaming me since I *did* request not to be in contact with Roman.

Everyone has a point on that– except for the sister-code oath breaker.

The Jaw's theme song breaks into my stare-off with the guesthouse. Since I have no penetrative superpowers, I give up trying to see through walls.

Jabbing the phone to my ear, "You're late," flows out listlessly when I was going for pissed off.

"I won't apologize," is Marc's standard response for everything. "However, I will explain why I'm calling late. I wanted your undivided attention this time, and didn't want to hang up because Jamie's texts would be rolling in."

"We're reluctant partners and lovers– people who don't want to like the other but can't help ourselves. I was thinking earlier–"

"That's terrifying," Marcus teases me. "Should I be worried?"

"Yeah, if you keep interrupting, you should," I warn. "Anyway, reluctant is the very word. You and I are so much alike, it's a wonder we hold a conversation. You're version of intimacy is fucking my head into a wall."

"As I said, it's terrifying when you think." Marcus releases a sardonic chuckle. "And here I was under the impression you liked your head being fucked into a wall, today notwithstanding– which I'll apologize for, if you'll allow it."

Snorting, I can barely force the words out. "I've got to hear this."

"I suppose saying I snapped won't cut it." Marcus pauses, waiting for an objection from me that never comes. Same shit, different day with this man. "Truth be told, I was jealous, but in an innocent way."

"Oh!" I huff so hard it hurts my lungs. "Fuck you, Marc!"

"Listen– hear me out," Marcus pleads. "We're both busy all the fucking time, and what little time we make for one another is interrupted by others. Meanwhile, I'm holding all these secrets from you, secrets that aren't mine to tell, and it's stressful on me. It's like I have an anvil hanging over my head, and I'm waiting for someone to cut the rope. So I share your attentions with your girls, with your job, with whatever sleuthing we're doing for the day, your training... then Cort is a charming motherfucker who entertains you and makes you laugh. Then there is Jamie, who has your undivided attention when he's in the room or on the phone."

"I don't get where this is leading, Marcus. You sound like a possessive friend who thinks I shouldn't play with others. I'm not the type of woman who gives all of herself to a man until she's just a shallow shell with no personality and needs and wants."

"I'm not saying that, Regina." Marc's voice is rough and grating. "The space Grant gave you was what kept you both happy. I'm explaining why I lashed out today– why I broke our agreement. Roman had decided enough was enough and wanted to see you, and don't think of blaming me on that one. I don't hold Roman's leash, so he could have seen you whenever he wanted."

"First, it's amazing how easily you can slip back into calling him Roman, after you called the man Alex for an entire year. Secondly, you don't need to twist the knife. I know Roman is a big boy and decides who he wants to see... or not see, as the case may be."

"That wasn't what I was trying to say, Regina." Oh, now he's pissed. "I knew two things were going to happen. One, you were going to be furious with me, thinking I betrayed your trust for not telling you about Roman Alexander. But I was abiding by your wishes handed down by Grant. As we established, if Roman wanted to see you, he could. Plus, I know we promised no secrets and lies and complete and total honesty no matter what. Every secret I have from you is not my own, all belonging to the man you idolize, which is why I spend my time in a perpetual cycle of being in love with him and hating him. Two, was my fuck-up for the day. I already fight for such a small sliver of your attention, and I knew Roman would take that away from me. So I snapped."

"Oh, God!" Rolling onto my back, I stare at the ceiling with my cellphone pressed to my ear. "That was what I was thinking about, you fool."

"You were?" Marcus sounds hella confused. "The voicemail you left was unpleasant, Regina, so pardon my surprise that you're not angling to chop off my balls."

"No more taking me without permission. I thought we discussed body language being an indication of a yes or no. I get it, though. I feel like a rape-monster myself after the shit I pulled with Roman."

"Explain," Marcus commands, and I'm surprised to not hear any judgment in his voice because I'm positive his name is Marcus Judgmental Zeitler. Well, the man is campaigning for the judge's chair.

"What a lovely impression I made on Roman, all marked up, while wearing a fuck-me dress with mussed up hair and cum on my thighs. After my shower, we took a walk, and Roman judged me, and you know how much I hate that. He was saying BDSM wasn't normal, so I snapped."

"You snapped?" Marc's voice is surprised, but it holds amusement as well. "Oh, this I have to hear."

"Something about it made Queen roar to the surface, to the point I can't put her away."

"Regina, you can't put *her* away, as you say, because you are Queen. You were just letting go of what was holding you back. So what happened?"

"I pushed Roman up against a tree with my will alone, then it's like I pumped my dominance into him, and rolled him over. Roman is a switch– he was fighting me off, but wanted to submit. I forced Roman to accept who he was, while making him hate himself for being drawn to BDSM."

"Oh, Regina." Marcus whistles sharply. "What I wouldn't have given to see that man knocked off his pedestal."

"Yeah, but– I did that to my childhood friend. It's wrong how I made him want me, how I made him see me, and now I'm ashamed of myself."

"You don't know Roman Alexander the adult. It's been a decade and a half, Regina. People change, and you don't know this version of him. Alex, Roman, whatever you want to call him, he is a great guy. Truly. But if he judged you, then he deserved it."

"Something about tonight made me realize you and I are a lot alike, and yet we separate ourselves from everyone and each other. I know you still have secrets you're holding, and I can feel it. But I want to be honest about what else I learned from Roman."

Without a moment's hesitation, I explain every detail of my conversation with Roman to Marcus. Then we spend the next half hour spinning every possible scenario like conspiracy theorists, and we come up with nothing. But we agree ignorance is not bliss, and our eyes are open while everyone treats us like fools.

"I can't wait until I'm not beholden to Grant's secrets anymore. But at the same time, it will feel like a little death when it happens. You're going to blame me, not him. I can feel it in my bones. It's like I'm acting as Grant's replacement, and you are filling a void he wouldn't fill for me."

"Along the way, though–" I decide to admit something, even if it is stupid. "Along the way, somewhere, somehow, you became more than Grant's replacement, Marcus. You're not Grant. You're his opposite, so I cannot compare you, which is what I needed."

"Same here," Marcus whispers. "But I worry that by the time you learn the truth, I'm the one who is going to be left broken and alone."

"I'm not like that, Marcus. I'm about as loyal as they come. I'd ignore my own happiness to keep my promises."

"I know, and I'm counting on that, because I'm a selfish asshole. But at some point, you're going to realize you're worth more, and then you'll leave me for what you really need. My biggest fear is you'll blame me, then see me for the man I truly am– the man I see when I look in the mirror."

"Do we need to restrain you to the frame, make you take your clothing off, and have Cortez humiliate you?" Laughing, I change my mind. "Never mind– you'd probably like that."

"I most definitely wouldn't enjoy *that*." Marcus pauses, and I swear I can hear fabric whisper in the background. "I have issues, Regina. Major issues, and they aren't going to go away overnight. So I hope and pray you're patient with me."

"I'm no prize– we can annoy the fuck out of each other."

"Deal," Marcus breathes softly. "Partner."

Chapter Twenty-Three

"Why so pensive?" Cort's question momentarily cuts through my musings.

Last night was one of the worst and best nights of my life. My body rolled with power. I wanted to hunt, kill, and fuck something. It took everything in me not to smash my belongings in a fit of rage. It felt even better to control the emotions. After I got off the phone with Marcus, I channeled everything into a sense of euphoria. I finger-fucked myself to XIV, and screamed my climax loud enough for Kristal and Roman to hear it in the guesthouse.

I was about to have another go when my phone pinged an incoming text message, long after our scheduled nightly session. I spent the next six hours texting Jamie. If I thought it, I sent it. It was a new kind of intimacy I've never experienced. I opened up and said words I'd locked inside myself. Jamie helped me come to terms with what was happening to me.

Jamie has always felt like background noise to me for well over a year, a supportive player. Maybe it's the resentment of not seeing him that has kept me from completely connecting to Jamie, whereas seeing Marcus but not hearing him has kept me disconnected from him as well.

I've been debased, fucked, beaten, and restrained at the hand of Marcus while Jamie played voyeur. I've failed and excelled under both their gazes. I've also watched movies, taken walks, and ate meals with Jamie in the background. I've talked about every subject while he absorbed my words.

Just as I truly connected with Marcus last night, Jamie finally feels real to me too. He's extremely bright, witty, funny, and kind. He gave me the advice that Marcus would have given me to get me to calm my emotions.

Jamie *hears* me.

It's taken everything in me not to climb the steps to Jamie's apartment and demand access to see him, to spend time with him. Learning Roman was Alex, having Kristal betray me yet again, connecting with Marcus on a deeper level, and then seeing Jamie as more than muted background noise, has made me reevaluate my life.

I'm sick and tired of playing games and sticking my head in the sand. I want answers, and I'm willing to put my foot on the bottom step, even if that means Marcus throws my ass to the curb.

But my plan was thwarted, almost as if Marcus could sense it in me, because he's upstairs with Jamie, keeping me downstairs until cooler heads prevail.

Staring at the ceiling, I wonder if they're directly above me.

"Pensive? I see you're using that huge vocabulary of yours, Mr. Writer Abernathy. When's the newest release?"

My body's wrecked. Marcus worked my aggressions out of me. My poor feet are smacked raw. Marcus isn't huge on inflicting pain, but we both needed it tonight. As my caregiver for the evening, Cortez is rubbing cooling lotion into my blazing soles, and I'm practically purring in bliss.

"Soon." Eyelashes shuttering his eyes, Cort turns shy, almost coy, and it's not an act. He has insecurities just like the rest of us. "Did you like the last book?"

Cortez always sounds unsure when speaking of his writing. It's the only time he lets down his cocky attitude. I only read his books and James Atwater's. It was exceptional, but I don't tell him this, though. Cortez doesn't need my validation when he should just believe in himself.

"I *loved* that twist at the end." Laughing with a sarcastic edge, I envision myself strangling the piss out of Cortez. "It really made me want to find you and beat the living shit out of you for ending with a cliffhanger. Not cool, asswipe."

"Be happy I give you the first draft." Cortez tweaks my pinky toe, and I yelp. "You could've had to wait as long as my readers."

"I'd just hack your laptop and get it myself. So thanks for keeping me legal." I change the subject because I was really contemplating doing it, and that freaks my ass out. Plus, Cortez goes postal when I'm in the same room with his plotter notebook— imagine if I hacked his computer. "How's the wife?"

Divina is Ezra's cousin, and Cortez married into the family to secure their future. It's a strange concept for me to understand, and I've lived in the upper echelon for the past decade and a half. I'll start to worry when I think it makes sense, but until then I just flow with it.

"Divina's really good. Her health is perfect right now. We had a scare a few months ago, though." Cortez's face is vibrant with happiness, and he flashes me a shit-eating grin. "I give the credit to her new boyfriend."

Groaning from the foot rub and the ridiculousness that is our life, I shake my head in disgust. "This is just too fucking weird for me."

"I see Divina as my family, Regina. It's not weird for me because it's all I've ever known. After you've known someone since you were born, and seen them ill and healthy, you can't really lust after them. Divina used to smash my Matchbox cars with a hammer. Ya just can't fuck someone who does that." Cortez's snickers say there's more to the story.

"What did you do first?" I accuse.

"Oh, there ya go again." Cort throws his hands up in the air dramatically. "It always has to be something I did first."

"Okay, then how did you retaliate?" I have no doubt Cortez didn't let the destruction of his toys drop.

"I may have burned all the hair off her Cabbage Patch Kids, first." Cort admits, looking sheepish as all get out.

"HA! I knew it!"

"I love Divina with all my heart, but not as the person I want to spend the rest of my life with. If I was allowed to pick, I would always choose Ezra. But since that ain't happening, I'm not a one-on-one kinda guy anymore." He gestures with his arms as if saying, '*what are ya gonna do?*'

"Me too. I don't think I could have one person as my world again. It hurts too much to lose them." Voice lowering, despondent, I hate how true my words are. "I've lost more than I've kept."

We sit for a moment, and I can tell my words affected Cortez somehow. I watch him and he watches me back, both waiting for the other to break the silence first.

Cort gives me a self-deprecating smile, because he can't stay quiet for long. "I almost lost Ezra once. It was the worst three days of my life. I've never gotten over it, and I got him back. We aren't the same as we once were, but at least he's still alive. I get it, Regina, and I'm so damn sorry."

Cortez looks like he's going to cry, but then he has to go and ruin it by pulling out the charm. "So Marcus was in an especially foul mood last night. I'm surprised that I can talk today. Not once, or twice, but six times I was subjected to his fury. Somehow I know it's because of you. I wasn't sure until he beat the crap out of you, and then made you return the favor. Never have I seen Marcus take swats before... so what'd ya do?"

"I don't know what you're talking about," I lie, refusing to explain how I was teaching Marcus a lesson.

Marcus has no concept of intimacy, always thinking his dick has to be inside another person to truly connect. At the end of our phone call, he begged to come over. I denied him, completely shutting him down by telling him sex would ruin the intimacy we'd built during our conversation.

Marcus was livid and horny.

I was patient by tolerating Marc's bullshit, because he does have issues. But I'm not his mother, or his doormat, or his cum receptacle, so I hung up on him when he wouldn't stop begging. Then I turned off my cellphone when he kept calling.

Poor Cortez.

"Sure ya don't." Cort tweaks all the toes on my right foot. "Marc's being comforted by Jamie right now. Soothing words just aren't the same when they're said with your hands," he teases.

"Do you think they are doing something naughty right now?" I look to the ceiling, yet again wishing for superpowers so I could see through walls and floors. It bothers me to think they're touching, which is weird since I like it when Marcus is sweet to Cort. "Jamie keeps denying it, and Marcus is always bitchy about it. But do you think Jamie ever gives in like we do?"

"No, absolutely not– never." Cortez laughs at the thought. "Jamie is Marc's confidant and comfort object. Of course Marc wants to tap that, but the only time Jamie is strong is when he's denying Marcus sex." Cortez smirks at me. "So what'd ya do?"

"Nothing," I lie again.

"Liar." Cortez calls me on it.

"Fine." I sigh heavily. "Roman Alexander is the owner of this house, and he happened to be a good friend of mine when I was growing up." Cortez has the decency to look guilty. "I didn't know Alex was Roman until I walked into my house last night, and there he was. It was embarrassing because of how Marcus marked me up. I wigged out on Roman during a walk when Queen wanted to play something fierce."

"I knew that Alex was dating Kristal, but I didn't know you knew him in the past," Cort admits, and I do believe him. "Since I know you've only been with two men, how much of an old friend are we talking about here?"

"My first kiss. If I hadn't gone with Grant, there was a good possibility that I would've ended up with Roman."

"Marc knows about this?" He arches a brow at me in shock. "Jamie knew about this?"

"Marc's been watching Roman since I was eighteen. Worried my attentions would turn to Roman, Marcus bit the shit out of me, dressed me like a whore, fucked me, and then sent me home for Roman to see. For *that*, I'm a bit pissed at Marc, but not because he kept the secret. But the real reason Marc's a grumpy asshole is because I wouldn't fuck him last night. All forms of communication for that man are during sex, and I refuse to have sex with someone who acts like an emotionally stunted four-year-old."

"I never thought I'd see the day." Cortez whistles sharply while gazing at me in approval.

"See what day?" Ezra's smooth voice flows in from the doorway, and Cortez and I startle like we're up to no good.

In the year that I've been training, not once has Ezra set foot into the brownstone. I was beginning to think it was a secret location.

"Where's our grumpy master?" Ezra strides in like he owns the place, so that answers that question. Not a secret. "Marcus was being despicable today. I could barely tolerate to be in the same room with him."

"Marc's upstairs conducting business." Cort answers Ezra's second question, but fails to answer the first question, which I wanted to know myself.

"Jamie gives me the creeps– I hate how dependent Marcus is on him. He needs to just give it up and move on." Ezra shakes his head and shivers. "Are you two the only ones here?"

Hitching his thumb to point at the next room, "Nah– we're having an orgy in the back," Cort answers sarcastically. "We scabbed most of your clientele from Restraint, and there's just mountains of fucking bodies everywhere. Can't you smell the sex wafting in the air?"

"Dumbass," Ezra chastises, but he ruins it when his lips twitch.

"Don't ask a stupid question if you're not prepared to hear a stupid answer." Cortez sounds teasing, but the resentment breaks through.

Sadness rolls over Ezra's face, but he covers it quickly, just not fast enough so that Cortez doesn't notice.

Sighing heavily, Cortez grabs for his partner's hand. "I'm sorry," Cort whispers softly. This is a side of him I've never seen.

"I think you should just record that and give me a copy." Ezra glances down to their intertwined fingertips. "It's all I hear these days. I don't hear from you for weeks at a time, and then it's just '*I'm sorry, Ezra.*' It's getting old. You need to come home and stop torturing us."

In my adult life, I've only seen Ezra three or four times, and only ever having held two very short conversations with him. But I've seen him from a distance many times, and he's always controlled, emulating Marcus perfectly. But I recognize a fissure in Ezra's control– Cortez.

Dropping Ezra's hand like it burned him, "Why are you here?" Cort ask briskly.

"If it's just you and Queen, then I guess I can get Marc's newest trainee. I picked him up at the airport as commanded." Ezra looks at me, trying to judge whether or not I can be trusted. "Why is Marc being a complete douchebag today?"

"Trust me, you don't want to know," is Cort's reply. "Bring in the fresh meat."

As Ezra leaves the room, Cort and I share a shrug. We didn't know we were getting a new trainee. Dexter usually takes everyone, since Marcus is very selective about who he trains.

Ezra walks back in with a short male following behind him. It's almost comical seeing the pair side-by-side. Ezra is tall and lanky with white hair and gunmetal eyes, and the only thing he shares with his companion is soft, pale skin. The new trainee is so underwhelming it's like he's camouflaged– indistinct brown hair and eyes, slight frame in frumpy clothing. Most people would look to him, and then look away, without a second glance. But for some reason, I study him. The trainee's appearance screams someone my age, but his skin is flawless. He must be around twenty, and no more. His face is beautiful beneath the disguise, and I know what I see isn't really him.

The trainee's eyes latch onto mine in utter defiance, acting as if he's playing dominant animal kingdom, but I'm not fooled. He's trying to divert my attention away from what's lurking beneath the surface.

That's fine, young man. Your new master will tell me your secret.

"Welcome to the brownstone," I greet politely.

Ever the gentleman, Ezra makes the introductions. "Dalton Thompson, this is Cortez Abernathy and Queen– don't ask her real name. Marc's rule is to never pry." Ezra sits next to Cort on the sofa, and Dalton sits next to me, opposing them.

Dalton looks at me as I did him– intent on studying me. Instead of allowing the youngster to intimidate me, I smile.

"Dalton, it's nice to meet you." I shake his hand, and he seems shocked by the display of respect. Dexter wouldn't shake my hand when he first met me, as if I were beneath him– hell, I haven't seen him since. Dalton's hands are so smooth and soft that I know he's barely legal. His appearance and demeanor may say thirties, but his skin says twenty.

Interesting.

"Are you two sleeping together?" Ezra asks out of nowhere, eyes flicking between Cortez and me.

It's so random, I bark a sharp laugh. With Ezra staring daggers at me, at first my guilty conscience kicks in and I think he means me and his adoptive father. But Ezra's eyes are glued to Cortez's fingers rubbing my feet.

"I'm not your boy's type." I mutter, then release a self-deprecating laugh.

Since our make out session in the Vanquish, I've received nothing but sisterly touches from Cortez, and we've beaten the crap out of each other on the equipment. That's par for the course– everyone wants to kick Cort's snarky ass, but I'm the one who actually gets to do it.

"Cort doesn't have a type. If it has a pulse, he fucks it." Ezra jokes, but it's tinged with truth and pain. "Actually, it probably doesn't need a pulse either."

"Well, I guess I'm the exception to the rule. I don't fit those *stringent* standards." I turn to sarcasm to hide my hurt.

I don't mind, but it doesn't lessen the rejection to know Cort finds me less than desirable, especially since I received the leering treatment at Restraint. Cortez may not find me attractive, but we share mutual respect and friendship now. That's a hell of a lot more valuable to me than another notch on a metaphorical bedpost.

"You don't shit where you eat," is Cort's only reply.

Pulling my feet from Cortez's lap, I fight back tears because he offended me, even if I have no idea what that saying means. I know I'm not hot or anything, but I'm not a troll.

With his hands hanging in the air where my feet used to be, Cort flashes me a strange look for my reaction.

"Marcus probably commanded him to leave her alone," Dalton says quietly, pointing between Cortez and me.

"Yeah, right!" I scoff. "Why would Marcus care?"

Cort gives me the *'you're a dumbass'* look.

"It's an effective way to reward and punish." The new trainee gets a devious gleam in his eye. "You must be very controlled, since I would assume Cortez would be your punishment."

Dalton says this with a straight face and a douchebag tone in his voice, but I see his lips twitch. He's playing a role for some reason.

I like this kid.

Ezra howls out a laugh so loud Marcus and Jamie had to have heard it upstairs. He's nearly in hysterics, but the jokes on him since Cort is his punishment.

"Laugh it up now, Ez," Cortez grumbles, offended. "You'd beg to be punished if that was the case."

"I would." Ezra sobers. Voice taking on a pleading tone, "Come home."

Cort looks away from all of us, and doesn't reply.

"Queen, could you show Dalton around the rooms?" Since Ezra asks politely instead of commanding me, I comply.

"Ouch– fuck me! that hurts." I hop around from foot-to-foot a few times in discomfort.

"Maybe you're a bad mistress." Dalton takes my elbow, supporting some of my weight. "Since you seem to have been punished."

"Be forewarned, you will play with everything and experience everything for the sake of instruction, and several more times for our master's enjoyment. Marcus is brutal. But in Queen's case–" it's weird hearing Cortez call me Queen in anything but a mocking tone "–she wasn't punished. Marcus is being a jealous brat, so he took it out on her feet and thighs, but he allowed her to retaliate on his gorgeous behind."

"Your master allowed you to work him?" The kid asks in awe. "What did you use?"

"Paddle– I didn't want to hurt Marcus." Lips curling, I smile like a Cheshire cat.

Ezra's staring at me intently, eyes traveling from my toes to the top of my head, and then back down again. It's creepy being visually examined by your best friend's fiancé and your lover's adoptive son, but there's nothing sexual about it– it's calculating.

I try to walk Dalton out to get away from Ezra's assessing eyes, but Cortez draws me into their bullshit. "Queen stays," Cort demands. "Her feet hurt, and Dalton can wander around the first floor unaided."

"No," Ezra is adamant. "I need to speak with you privately."

"Queen can listen in since I'll probably tell her anyway." Cortez looks at Ezra, silently saying, *'she either stays or we don't talk.'*

"Not about this, you wouldn't," Ezra murmurs smoothly while giving me another penetrating glance. He's trying to burn me to ash with the intensity in his gaze– like father, like son.

Jealous.

"You can't know that– Queen stays." Cort holds firmly and won't budge.

Ezra takes on the look of Marcus, and I wonder if he's going to choke Cort again like he did the last time I saw them together.

"Fine," Ezra concedes. "Dalton, you may explore, but if your feet touch those steps, I'll take my frustrations out on your hide. No one passes the first step except our master and the owners of this house. Understood?"

"Yes, sir," Dalton mutters respectfully as he flees the room.

Settling on the sofa, I close my eyes in preparation for a ton of dramatics. "Just pretend I'm not here. Just so ya know, I don't want to be here either, but I'd rather not walk around on bruised soles."

"I want to do this in private, Cort." Ezra's voice is so sharp it could cut glass. "You don't know what I'm going to tell you– it's important."

"I know what it's about. I may not be around all the time, but I do know what you're up to. If you don't think Marc pesters me at least fifty times a day, then you're insane. It's her. When is Katya coming?"

Now *that* gets my attention. My eyes snap wide open, and it takes everything in me not to sit up and beg them to answer. Katya Waters is the woman from Ezra and Adelaide's engagement contract. I've caught bits of conversation between Marcus and Cortez, about how Katya was included in their abduction and harmed. If Katya accepts Ezra's marriage proposal, Ade has to publicly dissolve their engagement.

"I have Katya in a position that will place her in my hands very soon. I need you to come home, because I don't want her coming here while we're still fighting. I'll acknowledge that you don't see me the same way as before. You blame me, and when you look at me, you see Raymond. All you see is what Raymond made you do to Aaron." Voice breaking, Ezra sounds on the verge of tears, and the mother in me longs to comfort him and remove his pain.

"I'm sorry, Cort. I'd turn back time if I could." Ezra's voice quivers with panic. "We all need to heal from this, and I'm doing the best I can."

"This has nothing to do with before." Cort's words lash out with violent intensity. "You've cheated on me twice, sorry if that doesn't make me want to trust you. My issues with the past aren't about you at all. Maybe– just think about this for a second, Ezra – just maybe, I feel some blame about what I did to Aaron."

Remembering the terror in Grant's eyes when the boys were abducted, and when they were returned, it's horrific to think it's still affecting their everyday lives. For the rest of my life, I'll never forget that day because it was the day Grant died.

I want to bundle Cort in my arms and comfort him. He has the same expression on his face as he did when we spoke of him losing Ezra for three days. Even though Ezra and Cortez still live, they lost that spark that made them feel alive together.

"Just come home," Ezra pleads, but I can hear it in his voice that he knows Cort won't come home.

"I won't sleep in a bed that you fucked that cunt in." Cort's vehement about Adelaide, but then he looks at me and his eyes soften in apology. "I can't sleep in the bed where you cheated on me."

"I've never slept with Ade in our bed, Cort– I promise I didn't. I used the spare room. Our room has lain empty since you left. I can't sleep without you. I spend most of my nights driving back-and-forth so I can roam Shadow Haven. Please…"

It's killing me to watch such a strong, intelligent man beg for affection from the man he loves. Understanding Marcus better, I want to do everything in my power to get them to see they are both crying out for the same thing– each other.

"Fine, I'll come home under a few conditions." Cort tries to look harsh, but I can see the relief lying underneath.

"I'll agree to anything– just come home." I hope Cortez isn't too crafty, or Ezra will wish he didn't say that.

"I will sleep in *our* bed, and you will sleep in the bed you tainted with that cunt. I won't be your lover, because you don't deserve my attention. I've never cheated on you. Once I understood, because I hadn't been giving you what you were craving. I understood because I know how rigorous and arousing training can be. Twice is unacceptable. I don't know if I can ever trust you after that. I had to sit at our family home while you fucked *her* in our apartment. You'll never know how powerless that made me feel."

"That's fair, and I deserve it." Ezra smiles like he just won the fucking lottery. He'd rather have Cort be an abusive asshole toward him than ignore him. "I accept your terms without limitations."

"I'm not finished," Cort warns.

Waiting with bated breath, I love Cort's ability to fuck with the ones he loves. This won't be good, and I'll be damn proud of him because cheaters deserve to be punished– repeatedly.

"When Kitten comes home, she's mine too. If you ever want to feel my touch again, you'll agree."

Ezra's head snaps back as if he were bitch-slapped. His eyes turn to molten silver and he drags in loud gasps of air through his nostrils like an enraged bull. "I'll think about that one. We will discuss what that entails in private. Just come home." He tries to calm himself and leash his emotions.

Interesting, Ezra doesn't want to share this woman for some reason.

"We've always shared everything. What happened with Katya affected all of us, not just *you*, so I won't allow you to keep her from me."

"Katya is not ready for your type of attentions. I'm not bringing her here to fuck her. I want to heal her the only way I know how– with therapy. Katya doesn't remember us at all, Cort, so I'm trying to coax it out of her. Just let me take the lead on this, and we'll discuss the rest of it at home."

"Am I hearing happy news?" Marcus chirps from the doorway, clapping like an ecstatic toddler. "My children are getting along. Ezra don't be so possessive." The jealous idiot chastises his son for being jealous– that's rich.

"Ms. Waters may like Cortez… you never know. Our Cort is very charming and entertaining after all. So don't fight over Katya, just let her decide."

Marc's mood has drastically improved from two hours ago. He's beaming with pride and happiness. It's fucking bizarre, like he was upstairs getting high, but I know that wasn't the case.

Gobsmacked, I turn lightheaded when Marcus comes into view. Apparently he showered and changed, now wearing painted-on, worn-in jeans and a white dress shirt that's unbuttoned. His bronze skin glows like the sun underneath the white billowy fabric. I want to peel it from his skin and devour his flesh and scent. I shudder when his whiskey eyes latch on to my green. He smiles brilliantly and my stomach flutters.

"I found our new trainee wandering the halls." Marcus tugs the boy into the room, with a hand on his shoulder. Both seem acquainted with one another. With intimacy issues out the ass, Marcus only touches those he trusts, and the boy looks like the skittish type. Both are relaxed, and Dalton's resting a hand on Marc's hip.

There's more to this story.

"Dalton, Ezra and Cort will take you to Restraint. I've prepared a few rooms for you on the second floor. If it's not to your standards, we will remodel, but it was the best I could do under such short notice."

"Thank you, Marcus. I appreciate it." Dalton peels away, wandering back to the hallway.

Leaning forward, Marcus breathes, "Son," against Ezra's forehead, and then gently places a kiss before stepping away. "Cort will meet you by your cars. I'll stop by your apartment before I retire for the evening, but it may be late."

As soon as Ezra and Dalton disappear out the front door, Marc pulls Cort off the couch by fisting the center of his shirt. "You will not kill each other when you get home. You will try to get along. I know this is a foreign concept for you, Cortez. But you will not fight over Katya Waters. It will be her decision if she wants either of you, because she's been raped enough."

"Yes, Master," Cortez mutters, looking startled by harsh reality.

All I can do is watch as Marcus unleashes the part of his dominant nature that is hyper-protective.

"Do you understand me, Cortez? I'm not only referring to Katya and you, but to how Ezra has been misbehaving. You need to go home to keep Ezra's issues in check. I'm not telling you to fuck him, just touch him as I know you're dying to do." Marc stares the younger man down until Cort's eyes drop to the floor in acquiescence. "Make sure Ezra behaves, especially for Katya's sake."

"Yes, Master," Cortez repeats, seeming to get with the program.

I wait for Marcus to reply, but he shocks the piss out of me instead. Snaring the nape of Cort's neck in his palm, Marcus holds him immobile for a passionate kiss.

I watch in shock as they kiss as lovers do– with dueling tongues and moans of pleasure. Enraptured by their display, two incredibly beautiful men– one gold, one bronze –share an intense passion I've never felt.

It's enough to make me weep, even if it's the hugest turn-on. I never thought I'd like to be a voyeur. But if Marcus and Cortez ever hook up, I want to watch, even if it emotionally murders me to watch.

Marc breaks away, and then roughly pushes Cort to the sofa. Marcus looks disgusted with himself, like he allowed his control to break, and the very fact pisses him off. And I can see he blames Cortez for his current condition– aroused, frustrated, and out of control.

"Behave, and make me proud to be your master. Go–" Marcus points to the hallway, toward the front door.

Wavering, Cort gets up and walks like he's treading through quicksand. His feet are laden, eyes heavy-lidded, and his face is flushed with puffy, swollen lips.

As pessimistic as I am, I wonder if Marcus turned Cortez on to benefit his evening with Ezra. It wouldn't surprise me that he'd go down that route. I could see Marcus making Cortez want him, only to push Cort toward the one he really needs. Marcus is a tricky bastard like that.

There's one problem with this plan. Cortez is Marc's Pandora's Box. Once he opens himself up to this, he has to watch Cort walk away to go satisfy Ezra. Marcus would deny this, of course, because who would admit such a thing to their own lover.

Marcus wants Cort with a single-minded desperation that he barely holds in check.

"Let's take a ride." Marc's voice is deep and husky with lust as he grabs for my hand. Being pulled to my feet, I yelp sharply as I try to stand.

Marcus eyes me like he's going to pick me up.

"Oh… no– don't even think of it." My voice quivers with fear of the mortification to come. "I'm too huge to be carry-worthy. I'd die if you couldn't pick me up!"

Marcus smirks at me in challenge, and I sprint from the room, pained feet be damned. I find my flip-flops next to the front door, and slide them on. It's fall, but I'm not giving up my sandals until snow flies.

Running out the door and down the front steps, I make my way down the sidewalk to my car. Marcus is right on my heels, laughing and growling as I try to unlock my door.

"We're taking the Spyder," Marcus breathes into my ear from behind, body curling over mine. "I want to drive *fast*."

Pressing his impressive bulge against my ass, a moan rolls out Marc's mouth.

If this were under different circumstances, I'd be flattered, but I'm not the one who put the steel in Marc's cock. A snarky, naughty author did.

I try to pull away, but Marcus doesn't allow it by pinning me to my car. "What? Are you still mad about our session earlier? About last night? I thought we got that ironed out." Confused, hurt rings in his voice, and I have no idea why.

While Marcus rubs a hard-on against me that Cortez supplied, I'm still feeling a twinge of rejection by Cort's '*I don't shit where I eat*' comment. I don't know what it means, but I know it's nothing good. Now Marcus is trying to use the arousal Cortez inspired in him on me, just as Marcus was trying to get Cortez to use the one Marcus gave him on Ezra.

I don't want to be used by someone who needs help in order to touch me. To say it stings is an understatement.

"What's wrong?" Marcus peppers the back of my neck with kisses and embraces me from behind. "Tell me," he commands. His breath heats my skin, with every kiss enlivening my nerves. My body tingles and breaks out in goosebumps, and it makes me physically sick.

I pull away without a word.

I walk around the block and down the alley with Marcus trailing me. His confusion flavors the air as if he's releasing a current that is readable. I quickly tap the security code into the garage door, and then slide it up. I wait outside for Marcus to get in the car and back it out, since I'll have to reengage the security system and slide the door shut after Marc pulls the car out. He walks by me, radiating annoyance and confusion.

Chapter Twenty-Four

We drive in silence as the Spyder hugs curves at outrageous speeds. It's dark, fast, exhilarating yet soothing, and it reminds me of Jackson's love of living on the edge because he was dying.

All roads lead back to the Whittenhowers, don't they?

"Why are you mad at me?" Marcus never takes his eyes off the road, but his fingers twitch on the steering wheel.

"I'm not." I answer with all honestly.

"Yes, you are." Marc's eyes flick my way, and an intimacy falls over us in the dark of the car. "I can feel it. Is it because of the way tonight's training went?"

"No, I needed to work off my frustrations just as much as you did, perhaps more. I'm still on edge. You know I see pain as weakness leaving the body as just another form of release. My feet will feel better by morning, but my thighs may take longer."

Marcus remains quiet as he absorbs what I just said, instead of being reactive. It comforts me some that he wasn't dreaming up what he was going to say next as I was speaking. Too many people hold conversations with themselves these days, only wanting someone else to hear them talk.

Watching the headlights caress the lines on the road, it entrances me into calmness.

"Did the kiss with Cortez turn you from me?" Marc's voice sounds hollow, more like shallow with shame. "I haven't kissed Cort like that very often– it's complicated. Do you want me to never do it again? I know you and I have never discussed exclusivity or monogamy."

Yeah, because I know monogamy is not an option when your married lover is Marcus Zeitler.

I'm shocked that Marcus thinks I'm angry, or that I'm revolted by what he did with Cortez. Marc was trusting me to understand and not judge him, and now he thinks I'm throwing it back into his face.

Shit!

"No, Marcus. You can kiss Cort anyway you want, because I have no right to say anything about your affairs."

"I-I-I–" Marcus stutters, at a loss.

"The kiss was beautiful– the way you touched each other. It was like living art, with how you're both so perfect. Your bodies and coloring together was a sight to behold. So don't feel shame over wanting to touch Cortez. Hell, Dominion's population couldn't resist Cortez's charms."

Marcus sits in silent contemplation, leaving me to fill the void.

"Cortez hit on me once. It was at Faith's sweet sixteen birthday party, and it was a lame attempt at best. He was probably trying to make either Faith or Ezra jealous at the time. I'm always the instrument used to exact jealousy, but never the one who is coveted. But I always wondered if Cortez would eventually grow into his charisma. He did, and I'm so glad that I know him. He may be an asswipe, but he's *our* asswipe."

Voice strained with a mix of jealousy and resignation, Marcus asks the dumbest question. "Do you want to sleep with Cortez?"

My sharp bark of laughter echoes around the car, because Marcus sounds exactly like Ezra, asking the same stupid questions.

Wow, what it must be like to be Cortez, to have two men jealous to have you. Both jealous of me, and Cortez wouldn't touch me with latex gloves.

"Why does it matter?" My tone is laced heavily with curiosity. "It's not going to happen."

"It matters," Marcus mutters in a deep voice– the deeper his voice goes, the angrier he is.

"I'm sure there's a supermodel out there you want– does it matter if you find her attractive when you'll never have sex with her? That is my point."

"You make no sense." Marcus white-knuckles the steering wheel. "Are you really comparing Cort to a supermodel?"

I can't help it– I start to laugh until tears fall from my eyes. Wiping them away with my sleeve, I try to blink my vision clear.

"Oh, I bet a lot of people at Restraint think he is." Chuckles keep bubbling up my throat. Could Marcus be any more jealous? "My point is that it doesn't matter, since it's unrequited. It'll never happen."

"You're confusing me," he grumbles.

"Just forget it, okay?" Now I'm frustrated, too. "No, I have no interest in fucking Cort. Happy?"

"Not really," Marcus mumbles, but at least he stops strangling the steering wheel. Lord knows, the dang thing is priceless.

"Do you want me to want Cortez?"

"No!" Marcus bellows in the confines of the car, echoing to the point it hurts my ears.

Yep, Marcus has a deep jealous streak when it comes to Cortez. It amazes me that he wanted Cort to go home with Ezra in the first place.

"We need to talk about what happened with Roman last night. How did you handle it when your dominance erupted?" Marc changes the subject to a more uncomfortable one.

"What?" I'm going to kill that mute nark. "I guess I know who not to talk to anymore. Thanks for the trust, Jamie," I mutter underneath my breath. "I honestly thought Jamie wouldn't betray my trust."

"Seriously, Regina? Jamie came to me because he wanted your training to be altered to help you cope. So many people betray you, to the point you see the small things as conspiracies. You're paranoid."

"Not all the time, I'm not!"

"Agreed," Marcus mutters gruffly. "Don't judge Jamie for coming to me, especially when he was coming to your defense by tearing me a new asshole. Contrary to popular belief, a mute can be very loud when furious. He also said you're pissed at me for marking you and dressing you like a whore. How did you put it?" Marcus taps his fingertips on the steering wheel, drawing information from his memory bank. "*Fucked, marked, and whored by your master, and left to be humiliated and ashamed.*"

Seething in silence, Marcus bypasses my street, and then drives right up to the main gate to Crestview. I'm so shocked I can't speak as we enter the Gates. Taking one look at me, the security guard waves us on, knowing exactly who I am after all this time.

Who would have guessed, Daniel never revoked my right to enter the Gates.

Wondering if it's possible to have a PTSD attack after more than a decade, I haven't been back here since the night Grant died– the night I left my first born behind.

The only movement I make is my eyes flicking left and right as we pass each and every gated driveway. Nothing has changed– it all looks the same.

Heart beating out of control, at first I think Marcus is taking us to visit Dexter, since we go straight, instead of branching left to go to Shadow Haven, or right to Misery Castle. My heartrate triples when I catch sight of the Whittenhower crest on the gate in my peripheral vision.

But we don't stop at the Victorian nightmare of a brothel. Marcus pulls the Spyder into a blind driveway alongside Dexter's home, and then slowly drives down a dirt road that's bordered by a tunnel of thick woods.

It's pitch-black except for the headlights leading our way.

"The dress was because it looked amazing on you." Marc's voice startles me in the dark silence. "I wanted Roman to see what he'd missed out on because the ass avoided you. The marking was my territorial urges coming through– I didn't mean to do it, but I lost control."

With his fingertips nervously tapping on the steering wheel, I know Marcus isn't through with what he has to say, so I don't interrupt him.

"The brutal fucking was from my lack of control as well. I never want you to feel ashamed for any reason. You're not a whore– you're a woman with needs, and any woman who puts another down for owning her sexuality was brainwashed by a man to think little of herself. If a man belittles you, it's because he's envious he can't be with you."

I can't help but to interject, "Hear! Hear!" Thank God, Marcus ignores me.

"Roman's nothing to you anymore, and eventually you may have a friendship if it survives the fact that he abandoned you. But, me? I'm the master who trained you, your lover, and partner. As someone who loves Grant as much as you, I have your best interests at heart at all times. I have the honor of being allowed to have sex with you, and I wanted Roman to know he isn't as fortunate. He's left with the pitiful scraps from Kristal's well-used table. I wanted Roman to know you're mine."

"Antiquated mine bullshit? I do take objection with that."

"Be that as it may, it doesn't change the fact that that's how I feel." Marc's eyes cut sideways to judge my reaction. "What I didn't count on was Queen wanting to stalk prey. I know you want Roman, but if you have sex with him, I can't be held accountable for my actions." Marc's voice is so deep I can barely hear him. "With or without a talk of exclusivity or monogamy, Roman

Alexander is not going to have what was once Grant's and is now mine. *Ever*."

With a roll of my eyes, I look out the windshield and gasp in shock. In front of us is a small lake and a dock. Its crystalline waters glisten in the moonlight, a deep so blue, it's nearly black. Beckoning, it invites me to jump in and experience the freedom that only water can offer.

Flicking my eyes, I look to Marcus to judge his reaction to the water, but his eyes are already on me. "It's beautiful." I whisper of the lake and the surrounding area.

"It is," Marcus whispers back, not taking his eyes from my face.

If I were any other woman but me, I'd think Marcus was speaking of me.

"Would you really harm me if I had sex with Roman?" It's meant as a joke to break the tension that has fallen in the car, but it only manages to ramp up Marc's intensity.

"No, not you," he breathes.

"What?"

"I told Cort that if he ever touched you again, I'd break any part of his body that came in contact with yours. If Roman touches you– he's dead."

"What?" I repeat because Marcus has never looked more serious in the entire year I've known him.

"It'll be your problem, Regina. I won't be held accountable for my actions since I've given you fair warning. Roman received his warning this morning. Never fear, we just talked as two gentlemen with a common interest. If Roman wants to play with you, he has to come to me and ask permission– don't look at me like that," he hisses, grabbing my chin between his forefinger and thumb, and I wince from the pain.

"You're mine." Marc's voice is low and menacing, and laced with a depth of possession I didn't think possible. "Grant was a pussy."

"Marcus," I growl in disgust.

"Grant may have loved you with all of his heart, but his insecurities ruled him until he sacrificed it all for you. He actually asked me if I wanted to have sex with you, saying he wasn't strong enough to meet your needs. But the dumb fuck didn't realize he was everything you needed and then some. I almost took Grant up on it, because I thought it would mean I could be near him while we touched you, and it would be enough."

Chin still gripped in Marc's fingertips, all I can do is close my eyes in defeat. "I know."

"My every breath around you is an attempt to escape Grant's ghost." My eyes open to witness tears tracking down Marc's cheeks. "Being near you is both a comfort and an exquisite form of torture. I feel closer to Grant than ever, and I see everything he sees in you. The longer I know you, the closer I get to you, the shorter our time together is until you learn the truth and leave me."

"Marcus, what the fuck are you talking about?"

"I warned you that I have issues, and I need your patience for when I act like a fuckface. So bear with me, because I fear my possessive streak will get stronger and stronger every day we spend together, with every intimate conversation we have. I've tried to keep you at arm's length by fucking you as a way to disconnect, but that's an impossibility now."

"If this is your way of reassuring me, all you're accomplishing is to terrify me instead."

"Good. Our time alone together is drawing to a close, because those who actually have a claim to you are going to take you back. Trust me– you'll go gladly with a smile on your face."

"Marcus?" His demeanor has changed, going from someone who is pouring his heart out to someone who is on the verge of desperation, and he's the one who called me paranoid.

"Then there's your odd fascination with believing Cortez thinks you're unworthy, or unwanted. Trust me– Cort wants you. I see you don't believe me, but I thought you had realized I am the one who decides who you sleep with and when. You chose this path a long time ago when you answered that phone call outside of the brownstone. Own it!"

With a rough shove, Marcus pushes me away, and then vacates the car like he can't suffer a second longer in my presence. Shocked senseless, I know I'm to follow Marcus, but I can't force myself to move a single inch.

Closing my eyes, I breathe through the jumble of thoughts flashing through my mind. Abruptly my door is opened, with my arm being wrenched until my body follows. Marcus traps me against the car while growling low and deep like a rabid animal.

I gaze into eyes that are normally soft and brown, yet tonight they swirl as a storm brews beneath the surface. Marcus is no longer in control. The dominant version of himself, the primal being who runs on instinct is firmly in control instead. Master. Just as I was last night when Queen took over in her quest to teach Roman a lesson.

Marcus is in animal-mode, primal and instinctive.

Staring deep inside me, Marcus is reading every thought that flashes across my face and inside my mind, as only he can.

I learned to school my true emotions after years in my neighborhood, followed by Hillbrook, and finally Misery Castle. The only way to survive the Whittenhowers was to suppress all emotion. Just as Grant did, Marcus knows me to my soul.

"You controlled Queen nicely–"

"Are you bipolar?"

"No." Marc's eyebrows scrunch in confusion, finding my segue from one topic to the next baffling, but if only he heard himself talk. "I'm not bipolar, but my son does have multiple personalities."

Huffing a laugh, leave it to Marcus to diffuse the situation with a good dose of inappropriate humor. An insane psychiatrist!

Yet again, Marcus finds me cute. "I'm proud of you, Regina. Jamie said you channeled all of those sensations into your control, and it gave you a high. There are three ways we feel alive. One is to do as you did. Another is to completely let the beast out to play and lose all control– people may get hurt in the process, but it feels fantastic. Freeing. Lastly is to channel it all, and dominate your submissive with absolute control.

"The rest of the time, we feel off kilter. That's why you don't feel right most of the time. This is why you'd rather command your programs– you get a sense of power in a world that makes no sense, in a world where you feel powerless. I understand you. We're one in the same, you and I."

"That's why you terrify me," I admit.

"Trust me," Marcus whispers, and then his lips latch onto my neck and suck. Knees giving out, Marc holds me up by pinning me to the car with his hips. Eyes rolling back, I quiver uncontrollably while hissing his name in ecstasy.

"You don't like my marks on your neck?" Marcus teases, and I whimper as he nips at a tender spot. "I think you do." He pulls harder on a spot he ravished the night before. Head falling back against the car, I give him greater access while groaning like a wanton whore. Distracted by the vampire routine, I don't notice his fingers are busy pulling off my jeans until it's too late.

I stay passive as he undresses me and suckles at my neck. "Marcus," I breathe reverently, need coursing through my veins.

"You have no idea how much I love the sound of my name from your lips, Regina. I hear Mr. Zeitler all day by associates, Marc by my family, and Master by everyone else." His voice is heated, nearly scalding me with its intensity. "When you say my name, it melts me."

Warm lips follow the path of Marc's fingers as he unbuttons my blouse. He slides it free of my arms, and then tosses it into the car to land on my seat. My jeans follow the arc my shirt took, until I'm left standing in flip-flops and a lacey bra and panty set.

Marc's teeth bite my necklace, shaking the prize like a dog with a bone. He rolls his eyes up to mine, mouth curling into a devious smile.

"I like that you wear these around your neck. It makes you feel close to those you lost." Marcus lifts the necklace over my head and fondles the three bands that hang from it– my parents' wedding bands and the infinity ring Grant gave me when he asked me to marry him.

It was my last moment with Grant.

"Ah– now… no sadness. They all loved you. I bet they miss you as much as you do them– I know Grant does." Marcus leans away from me so he can see me better. "Even though I hated them, I miss my parents and Dexter's parents. I miss my grandmother the most, because she was the only family member who loved me unconditionally."

"I'm sure Dexter loves you, Marcus," I murmur to comfort him.

"Dexter does, but he doesn't truly know me." Marcus cocks his head slightly, gauging whether or not he should continue. "I know how you feel the Regal line dies out with you because your children are Whittenhowers. I feel the same way, being as Dexter is a Hayes, and my only child will take her husband's name."

"Not necessarily." I point out some antiquated customs no longer apply.

"I was thrilled to adopt Ezra." Marc's eyes glow with wonder. "It made me feel less alone knowing his future children and wife will have my name. As we've discovered, I'm a possessive person. So this makes me infinitely happy to know my name will never die out."

"You could always remarry a woman you love and have children." Marcus barks a laugh as if that's the most absurd thing he's ever heard. "It's not *that* odd of a concept. It was what I wanted out of life."

"To marry a woman you love?"

"Jackass." Lips quirking, I can't help but smile when Marcus banters with me.

Eyes glinting with mischievousness, Marcus slides the infinity band over his pinky finger and smirks. I know that wicked grin– Marc is going to say something I will regret.

Always pushing the limits of my emotional restraint, "Did you like this ring?" Since I don't know where he's leading with the question, I can't do damage control.

"I love it." I murmur in awe. "It was the perfect ring for me. Understated instead of ostentatious."

Apparently dead-set on murdering me from the inside out, like his demented version of aversion therapy, Marcus slides the band on my left ring finger, and makes a pleased sound in the back of his throat as it slides into place.

Gazing up at Marcus in suspicion, I'm not going to like where this is going. When Marcus is uncomfortable, he razes my life to the ground. Partners– we both have to hurt if he hurts.

"I love how perfect it is on your finger, right at home. I should make you wear it for me," he teases with a voice heavy with emotion.

"Are you trying to make my heart bleed?" Breath hitching in my throat, the suffocating grief nearly takes me to my knees.

"Grant and I picked it out for you," Marcus confesses. "Every jeweler we went to took one look at us and knew who we were, and they tried to get us to buy carat after carat of diamonds. It was an honest to God struggle to find something you'd be able to wear every day for the rest of your life." Puffing his chest out, Marcus destroys me. "I found it, and bought it, and Grant was so excited he didn't knee me when I kissed him."

My heart jackhammers in my chest. I think I'm going to be sick. The only possession I have of Grant's is this ring, and it isn't even his. They tossed me from Whittenhower Estates directly after his death. I wasn't allowed to gather my things, and the only things I left with were the clothes on my back, the ring on my finger, and the necklace holding my parents' bands. I didn't even get the album from my childhood. According to Ade, Whitt stole it and hid it for Niel to have.

"I love knowing that you wear something around your neck that's from Grant *and* me. It's perfect symmetry. I think you should wear it."

"Marcus, no. Why are you trying to hurt me right now? What did I do? What is causing you to turn into the fuckface you warned me about?"

"*You* are," Marcus snarls. "You are, Regina. I wasn't supposed to fall for you, especially knowing you'll leave me without a backward glance."

Tugging at the ring, I try to dislodge it, but Marcus stops me. "I don't think you'd like me marking your neck constantly, no matter how good it feels for the both of us. You're a professional woman, and I want people to know you're taken." Leaning in, Marcus whispers possessively across my face. "I don't want anyone trying to take you from me. Jamie is one thing, Pretty Boy is another. But everyone else must have a death wish."

"Jesus Christ, Marcus! Get ahold of yourself." I hitch my chin up and glare at him. "You're a goddamn dominant who prides himself on restraint. It's almost been over a decade since I lost my virginity, and I've only given it up to you and Grant. This hasn't been an issue my entire life, I highly doubt it will turn into one. I'm a big girl, so I can take care of myself."

"I like the looks of it on your finger," Marcus murmurs, affection thick in his voice. "It's where it belongs."

"You need to have Ezra refer you to a psychiatrist. But then again, I doubt a bipolar person goes through so many moods in seconds flat."

Ignoring my outburst. "Wear it, Regina. Please."

"It hurts me to look at it," I grit out between clenched teeth. It's like Marcus is trying to emotionally torture me.

"It shouldn't– I want your memories of Grant to be good ones. This is a good one." He taps the ring with a sad smile flirting with his lips.

"It's also the last memory I have of Grant." Wrenching my hand away from his, I thrust the ring into Marc's face. "Two minutes after this ring was slid onto my finger, I fell into a pleasure-induced coma. I woke and Grant was gone. Dead. It's not a good memory for me."

"You'll wear it for me." Marcus uses his '*end of negotiations*' voice.

After tossing my necklace on the seat with my shirt and jeans, a second later, my bra, panties, and flip-flops join them.

"Why am I naked? Why are you getting naked?" After a decade of work and being around estrogen, I'm never bored around Marcus, that's for sure. Off-kilter is another matter. "Not that I mind the view, but what the fuck, Marc?"

Pulling off his shoes, Marcus tosses them into the car, then his pants and socks follow. I watch his elegant, nimble fingers unbutton his shirt like an expert, revealing perfectly bronze skin and a few wiry hairs.

Marc's skin glows in the moonlight, and my mouth waters at the sight. I'll never get used to seeing the taut lines of his muscles and gorgeous skin. Other than having what Grant once had, I can't fathom why Marcus would want me. I wish I could call him mine, but there are too many people vying for his affections. It's an impossibility to call a God among men mine.

A smug smirk pulls at Marc's lips as he gazes at the dumbfounded expression crossing my face. Marcus always gets amused when I watch him undress, like I'm a dieter and he's the most decadent candy. It's the same look Cort gives Marcus, and the look Marcus gives Cort. I wonder what it feels like to have that kind of gaze directed at you, the kind of power it would possess.

Taking off while my mind spins, "C'mon, Regina!" Marcus yells over his shoulder and jogs to the dock buck-ass naked.

Giggling the entire way as I follow, Marc's ass cheeks are bright red from the paddling I administered earlier. No sight could be as erotic as watching the tight muscles contract and flex as he jogs. Other parts of Marc's anatomy are visible as he runs– the heavy weight between his legs swings like a pendulum and drives me crazy with need.

Waiting on the edge of the dock for me, skin glowing in the moonlight, Marcus is devastating to gaze upon.

Once Marcus is in arm's reach, I smack his firm ass, stinging my own palm with the force. Marcus grunts, and as he turns his eyes on me, I wait for anger. Shockingly, I receive none.

Marc's eyes are heated, with his mouth parted on a raspy pant– he liked the swat. Shifting his hips, Marcus shows me what's waiting for me. Standing at attention, he's the firmest I've ever seen him, with his cock grazing his belly. Marc's gaze is pure animalistic hunger. If a brick wall was between him and the object of his desires, his cock could drill through it until it got what it wanted.

Clenching my thighs against the need and ache blooming in my lower belly, a trickle of arousal slides down my leg, tickling the back of my knee. Nothing turns me on more than Marcus when he's Master.

"It's autumn– be prepared." Flashing me a wicked grin, Marcus jumps without hesitation. His loud grunt of shock resembles the noise he makes when he comes

"What the fuck? You only live once." With a running start, I jump without a thought or care in the world.

My scream cuts the night as the frigid water engulfs my body. With hasty strokes, I swim to warm myself up. Temperature stealing my breath, I know we can't stay in here long.

"Lake Serenity is my home," Marcus forces the words out between chattering teeth. "I left my grandmother's house and went straight to Shadow Haven. I went from one mother figure who loved me unconditionally to another boy's mother who was as cuddly as a snake and didn't want anything from me but my family name."

Always finding the oddest ways to open up to me, most people wouldn't see it as the gift it truly is. "Jesus, Marcus." I try to swim closer to him, but his strokes have the water propelling me away.

"Dexter built his house as a warning to all those in Crestview, because Serenity was burnt to the ground by arson. The house stood sentry on this ground for over one hundred and fifty years, and I blame our shady parents and the games the founders play."

Swimming against the current, I struggle to keep my head above water long enough to speak. "The arson is connected to what we've been uncovering?"

"I believe so." Marc's voice gets closer and closer, causing water to lap against my cheeks. "Dexter knew I'd never have a home anywhere but here, so he left this land undisturbed for me."

I swim around trying to get warm while Marc plays Jaws. He even hums the theme song as he circles me in the water. It's laughable because he's made me watch the movie so many times I made it his ringtone.

"I never like making long-term plans with you, because I never know if you'll be out for my blood, but next spring we should come back and swim often."

Teeth chattering, I try to force the words out. "You keep hinting, and I keep ignoring. One day, your cryptic shit will make sense."

"On that day, I hope you can forgive me for always putting Grant first, even if I want to place you in that position." Marcus breathes out from between pale lips. "Maybe we could bring the rest of the gang– it would be fun. You and your ladies could come up here for a picnic, or maybe hijack all the Whittenhower heirs."

"That will never happen." My shiver isn't from the cold.

"You'll have your family back sooner than you realize, Regina." Before I can ask what he means, Marcus changes the subject as always. "I love swimming. It's so freeing. My body turns to fluid with the water– buoyant."

Arms hooking on the dock, he lifts himself out of the water, and then kneels on the dock. Surprisingly, the cold water had no effect on his arousal. Marc's cock is pointing his desire at me.

Offering me a hand out of the water, Marcus yanks and I stumble onto the edge of the dock to land on my back. He quickly covers me with his body.

"I'll warm you up, Regina," Marcus murmurs, affection lacing his tone.

Blazing hot, Marcus was in the same frigid water as me, yet his skin is scalding against my chilled flesh. Moaning at the juxtaposition, we wrap ourselves around one another.

Wiggling until he's where he wants to be, without any preamble, Marcus enters me. Gasping, I marvel over how Marcus doesn't believe in foreplay, at least never with me. The cold and the water removed any moisture I had to offer, so he only makes it halfway in before he has to stop, or go further and hurt me.

Neither thrusting nor moving, Marcus blankets me with his body while his cock rests halfway inside my body. Seeming content to just connect, this is a very different side to the man I've come to know.

"In all the years since Grant found you, I've been running interference." Shifting slightly, Marcus raises over me while resting his elbows on the dock. "I've had four people ask permission to have sex with you, Regina. I'm honored that you allow me to make love to you, and it honors me that you chose me after only being with Grant. It makes me feel closer to him *and* you, and I don't want to lose that."

"Marcus," I tread lightly. "You're the one who has told me time after time that the measure of a woman isn't by the amount of men she's allowed into her body. If I have sex with anyone else, it won't diminish who I am or how I feel about you or Grant."

"I'm well aware of that, Regina." Sighing, Marcus organizes his words, which means he's also managing me out of fear of my reaction. "But you're not like Kristal, and I'm not judging Kris. You are a one-man kind of woman."

"And you're not a one-woman kind of man," I add to bring us both down to Earth.

Husky laughter flows from between smiling lips. "Oh, I could most definitely be a one-woman kind of man, but I have a problem with the fact that I'm also drawn to specific men. We both know I associate affection and intimacy with sex. So said woman wouldn't find that fair, I'd wager."

"You'd wager correctly."

"As I thought, which is why exclusivity and monogamy will not be discussed."

Furious and hurt, I try not to allow it to show. "Yet you're threatening anyone who wants to have sex with me, as if you own my body."

Marcus shrugs, but has the decency to look sheepish. "The four men: the first is the one who had to give *me* permission. Yes to one, never to another, train and I will think about it, and finally, I don't think that's a good idea to the last."

"Who?" I want to know who the yes was because it scares the shit out of me. Don't I get a say in who I take into my body?

"I can read your thoughts as they scroll across your face. Initiation into Maître du Jeu is tricky, and the Masters of Restraint have all paid their dues and will want you to do so also, which is why I've dragged my feet for so long. In Vegas, my spawn's mother made us all fuck each other while she watched, whether we wanted to or not. Sex is usually involved, and I don't want to share you. The only consolation is the fact that they are all close to me, and I trust them infallibly."

"Lovely," I mutter in defeat. "Initiation is a goddamn orgy."

"Sometimes, but not always." Marc's playing the sheepish act again. "After your car ride, I told Cort never, but that depends on how your initiation goes. If anyone catches wind that you're my lover, it will be uncomfortable for the both of us."

"Marcus?" I reach up to cup his jawline, and his eyes soften. "I could easily go for the rest of my life without doing Cortez. I value his friendship more."

Smiling brightly, Marcus murmurs, "Right answer... so Roman came to see me this morning, totally freaked the hell out over what you unleashed in him. He actually had the audacity to sit down with both Jamie and me and ask if he could screw you."

"That would be where your bad mood came from." A growl reverberates against my chest, and it takes a few heartbeats before I realize it's emanating from me. "How... what an asshole."

"Exactly. Since Roman is so against BDSM, I said yes only if he would train to become a Master of Restraint. I also said if you ever have sex with him, it will be your choice and on your terms."

Touched, I whisper, "Thank you."

"I'm not a disrespectful monster, Regina– I do have a few good qualities," Marcus teases me. "Roman was very candid about the affect you had on him last night. He was tempted to say yes to the training, more so because of what you unleashed than to have you. I promised it would just be he and I, and no one would need to know until he was comfortable. He'll get back with me, but I know he'll agree."

Before I can reply, Marcus kisses me softer than he has before. Usually our kisses are violent passion with extreme fucking. Tonight, Marcus kisses me as a lover, while rocking slowly into me to prepare my body to fully welcome his. Resting his forehead against mine, Marcus groans into my mouth.

"I won't last long– I fear," Marcus reluctantly admits. "I've been crazed for days because Roman was coming back into your life. I'm sorry about how brutal I was toward you, and it's rubbed my conscience raw. Last night when I was begging, it was because I wanted to be soft with you to erase how I was earlier."

"I get it– if I didn't, I wouldn't be here with you right now, and your cock would be somewhere at the bottom of Serenity Lake."

"I love how you get me." Marc's laughter is strained, and what he says next explains it. "The reason I told Roman he needed to train with me is because I know you'd love to dominate him. Queen specifically picked Roman out for you, so I won't begrudge you the pleasure should you decide. I told Cort no to sex because you're better as you are– your friendship and the closeness and connection would be ruined by casual sex, because you're not a casual person, Regina."

"I know," I whisper in agreement.

"Since Pretty Boy figured out who you are, he's been manipulating the hell out of me. Goddamn him, and it only makes me respect him all the more. I swear to God, even though he's frustrated, Jamie's been walking around with his chest puffed out like a peacock with pride. Pretty Boy is putting me into an impossible position with his demands. He wants you during your initiation, and it's wrong and right all at the same time."

"Initiation or not, I am the only one who decides what happens to my body," I seethe, suddenly annoyed at this Pretty Boy.

"It's killing me, Regina, and it's making me snap all the time. I don't want you to do it because your connection to Pretty Boy is stronger than the one you have with me. I'm fucking furious at Kristal for telling him your identity, to the point I can't look at her without wanting to spit in her face."

"You have no idea how badly I want to punish Kristal," flows huskily from my throat, and truer words have never been spoken.

"Be careful of Pretty Boy. I've had to negotiate to get him off my back. He's very shrewd and calculating– a genius. He's an amazing man, and I'm extremely proud of him. I would applaud his efforts if it wasn't for the fact that we're bartering over you, and I fear for your emotional state if you do have sex with him."

Voice cracking in fear, "Why, will Pretty Boy harm me?"

"Um– no…" Marcus barks a single, sharp laugh. "Pretty Boy has thought of every angle, except for one. You're truly Queen now, so I know you'll kick his ass the instant you see him. While I'm worried over your reaction, I'm not worried about him hurting you but you hurting him."

Burying my face against the side of Marc's neck, I try to come to terms with what I'm feeling. I'm confused, shocked, and scared. The one emotion I feel and would never admit aloud is arousal. It's flattering that someone has begged and plotted for a chance to be with me.

I don't want to feel aroused over something so sick and twisted, but it's obvious when Marcus starts to take deeper, smoother thrusts as my body floods my core with moisture. I'm mortified because Marcus knows why he no longer has to fight my body. Blushing, I flame with embarrassment, and I'm thankful Marcus will never judge me.

I'm no longer cold, that's for dang sure.

"Pretty Boy would please you, Regina. I have no doubt of this. Everything would be about your pleasure and happiness– he's waited a long time for the chance. But my issue is that Pretty Boy doesn't want you to know who he is until *after* he's entered you, and that is where I'm torn."

"No," I gasp out in shock.

"As a woman, you have every right to know who you're bedding, especially since I know with one-hundred-percent accuracy that you wouldn't say yes to Pretty Boy if you knew who he was."

"Then I won't do it," I mutter defiantly.

Marcus drops the bombshell. "Your initiation hinges upon it, Regina… Will you feel pleasure and connection? Yes. Afterward will you feel sick? Absolutely. I'm not the only one with concerns. Jamie is counseling me on what to use as ammunition to get Pretty Boy to back off. We agree that it's good and bad, wrong and right, and that you will undoubtedly react when it's over. Jamie doesn't want you to do it, but he understands. It's out of our hands now, and entirely up to you during the initiation."

Allowing silence to descend, Marcus makes slow love to me on the dock, at complete odds with how he usually takes me. The water lapping against the dock's wooden supports is in time with our rocking. The night air is brisk, but Marc's intense heat warms me from the inside out.

Marcus had said he feared he wouldn't last long, but he's going slowly, taking his time and making it count. He usually pounds like a jackhammer with no off switch. Tonight, Marcus wants our coupling to last. Every few minutes, he stops to chat, to connect us in every possible way.

Marcus is apologizing with his body while connecting to me on a level we've previously never reached. The intimacy is affecting him greatly. He keeps kissing every part of my body he can reach without moving from my embrace, all the while whispering my name reverently.

"Jamie wants you in his bed, but he's not ready for this type of sex until after you see his face." Marc's voice is quiet as a way to hide the conflicting emotions lurking beneath the murky surface. "It's the only thing that's fair for you."

Unable to deny it, my body informs Marcus how I truly feel– my pussy pulses at the suggestion. After an hour of text messages every single night for the past year, not counting his constant presence when I am inside the brownstone, I can't deny the hold Jamie has on me.

The reason I'm not pressing for exclusivity isn't just because Marcus has no plans to ever stop touching Cortez, it's because one day Jamie will show me his face, and I know my world will tilt on its axis yet again.

"Your silence speaks volumes, and I'm not upset." Marc is no liar, and he promised to be truthful when he could be. In this,

Marcus actually sounds relieved that I'm not angry that his friend wants to bed me, or maybe it's because I'm owning what I want for the first time ever.

"Hold me tight Regina," Marcus murmurs against the side of my neck. "Tighter."

Wrapping my arms and legs around Marcus in a near stranglehold, his hands slip beneath me to grasp my ass. Lifting my hips at an angle, he slides deep within me– deeper than ever since he's more aroused than ever before. Both his length and girth have expanded, filling me past the point of pain.

With bated breath, I wait for Marcus to turn into a beast and ride me ragged. He doesn't. My nails bite into his tender backside as I moan into the wind. He roughly pants in my ear and offers words of affection. I dig my heels into his back and press him as tightly to my body as humanly possible. My core struggles to accept him, and the pain is exquisite– it means I'm alive.

My orgasm builds slowly, the pressure maddening. My skin prickles as my nerves try to interpret all the sensations they're fielding. I swear even my hair and nails throb. One moan mingles into the next cry, creating a symphony of pleasures to fill the night sky.

Marcus howls as his release scalds me inside, and for once I welcome it, because this is what sex should be. Marc's climax brings on my own. The undeniable truth of my dominance, I have difficulty finding release until my partner does.

Marc's orgasm extends mine, and mine extends his, with my core milking at his cock as he throbs and releases into my body. It's a never-ending cycle. My body is wracked with waves of pleasure so intense that it's bordering on pain.

We simultaneously go limp, and laughter rumbles from Marc's chest to vibrate against mine. "That was intense– that was the first time I've tried to make love instead of fuck," he admits, and I feel sorry that that is the case for him. "My God, that was intense."

"Understatement, that!" My chuckles join his. "Thank you for going slow for once."

"Oh, that was just me warming up. I've been nuts for days, so I still have another one in me."

Clutching Marcus tightly, my voice quivers in fear. "Oh, shit!"

"I think a *fuck* is in order this time." Marcus flexes his cock inside me, proving he never softened. If anything, he's harder than before, which I find impossible. Sitting up abruptly, he draws me to straddle his hips without disconnecting us.

"I don't want you to get slivers in your back from the dock, so hold on tight to my shoulders," he commands.

Complying quickly, I know what that naughty gleam in Marc's eye means– I'm in for it. Wrapping my arms around his shoulders and my legs around his waist, I anchor myself to him.

On the dock with water rushing around us, Marcus sits on his heels and pumps into me from beneath. Each thrust is harder than the last, and then harder still. Pressing his hand into the small of my back, he twists his hips in a way that has his pelvis grinding into my clit. A howl flows from my throat when the contact is made.

I'm sore from the last time, but it hurts so good.

Love making for Marcus is words of affection. I've noticed this phenomenon when he's gentle with Cortez. I've heard stories of Cort's punishments, or rather Marc's frustrations. He's brutal with Cortez while spewing words of lust. This is the first time I've experienced both back-to-back, and never before tonight have I heard either.

Shocked, all I can do is hang on and endure Marc's vicious onslaught.

"I love the way my cock feels in your tight cunt while we fuck." Marcus grunts sharply, thrusting up violently while shoving me down, forcing a cry of pain to tear from my lips. "You have no idea how much I masturbate reliving how this feels, knowing Grant was here first."

Pulling my hair back roughly at an angle, Marcus bites my neck hard. Digging his teeth in viciously, he moves his head from side-to-side, making sure his mark lasts. Scarring me, branding me for life.

The pain hurts like a sonofabitch, to the point it steals my breath.

"Your cunt is mine– all mine now. Master is so pleased you're not a dirty whore. Children shouldn't come from an overused pussy, because it'll taint them." Wrenching my head backward, he sinks his teeth in again, forcing a scream from my throat. "You saved yourself for me all those years, admit it. Just one look into my eyes when you were young was enough to make you dream of me for years to come."

"Jesus fuck, Marcus!" A scream is torn from my throat, the thrust so hard no doubt blood flows.

"If anyone other than Grant had come before me, I would kill them with my bare hands." Fingers tightening on my breasts in a bruising grip, Marcus twists his hands until my tits feel like they are going to rip off.

"These are the most beautiful pieces of flesh I've ever seen. Your tits are mine, too. Did you like Jamie sucking your tits? He relives that night over and over, rubbing his cock raw." Voice turning snide, "Did you like Pretty Boy's hands on them? Did he touch you softly?"

Twisting harder, Marcus demonstrates he's not Jamie or the other master. I cry out, and he twists harder in punishment. Being a fast learner who places self-preservation above all else, I keep my damn mouth shut.

There's no answer to his questions because Marcus is lost to his rage. Said in jest, I've often wondered if he truly is bipolar. One moment Marcus is calm and loving, and the next he's calm and deadly.

Taking me roughly with brutality, it's not borderline violent— it *is* violence. I thought last night was bad as he pounded me from behind while I gripped the chair rail, but I was wrong.

Marcus has transformed into a feral animal lost in the mating.

Out of nowhere, my orgasm hits with the force of a freight train. Screaming, I dig my nails into Marc's back, scoring his flesh in furrows.

Marcus roars to the night sky with power and possession. "Come for me, bitch," he demands, pounding harder and harder with every thrust. "No one will ever make you come like I do."

Lost in the agony, if I could talk, I'd agree with Marcus if it would make him stop. It wouldn't even be a lie. The most powerful orgasm of my life has me writhing above Marcus as he pounds me from beneath.

All I can do is whimper in a mixture of agony and pleasure, and just take what Marcus gives me.

"I'm going to cum inside my cunt– *mine*. If anyone besides Jamie and me ever releases inside of you, I will kill them. I've wanted to kill Pretty Boy because that is one of his provisions. The only thing stopping me is the fact that it would hurt you and Jamie if I did."

Raging while climaxing, Marcus turns into the most possessive creature on the planet.

"Grant– he made me love you to save you. If I ever come face-to-face with Gwen, I'll kill the whore on the spot for ever touching him." Jabbing me so harshly, I bleat like an animal. "This pussy is for Jamie and me. Your cunt is for us— my cunt! MY CUNT!"

Tears flowing from his eyes, stuck in a loop of misery I'll never understand, Marcus screams as he pours molten lava deep inside of me. Pump after pump of semen floods my flesh. It's a never-ending torrent, and he doesn't stop screaming until he stops releasing.

Chapter Twenty-Five

We ride back into Crestview in contemplative silence. Sore doesn't properly explain the toll Marcus put on me. I understand Cort better now, because Marc's violent frustrations are usually taken out on his mouth and throat. My neck has a bloody necklace of bruised teeth indents. Reminiscent of more than a year ago, my chin has fingertip marks again. My hips, back, thighs, and buttocks are covered in fingertip bruises. I tried to put my thighs together and almost screamed in agony.

I had blood on my thighs from the pounding I took.

It's as if I finally lost my virginity. The first time around, I didn't experience any pain or discomfort, and Grant didn't make me bleed. Back on the dock, when I crawled to my feet, Marc's semen was mixed with my blood, trailing in rivulets to my ankles.

As soon as the release ebbed, Master fled and Marcus returned. I could tell he was grief-stricken over the condition I was in. He took his boxer briefs and dampened them in the lake so he could dab the blood and semen from my legs. Then he redressed me and tucked me in the car with the heater blazing before he dressed himself.

Marcus never apologized, though. He's of the school of thought that actions speak louder than words, and I tend to agree with him. He didn't say it wouldn't happen again, because we both know it will. A sick and twisted part of me looks forward to it, because it was the best sex of my existence. And by the look that's trying to break through Marc's shame, it was the best for him too.

"May I ask you a question?" I ask in the quiet of the car.

"You just did." Marcus chuckles beneath his breath. "Yes, you may," he offers.

"Almost positive, but not quite, I thought I should ask instead of assuming. Is this Katya Waters the female from Ade and Ezra's engagement agreement?"

"Yeah…" Marcus seems surprised that I'm not totally ignorant for once. "I didn't know you knew about that. I'm sorry."

"So Katya Waters is a real threat, and Ade is screwed." Glancing out the side window, I watch as we pass by Crestview's driveway gates.

"I'm sorry. Adelaide Whittenhower is a beautiful, intelligent female. She will be perfectly fine. I'm sure Adelaide and her girlfriend will console each other over their failed plan."

"How about you just tell me who Ade's girlfriend is instead of playing mind games."

"You don't know?" Marc's voice pitches high with an upward inflection of surprise.

"No, I don't. I've come to realize my best friends hold me at arm's length, completely leaving me out of their lives."

"Well, in this, it's understandable considering how you and I are doing each other." With a wave to the security guard, Marcus drives out of the Gates, and then bypasses my neighborhood.

I'd left my car at the brownstone.

"My wife," Marcus breathes so softly I'm not sure I heard him correctly.

"Come again?" Leaning forward and to the side, I try to see Marc's facial expression better. "What?"

"Adelaide Whittenhower has been with Diane Holden since you hooked up with Grant." Marcus says this in a cool and collected voice, as if it doesn't change anything in our lives.

"How many of my so-called friends will betray me, lie by omission? It's disgusting, considering I have few friends."

"Truthfully, everyone in your life has lied to you by omission." Self-loathing rolls off of Marcus in waves.

"Thanks a lot, Marcus," I mutter, annoyed beyond words. "Explain why the marriage was so important."

"Diane wanted her lover in Shadow Haven, and her fortune secured. Ezra is unstable, and uncontrollable. If they married, the entire Holden fortune would have been in Adelaide's hands, meaning back in Diane's. Once Ade and Diane got a kid or two out of Ezra, they wouldn't need him at all. This was more important than marrying Divina to Cortez to secure the legacy. The double-whammy was that Diane and Daniel are closer than you and I, minus the sex. Added to the fact that Diane and Ade have been lovers since the betrothal was made."

"Jesus Christ." On the verge of suffocating, all I can do is listen to Marcus speak.

"Ezra forging his own path will upset the balance. As I've said over and over again, Ezra deserves to find his own life. I never wanted Cortez to marry Divina, nor do I wish the type of life I've led on Ezra. I want everyone to be happy. In a different world, Ade and Diane would be married, and Cortez and Ezra would be married, and I'd be... free."

I start to cry out of nowhere. Great sobs echo from my chest to fill the car. All of the stress of the past few days spills from me, combined with the stress of my entire shitty life. Everything tumbles out at once. Marc's mercurial moods. Roman being Alex. Kristal breaking the sister-code. Marcus fielding sex requests, and my impending orgy of an initiation. Added on top of the shit pile is the fact that I went down this path of utter destruction to save Adelaide, and all along she was lying to me. A lifetime of Adelaide lying to me, of her plotting with Ezra's own mother to rip his legacy from his grasp.

The lust, gluttony, greed, sloth, wrath, envy, and pride has me sobbing. Life is too short to be the passenger driven by the deadly sins.

Marcus veers off the road, throwing the Spyder into park, and then yanks me into his lap. Rubbing my back in a circular rhythm of comfort, Marcus holds me as I cry.

I'm pretty sure I scared Marcus, since I never cry in front of anyone. Shit, I went five years without shedding a single tear. The moment my mother died, I couldn't cry. The moment Grant died, I couldn't stop the flood.

"I wasn't aware that it was so important to you that my son marry your friend. I didn't know you were playing for the other team." Marcus murmurs lightly, but I can tell he's joking to calm me down.

"It's not that. If Ezra really loves this woman, then a love marriage would be amazing. Life is way too short not to grab what you want and keep it safe– cherish it. There are no guarantees there will be a tomorrow for some of us. To plot for so long, to bring so many lives into a quest to steal money of all things... it makes me sick."

Rubbing my back in soothing circles, Marcus surprises me at how gentle and caring he can be. "Is this why you cry? Do you feel as if you took the life you had with Grant for granted?"

"I miss my life," I gasp out, not even realizing it to be true until now. "It was torn from me. I was supposed to marry Grant, and I didn't even know he had bought me a house in the neighborhood my father promised. I was supposed to raise my son with my daughter, with Grant at my side– my future died the day Grant did, and I've just been in a constant state of stasis, with everyone around me being lying plotters with hidden agendas, and I just want to run the fuck away."

"To be free?" Marcus whispers against my cheek. "Whitt's of age now, trying to break free of his own chains, and he'll be coming for you, Regina."

Shaking convulsively, I can't form words to reply.

"You know I love Grant in an unnatural way– not that loving a man is unnatural. But it is when it's an obsessive form of love, and the man can't love me back the way I want. I've raised Grant's sons as if they were my own, Regina. Every day. Every damn day, I see both Whitt and Niel. That is why I asked for pictures of Ella and for you to tell me about her, because I wanted to know Grant's daughter as if she were my own too."

"Marcus," I cry out, curling against his chest to hold him tightly.

"If there is anyone on this planet who understands what you've lost, it's the person who wanted it in the first place and never even got a taste. That's why I know you made the most of the five years you spent with Grant, and why I've been trying to get you to *live* life. If you can truly live, then maybe I can."

"Tell me about my son," I whisper, asking for the first time since I lost Niel. "The majority of my grief over losing Grant is because I feel guilty for abandoning our son, even if I had no choice."

"Niel is a lot like you," Marcus murmurs with affection thick in his voice. "Reserved, book smart yet physically strong-willed. Once in a while, when he's comfortable, Grant's playfulness erupts and it's so cute. I can't wait for you to see Whitt and Niel together. It's interesting–" Marcus laughs, chest rumbling beneath my ear. "Regina, I promise it will be sooner than you expect. I promise you, you will have them both back in your life permanently."

After kissing me softly on the lips, Marcus has me slide back into my seat. As Marcus pulls away, he gives me a look that speaks volumes.

More is coming.

"I'd love to take you home, crawl into bed with you, and make love one more time, then fall asleep in each other's arms. I've never done that. I've never slept with my lover and woken up beside her. The closest I've come to that is holding the boys for weeks while they cried and screamed through their nightmares after their ordeal."

My heart is breaking from the pain in his voice. "Oh, Marc." I feel sad that he hasn't experienced much intimacy. If Marcus honestly believes caretaking traumatized teenagers is even close, then I'm scared for him.

"I'd love to experience what true intimacy feels like, but it won't be tonight. I have to check on the boys to make sure they're both still breathing. Ezra has the propensity to choke Cort– often." There's a joking lilt to Marc's tone, but he's being serious.

"I hope they work it out, really."

"Me too… Dalton Thompson isn't Dalton Thompson." Marcus announces loudly in the quiet of the dark car.

"I know," I admit, startling Marcus. "Dalton's disguised to cover up the fact that he's very young and beautiful in a fragile way. He wouldn't look at me, yet he challenged me to look away, which is why I noticed."

"Ah, Regina… you and I are perfect for one another. I should have known you'd see through it. Dalton is my daughter's older brother. His mother sent him to spy on me. I know it, he knows it, and we're both going to ignore it for now."

"That's the story of my life with me and my girls."

"If it wasn't for Spyder, I would wish I never met Olivia Fontaine. She reminds me of a black widow spider. So gorgeous she could tempt the Pope, but then she kills you after you've fertilize her eggs. Another reason the product of our union should be named Spyder."

An irrational surge of jealousy pounds in my veins, the possessive need to keep what is mine all dominants feel. But then I remember what Marcus told me over a year ago– not only is Olivia Fontaine a black widow spider, she's also a billion dollar sperm thief who keeps her victims captive until they produce another in the bloodline.

"Don't trust Dalton until he comes clean," Marcus warns, cutting off my ruminations.

"Do you know much about him?"

"His name is Dalton Anthony Fontaine Marconi. He's the head of two major crime syndicates– Fontaine and Marconi. But he's also Stanton Green's son-in-law, married to the little girl you used to babysit, which means Dalton is Whitt's brother-in-law– Fate's too."

"Jesus Christ, what a small world. Will Bianca be coming to Restraint?" I try to wrap my mind around the fact that the baby ballerina would be into BDSM. Binks?

"I doubt it. Yet another bloodline marriage, and I'm pretty sure Dalton's gay, anyway."

"I wanted better for Binks, so much better," I muse. "I thought Stanton was stronger than that, stronger than giving in."

"Sometimes it's not about strength when what you love most is used against you," Marcus speaks from experience. "Dalton just turned twenty, and he earned the right to be called the crime boss on his birthday."

"How?" I'm taken aback.

"A few days ago, Dalton's father was murdered in front of him. Then his grandfather disappeared, as did the grandfather's associate. Both of which were accused of Tony Marconi's murder. Olivia sent Dalton here to get him out of Vegas to safety. I know as much of him as I did you. I know everything before I train someone, because I don't like surprises."

I laugh. What an understatement– Marcus not liking surprises.

"Dalton's an exquisite creature. Small and androgynous, with huge green eyes, black hair, and pale skin. He will make someone a very lucky man someday. He's more striking than his mother. It's a shame he's in that ridiculous disguise."

"Why is Dalton really here? There are better places to hide."

"Going by what we've been uncovering about the founders, they're harboring one of their own. I doubt Dalton knows any more than we do, so I'll forgive his ignorance and turn him to our side."

Nodding, I murmur, "I have a good feeling about this kid. I liked him the second I laid eyes on him. Dalton's here to tilt someone's axis, but whose?"

Chapter Twenty-Six

Emotionally on edge as it is, Queen erupts like a banshee the moment I walk in my front door. The rhythmic thumping and squishing noises should have clued me in. Queen's enraged with territorialism, and surprisingly not for what I'd think.

I stare in wonder at the firm, russet-skinned ass pumping into a bent over Kristal. Together, they look like porn actors, but hotter in a less sleazy sort of way. Every hard thrust has them both moaning. Roman has a nice ass, but nowhere near the perfection of Marc's chiseled marble.

There are so many things wrong with this situation. So many. Kris and Roman are both being assholes for varying reasons, and Queen will have none of it.

Time to learn some manners.

"Don't mind me– carry on." Queen's voice purrs from my lips as I sit on *my* sofa– the sofa they're fucking on. Kristal kneels on the cushion next to me, with her arms braced on the back of the sofa, with a stalled Roman standing behind her.

"Seriously, don't stop." I shift, curling one calf beneath the other thigh. "I figured you wanted me to watch since you're in *my* living room, on *my* sofa, where I eat cereal and watch cartoons with *my* ten-year-old daughter."

"I–" No need for me to cut Roman off, because he doesn't have the balls to continue speaking once his eyes connect with mine.

What happened to the Roman Alexander I used to know? Everyone is so reactive, like toddlers throwing tantrums, because their emotional maturity is stunted.

"I mean, c'mon, Kris." Eyes roaming her bent body, I decide to mortify her. "Nice tits, by the way– perky now, but give it a few years. Once you have a kid, those bags will sag."

"Regina!" Kristal's hands cup her perfect tits while her paler than usual face blooms with embarrassment.

"It's not like I didn't build you an entire house in the backyard for your exploits. Is the guesthouse being fumigated for STDs? Or didn't you want Roman to see the orgy palace?"

Turning slowly like a soon-to-be murdered victim in a horror flick, an inky eyebrow raises in my direction. "Resorting to slut-shaming, are you now?"

"Me?" I point at my chest. "Roman, my man… Alex, whatever your name is tonight. Xander? You're the one who just called your girlfriend a slut, because that word never once slipped past my lips. In fact, nothing I said wasn't the truth."

"I– wait?" Confused and acting as dumb as a box of rocks, maybe because all the blood that usually nourishes his brain is swelling in his cock, "What?"

"You're an educated man, Xander. You'll figure it out."

Balls dropping, Roman gets insulted. "Stop calling me that!"

"You're pissed?" I challenge Roman. "Why are you fucking on my sofa? Why? Fate lives here with Ella and me since she has the common decency to stay at her lover's homes for the evening. I've never fucked on this sofa. Hell, I've never fucked on this property. But, by all means, fuck away while my daughter and Fate are sleeping down the hall."

Roman finally gets the gravity of the situation, how disrespectful and disgusting their actions are. He tries to pull out of my housemate, but I stop him with a smack to the ass. Firm, but the cheeks jiggle a bit.

Roman freezes, and I watch with vindictive satisfaction as his pupils turn to pinpricks and then blow wide with lust.

"Continue," I command, smacking Roman's ass once again. Then I add insult to injury, "Xander. Roman was my childhood friend who respected me. Alex is the man who avoided me like a spineless coward. Xander is the disrespectful fuckface who would screw the resident sex addict on his childhood friend's sofa while her daughter was sleeping down the hall."

Roman's turquoise eyes look uncertain as he watches my face for an indicator on how he should proceed. I want to scream and shout and beg him to explain what he's doing and why, because this is not the kind and considerate man I remember.

With hesitation, Roman begins by moving slowly. His muscles coil and bunch beautifully, and I try not to have the sight distract me from what I must do.

Honest. I don't want to fuck Roman. Ever. I want my friend back, but that doesn't mean I won't enjoy the view.

Scooting up the cushion, I make myself comfortable. Just to be an ass, I make sure my eyes are trained on Kristal's tits, and then between her thighs where Roman's hiding his limp sausage.

"Now's a great time to talk, don't you think?" I smile sweetly while folding my hands in my lap.

"What's wrong with you?" Kristal's voice is strained, like she's trying to talk through a straw.

"Why? Did you expect me to beat you? Maybe yell at you and make you feel like shit? Throw you out of my house and my life, so you won't have to look me in the eye while you lie to me anymore?"

"What are you talking about?" Roman stares at me, no doubt terrified I'll say Voldemort's name again, like I did on our walk several times. I give a point to Roman for not telling his partner in crime that their jig is up.

"I'm not going to give you what you want, Kristal, because that's not how Queen rolls. Don't you like her?"

"Queen's scary like Master." Kristal's hazel eyes are bugging out, albeit a bit glazed looking. She may be scared of Queen, but she's a naughty submissive who will only respect a dominant who can put her into her place.

"What happened to you?" Roman's eyes are tracking across my body. At first, I think he means my demeanor, but then I realize I'm looking rather beat up.

"A jealous Marcus happened– he was reasserting his and Jamie's claim on my body."

"Why?" Now Kristal is looking at me like she's never seen me before. "Did you really fuck somebody else? I doubt there's a man alive hotter than Marcus."

"Really?" I mutter in disgust. "I'm not fucking around on Marcus, and way to insult your boyfriend."

"Marcus has even conned me into oral with him." Roman looks like he's going to be sick, as if he meant to think it, not say it aloud. "I mean– I'm not insulted." Whispering so softly I have to strain to hear him, "And it was only the one time."

"I know– way to go, you!" I taunt the idiot. "Kristal, it seems that just this morning your boyfriend asked Marcus *and* Jamie for permission to fuck me. Did you know that?"

Smirking at the lovers, I feel power coursing through my veins– addictive power. I don't rat Roman's ass out because of jealousy, or a way to stick it to Kristal. I do it because what good is this bullshit relationship if she's hosting orgies on my property, he's getting sucked off by Marcus, and then asking to do me?

Roman treated me with respect when we were kids, now he disrespects me every time I turn around, and it makes me sick.

After the shock fades, Kristal flinches, then tries to crawl out from beneath Roman as he curls around her back in the doggie-style position.

"Tut-tut… No." I tug Kristal back to where she was, placing her palms on the back of the sofa for good measure. "We're going to talk, and Roman is going to fuck you." I slap his ass to get him moving again.

"I guess Kris didn't know, Xander. The Roman I knew wouldn't have done that. It was very naughty of you, wasn't it? Stupid? Do you have a death wish?"

I implore Roman with huge green eyes, while waiting for a reply.

Goddamnit, I feel alive! Not only am I dominating Roman, but Kristal too. It's a powerful, heady sensation.

Addictive.

"Yes, Regina– I'm a fucking idiot, and I deserve whatever you throw my way."

"Queen– it's Queen right now, *sweetheart*."

Flinching, Roman looks on the verge of puking his guts out. "Queen suits you, and I mean that in the best possible way. I'm a rotten asshole, and I don't know why I allowed Kristal to talk me into this– I should have known it was a trap."

"I didn't trap you into fucking me!" Kristal snarls, and I don't blame her for being angry. Her boyfriend is sacrificing her while trying his damnedest to side with me so she'll take the brunt of the blame.

Dick move, that.

"Own your choices, Xander, or else it looks an awful lot like slut-shaming." Head hitching backward, I let the ironic laughter fly.

I don't need a paddle and a bench, or ropes and chains, or gags and toys. I only need receptive people to do whatever I say, while I show them the error of their ways. I don't need a dungeon, because as sick as it is to admit, my kink is playing God.

"So, we're going to play a game. I'm going to ask questions, and you're going to answer them. There is *no* option not to answer truthfully. Simple. Roman, Kristal, do you agree?"

"Yes, Queen," comes in unison.

Smirking at them, they wince. I feel like a predator that's cornered its prey. My God, I could become addicted to this sensation. No wonder Marcus is fucking crazy.

"Roman, how many boys and girls have you been with?" I lean forward and get into his personal space. I'm really curious to know.

"Four girls, and a guy gave me a blowjob while I sucked another dude off–just the one time, though…" Roman's voice trails off, getting quieter and quieter as he speaks. Face blooming red with embarrassment, he stops fucking Kristal again.

I give Roman another thwack to the ass to start him up again.

"Kris, answer the same question, please," I coax, knowing it's not going to be good. I'm not trying to shame her. I'm trying to get her to admit it out loud to hear that she may have a problem that needs to be addressed.

"Seventeen girls and six-hundred-and-forty-three guys." Defiant in the face of her addiction, Kristal admits this without a shred of shame. I'm not entirely sure how she would keep track of such a high number. During an orgy, how do you remember to add them all? So I'm terrified that's a conservative estimate and not a factual number.

"Hope you're double-bagging, Roman." I say this not because I'm shaming Kristal, but because I want to take note of his reaction. I've noticed Roman likes to call everyone else out when he feels they are being judgmental, while simultaneously judging them.

Hypocrite.

"I am," his voice deepens in disapproval, eyes turning stormy with his anger. I can sense Roman doesn't want to fuck Kristal anymore. He looks disgusted, and that pisses me off.

"I see your disgust, Mr. Don't Slut-Shame," I twist my words with anger. "Next question. What do you think of me?" I fire off.

"I don't like how you're like Kris now." Roman answers without hesitation.

"Like Kristal how?" Voice warping with confusion, I'm at a loss. "I'm nothing like her. What the hell, she's your girlfriend?"

I wouldn't be ashamed if I were like Kristal. I just don't want someone thinking I'm a pathological liar who has no issue breaking the sister-code.

"This BDSM bullshit, and all the guys you're fucking. Look at you for Christ's sake," he whisper-shouts and points at the marks all over my neck and my mussed up hair.

"You're a goddamn hypocrite, Xander! So you don't like me anymore because I'm a whore, is that what you're saying? Your friendship is conditional? You were begging Marcus to train you in this BDSM bullshit just this morning, you judgmental prick."

"God, no, Regina– that's not what I meant," Roman mutters in a panic, and I can tell he's being genuine.

"Regina left the building when she found her childhood friend fucking her girl on the very sofa her daughter takes naps on. You'll give me the proper respect by calling me Queen."

"I apologize, Queen," Roman says, properly cowed.

"You think since I'm in this lifestyle that I'm a whore, I gather. I'm a whore because I signed a contract to have sex with a rich man and produce an heir, not because I had sex– get that straight, Roman."

"No, Reggie!" Roman protests. "Grant didn't make you a whore– you're *not* a whore!"

"It's a fact that I am the very definition of the word," I mutter with a shrug. "FYI: Kristal added those numbers to her tally before she was embraced by the community, not during her time with us."

"That's mostly true, actually." Kristal looks scared to speak, but she does anyway. "I've been doing the same guys over and over again, instead of random strangers."

"Roman, I've been with two men. Does that surprise you? *Two.* The first was the father of my children and the second was his best friend. Both were born out of mutual respect and honor. Regardless, I may fuck my way through the ranks of Restraint if I feel so inclined. It's of no concern of yours, nor does it signify my value as a human."

"Yeah, but… is that sanitary? I mean, do you really want all those men touching you? Then there is that bizarre shit you guys are into. It's not normal."

"Xander, if you're going to fuck Kristal on my sofa, then you best have the balls to finish what you start." Without thought, a punishing smack reverberates up my arm and stings my palm– its sound cracking through my living room.

Roman grunts loudly, but doesn't scream, and he gains a bit of my respect for that.

"First, I need to say your bias toward BDSM is fear-based, because it probably seeps into the edges of your consciousness when you're jerking off, and it terrifies you that you're not normal."

"That's not–"

"Save it– the reason I'm bringing numbers up is to show how you and Kristal will not be compatible until you're honest about your relationship. If you love each other and want a future, you cannot continue this charade. You spout this no slut-shaming attitude while simultaneously judging Kristal and me for having sex because BDSM may be attached to it. You also need to recognize that Kristal is a sex addict and a habitual liar."

I caress Kristal's cheek to lessen the dig– she knows I love her, and now she understands I *get* her. Reaching over, I place my hand on Roman's back to connect us.

"I loved you, Roman," I profess, and I'm shocked at how easy it was to say the words. "You were my protector and friend. But now I realize I don't know you anymore, and I'm not sure I even like you. I was going to ignore that fact while we reconnected, but once it's fucking on my beige sofa, it's hard to ignore."

"Fuck– you're right." Roman's words match the self-disgust etched across his chiseled features.

"Did you know Alex was the Roman from my list?" I ask Kris, getting to the heart of the matter– the betrayal that hurts the worst. Not because it was Roman, but because I saw Kristal as one of my partners in life.

"Yes." Defiance glares back at me from hazel eyes.

"Why?" My voice breaks for the betrayal.

"Gwen was like a cool older sister to me. Just before you came into our lives, I tried to get with Grant but he said no. Then I tried to seduce Marcus into noticing me, but he looked right through me. I've known Roman for a long while, so I seduced him knowing it would hurt you. I'm with Pretty Boy to hurt you, too, but he refuses to fuck me. Yet again, someone is saving themselves for *you*."

"Jesus Christ, why in God's name would you be jealous of me, Kris?" Beneath my anger is sadness.

"Everything is yours, and I'm just your hanger-on-er. I'm disposable to you, interchangeable with Fate or Ade. That's why. And I know when you figure out who Pretty Boy is, you're going to want to kill me, and you'll finally see me for the trash that I am."

"Who the hell is this Pretty Boy?" I hiss in anger. "And you're the one who makes yourself look and feel like trash. No one will respect you if you can't respect yourself."

"I want to be wanted, and the men who fuck me never do. I'm always a placeholder, just as I am to you."

"That is such bullshit– I don't think that at all!" Furious, I ask something I shouldn't. "How many people have you fucked today?"

"Three. I was with Cort, Ezra, and Pretty Boy," pride and shame war in Kristal's tone.

"What?" Shock and awe heavily lace my voice. "And you're jealous of me? I have no idea why. I'd kill to look like you. Cort? Ezra? Pretty Boy?"

"They want to fuck me," she hisses. "But they want to *possess* you. There is a distinction."

"I smell self-inflicted emotional bullshit." Noticing Roman has stopped, I tap him in the ass to get him going. "Hey, keep thrusting."

"Alex is limp," Kris murmurs in defeat.

No shit. It's like fucking a cesspool.

"All three at once?" I ask in amazement.

"Yeah," Kristal announces with pride. "Cort fucked me from behind while Ezra went down on me, and Pretty Boy screwed my mouth. Ezra usually doesn't do that kind of thing. It was the first time ever, actually. I felt damn great about it afterward, until Cort said he was done playing. I was hurt, and I asked if I did something wrong."

Both Roman and I are riveted, our heads cocked to the side as we listen to Kristal's sexual exploits.

"Cort and Ezra are no longer playing with anyone but each other. Something about how their woman wouldn't like it." Kristal shrugs. "I didn't think they had a woman– that's something Ade needs to know."

"Ezra's gay for fuck's sake!" Roman interjects. Kristal shrugs in answer, but I want to know how Roman knows Ezra.

"So I watched Cort dump us, one right after another. Monica slapped Cort when he got around to her– they had been together for years. Since Monica's a really good submissive, he comforted her instead of punishing her," she says in a voice tinged with jealousy.

"Holy fuck!" I whisper-shout.

Who is this Katya Waters chick? Cort being monogamous? I give him a week. Tops. Oh, no! Marcus. If Cort doesn't have an outlet, he's going to drive Marc crazy.

Shit!

If Marcus doesn't have Cortez as an outlet…

I realize I've spaced out for a few minutes when I feel both of them staring at me. Roman's no longer inside Kristal, and his dick is resembling a slug, completely limp and sad.

Pity.

"Sorry, I was thinking. Okay, Queen's back." Pointing, I order him where I want him. "Roman, sit on the sofa."

Roman sits next to me, and a scent I've never smelled on his skin wafts up– sex. Sex mixed with his clean scent is even more intoxicating. Jesus. My eyes flutter shut and it takes effort to keep them from rolling up.

"Touch yourself. I want to see what you look like erect," Queen purrs at Roman.

Roman needn't bother masturbating, because he grows before my eyes to an impressive length. He isn't thick, but very long, and perfectly curved to reach that extra hard to reach spot. My mouth dries up yet waters instantly. I wish I would've sucked Roman off when I was eighteen. No such thing as do-overs.

Roman's laugh draws me back to myself. The lusty expression on his face and the angry one Kris is sporting, tells me that I didn't think that last thought, but rather spoke it aloud.

"Condoms?" Roman shucked the last one when he went soft. Kris hands him two. He wasn't lying when he said he'd double-bagged it.

"I work at an inner-city community outreach program. I've never gone bare. Not even for a blowjob."

"I respect that. Just take note, wearing two condoms increases the likelihood of the condoms tearing. So you're wasting money and exposing yourself to risks."

"So much for what they're teaching at Transcend," Kristal mutters sarcastically, and adds an eye roll for good measure.

"On the flipside, I've always gone bare." I don't know why I feel cocky about not wearing a condom. It's ridiculously stupid, but we're safe. I like the closeness of being skin-to-skin.

Tossing the unused condom on the floor, Roman only uses one. "Never?" he asks with concern thick in his voice.

"Um–no… You can't make babies with one on, and Marc's my only lover, and I'm his, aside from blowjobs, apparently. He requires us to be tested every three months, and the females have to be on birth control. He *suggests* condoms."

"But you don't wear one?" Roman asks, causing Kristal to snicker.

"Not between him and me– no…" I draw out.

"Why?"

"It's an ownership kind of thing– literally marking your territory." I smirk at his reaction.

"You're okay with that?" Roman's eyes widen. I can see him trying to come to terms with submitting that much for another being.

"No, it's a major battle between Marcus and me. But it's *Marcus*. I either deal with his fits and tantrums, or give in once in a while."

Quickly glancing at Kristal, I find her looking sad as she nibbles on her bottom lip. I'm about to make her very happy. Lesbian 101 is about to start a few days early. I'm going to do this at my own speed. If it were up to Cort and Marc, I'd be munched on after five minutes– Na-huh.

"Condom up, cowboy." I command with a teasing lilt, then I add sweetly, "Kris, reverse cowgirl, please,"

"And to think I thought you were a frigid bitch." Releasing peals of pure bliss, I can see why every guy falls head over heels with her. It's just too bad she doesn't realize her true worth.

"I know. I was just in mourning. What I do with Marcus is no different than what I did with Grant, just in the reverse… and with no cocksuckage." A frown curves my lips as the disappointment in my voice becomes recognizable.

"What?" Kristal gets into position. Roman grunts, spasms jerking his muscles as she slides down his cock. I watch in avid fascination as her hungry pussy swallows his thin cock whole.

"Marcus says a blowjob is demeaning and disrespectful. He wouldn't allow me, even after I told him I loved doing it."

"Bastard," Roman snarls, no doubt realizing he was just disrespected. I don't know who was pitching and who was catching, but either way, Marcus only saw Roman as his bitch.

"Um– that whole statement baffles me." Working herself on Roman's cock, Kristal is already breathless. "I'm shocked that Marcus doesn't want you to do it, and even more so that you *like* it."

"Why wouldn't I like it?" Annoyed, I command them, "Fuck!"

While Kristal really gets into it, and poor Roman is hanging on by the skin of his teeth, I strip down to my bra and panty set. Two sets of eyes drink me in– I know Kristal's seen the show, but Roman hasn't.

"You look like a bone a dog has worried for hours, or like you were in a car accident. Are you sure Marcus isn't a vampire?" With wide eyes, Roman stares at me in horror, and I hope it's just because of the bruises and not because I'm mannish with huge tits.

"I'm beginning to wonder that myself," I muse, straddling Roman's thighs.

Kristal is slowly rocking in Roman's lap while facing me. Pressing Kristal's and my tits together tightly, I ignore the fact that Roman's hands were gripping her tits moments ago, and then he quickly flipped them over until they were palms out. I stifle the moan that tries to break free from my lips as Roman kneads my breasts.

Locking eyes with Roman, he looks drugged on the deviant game we play. Hopefully this doesn't get out of my control, because I like it too much myself.

"I like your hands on me," I purr. "Train," I demand. "Then you'll be at Restraint with me and we can play reindeer games. Marcus is going to allow me to run the dungeon, and Cortez wants me to run the club. You and I could make a good team."

Roman's eyes widen, and then glaze over in lust. His full, ruby-kissed lips part and his pink tongue peeks out, begging for me to suck it.

Inching forward to take something I would regret until the end of time, Kristal's warning halts me. "He's going to come already."

Leaning backward as if burnt, I try to get myself under control. "Stop moving for few seconds, and let Roman's cock rest. That should do the trick."

Inhaling sharply, I go in for the kill. First thing you do with a lover is kiss. The only rule Marcus placed on me for when I go to Restraint is I have to playact the lesbian. Kissing Kristal experimentally, I groan into her mouth, sucking at her lips with Roman's taste blooming on my taste buds.

"You sucked him off before I walked in, didn't you?" I gasp out, licking my lips.

"Yeah… I'm sorry." Kristal whimpers, worried I'm going to pound her. "Your boy really is a hypocrite. He won't let me suck him without a condom, but he likes to squirt into my mouth."

"Thank God." Releasing a low moan from the back of my throat, I attack Kristal's mouth, sucking Roman's taste from her tongue.

I have to get rid of this nagging need that Marcus has ignored for more than a year. I love oral sex– Grant and I were crazy for it. Even after years together, there wasn't a day that passed where we weren't sucking each other off. Finally I had a lover after a decade without, only to have Marcus deny me the most fulfilling aspects of sex. No foreplay– no sucking, or touching, or caressing. All fucking, all the time.

If I was allowed to kiss Cort, I'd be attached to his lips, just so I could finally get a taste of Marcus. I even tried being naughty to get the mandatory skull-fuck punishment. But Marcus knew what I was doing. Instead, he denied me sex for three months. I thought I'd get Carpal Tunnel Syndrome from finger-fucking myself constantly during that time. Training with no release is pure torture.

Kristal and I take turns sucking each other's tongues, mimicking a blowjob. I press into her perfect breasts, luxuriating in Roman's hands between us.

Our mounds are fused together, and Kristal keeps tilting her hips to grind her clit on me. I rock with her, as if we're both fucking Roman. He's inside Kristal, but only halfway. His sack, the base of his cock, and about three inches of his length are resting against my soaked panties.

My tender, tortured flesh screams in agony. I'll never be able to come after the pounding I took earlier, but knowing that Roman's on the other side of that silk barrier is almost enough to bring forth a release courtesy of my fucked up mind. Usually it's not the physical, but the mental arousal that gets me off.

"Queen," is rasped against my throat as Kristal reaches her peak. Biting me hard, she muffles her scream, no doubt adding a small, delicate mark along with all the others branding my neck.

Falling against my chest, completely limp, I pick Kristal up and place her on the sofa. It creeps me out how I'm a woman, yet I can easily move my friends around with little effort.

Freed from Kristal's pussy, Roman's cock pulses on his belly, jumping toward me in greeting. His hands find my hips, and he tries to pull me up and over him.

"Nah-uh, Roman. Take off your condom and stroke yourself for me." Queen's voice is deeper than ever before, a seductive purr that Roman can't deny. "I want to watch cum pour out that beautiful dick of yours."

"What about you?" Roman pops a perfect inky brow above those mesmerizing turquoise eyes.

"Are you questioning me?" I ask in a cold voice. "This isn't about me." Queen's voice erupts from my throat again.

"No, Queen," Roman murmurs in acquiescence.

Roman's a switch, and he submits better than the submissive Kristal. I haven't seen him find anything he deems worthy enough to fight for yet, but I know there's something deep down inside him that he'd battle me over. I remember the hard-assed Roman, and I miss that guy. But he isn't the one who wants to play with Queen.

I watch in morbid fascination as Roman's long, gorgeous fingers glide up the length of his cock, and back down again, over and over in a slow rhythm.

I've never watched anyone but Grant masturbate. Cort always shoves his hands down his pants, so there's never anything to see but his orgasm face and sticky fingers.

Roman does it differently. He only uses his fingertips to pull his foreskin back and forth over the head of his penis. Grant wasn't circumcised either. Marcus is, and he won't let me touch him to experience the differences.

I just now realize I've never touched Marc's cock except with my pussy. Sex is immediate with him– no foreplay of any kind. Marcus just shoves his dick in, and I hadn't realized how disappointed I've been about that until now.

It doesn't take Roman long before he's panting in need of release. His cock-slit is dripping onto his belly. I yearn to lean forward to lick his abs clean.

My body is a wick for the lust that flames inside of me.

A whimper bubbles up my throat every time Roman's fingers slide up and down that gorgeous shaft– he'd let me do whatever I wanted to him, I instinctively know that.

I need more than the rough sex I've been having, so much more, and it has nothing to do with Roman– I won't use him as replacement.

Holding my eyes, the electric spark flares between Roman and me– maybe stronger than ever. He shows me how he's submitting because he wants to, not because he must. I see the banked fire in his eyes– the dominance trying to overcome Roman's need to submit.

Abruptly grabbing my hips, Roman yanks me to him. Before I can protest, he's growling out his release with my slit resting on the length of his cock, with only his cockhead peeking out. Arc after arc of semen shoots out of his cock to land on his chest and neck– the first one landing with a splat to his chin.

Roman throbs and pulses beneath me so strongly that I wish he was inside me, just so I could experience it from the inside out. My eyes flutter shut in desire to know the sensation of that powerful orgasm firing hot inside of me.

Even with his head tossed back in ecstasy, Roman's eyes never leave mine. The moment is intense, yet not entirely sexual. Roman is trying to connect with me the only way he can in this moment. He groans and gulps for air, but he isn't loud as he comes. His neck cords with stress as he tries to be quiet, ensuring the rest of the house doesn't hear his cries of pleasure– that earns my respect.

"Clean it up, Roman." I command as soon as he quiets.

Roman doesn't ask what I mean. His fingers quickly scoop up the milky fluid covering his chest, abs, and chin, then the fingers disappear into his mouth covered in cum, only to reemerge spotless. He repeats this process until he's sparkling clean.

Patting the top of his head, lingering a bit on his perfect hair, "Good boy," I praise Roman, and he beams back at me with sparkling eyes.

I have to get Roman away from me before I kiss him, or do something equally stupid. It's just lust, and Queen doesn't fuck because of lust. She respects the fact that Regina Regal is a woman who wants a deep connection with her lovers, not a quick fuck that may cause regret.

I'd regret fucking Roman, just as I would Cortez, because their friendship has a higher value than a ten second release.

"Go to the Guesthouse and rest." With awkward movements, I climb off Roman's lap. "I need to speak to Kristal in private for a moment. She'll be right out." Gazing down at him, I speak the truth. "I really enjoyed this, Roman."

"Me too, Queen." Roman kisses me on the cheek, and that electric zap returns with a vengeance. He smiles at me, and says, "Regina," because he noticed that Queen has left the building.

But Queen really isn't gone. She's lurking beneath the surface, and as soon as Roman leaves, she'll be back for Kristal.

I wait patiently as Roman redresses, then my gaze follows him through the picture window as he crosses the lawn. Then I wait until he disappears behind the guesthouse's front door, and longer still until lights pop on.

Grabbing her scattered clothes from around the room in a hurry, "Regina, I don't want to listen to this shit!" Kris whisper-shouts with defiance.

"Wrong bitch, Kris," I snarl. "You *will* listen right this instant."

Glaring Kristal down, she drops to the floor. "Queen, I'm so sorry," she grovels.

I don't yell. My voice is low and seething with menace. Controlled.

"Never again, Kristal. I fucking mean it," I spit. "This is my home that I share with my daughter. Roman was my friend. I don't know what other jealous plans you have in play, but they stop this instant. If you do anything else, one more thing, no matter how big or small, you're out of my life," I promise.

I wait for it to sink in, then Kristal begins to weep and beg. I don't have the time for her groveling. She knew better when she did it. It was in direct challenge of me, and it was to feed her addiction.

I'm not finished, and I need Kristal to pay close attention. I grip her chin as Marcus does mine when he needs my undivided attention.

"I've loved and cared for you since I met you, Kristal—unconditionally." I hate how soft my tone has become, showing my weakness. "Even in my private thoughts, I don't shame you for your actions. I'm the only person on this planet who sees the good in you, the potential, and I've tried to drag it out of you kicking and screaming. But you would rather show the world how you see yourself."

In this moment, I realize this was the lesson Marcus was trying to teach me over a year ago about my appearance. My body-image insecurities were infecting how I thought others saw me, when it was just how I saw myself.

Because it didn't fucking matter how anyone else saw me, as long as I didn't accept who I was.

"You have a problem, Kristal. A big fucking problem, and I think you need professional help. Your worth is not centered between your thighs." Jabbing a finger to her temple, I seethe. "It's here— your mind. And here," pointing at her heart. "Every woman has a vagina, and it's no big feat to have a guy fill it with a dick. What is a feat is respecting yourself enough to know the difference between a guy who gives a shit and a guy who is using you to get off."

"Sex doesn't make me a bad person." Kristal sounds like a disillusioned child.

"No, it doesn't. If you're having sex for pleasure and connection, not if it's for validation. Go to work, hug your mother, or take a painting class. You don't even have daddy issues, because Albert is your biggest fan. You don't need some random dick making you feel worthy because he gets off on you– that's just disgusting."

Hitching her chin up in defiance, Kristal doesn't surprise me with what she says next. "I'm not going to apologize because I'm not sorry."

"I know– I didn't care that you were a sex addict as long as it didn't affect me or mine."

"Me fucking around doesn't affect you at all!"

I ignore Kristal's outburst. "Just as I don't care that you're a pathological liar unless it's directed at me. But this stunt tonight crossed several lines. What if Ella had come out to get a drink? Or wandered in here because she heard a noise? She's at an impressionable age. We sit on this couch! My daughter will not be a part of this bullshit. She is a child!"

Kristal has the decency to turn her back on me, never looking more ashamed in her life.

"First things first, I expect a new couch in this spot by tomorrow afternoon. I want this one gone– tonight! Second, I didn't play with you to reward you, Kristal. I played with you so you would see what you'll be missing out on. Never again will I touch you in this manner. I played with you both so Roman could understand his needs and see the real you for who you are."

Whipping around, "You want what I have!" Kristal has the audacity to accuse me.

"The only thing I want from Roman is friendship, Kris. That's it. I'm not built like you where the only purpose I see in human beings is a cock and vagina. I don't want to break you guys up, because I love you both. But I do want respect and honor to be between you. It's like watching a train wreck. I see the train up the tracks careening toward Roman, but he's too blinded by lust and infatuation to get the fuck off the tracks in time. He's a big boy, so I'll wait for the aftermath."

"How dare you say that to me?" Voice stiff with anger, if I was anyone else, Kristal would have attacked me.

"How dare I? Are you shitting me? I said I loved you unconditionally, Kristal, but that doesn't mean I'll put up with your destructive behavior. Until you come to terms with your wrong in this, I don't want you in this house. Come morning, your fingerprints will be removed from the security system and you'll have no access to this house with my daughter in it. Fucking on my sofa showed that there are some major issues between the two of us. Until they're fixed, I can't trust you, especially around Ella."

"Are you terrified she'll catch the sex bug from me?" Kristal spits.

"No, I'm terrified your misguided resentment toward me will be felt by my daughter, that's what. All I've ever done is love you, care for you, and try to make you see your worth, and all you've ever done is throw it back into my face. There is unconditional, and then there is disrespecting myself by putting up with your shit." Turning away from Kristal, I say over my shoulder. "Good fucking luck, Chica!"

I rush from the living room before I start screaming and physically harm Kristal until she gets a clue. The loss of me is her ultimate punishment, because I was one of her positive validators. If she does anything else, I will not hesitate to exterminate her entirely from my life. It will hurt me, but my child comes first.

It takes everything in me not to go back out there when the sister-code hits my mind with the force of a tsunami.

My list had four men: Grant, Roman, Whitt, and Niel.

I just found out Kristal tried for Grant. When? She was fifteen when I entered Whittenhower Estates. My intuition screams that she tried *after* I moved in. Now she's fucking Roman. If she touches either of the boys, I will thrust her from my life so fast she'll have sidewalk burns on her asshole.

Chapter Twenty-Seven

After my shower, I'm taking a long soak in my bathtub. The shower was to clean a night full of sex from my body, followed by a douche to clear Marcus from where he doesn't belong. The bath is to warm the chill that has seeped into my soul. I can't even think of Kristal without wanting to spit nails. While at the same time, it breaks my heart that Kristal's hurting so much she's trying to destroy our friendship to prove I didn't find her worthy in the first place.

I wonder if we should get Ezra on retainer for our psychological needs, because Roman isn't using his education to help his own girlfriend cope with whatever is infecting her.

The whistle of my text message alert pings from the edge of the tub. After drying my fingertips on a towel, I reach for it already knowing who's making the request.

Jamie: *Regina, I'm sorry for discussing Roman with Marcus. Will you still converse with me?*

I don't even hesitate before responding. Jamie gives me what no one else does. Softness. Tenderness. Comfort. He makes me feel like a woman instead of an acquisition. It feels like Jamie puts me first, always worrying about my comfort, and somehow sensing when I'm upset. Every woman needs a rock in her life. Jamie's mine, even if he won't allow me to see his face.

—Hi, Jamie. Glad to hear from you. You know you're the highlight of my day.

Jamie: *I'm glad to hear that. How are you?*

—Ah, the same greeting as always. How predictable, Jamie. Why?

Jamie: *Marcus.*

–Oh, are you spying again?

Jamie: *No, Marcus said he was afraid he'd hurt you. Um… sexually, so probably emotionally and mentally too. I know better than anyone how Marcus can lose his head and not realize the harm he's doing. I'm checking in because I care, but also because Marcus left to do a wellness check on Ezra and Cortez, and I know you need someone to do one on you too.*

Even though you can never tell the tone a text is written in, I laughed at that. I don't know if Jamie's being serious or sarcastic. I envision Cort's neck fisted in Ezra's hand while they… yeah, not going down that route.

–I fucked up some tonight. Marc will probably kill Roman.

Jamie: *You didn't sleep with him, did you? PLEASE tell me you didn't! I try to never judge you, but this is in your best interests. You would regret it, Regina. Truly, you would. That's not some possessive asshole talking. It's me, knowing you better than anyone else.*

–No. I didn't sleep with Roman, and I know exactly what you're talking about. After the night I had, I walked into my house ready to sleep the night away, only to find Roman banging away at Kristal from behind… on my sofa.

Jamie: *Was Ella on a playdate? Please tell me she was.*

–No, Ella wasn't, and that's the reason it was like walking into my home and getting sucker-punched in the guts.

Jamie: *Did Roman know Ella was home? It's not like him to be so careless, to disregard other human beings in such a disrespectful manner.*

–I have no idea if Roman knew or not, but he was in a mood tonight too. Both of them were testing my patience for some reason.

Jamie: *I'll have a talk with him, because that is unacceptable. First he disrespected me by asking such a heinous question this morning, as if you were property who didn't have a say in who you* had sex with, then he rubs it in your face that he's screwing Kristal... with Ella in the fucking house!

–Jamie, I've never heard you swear before– um, you know what I mean. Normally you're so calm and forgiving.

Jamie: Some things are not forgivable. What was your reaction to their blatant disregard for your sanctuary?

– Queen wanted to toy with them, so I let her teach them a lesson. I was wicked pissed. Not that Roman was with Kristal, but where and how. Ella would've had to walk through the living room to get to the kitchen if she was thirsty. I just... I don't even want to talk about it because it makes me so livid. My daughter doesn't need to see that shit. I mean, Ella's only ten but she already started her monthly. Her body is already more mature than her age, and I don't want her to think that is how love is supposed to be.

Jamie: Ella will fall in love the way none of us have been allowed, and she'll have a life worth living, and I know you'll protect her from everything you can, Regina. You're the best mother Ella could ever have– Niel too.

–You're going to make me cry, Jamie.

Jamie: No crying necessary, because I was only telling it as I see it. So what did you do?

–It's like something clicked inside of me. During training, nothing fit. I was apathetic about all the BDSM equipment and toys. Tonight, directing and watching made me come alive.

Jamie: I was waiting for you to come to that conclusion. I knew it from day one, even if Marcus didn't believe me. Instead, Marc kept forcing you to repeat the training, hoping for something to stick, and I was just waiting for him to get a clue. What happened next?

–I played them as my personal puppets. I waited for Kristal to get off and then made Roman masturbate in front of us. He did touch me– no sex of any kind.

Jamie: *Where did he touch you?*

–My breasts through my bra, and him against me, but I still had panties on.

Jamie: *Okay...*

–Are you angry?

Jamie: *What does it matter if I am?*

–It matters. Are you?

Jamie: *I'm trying not to be. As I said, I won't judge you and I do understand, but I'm still a man. I do have feelings, ya know?*

–I'm sorry. You're right– I would regret being with Roman. I want to rebuild our friendship, not have it destroyed by lust. Do you think Marcus will be angry?

Jamie: *No, Marcus was testing you with this. Sometimes he confuses me, and I'm the one person on this earth who knows him better than anyone, enough so to be able to calculate how he'll react. So don't fret, Regina. Marcus won't be angry– he'll be impressed with your control.*

–I didn't feel in control. I felt like the dominant part of me was in charge and I was its passenger. I was so livid, I was suffocating on it.

Jamie: *What are you going to do about Kristal? I could help you with her, contact someone who should get her in hand.*

–I'll deal with my own shit. In fact, if Kristal does anything like this again, she's out of my life. I've had enough. If I'm dominant enough to enter Restraint, then I should be master of my own home, and allowing Kristal to disrespect me proves I'm not worth the title.

Jamie: *I agree. Regina, Marcus is close to cutting Kristal loose. She has been doing things he finds inappropriate. When she told Pretty Boy who you were, I wanted to kill her, and I don't say* *that lightly. I mean that as the very definition of the word. Kristal meddled out of jealousy, because if she was on your side, or Pretty Boy's side, she would have kept her mouth shut or came clean long ago. Her bullshit has created so many issues, and we can't stop them. There is too much riding on this. Our worlds will collapse, and a loose cannon is a liability.*

—What are you saying?

Jamie: *I know what you and Marcus have been up to, Regina. When Marcus keeps secrets from me, he behaves a certain way. I know he doesn't trust me anymore, when every fucking breath I take is to protect him— to protect you.*

—I honestly don't know how to respond to that, Jamie. Because what we've figured out means nothing in the grand scheme of things.

Jamie: *Kristal's behavior is the perfect example. She'll do anything she can to obtain anything she wants, and anyone in her way is just an obstacle she'll remove with any means necessary. You're on the correct path with what you've uncovered. Seven sociopathic billionaire families are experiencing ennui, so they destroy and rebuild each other over and over again to remove the apathy and feel alive.*

—That's along the lines of what I figured, actually, and Marcus calls me paranoid.

Jamie: *I know you understand the loneliness. But if you were born to this life, then nothing is extreme enough to make you feel alive. You can buy anything, do anything, and go anywhere. Added on top of that, the sins of the father are visited upon the son in an endless cycle of mental, emotional, physical, and sexual abuse, where your life is not your own even before your conception. When that bored and warped, things go awry.*

—I'm that rich, Jamie, as is Marcus, and neither of us is moving our loved ones around an imaginary chess board.

Jamie: *Marcus channels this by owning people. In the sense he wants to take care of them and elevate them to meet their potential, because he believes in them. Marcus can be unstable at times because he was born into this life whether he realizes it or not, which you've experienced, but he is nothing like those who are moving us all along the living chess board in Dominion.*

—Way to make me terrified when I speak to you because it's a comfort. Soothing. A way for me to relax and feel normal.

Jamie: *Maybe I felt it time to tell the truth, what little I can tell. What I just said to you, I've never even said to Marcus. It's my boon to you, because you have no idea how much this past year has meant to me. Seeing you, being near you, conversing with you… touching you.*

—Same here. It's too bad you won't let me see your face, because I'd reward you beyond your wildest imaginings.

Jamie: *Are you trying to charm me, Regina? Because if you are, it's working.*

—What's this I hear about you playing whack-a-cock?

Jamie: *Now who's pissed at Marc's loose tongue? Is nothing sacred with that man?*

—Um… I'm going to have to go out on a limb and answer no to that question.

Jamie: *<laughing> By the way, I'm engaging in a round of whack-a-cock right now actually…*

—Seriously? You're whacking off?

Jamie: *Y E S! I like talking to you. If I've done it once, I've done it a thousand times thinking of you, or listening to you.*

—Is that what you do when you're lurking in the shadows?

Jamie: *I do not lurk! I wait patiently, and as I wait, I engage in whack-a-cock. <I'm laughing>*

—What do you wait for?

Jamie: *Y O U*

—Why the wait? You can have me anytime you want me…

Jamie: *You'll see me.*

—So?

Jamie: *I'm not ready for that. I'm disfigured.*

—I know, and I don't care. It's been a year and a half, Jamie. It's time.

Jamie: *I would love to give in if I could figure out how to do it without you seeing me.*

—Fine, I'll tempt you.

Jamie: *Tempt away… It better be earth-shattering to get me to give in.*

—That's not very submissive of you, Jamie.

Jamie: *I know all of your tricks, Regina, even the ones you haven't used yet.*

—Omnipotent, are we?

Jamie: *Marc's rubbing off on me. But not in the literal sense.*

—Too bad for Marcus, right? So I came to a realization today. Maybe you can help me out. Why won't Marcus do foreplay? No oral sex or touching. It's straight to fucking. I mean, I've never touched his cock. Don't you find that odd? I know I do.

Jamie: *Marcus has some issues, which I can't discuss with you because they're not my secrets to tell. I can understand why this would make a woman like you feel unwanted if all you do is get* *pounded. But this doesn't mean Marcus doesn't want to be touched or touch in that manner. He doesn't know how, and he's terrified. For Marcus, oral is for submission and punishment. He's always more frustrated after his sessions with Cort than before, because he does it for Cort, not himself.*

–Have you seen it?

Jamie: *No, it's always in private. No one has.*

–Is Cort the reason he won't do foreplay?

Jamie: *No. Close, so close, but no cookie for you. I cannot keep speaking of this, Regina. You're trapping me into a corner. Why is it bothering you– the no foreplay?*

–I went almost ten years without sex of any kind. Marcus has been more rough than gentle. I'm not complaining. But I miss the build-up to the finale, and the intimacy of exploring a lover's body. I miss the attention and pleasure of oral. I want to get lost in the connection of sex, not be its passenger. Marcus won't do any kind of anal anything, either. Why?

Jamie: *Ah– same answer as above. You could always do those things with someone else.*

–Who? No one would want to. Plus, Marcus would murder them in a possessive temper tantrum.

Jamie: *Would you like us to take a number? Maybe form a queue in front of the brownstone on the sidewalk?*

–What?

Jamie: *<laughing at you> Regina, you were always so sure of yourself. Why did that change?*

–How do you know that?

Jamie: *Your tempting worked. You have ten minutes to get to the brownstone– starting now. Door at the top of the steps. Enter, then remove your clothing. Walk three paces forward and climb on* *the bed. It will be pitch-black. I will give you your foreplay. Unlimited, unending amounts of foreplay.*

–Holy mother of God!

Jamie: *You're not Catholic, Regina.*

–You just made me a believer.

Jamie: *9 minutes, Regina. I'm playing whack-a-cock. When the clock strikes, I'll come without you. No fun sucking a limp dick! HURRY!*

Chapter Twenty-Eight

I sit in the bathtub in stunned silence. I'm rendered mute as my mind swirls with endless possibilities. Jamie is finally going to let me touch him.

Holy shit!

Oh fuck, I just spent two minutes of wasted time on musing. I jump from the bathtub, not bothering to dry off or drain the damn thing. I pull on a cotton dress with no underthings beneath, and find a fresh pair of flip-flops. I quickly check to see Ella is still breathing and that Fate's still in the house for babysitting duty.

Driving like a bat-out-of-hell, I can't believe I'm doing this. My car lurches forward when I throw it into park. Jogging up the sidewalk, I can't remember if I hit the fob or not– fuck it, the natives can jack the thing for all I care.

I quickly unlock the red door with the cheery gargoyle with the evil smile staring at me the entire time. The key misses the hole several times as my hands shake. I feel like a virgin male during his first time– I almost cry when I get it in.

My foot hesitates before touching the bottom step. After countless lectures about the perils of entering Jamie's sanctuary, I have permission. Charging up the steps like a woman on a mission, I notice nothing but my destination. I bang the door against the wall as I enter, and catch it before it smacks me in the shoulder.

My phone whistles.

Jamie: *One minute. You were in the bath, weren't you? Very good, Regina. Shut the door, and get your ass in this bed! You think you've waited a long time… My dick needs to be sucked!*

Lounging on the bed, Jamie is haloed by the light from the hallway. He can see me, but I can only see the fuzzy outline of his silhouette. I could step to the side to illuminate him, but Jamie would lose faith in me. We're building trust. When Jamie trusts me enough, he will let me see him.

Flicking my sandals off, I let them fly without care where they land. Heart beating out of control, it's like the past year has been building to this moment. Without hesitation, I yank the dress over my head, and stand nude before Jamie with the light from the hallway eclipsing me.

Jamie always makes me feel beautiful, no matter what.

A hollow sound rasps from Jamie's chest– the kind of noise that would frighten children. It's ghostly and haunting, as is Jamie. It's the sound he makes when he climaxes, or when we're talking and he wants Cortez or Marcus to read his hands so he can join in. I love that ghastly sound more than I could ever admit.

Standing in the doorway, I allow Jamie to look his fill for a few moments, because I know he liked the view, or I would've never gotten that noise from him.

The Whistle sings again, and the message is opened before the alert finishes.

Jamie: *Beautiful. Let me show you how beautiful you are, Regina. I beg of you.*

I lock my cellphone as my heel hooks the edge of the door. Kicking it closed, I hop the span between me and Jamie, and then I crawl on the bed. Shivering from a nervousness I can't explain, I wish Jamie could speak words of reassurance.

I huff a laugh.

Jamie's the submissive, and I want him to reassure me. Damn. Bad dominant– bad Queen.

But this moment isn't about dominance and submission. It's about a man and a woman connecting on a higher level in bed.

"I'm really nervous." My voice quivers as I crawl up the bed, trying to locate Jamie in the total darkness of his bedroom. "It's been a long time." Filling the silence with rambling, my nervousness is obvious. "I'm probably really rusty at it. Let's hope it's like riding a bike. See, the problem is, I don't know how to ride a bike."

Seeking me out, Jamie gently touches my hand, clasps it, and then pulls me up the bed. I can't see a thing, but I know we're facing each other because his sweet breath warms my chin and his bare chest is hard against my softness. I snuggle closer, marveling that I'm finally in Jamie's arms at last. He's gasping for breath too, as if he's as majorly affected by our closeness as I am.

Jamie's maybe an inch or two shorter than me, judging by the way our bodies align. I want to squeeze him close, but I'm frightened I'll spook him. My hands skim up Jamie's back, fingertips encountering the softest skin I've ever felt. He isn't overly muscular, but I can feel the definition.

Curiosity getting the better of me, I slide my hands down to cup Jamie's ass, needing to know where it falls in the lineup of asses– Marc's being perfect, and Roman's being a close second. I don't want to think of Grant in this moment, but his ass was devastating. It was the most beautiful sight on the planet. He always made me wish I was a man so I could fuck it– so I could possess him, which is why I understand how Marcus feels.

Making a sound of appreciation in the back of my throat, I cup Jamie's ass. Full and round like a female's, I can envision my fingers clenching it in the throes of passion. It's just as amazing as Grant's, and I whimper in pain for comparing the two.

It's not healthy.

"Your ass is the best one I've seen all day... well, felt up." Laughing softly, I give the punchline to my joke. "And I've seen many asses today. I'm not used to such a bounty."

Enjoying my thorough touch, Jamie scoots closer to me, allowing me a better grip. In the process, his arousal nests between our bellies. He's hard enough that it dents the pudginess of my tummy. That part of him feels perfect, too. Not too big or too small– just right for Regina Regal.

It's strange, the silence in the room. It's like when you're a child and you play the silence game with your parents. The pressure mounts to the point you have to speak or explode, even though you know they wished for quiet. I was never good at that game, and I'd get into trouble. Jamie being mute makes me want to fill the void. It's not awkward or anything. It's so intimate that I don't know how to handle it emotionally.

After Grant died, I didn't even allow the girls to comfort me. The first time I hugged someone was after Ella's birth, when I placed her on my breast to suckle. I was loving and affectionate toward Ella, and Ella alone, for a very long time. Fate and Kristal avoided touching me.

The longer you go without touch, it's almost a painful sensation to feel an embrace. Ade was the first to begin slowly, as if I was a wounded animal. Marcus isn't the cuddly sort, except on the rare occasions when he tells me to hold him. Jamie is a cuddler– I can tell.

"Does Marcus hold you sometimes?" The thought springs out of nowhere. Marcus knows Jamie will never expect sex, and won't give it up when pestered, so he would be comfortable taking comfort instead.

Jamie nods his head up and down, the fine hairs of his whiskers brush my cheek as he moves. Damn– even his whiskers are as soft as downy feathers.

"This is a weird question. You don't have to answer if you don't want. I'm curious, though. I just want to know you both better. Is it sexual for the pair of you? Marcus says it's not, but he wants it to be. But I also know he's known to fib, judging by the lack of dishes in this house."

A noise I've never heard before rattles Jamie's chest, and I fear I've angered him until I notice the telltale signs of laughter.

Jamie's laughing at me.

"I'll take your laugh as a no. I like your laugh, by the way," I mutter absentmindedly as I caress the back of Jamie's neck with two fingertips.

Laughter echoing, fingertips walk up my side to linger near my breast. Jamie waits to see if I'll reject him before he encompasses my breast, and I respect him more because he's respecting me. When I don't tell him to stop, Jamie circles his palm over my budding nipple with expert precision, and I go lax in his arms.

I lean in for a kiss, but Jamie turns his face away from me.

Rejected, my voice is filled with hurt. "Why?"

Hand seeking out mine, Jamie latches onto my index finger, and then lifts it to his lips. He runs it along his top lip first, and I feel the indent of a scar. It's wide yet deep gash, nearly bisecting his upper lip in half at an angle. Then he slides my finger over slightly, having me feel a dimpling of scars marring the other half of his upper lip. Tracing, I feel Jamie's bottom lip, and the majority is the same pattern.

"Acid?" It feels like an acid burn. My father was injured at work while he was changing a bus battery, and he had the same marks on his wrist and forearm.

"Cortez tried to explain this to me the best he could. Is this why you can't speak?"

Jamie nods yes against my fingertip.

"I'm sorry, Jamie. Please let me kiss you. I don't care, because I like you as you are. I'm nowhere near perfect. If you were, I'd wonder why you'd want to be in bed with me."

The soft press of Jamie's lips against my own is the purest thing I've ever felt. So sweet, I want to cry for some unfathomable reason. The kiss is tender and filled with intense longing. I know instantly that I'm the first person to have had the pleasure of Jamie's kiss since his injury.

Using my low moan to open my mouth, Jamie gains access inside. Remembering the feel on my breasts from well over a year ago, I now know Jamie's tongue is scarred, too. It's a sandy texture, but not unpleasant.

Wrapping my leg around Jamie's hip, I realize how amazing his tongue would feel somewhere else. "Jamie, I know you worry about your scars, but I think the ones on your tongue will be to my advantage," I tease him salaciously.

His deep, spooky laughter vibrates my chest, then he playfully licks me from collarbone to chin like a big cat. Rasping against my flesh, he makes me want to purr.

Fingertips gripping my hips, Jamie rolls me onto my back. Parting my legs as I lay on the bed, I allow Jamie to cradle between my thighs. Cock jerking like crazy from the contact with my heat, it's incredibly flattering and turning me on like mad.

Pulling Jamie's hair, I anchor my fingers in the downy softness. Holding him firm, I steal a kiss that explores the depths of his mouth, and even the roof– all scarred.

A ghostly sound rumbles from Jamie's chest as he bathes my cunny with the hot wash of his release. Jamie proves his submissive nature as he climaxes just from the force of my hand yanking his hair.

"That was very naughty of you, Jamie," I sing in a light and teasing tone. Eager with anticipation, "Clean me up," flows as a demand as Queen's voice drops low and turns husky. I'm rewarded with another spurt, and I motherfucking giggle. "And now you have even more to lap up."

I loosen my fist from Jamie's hair, and he immediately shimmies down my body like a well-trained pet. His tentative touch eases my nervousness. My thighs part as far as humanly possible, giving him unlimited access to places only Grant has gone before.

I wait for the rasp of Jamie's tongue on my slit, but I'm rewarded with a nip to my ankle instead. I jerk my foot back, and giggle. Again. I'm extremely ticklish. He nips my calf, and then behind my knee. It's sexy as hell, but I can't stop wiggling around and giggling.

Jamie's strange laugh fills the room, and just the sound of it makes me break out in goosebumps. Anyone else would probably hide underneath the bed, thinking a monster was in their closet, but I'm not normal.

Playful and exploratory, Jamie nibbles a path up my leg from ankle to inner thigh. I squirm and hiss with every bite. Just as I suspected, Jamie will turn a session of oral sex into a feast.

A long, wet lick from thigh to foot has me writhing on the bed and gripping the sheets in my fists. Unable to stop moaning and thrashing about, I've yet to feel his tongue on me.

When Jamie repeats the torturous process on my left leg, I think I'm going to die.

I grunt like an animal when Jamie's tongue finally licks me from asshole to clit. His kiss was gentle against my mouth, and that is what I expected on my nether lips. I was wrong. Jamie sucks my labia into his mouth and pulls with his teeth. That magnificent tongue dives inside of me, collecting all the cream that spills just for him.

Jamie's making a sound I can only describe as a growl– that is if you have an enraged monster from the Syfy channel chasing after you. The animalistic sound raises the small hairs at the nape of my neck, yet enlivens me. I moan in hopes he'll make it again.

Drawing my clit into his mouth, Jamie sucks the bundle of nerves expertly while biting at its root. Without letting up, he flicks it with his tongue. A long nonsensical word flows from my lips, it may have been *holyfuckingshitjesuschrist,* but I may be wrong.

After waiting so long for a taste, I never want this moment to end. "I need to taste you before I cum." I'm not too proud to beg.

Jamie has a hold over me, a powerful hold, and I want him to have it. I've never truly understood the dynamic between the dominant and the submissive before this very moment. It's all an illusion. We both provide a service for the other. One taste of Jamie's pleasure and I'm already addicted.

In the blink of an eye, Jamie's no longer between my thighs. Stronger than I envisioned, I'm flipped and inverted until he's underneath me with my cunt pressed to his mouth and his cock is an inch from my face.

I'm shocked that Jamie could move my large body so fluidly without my help since I was stunned stupid. Without missing a beat, Jamie resumes his skillful oral ministrations to my very happy cunny. I have no idea what to call that technique he masterfully uses besides divine.

Somehow I managed to forget that I asked to taste Jamie's cock the second my clit is sucked into his mouth. Spearing my body with two fingers, Jamie adds one in each hole.

Experiencing a mini-orgasm that starts at the tips of my toes and rages through my core, I scream that word again, *holyfuckingshitjesuschrist* and Jamie growls for me in thanks.

Tongue cleaning the mind-altering wet, stickiness from Jamie's thighs and abs, I finally lick him clean like a lollipop. The more I lick his perfect cock, the harder he sucks me and makes a continuous growly sound.

It's the most animalistic noise I've ever heard, and it's a shot of ecstasy to my system. Queen and Regina are one in the same, and we both love primal men. Jamie's muteness isn't a disability to me. It's the emergence of his true-self– the self we hide from all of our lives, the one that scares us the most. Queen is mine, Master is Marc's, Roman is fighting tooth and nail to pretend his doesn't exist, and Jamie is always his.

Deep-throating Jamie, I groan from the sensation of finally being filled. I've missed this so much, to the point I would beg Marcus until I angered him. That moment where I knelt on the dirty, ripped linoleum in Roman's apartment, waiting to suck him off, opened a door inside of me, and when it was long denied, it went rabid. I spent a lot of time devouring Grant like a ravenous fiend. I've missed it so much that I could cry in relief.

Exploring Jamie without shame, every inch of his length is licked, sucked, and nibbled. I gently warm his testicles, and he almost orgasms when I suck them into my mouth one-by-one. I pull them away from his body to still his impending release.

When Jamie doesn't protest my tongue on his taint, I venture further south. Then I realize he's so submissive, he'll never protest anything I do, so I better ask first.

"Um– are you against this kind of thing?" I circle a finger around Jamie's pruny opening, waiting for permission. "I know you're adamant about Marcus, but what about me?"

I'm too bashful to say it out loud, but it's not like Jamie doesn't have his finger jammed inside of my asshole. Some guys like it, but most don't.

Sometimes my mind and body don't agree. My body's a female, but when I'm in control, I want to control everything. It makes me envious of men, because I feel like I should have a dick to mark my territory, too. I want to impale Jamie somehow, and all I have are fingers.

Jamie rocks his hips against my hand, and I take the movement as a yes. Dipping my head, I give him a few licks to moisten him.

Jamie makes the loudest sound I've ever heard from him– it's pure agony. His cock jerks against my chest, but he can't release since my fingers are pinioning his sack. Working my middle finger inside of him with his help, Jamie moves until it's where he wants it.

I decide since Jamie's multi-talented, then I can be, too. He uses two hands and a mouth on me with expert skill. My mouth sucks him down my throat. I draw back until the plum of his cock runs across the roof of my mouth, and then I slurp him back down again– over and over I repeat the action. One hand controls Jamie's release from pouring out by gripping his sack directly next to his body, while the other performs the action that's driving Jamie crazy– the three fingers I'm pumping into him so hard that my hand is threatening to cramp.

Jamie puts me at ease. When we text, I feel like I can say anything and never be judged, and that feeling rolls over into our sexual escapades. I feel like I can do anything, even the kinkiest shit that comes to mind, and not only will Jamie love it, he'll thank me for it.

My orgasm slams into me fast and hard. It's exquisite to be filled in my mouth, ass, and cunt, with a mouth suckling my clit. My body explodes, and I manage to come in every way imaginable– even my hair has an orgasm.

I scream out, but it's garbled as I allow Jamie to pour hot down my throat. His cock throbs with every pump of ambrosia, and his ass tightens hard around my fingers.

I no longer sound like me as I cry my orgasm around Jamie's cock. We take on the same cadence, animals bleating in pain, agony, torture, and pleasure.

Falling back to the bed, I slowly turn upright to join Jamie. The instant I'm near him, he pulls me close and holds me tight, hands caressing every inch of flesh he can reach.

I lean in to kiss Jamie, but hesitate because some men don't like to kiss after oral sex. From somewhere deep within his drained body, Jamie summons dominance– he fists my hair, pulling my mouth down to his. Kissing me passionately, Jamie licks his taste from my mouth while transferring my taste to mine. We become a mass of tangled arms and legs writhing in pleasure.

"Whoever says oral isn't sex, is a fool." I gasp out when I come up for a breather. "That was more than sex– so much more."

Rolling me to my back, Jamie settles between my thighs again, holding me so tight I can barely breathe. Drawing my left hand up to his mouth, he places a soft kiss to my palm, and then to each finger. When he's through, he intertwines our fingers and sighs contently.

Jamie communicates without spoken words, allowing his body language to speak the thoughts his ruined voice won't allow.

Drifting off into a pleasure induced coma, I fear Jamie won't be here when I wake up. The last time I entered this space of pleasure and sleep, I awoke a widow. Wrapping myself around Jamie, I pray he's still here when I wake.

In a state between wake and sleep, "Don't leave me again," flows softly against Jamie's neck as we hold one another. "I couldn't survive it."

I drift in and out every few minutes, checking to make sure Jamie hasn't poofed into the ether. He isn't asleep, but I can tell he's content by his breathing. He also hasn't lessened his hold on me, either.

The creak of a door opening draws me out of my meditation. Jamie's head moves in that direction, so I'm not worried about the visitor.

"How was it?" Marcus whispers.

A moment later, cold plastic is at my back as Jamie types lightning fast on a cellphone.

Marc chuckles. "Did you have sex?" He asks softly, trying not to wake me, even though I'm only on the cusp of sleep.

"Ah– Regina would say that." Marcus laughs again. "She was your gift to me, so it's only fair. I've monopolized her long enough. I don't want to share with anyone else, but this is different because it's you."

A hand rubs my back and shoulders, and I'd know that hand anywhere– Marcus. He's never gentle or tentative. After moving my hair to the side, he kisses my throat. I sigh and drift to sleep.

"Roman did what? I thought you had him in hand." Voice tinged with fury, Marcus grows impatient. "Just let me read the messages. Oh, c'mon, don't be stingy with Regina's words. Fine, just the ones about Roman."

The bed dips as Marcus sits next to me. I can feel the anger radiating off of him, so I scrunch closer to Jamie and away from him. He's going to kill me. I start to shake, and Marcus rubs the tension from my shoulders.

"I've had just about enough of Kristal. She's becoming a real problem. I don't like her near Ella, and I know you agree. Ah– Regina's had enough, too, I see. Good. I'm curious to see what

Regina does to Kristal when she figures out who Pretty Boy is. Kristal better fucking hide." Marcus chuckles evilly.

"Jamie…" Marcus uses his '*I'm disappointed in you*' voice. "That's my secret, and you came very close to letting it slip. I'm going to tell Regina, but I'm waiting until after her initiation. She'll need to hear it if Pretty Boy gets what he's after."

Marc's heavy sigh fills the room as he hands the cellphone back, then Jamie's hands tickle my back as he furiously replies.

"Tomorrow is another day." Marcus sighs again, sounding physically and emotionally exhausted. "Can I stay here? The house feels empty now that Cort went back to Ezra. I have no allies in that house."

Rolling slightly, I slur out, "Marcus?"

Moving my hair to the side, I can feel Marcus gazing down at me. "Yes, Regina?"

"Now's your chance to spend the night with your lover, make love to me, and fall asleep with us." I whisper into the intimate dark of Jamie's bedroom.

Marc's sharp intake of breath surprises me. "You honor me, Regina." His voice is filled with unfathomable emotions, desperate longing, and loneliness.

I worry Marcus will leave now that I've brought up true intimacy, but I hear his clothing hit the floor, and then he's sliding behind me and cuddling up close.

At last, my body envelops his within my moist heat. The events of the day have me fading, and I start to fall asleep while clinging to Jamie as Marcus rolls smoothly inside me.

"Roll over, and face me." Marc's husky command jolts me back to consciousness.

I do as I'm told. Instantly rolling into Marc's body. Clinging tightly, I go to kiss him but flinch back. Kissing Marcus with the taste of another man in my mouth would be wrong.

As usual, Marcus reads my mind. Practically pinning me to the bed, Marcus devours me, tongue removing all traces of Jamie's taste from my mouth, where he swallows it down as if Jamie had given him the gift instead.

At first, I fear Marcus is turning into that possessive fuckface, but then I realize he was starving for a taste of Jamie. The man in question realizes this at the same time I do. Growling, and not in a nice way, Jamie's pissed.

"Share and share alike," Marcus croons smugly, causing Jamie to growl again. Snorting, "Deal with it– we've got Regina in this bed. I promise not to touch your precious dick, but I'm not going to promise I won't enjoy what you leave behind in Regina's body."

I quickly reach back to grab Jamie's arm, fearing he's going to flee from his own bed, but he relaxes into me, even going as far as to pat Marc's back intimately but not sexually.

Taking the initiative, Marc's hand skims up the back of my thigh and hooks it around his hip. Without preamble, with a smooth thrust, he roots himself deep inside me. Gasping, I sigh in pleasure as my body welcomes his home. We fit together perfectly, but a part of me prays Marcus won't go caveman on my ass and harm me.

"Regina, I read how you wanted anal pleasures. But I wasn't aware that was something you enjoyed." Marcus sounds mildly accusatory, and I have no idea why. "Have you had anal sex before?"

"Yeah…" I mutter bashfully in the quiet of the dark bedroom. Hiding my face against the side of his neck, Marcus smells so good. Embarrassed, I flutter a kiss to his skin.

"Did you enjoy it?" His voice is sharp with curiosity.

"Yes," I say shyly.

"Only once?"

"All the time…"

"All the time, huh?" Yet again he sounds suspicious. "I wonder why I wasn't aware of this. Hmm… no matter now, I guess. Jamie will happily give you what you seek."

Throwing caution to the wind, I kiss Marcus while holding Jamie against the back of my body. Marcus groans into my mouth and tilts my hips to get deeper inside of me. My nails bite into the fleshy muscles of his back, and he moans louder.

Marcus reaches past me, grabbing for Jamie, who presses tightly along my back. Panting through the invasion, my eyes pop wide as Jamie's cock explores from the bud of my ass to the opening Marcus dominates.

The sound of someone rummaging in the nightstand fills the air, and moments later I'm saturated with lubricant. Using his cockhead to smear the lube around, Jamie comes into direct contact with Marc's dick.

Jamie freezes while Marc's reaction is as intense as an epileptic fit.

"Jamie was giving you a freebie," I say to remove the tension that has fallen. "He'll do it again in another twenty years or so, so I hope it was worth it."

"It was," Marcus breathes against the side of my neck, squeezing me tightly, no doubt reaching for Jamie.

I wait for Jamie to be unsure of himself, but he knows what he's doing. I don't know how long ago his accident was, but prior to that, he must have been ravenous to have picked up this level of skill. Jamie slides into me easily, and without any pain.

Gasping in shock, I realize I have two men inside me at the same time. Never have I had a threesome. It's so unexpected that I want to weep, and I believe Marcus really is crying in relief.

Marcus groans into my mouth as he tries to devour my tongue and lips, arms gripping the man curled behind me. Jamie's haunting growl reverberates against my back, no doubt because Marcus is tugging and releasing him, forcing him to rock into my body. Relenting, Jamie holds Marcus back, sandwiching me in between them. We release a long string of whimpers and cries as they begin to thrust in tandem.

The exploits of my evening mount up, as if it's all been foreplay for this main event. A sensation builds inside my lower belly that I've never felt before, probably because he never goes slowly or marathon-long. Marc's hitting me at a different angle than usual, and it's on the edge of pain. Worrying I'm going to have an accident and pee the bed, I start to panic, but neither man slows their onslaught.

"Shh… It's okay." Marcus coos at me in a soothing tone. "Enjoy it."

"I think I'm going to have an accident." I push at Marc's chest, but he'll have none of it. "You better stop," I issue weakly. Jamie's lost in his own world, fused to my back while kissing my nape and slowly rolling his hips against my ass, being propelled by Marc's hands.

"It's just another type of orgasm. Relax." Marcus commands in a tone that immediately removes all my fear.

The sensation strengthens, building and building until I don't think I can bear anymore, yet the pressure keeps mounting. I bite Marc's shoulder in warning as the pressure reaches its peak. In reply, Marcus pulls from my body, allowing a flood to pour from between my thighs.

Thrashing and writhing between them, I scream as the most painful and strongest orgasm of my entire existence tries to rip free from my body. My nerves are on fire, to the point I become a wick for my release's flame. The pressure isn't abating, and I whimper in pain.

Marcus gives me much needed relief with several sharp thrusts of his cock. I flood again in a large whoosh, and this time it's a true release of the pressure inside my body. My orgasm flows in a tide with the flood between my thighs.

Jamie never stops his pleasure inside my behind. He's throbbing for release, yet he holds it at bay, proving he can go for hours and hours, and he'll only finish when I'm ready for him.

Marcus seeks the refuge of my clenching passage, giving a few more thrusts, then he spends himself in a scorching wave. His grunt unleashes something in Jamie, signaling the end. Hesitating, I can tell Jamie's unsure if he's welcome to fill me, so I reach back and don't allow him to pull free of my body as he orgasms.

For once, I want Marcus to leave a part of himself behind, because it's about damn time Jamie did.

Satisfied male laughter fills the air– Jamie's strange animalistic sound and Marc's impressive, husky laugh from deep within his chest. I'd join in, but it would take too much energy.

"Wow… that was unexpected fun. I wasn't sure you'd be willing to share with both of us. I needn't have worried." Marc kisses the tip of my nose, then slowly pulls from my body, grunting every time I constrict around him in aftershocks. "I should thank you for finally getting Jamie to loosen up and get some." Giddy, Marcus shouts, "Jamie crossed swords with me!"

Jamie's answering growl echoes around the bedroom.

"I didn't think you had the capacity to sound like a teenage boy, District Attorney Zeitler, but you just managed it."

"Sorry, not sorry. I've been waiting for a lifetime." Marcus sounds so satisfied that Jamie actually laughs instead of growling in protest.

"Well, I don't think I can have sex for at least a week. This has been the busiest night of my life." I find a burst of energy to give a weak giggle.

"We'll let you rest up, especially since I hurt you some when we were at the dock." Marcus falls to his back, and releases a heavy sigh.

Jamie pulls away from me and gets out of bed, and I fear he's leaving us alone. I don't want to push him from his own bed, because I want Jamie to sleep next to me. I want to be able to wake every few minutes and hear his breathing in my ear, being comforted by the knowledge he didn't disappear.

Thankfully my fear was unwarranted, because Jamie returns moments later with a warm, wet washcloth. I try to take it from him, but he swats my hand away.

Marc makes an odd 'oof' sound, and then snickers. "Thanks, Jamie. A man loves a wet washcloth to the nads."

Jamie bathes me efficiently yet gingerly, like I'm something precious he wants to treat with special care. After he cleans himself, he crawls back into bed, curling around my back. Jamie even throws Marcus a bone by resting his hand on the other man's back.

Chapter Twenty-Nine

We sit around the table eating dinner– Ella's favorite, spaghetti. Kristal isn't with us this evening, as she hasn't been for the past week. When I got home from the brownstone in the wee hours of the morning, my soiled couch was missing and a new one was in its place. It was a hell of an upgrade, too. In the place of my three-seater beige sofa is a U-shaped sectional. Its plushy awesomeness is perfect for Fate to lounge on one end while reading, with Ella and me cuddled up watching television on the other. Just as we've done all week long.

The house flows with a harmony now that Kristal won't pass its threshold. I feel a twinge of sadness, but not enough to go back on my decision. Kristal can stay in the guesthouse, but she isn't welcome inside my home until she redeems herself.

Ella and Ade do their weekly chat about the boys, and I try to ignore it. But it's nearly impossible now that Ella has been hanging out with her cousins at school. She's asked if she can have a slumber party here at the house with Kate's girls– Whitney and Prissy. Fate is even excited over the prospect, always in nesting mode like a mother without a chick. Ade? Ade is practically glowing over having all the Whittenhower ladies in one place, even going as far as to ask if she can stay the night too.

The guilt of keeping the secret that Katya Waters will soon grace us with her presence is eating me alive. I don't want to worry Ade any more than she already is. I do agree with Marcus, how Ezra should marry who he wishes, and not be held to antiquated betrothal traditions. But I fear for the woman I see as a sister. What will happen to Adelaide, when her entire adult life has been about marrying Ezra Zeitler?

Nervous, Fate shreds her Italian bread as Ella tells a story about Niel that Prissy had relayed to her. We're all inside our own minds tonight, only Ade is paying my daughter any attention.

Fate's fretting because tonight is the first night I train with my submissive. I've tried to change my mind and just go to Restraint as myself. But both Jamie and Marcus said that it would be in my best interest to portray a master with a proclivity for female submissives. They're under the impression that I can't field manly advances. I don't like pretending, but it doesn't matter because I'm not going to Restraint to get laid– I only want respect.

With his weird sense of helping, Cort said that sometimes you're made to do things you wish you hadn't, and he didn't want that happening to me. Marcus actually shuddered at the thought. My main goal is to be the strongest of the strong, then no one will be left to tell me what to do, even Marcus. Restraint is going to be my bitch.

"Here's the newest tattoo Whitt inked a few weeks ago." Ade explains to Ella, showing her a photo of a large creature with green eyes.

"Hey, let me see that!" Tugging the album across the table, I stare down at the tattoo. The green-eyed monster is inked across a woman's tan décolletage. I've seen it before.

Fate freezes, as if she's ready to bolt. The more dominating I get, the meeker she becomes. It's disturbing.

Snatching the image from the album. "No," Ade mutters as she hides the photo underneath her shirt. "No," she repeats.

Ade and I are equals when it comes to battle-of-the-wills. "Why?" I ask in suspicion.

"You never want to know what's going on with the boys, so I'm just doing as you ask." Ade hits me back with my own demands, and it's annoying as fuck.

"Yeah, right. You make sure I hear you every week regardless." I let the subject drop. If Ade doesn't want me to see it, then it must be in my best interests not to look. I do trust Ade on most things. Whitt's an adult now, and he can choose who he wants to tattoo– it's none of my business.

"I'll clear the table." Fate starts gathering our dishes, scraping the plates, and then stacking them. "Will you help me, baby girl?"

"Yeah," Ella chirps, hopping up to help. "But you have to teach me how to make soft pretzels like you promised."

"Tomorrow afternoon. Deal?" With Ella's nod, their negotiations have been finalized. "Okay, go get the Pyrex and put the leftovers in the fridge."

The rule of the house is that whoever cooks doesn't clean up. I cooked tonight. My ten-year-old daughter isn't living the spoiled lifestyle like her brother. Ella has weekly chores, helps clean the house, does yardwork– her favorite is helping me clean the pool – and watches Fate and me as we cook. I promised Ella once she turns twelve, she can cook one simple meal for us a week with no help from any of us.

Ella's a very independent girl.

With the girls in the kitchen, Ade and I are left alone, and I can tell she wants to say something to me and is chickening out. Looking sheepish, her eyes dart in my direction, and then away.

"Out with it– I don't have all night for you to garner your courage. I have to go to the brownstone in a few minutes and I'm not looking forward to it."

Ugh! I don't want to touch Fate sexually. Since last week's marathon sex night, I haven't even had a twinge of arousal. Marcus seems content, more confident even, and Jamie and I are now texting before I go to bed and when I get up in the morning, then again at lunch. We're logging in about four hours a day. We haven't even trained all week. Marcus and I, with Jamie in the shadows, converse and watch movies while we snack.

"Have you met the newest recruit yet?" Ade's voice is smooth as silk, and I go on high alert. "I believe his name is Dalton."

Marcus was right. I can see it in Adelaide's eyes. She's trying to draw information from me for some reason.

"Yes, I met Dalton last week." I infuse my voice with curiosity to mask my suspicion. "Why?"

"I was just wondering," Ade mutters underneath her breath, pale skin flushing pink.

"How would you know about Dalton?" I act as if the answer doesn't matter to me either way. I'm getting better at subterfuge. It's too bad that I have to use it on my best friend. I trusted Ade before, even though Marcus told me not to. Now any trust I may have had disappears in an instant.

"Ezra was talking about him earlier." She lies flawlessly. If a man is looking to replace you as his wife, he sure as fuck doesn't talk about random people who are joining his BDSM club.

Ade stares at her hands while shuffling an envelope back and forth between them. She appears nervous, which worries me. She showed no weakness when asking of Dalton, but that envelope scares the crap out of her.

Raising an eyebrow, I point at the envelope. "Is that for me?"

"Here," Ade mutters bashfully, pushing the manila envelope across the table. "I'll be in the kitchen." She gives me privacy, and I eye the envelope while waiting for it to explode.

Gaining courage from my metaphorical balls, I open the envelope. Inside is a black document folder, and quickly open it before I lose my nerve. My breath whooshes out and dies in an instant.

It's a portrait drawn by an amazing artist, and I immediately recognize it as Whitt's work of art.

Almost three-dimensional and lifelike, a grown man with sandy blond hair stares at me from the paper. Angelic is the only word to describe the face, with his crystalline blue eyes twinkling with mirth. A set of dimples bracket full, luscious lips. It's the twitch in the upper lip that informs me the portrait is of Whitt and not Grant.

Whitt looks exactly as how I remember Grant. They could be identical twins with the exception of the expression the mouth holds. It's taunting, calculating– powerful. Grant's smile was always self-deprecating. Even when Grant was teasing, he still emitted a somber feeling. Whitt has all the confidence Grant lacked, plus his own healthy dose.

Whitt's no longer the boy I remember him to be. He's a grown man, and it scares me to death. Fingers tracing the edges of his face, I stare at the inscription for a very long time.

For our Queen from her King– Daniel Whittenhower II.

I don't know what to make of this, or what to do with it. Whitt knows Ade brings us weekly photos, so why would he make me a portrait? Does he still know me well enough to assume I'd never look at the pictures because it would hurt too much?

Premonition.

A coldness breezes over my soul, eliciting a shiver to roll along my spine– the cold hand of a premonition manifesting from the one-dimensional drawing.

Tucking the portrait back into its envelope, I hide it in my office. It scares me for some unknown reason. It shows me all I've lost, and what I can never regain.

Grant. Gone forever, never to meet his daughter. The future we dreamed will never be realized. The boys are now young men, with their childhood lost.

Chapter Thirty

Fate trails behind me, gripping my elbow. She's shaking and her teeth are clattering. A memory flashes from the depths of my mind: Fate holding my hand, scared shitless, as I barter with a pawnbroker. I don't know how I didn't see it earlier; she truly needs a protector.

After her father went to prison, Fate came directly to me, knowing she could seek solace under my protection even though I could barely protect myself from the Whittenhowers.

The trust Fate places in me is as scary as it is exhilarating. I could see how it could become as addictive as a junkie's need for crack, or Kristal's need for sex. We all have needs, and the more you feed them, the more the needs grow, and the more addicted you become. It's the payoff that makes it so dangerous.

"Two wannabe lesbians reporting for duty!" I call from the foyer. "Yo, where is everybody?"

Fate relaxes exponentially when she sees the ordinary hallway. Maniacal laughter bubbles up my throat as I take Fate to the restraint room. They're going to have to restrain me if I can't muster the courage to touch my best friend.

My metaphorical balls have shriveled up, and I'm chickening out.

Fate's sharp gasp makes me feel bad as her earlier comfort dissolves in an instant. I worry she may wet herself, so I pull her into the safety of my arm and cuddle her to my side.

"You don't have to do this, you know? I won't be disappointed. This is too much for me to ask of you."

"I trust you, Regina. I know you won't hurt me." Fate's naiveté petrifies me. No, I'll never hurt her, but someone else could, or someone else could try to command me. I silently vow to do my very best at protecting Fate always.

In that second, I realize that in a way I've always taken care of Fate since we met. She was sure and forceful at Hillbrook, but that was her people and her environment. Fate was doing her father proud. But outside of Hillbrook and her affluent family, Fate needed my shelter.

Ignorantly so, I thought power-exchange was about sex and control. I was a fool. It's about ownership. There are good and bad owners of all things. Ade with how she kept her room as a teenager, not caring for anything– she is a bad owner. The adults who keep a dirty house, or break their belongings in a fit of rage, then later complain how everything is shitty– shitty of their own making. My mother and I were beyond poor, but our environment was clean and in good repair– clean is free.

Masters are just owners, and our personalities dictate how we treat our property. No, this has nothing to do with sex. Respect and trust are fundamental. Dominants and submissives have a unique relationship built on years of small gestures that aren't obvious building blocks, but they strengthen the bond. Fate and I have seventeen years of mutual respect and trust. I've never doubted her, and she'll never doubt me.

"We can do this, girlfriend," I reassure her. "Together." I kiss the top of her head and smile against her hair.

"Warming up already?" Cort's snarky voice permeates the room. "Interesting choice of location, Regina. You make me feel like a proud papa."

I wait for Marcus to follow Cortez into the room, and I stare out the doorway and into the hallway for a moment in disappointment when Marcus doesn't show.

Cort kisses my cheek, and turns to Fate. He kisses her full-on the lips, and I stare in shock. He goes as far as to add tongue, turning my poor girl into a puddle of whimpers. Enraptured, Fate follows Cort's lips as he pulls away.

Cortez's pouty, ruby-kissed lips hold the pull of the moon on unsuspecting females, even I'm not immune.

"Hmm… you were the best virgin I've ever had." Cortez murmurs while wearing a dreamy expression on his face. That was sweet in a weird kind of way, until he goes and ruins it with, "Your sister was a close second."

Punching Cortez in the chest, I order. "Behave!"

"I like you when you're pissed. It makes me hot." Cort jacks up his pant leg. "It's too bad you dampen your power. I bet you could kick Marc's ass if you were angry enough." His eye twitches.

"Behave," I issue weaker this time. Cortez misbehaves, and you want to kill him. But after one look at him, you want to hug him and laugh instead. He leers at me in a strange way, when he hasn't looked at me with heated eyes since we made out more than a year and a half ago.

"What's up with the sexual connotations? You never act like this around me." I feel like Cort's playing with me, and not in a good kind of way.

Immense sadness and guilt flash over Cortez's face for a moment, causing dread to coil in my stomach. I don't understand, but my instincts pick up all sorts of warning alarms.

"Shall we begin?" Cortez gestures to me, looking to me as if I'm already Fate's master. The irony is the fact that he's asking for permission after he already molested Fate's lips. My question must have brought up something painful for him if he's decided to play fair again.

"Where's Master?" I ask with suspicion.

"Master decided it would be for the best if I supervised you with Fate. He wishes to remain nameless." I can tell Cortez is lying, and he realizes it, because there is no one in my household who doesn't know Marcus has been my lover. Cortez looks away in guilt, and then walks across the room.

What makes that statement all the more untrue is the fact that Cortez would never be allowed to instruct anyone because of his taunting personality. Also, Marcus would never allow Cortez access to someone he deflowered in front of her horrified sister. Lastly is Cort's strange sexual behavior toward me, when he hasn't even batted an eyelash in my direction for fear that Marcus would yank the hair out at the root.

The dread screams louder in my ears.

An ache forms between my breasts, and I stifle the need to run up those steps and seek Jamie out, or run screaming from the brownstone looking for an AWOL Marcus. The training was supposed to be about *us*, Marcus and me with Jamie watching.

I push the pain away and focus on the task ahead.

"So I've been brainstorming," I inform Cortez who is now lounging on the sofa like Cleopatra herself.

"That's utterly terrifying, Regina." Cort is a fuckface– literally.

"D/s has many forms. It isn't uncommon for a couple not to wish for voyeurs. I'd like to figure out a way for Fate's and my relationship not to be sexual. I want our relationship to be true dominance and submission, like we are at home and work."

"Ms. Bossy is bossy all the time, eh?" Cort directs to Fate, who shakes her head no and blushes.

I ignore him. "I think we'd blow it if we had to play besotted lovers. But no one will know we aren't behind closed doors. Does this make sense?" I decided to deal with the problem at hand, and try to push the screaming alarm bells to the depths of my subconscious mind.

"It would work." Cortez actually takes me seriously for once. "You'd still have to be affectionate, maybe touchy-feely. If your bond is strong enough, no one would question it." Cort takes on an expression of cleverness. It's easy to forget when you banter with him that he has a strong, intelligent mind behind the bravado.

"I need to see how much Fate trusts you, and how well you respond to her cues. If Fate can follow your lead and do as she's told, then you won't have any problems. I know you're both smart, and I can see that she's highly submissive, but I worry the club will be too much for her."

I understand what Cortez is saying. Another misnomer with the lifestyle is that anyone who isn't familiar with the scene believes it's only in the bedrooms, clubs, and dungeons that we engage in D/s or BDSM. It's a lifestyle, and not one of our choosing. You're dominant all the time. You're submissive all the time. The only exception to the rule is a switch, and they are usually a dominant who wishes to relinquish control as a way to feel more in control.

Fate may be submissive, but that doesn't mean she'll fit into Restraint. I'll have to monitor her reactions. At home, Fate loves structure. I tell her when and what to work on for Empowerment, and she does it flawlessly with competent efficiency. We have chores around the house, and hers are always completed. She even asks my opinion on who she dates. Just because Fate needs a master in life, doesn't mean she needs one in the bedroom, or that she ever needs to step foot into a dungeon.

"What do you suggest?" I ask Cort in a businesslike, fashion, both of us ignoring the fact that the elephant is *missing* from the room.

I'm ready to conquer this so I can move on to the next step of this journey. Work has been slowing down, or perhaps I'm losing my knack for it. Ella's getting more mature and wants to spend time with her cousins instead of me. So now I have time on my hands and empty blocks of time where my training used to be. I need Restraint, because an idle Regina Regal feels dead inside.

"Kinbaku." Cortez throws the gauntlet down.

I want to freak out and scream, but Fate will feed off my energy. Ever so slowly, I draw air into my lungs and exhale quietly. I repeat this until I'm calm. I mustn't upset the submissive.

Kinbaku was what I was the worst at during my training. It's the Japanese art of rope binding. Art and I are no acquaintances. I can command a computer to draw me a picture, but I can't draw one from nothing. I'm proficient tying the knot-work, but not the *art* of knot-work.

Both Marc and Cort tied me up for weeks on end, and I tied Cort up in return, only to fail miserably time and again. We moved onto another subject, and came back to it– twice. Marcus gave up when I couldn't tie him up, either.

The final.

I sense this is the last step of my training, and Marcus isn't here to witness it. It's two-fold: if I can conquer the rope and prove that Fate trusts me infallibly, I will finally earn the title Queen.

My mind goes into the mode I use when working. I've never delved this deep while playacting the dominant, and I know why. I'm not playing anymore. Queen and I are one and the same, and Fate really is my submissive. I'm not going to be tying up a master playing submissive– I'm going to tie up the real thing.

Fate's face is flushed and she's breathing in tiny pants of air, yet her eyes are clear and trusting. I smooth her dirty blonde locks back from her face and braid it. I don't want to accidently knot one of her hairs in the rope. Having your hair pulled can be thrilling and pleasurable, but there is something ridiculously painful about just one strand being yanked. I don't understand it, but it should be a form of torture.

Fate calms under my touch, and I can sense her trust in me permeate the air, and it calms me in return. Whereas she feeds off my emotions, I learn I can feed off hers, too. We calm each other.

Fond of dresses, Fate loves billowy, soft fabric that floats around her small frame. I pull her dress off only to discover that she's nude beneath. I smile when Cort hisses in a sharp breath of arousal.

Yeah, how's that abstinence treating ya, Cort?

Fate and Ade used to strive to be rail thin in a quest to reach the perfect size zero. I made Fate eat healthy, stating that I was raising a daughter and I didn't want her to feel bad about herself. I know how horrible it is to feel uncomfortable in your own skin, and I didn't want Ella or Fate, or any other human to experience it. I don't like my body, but the difference between me and Ade is that I accept that I can't change it.

Fate looks incredible with the healthy weight gain. Her breasts have filled out to a large B-cup and her hips are shapely. The best thing I could have ever done for Fate was making her eat. Thin didn't suit her. As she is now, she's gorgeous.

"Which do you prefer, Cort?" Voice a teasing lilt, I go in for the kill. "Teenage Fate, or the new and improved adult Fate?"

Cortez licks his lips a few times, but otherwise doesn't answer. The tent in his dress slacks does all the speaking for him. Flashing him an evil grin, I laugh over the whoremaster who isn't getting any because of Ezra's monogamy or celibacy demand.

My mind slips back into the peace I find when I'm deep into creating a program from nothing. I begin by drawing Fate's elbows behind her back until they touch, then I weave the rope slowly with precise placement. The pattern begins to take shape, and I refrain from smiling. I worry that gloating too soon will break my concentration and jinx me.

Fate's huffing in huge breaths of air, and it worries me that she'll hyperventilate. A flash of silk in the corner catches my eye, so I make a grab for it.

Holding Fate's clear, blue eyes, I wrap the Rococo-patterned scarf around her neck. I tighten it to the point that if she continues to gasp, she'll asphyxiate.

"Look me in the eyes, Fate. Do you trust me?" Her eyes snap to mine, and she ceases to breathe. "I'm not hurting you. It's an ordinary silk rope– when it was lying on the floor, it was just an inanimate object, but now it is an extension of my fingers. Think of the rope as your master's caress. Think of the binding at your neck as your master's soothing hand commanding you to calm yourself." My voice is lulling– a tone I've never spoken in my entire life, yet it's still a cadence of Queen's voice.

Fate's eyes cloud and glaze over, while a satisfied smile flirts along her lips. She relaxes to the point that I have to hold her up to keep her standing. Reaching over, I attach her bound arms to an eyebolt set into a hardwood beam on the wall. When Fate's stable on her feet, I resume my knot-work.

Kneeling at Fate's feet, I begin knotting her legs together. Since I don't trust a horny yet frustrated Cortez around my submissive, I create an intricate design that ensures nothing larger than a fingertip could penetrate Fate's bare folds.

Breathing peacefully, Fate never takes her eyes from my face. She looks so serene that I understand the switches better. Dominance is a huge high, but submission is a release on a level like no other.

Snaking the rope between her thighs, I note the threads glisten with Fate's arousal as the rope passes her slit. I attach her thighs to her hands through the split between her legs. If she moves without permission, it will rub her raw. I don't want Fate to move– I just need her to trust me.

I stand to check Fate's eyes and lips, making sure she's getting enough air. I tighten the scarf one more notch, and her eyes widen and a moan spills from her lips. Who would've guessed that scared, submissive Fate likes the lack of oxygen?

Administered correctly, you'll reach a level of euphoria upon climax. Marcus taught me this neat trick by allowing me to choke Cortez with my bare hands while Cort touched himself though his pants. It was a pity I couldn't see anything, but I enjoyed the sensation of finally choking my frustrations out of Cortez. He sagged to the ground when it was over, and then begged me to do it again. It brought a whole new meaning to why Ezra chokes the instigator.

Fate's lips pout as she pants without moving her throat. I decide her lips are near perfect, the bottom one slightly fuller than the top, which is a curved cupid-bow. I place a tender kiss to her parted lips, and she relaxes further. Fate's so languid, I worry she'll spill to the floor into a pile of goo.

There is one more part of Fate's body left to knot– her breasts. I begin with a figure-eight pattern, binding them up and out, and then apart. As my fingers weave, I notice how beautiful Fate looks as I bind her, truly a work of art. I'm no longer afraid that I'll fail, because I've already succeeded.

Regina Regal always succeeds– eventually.

Fate's skin is flushed with arousal, and I can smell her musky scent wafting up– it's not unpleasant. It arouses me to know that I arouse her in return. As a dominant, it's my responsibility to provide Fate pleasure, peace, comfort, stability, safety, boundaries, punishment, and discipline. It's a huge undertaking, but for each that I provide, the sense of pride that infuses me is astronomical. Fate's arousal is the sweetest scent to my nostrils.

Her breasts are perfect handfuls with pearls raised at the tips, and I allow myself a taste of one of her buds. Fate groans deep in her chest and falls lax, and I decide I can provide the sexual side of her needs after all. It's a thrill.

I'm not one who particularly finds women attractive, but the act of dominating Fate overrides my natural persuasion. Her need to please me creates a need inside of me to please her in return. I understand why the lines blur, even for the straightest of masters. You're their master, and you don't want anyone else to provide what you should be giving freely. It's territorial, possessive, and all about pride and control.

Fate's breasts are turning red from the restrictive blood flow, so I nip her skin. She shudders– the sensations are stronger, livelier with the bindings.

The ache in my chest returns with a vengeance when I realize what I've missed out on during my training. Marcus must have never thought I deserved this glorious sensation of having my skin touched when it was at its most sensitive. It was the same with the latex– Marcus gave me a sample of a taste, and then selfishly took what he needed.

I won't treat Fate with that level of disrespect. She's done no wrong, she's put her life in my hands, and I'll damn well reward her for it. The difference between Fate and me is that I should have demanded the respect the instant Marcus disrespected me. Since I didn't protest, I doubt Marcus will ever respect me again for my lapse.

I feel sick inside, but this isn't about me– it's about Fate.

I kiss her sensually, and allow my fingers to trickle down her abdomen. Wiggling my index finger between her folds, I marvel at how difficult it is with the bindings. Reaching behind Fate, I tug at her hands. The movement flows down to the rope between her thighs, but I make sure it doesn't rub her too roughly. She groans loud enough that it echoes around the small room.

My finger circles the swelling nub between her thighs, and my ears register a whimper behind me. Gazing over my shoulder, I notice Cort looks sick with lust. His face is pale, his neck is red, and his hips are gyrating against air with no relief in sight.

"Cortez," I command, and his eyes snap up to mine. "You can relieve yourself. We won't mind, especially since Fate's had a front row seat to this show before." My voice is rough and husky from barely contained lust. "I wouldn't mind seeing you in the flesh for once,"

Hand ripping open his trousers, with a groan of immense relief, Cort's dick pops out of his fly.

"I thought I was going to die, it ached so badly. My pants were crushing me." Cort lies sprawled out on the sofa in obvious relief, but I can't take my eyes from his crotch.

"Very nice," I murmur modestly.

"Exquisite," Cort chastises me. "I prefer to call it exquisite."

I wait for a smirk, but one doesn't follow. I'll agree with Cortez– exquisite. When we made out, my hand was shoved down his pants as I stroked him off. But his pants kept me from seeing him, or truly feeling him. During training, when he couldn't take the pressure anymore, he would touch himself. But it was always either through his clothing, or with a hand down his pants.

I've never seen Cortez in the flesh. He's long, thick, and perfectly exquisite. I wonder how that big thing fit into tiny Fate, but he was only sixteen at the time. I'm sure it's grown since then.

"Regina, don't look at me like that." Cortez releases a long moan as he begins to touch himself in earnest. "That road leads to trouble."

"Like what?" I ask innocently and widen my eyes.

"Like you want me in you, any way you can get me. You and I both have a proclivity for a cock in our mouths. Please look away before I let you." Cort sounds desperate, so I give him the privacy for which he begs, especially since his begging is a new occurrence.

Since I can't have a cock in my mouth, I try something new, something Fate will undoubtedly love. Dropping to my heels, I push two fingers into her slit as far as the bindings will allow, and then scissor them apart. I see her nub peeking out at me in attention, so I draw the protective skin away from her clit and give it a tentative lick. She thrashes in her bindings, groaning and panting with exertion. I worry Fate will asphyxiate, but she calms enough to regain her breath.

Tongue exploring her folds, I can't reach much because of the rope, but I gain enough room to give Fate the pleasure she deserves.

I worried that I wouldn't like the taste of a female. It's strong and musky, with a slightly sweet and salty aftertaste. I decide it's an acquired taste, and it could eventually grow on me.

Her nub engorges beneath my tongue, and the heady feeling makes me lightheaded. I'm doing this to Fate– *me*. I'm the one giving her pleasure. She's so swollen that I'm able to suck her clit into my mouth. I decide I'm rather fond of that, because it's like giving a mini-blowjob.

Power course through my veins, as Fate whimpers with my every lick, with Cort's moans echoing in the background. I find myself speaking words that are truer than any I've ever spoken before.

"If I had a dick, I'd fuck you and cum inside of you, Fate. I'd prove I owned you." I growl like a feral animal.

I mean it. When I'm Queen, I feel like I should be a man. I have a hard time separating dominance and testosterone. Maybe that's what makes a woman more dominant– high levels of testosterone flowing through her veins.

I envy a man who can freely take their submissive. They don't appreciate the act of dominance they take for granted each time they fuck. No, it isn't about sex. It's about power and control. Domination. Can I really control Fate– empower Fate –if I don't have a cock?

"Oh. My. God. Regina, shut the hell up!" Cort shouts at me. "I'll buy you a strap-on for Christmas."

Cortez doesn't sound angry, more like he finds the idea appealing. It feels more natural to use it on a man than a woman. Maybe I'm a gay man trapped inside of a female's body.

"Will you let me use it on you?" I ask, not expecting a reply.

And I don't get one that I expect, either. Cortez starts to come, crying out as the first wave spurts from his cock with enough force to hit him in the forehead, with the next on the chin.

Sucking hard, I attack Fate's clit. For some reason, I want her to come while Cort's still climaxing. It would feel as if I've made them both come at the same time by my prowess alone.

Regina Regal never fails.

Cort's cries and Fate's whimpers fill the air to echo around the room– it's the symphony of a master's achievements. My body fills with pride, and Queen and I mesh as one. We're no longer either/or. We were always one, but I couldn't accept who I was until now.

I'm ready to be Queened.

"I'll take that as a yes," I murmur in Cortez's direction as I begin the arduous task of untying Fate.

"Don't temp me, Regina. That's the only part of my virginity I have left, and Ezra would kill you if he found out. Right now, though, I'd love to bend over for you."

"How did you manage that feat– never bottoming?" Voice laced with shock, I always assumed Cortez and Ezra were playing doctor in their cribs.

"I know Ezra's in charge. He knows he's in charge. Sex for us isn't about this–" Cortez gestures around the room. "It's about pleasure and connection."

I feel a pang of jealousy and agony when Cortez sounds just like Grant used to, when he says words that Grant had spoken to me on our first time.

"I've seen firsthand how much Ezra loves bottoming, just as I've seen Aaron taken by force fall to its charms. I won't allow myself to fail prey to its pleasures. Whoever took me would own me."

Tugging the silk rope, I try to remove a snag near Fate's arm. "Shit, I never thought of it like that."

"I used to give myself over to Ezra. It was a choice I made. I've seen Ezra cheat on me just to feel that rush of sensation again, just as I've heard my victim beg me for it. I can't do it, even for you– not even for Ezra."

Chapter Thirty-One

It's been two months since my last visit to the brownstone, and I've heard nothing from Marcus, the man who said he was my lover, equal, and ally. Partner. Whatever moniker I place on Marcus, I haven't heard a single word from him in eight long weeks.

After I successfully mastered Kinbaku, I went back to the brownstone on my regularly scheduled training day, expecting the usual reception from Marcus, Jamie, and sometimes Cortez. I won't lie, I had hoped to get an ounce of praise or recognition for my efforts with Fate. I wanted nothing more than to make Marcus proud. But what I found was an entirely different situation. Marcus and Dalton were sitting on the sofa, discussing the proper way to discipline a misbehaving submissive. Dalton looked at me with kind eyes, and then gave me a tight-lipped smile. In retrospect, Dalton looked worried for me, and I had no idea why.

Marcus wouldn't even turn to look at me, ignoring me for a few seconds as I greeted him and Dalton in turn. Keeping his back to me, Marcus asked what I was doing there since my training was now complete, then he continued to explain behavioral conditioning to Dalton.

I didn't say a word. I'm not daft. You don't need to hit me with a sign. I get it. I'm on my own again. I walked out of the brownstone, leaving my key on the end of the banister without saying a word.

I went back to my old atrophied life, where I'm completely apathetic about everything but my daughter. Only now my life is devoid of Kristal, and I know secrets that don't make sense, and sense betrayal just beneath the surface of my relationships with everyone.

I work twenty hours a day again, because my sleep is filled with dreams of the ones I ache to be with. I cuddle and play with Ella as if my heart doesn't bleed. I help with homework and teach Ella how to cook because her interests lie in that direction. Fate and I work side-by-side at Empowerment when I'm not hiding out in my home office, and we spend our evenings with my daughter. We watch cooking competitions, play board games, and practice nail art. Sometimes Fate goes on dates, or visits with her family, or goes out to dinner with Kristal. On those rare occasions, Ella and I will walk and talk for hours, reminding me of the solace I always found with Grant. Kristal avoids me, and I her, but I have no issue with Fate and Ade maintaining contact– I'm not that type of person. Ade doesn't know about Ezra's mouth on Kristal's cunt, but if I can keep one secret, I can keep a billion.

Instead of mentioning my daughter's extra chub and forcing Ella to go on a diet, I've been adding more vegetarian dishes to our lessons and I started teaching her how to swim in our pool for the exercise. Ella's weight isn't an issue as long as she's healthy. I want her to be comfortable in her own skin, so no diets and backhanded compliments about how she would be beautiful if only she lost some weight. Restrictive diets do more harm than good, and I won't push lifelong insecurities onto my daughter. So it's healthy choices, and that's the end of that, because my daughter was not put on this planet to be someone's eye-candy and pleasure-giver. Ella will be her own woman, chubby or not.

During our first lesson in the pool, I almost cried remembering the time Marcus took me to Serenity Lake. As twisted as it sounds, it was the closest thing to a date I've ever been on, and I realize now it was just smoke and mirrors.

Grant never took me on dates because I was his dirty secret locked away inside Misery Castle. Yes, I believe Grant wanted to marry me, but was it out of duty because I was the mother of his children, or because he truly loved me? He's gone now, so I'll never know. While our beginning was tainted with coercion, my love for Grant was pure.

Roman spent more than a decade knowing exactly where I was, then avoided me for a year in his own home– I can take a hint. I didn't want a romantic relationship with him, but a friendship can't grow in that environment.

Marcus was yet another man who wanted me in his life on his own terms, hiding me away in the brownstone, or doling out small treats like Serenity Lake to keep me addicted. Married and possessive, Marcus liked the *idea* of me being at his beck and call. Marcus not only loved Grant, he was *in* love with him. Marcus only saw me as a possession of Grant's, a toy that wasn't shared, which he was now in possession. In an odd form of revenge, Marcus got satisfaction from the fact that I was falling in love with him, becoming dependent on his presence in my daily life.

Jamie, while we still text back and forth at specific times every single day, his inability to allow me to see him is no different than how all the rest of the men in my life only want me on their terms, never in public– always the dirty secret. They always want me to be dependent on what they are offering.

I won't deny it, I've been closing Jamie out of my private thoughts and emotions, knowing he's just like the rest of them.

In the past, I was grieving for Grant, allowing the girls to shoulder my burdens, and I was emotionally closed off. After almost a year and a half with Marcus, I can see clearly now, and I can't shut off the part of me that sparks life.

For eight weeks, I've been on my own. Feeling alive while seeing clearly, not being dependent on anyone for any reason, and I'm stronger than ever. I conquered the ache the pool caused by repeatedly torturing myself over and over every day while Ella learned the backstroke.

Sometimes when Jamie and I text, he doesn't do his usual '*are you okay?*' routine, where we banter back and forth about meeting like this. It feels like an interrogation, and at other times, it's as if he's asking of the weather. During those texts, I know Marcus has Jamie's cellphone, and it makes me furious at the both of them.

I don't have the balls to ask what I did that was such a bitter disappointment. But I realize it started the day after the three of us were together. Marcus and Jamie had started to distance themselves from me slowly over the week before my last session with Cortez. I realize why Cort was behaving differently toward me that night– Marc had given him the go-ahead to touch me.

I stopped crying last week.

What makes it difficult is the fact that I have no idea what I could've possibly done wrong, and I honestly don't believe I did anything wrong in the first place. It's the most frustrating feeling in the world, and it makes me feel out of control. I can't control what I don't know. For a dominant, ignorance isn't bliss.

I wasn't told my training was finished, and Marcus spoke to me as if I should've just known. Since I'm not clairvoyant, it's yet another thing that frustrates the ever-loving hell out of me.

I haven't been to Restraint, since I was forbidden to do so until my initiation. I know the mysterious Pretty Boy trained until the day he was called a Master of Restraint and member of Maître du Jeu– the mother of all BDSM groups. Even while training, Pretty Boy was allowed inside Restraint.

I realized I've failed when Regina Regal fails at nothing. It's a bitter pill to swallow after training for more than a year, while forging relationships that didn't stand the test of time.

After learning my training was complete, I waited a week for my initiation. When it never came, I knew it never would.

I failed Queen.

A whistle fills the air, followed by the telltale vibration of my cellphone against my wooden desk. Already knowing who's requesting my undivided attention, even though it's outside of our texting schedule, I pick up the phone with fury raging inside of me.

Jamie: *What are you doing?*

And it's not Jamie, because he didn't start the conversation by asking if I was okay, and it's an off time. Jamie prides himself on texts that hold no emotion, yet this one sounds demanding.

Marcus.

–Working, of course.

I lie– I'm watching the guesthouse from the window in my office. Roman is chasing a giggling Kristal around the yard. With a satisfied, predatory smile across his full lips, Roman takes Kristal to the ground, and then covers her body with his. It's an oddly warm night, so they're making the most of it.

Their giggles turn my stomach. I want Roman and Kristal to be happy, and I hope they truly are. But I know they're living in a fantasy world with rose-colored glasses filled with lust and lies. First the sofa in my living room, now they always make sure they're in full view of wherever I am in the house, which pisses me the fuck off. If you're so happy, why do I need to be forced to play voyeur?

What nauseates me the most is that I want to be happy too. So seeing happy, no matter how false, it's a punch to the gut. I've never felt it, not really.

Happiness is a foreign concept to me.

Jamie: *Have you seen Roman?*

Paranoid, I look around, wondering how Marcus knows I'm watching Roman and Kristal engage in foreplay in my backyard.

—Yeah, I see Roman right now, doing depraved things to Kris in my back lawn. If you mean... Have I spoke to him. No!

Jamie: *When was the last time?*

—Why are you interrogating me?

Jamie: *Regina!*

—That's not very submissive of you, Jamie.

Jamie: *I'm not your submissive, am I? Answer the question.*

—I shouldn't. I want to hurt you right now, Marcus, but I'll answer. After this, don't text me ever again. Don't call. Make sure you relay that to Jamie, as well. Because if Jamie cared about me, he wouldn't have allowed you to commandeer his cellphone to pretend you're him.

Jamie: *Don't be that way.*

—I am that way, so deal with it. To answer your question, the last time I spoke to Roman was when he was fucking Kristal on my sofa. The man sure does want to reconnect our friendship, doesn't he? That was sarcasm, by the way. To take a page out of your playbook, you won't be hearing from me again. But at least I'll be compassionate enough to explain why and say goodbye. You're a fuckface who wants nothing to do with me, so bye!

Angry with tears streaming down my cheeks, I place my cellphone back on my desk. When it whistles again, I throw it on the floor. When the Jaws theme song fills the air, I smash it with the heel of my boot.

A sick sense of elation descends as I destroy a digital device. It's like murdering my own work. I scoop the powdered remnants of circuitry into the wastebasket, and then I pull a new phone from the drawer of gadgets I've been testing. Who needs a phone company when you can do it yourself? I program a new Sim card with a blocked number no one knows, and then I quickly text my new number to Fate and Ella. Everyone else can fuck off.

Did I mention I was stronger– yeah, I'm more ruthless too.

The liquor cabinet is calling my name as I watch Roman make love to Kristal within fifty feet of my window. Kris keeps looking at me as if she strategically placed herself in my view, just so I'd have to endure the torture. I don't want Roman anymore, not in lust or friendship. I've lost all respect for Roman as he continues to eat from Kristal's dirty hand.

Submissiveness doesn't equate weakness. There's a silent strength in submitting. What Roman is doing is spineless. I don't care if Roman loves Kristal, because what good is it to be treated like that– for either of them?

Unable to work with their moans and Kristal's gaze pinning me through the window, I pace the hallway. I'd love to go for a freezing swim, but they're a few feet from the pool. I need to be farther away, not closer.

I could drink myself to sleep, especially since it's been days since I visited the Sandman. I can't drink, because one taste and I'd be drunk off my ass. Plus, it's irresponsible to give my power away to a substance and lose all ability to control my faculties. I'm not sure when I ate last, either. Ade and Ella went on a trip for the weekend, along with Kate's girls. I guess I ate with them last, whenever the hell that was.

My eyes seek out the wall safe. The safe is my version of Pandora's Box. I tap the code in before I can change my mind. I finger the three rings that now live in there. Last I touched them, Marcus had placed the infinity ring on my finger, telling me how he purchased it for Grant. Marcus wanted me to wear it, saying he needed everyone to know I was taken. Then the next day, I wasn't worth keeping anymore.

I removed the rings from my body, placing them in the safe for safekeeping. I let my parents go at the same time I finally let Grant go. Incidentally, it was when I decided Roman was weak. I have no need for a man.

Queen is nothing if not self-reliant.

One other thing hides in the depths of the safe– Whitt. That portrait scares the shit out of me for some reason. I slam the door shut, then test the handle to make sure the safe is locked.

I swear I can hear my parents, Grant, and Whitt's voices howling from inside the safe, a hollowing sound because they don't want me to let them go. The sad thing, I don't remember any of their voices. The first thing that leaves when you lose someone is their voice, then slowly their features meld, and last to go is their scent. Once in a while, a smell or sound will trigger a memory, but when I try to conjure them– nothing.

The more years that roll by, the stronger the loss. Time doesn't heal all wounds– it replaces it with more wounds as your memory fades. The pain will always linger in your soul. Forever.

Chapter Thirty-Two

After my only indulgence, I lie in bed naked. I'm not the kind of girl who wears makeup, or designer clothing, but I do primp like a bitch. A few nights ago, I cut my hair off to only a few inches, then I smoothed it back against my skull with product until my natural color isn't discernable. The strawberry blonde is nearly black. My hair was ugly any way I tried to fix it, at least now it's manageable.

Now I feel like Queen, initiation or not.

Blasting music into my eardrums, I try to block the howling from the safe. Lying naked in the dark, I tap my fingertips on my thighs in time with the beat.

A shadow startles me to attention, but I only move my eyes as I school my breathing and continue tapping to the beat of my heart. I no longer hear the music– my blood pounding in my veins overpowers everything.

I find myself waiting patiently as a predator does its prey, except I'm the prey. Courage and bravery are ill-advised, but I value it. I recognize that if they got in here through my state-of-the-art security system, then I deserve to be invaded.

And it is they– many *theys*. Six theys.

I've laid here for hours, to the point my eyes have adjusted to the darkness. My night vision is excellent. I always joked that it was my dominant nature's way of creating the perfect predator. As I pretend I don't see them, vague shapes coalesce into people. But I can't see faces because they're masked, but not traditional masks. My mind computes the difference– night vision goggles.

With my lips curling into a taunting smirk, I address the gathering crowd in my bedroom. "Hmm… I can see you without those silly goggles. I wonder," I muse in a light voice. "Who's stronger, smarter, and better since I can see without help?"

Someone tries to suppress a chuckle– Cort. God, how I've missed him. The sound of his laughter is a shot to the heart. Without Marcus, I was cut off from seeing not only Jamie, but Cortez too. After a year and a half of seeing them as often as the people in my own household, it was like a small death occurred, and I've had to endure a mourning period.

"I know what's going down. Excuse me while I make myself respectable." I gesture to my nakedness. "I'd offer you all a seat, but I'm not feeling all that hospitable to the Masters of Restraint who broke into my home to haze me."

I never raise my voice from just below normal volume. It's the tone you use to speak in the dark– not whispering, but not really speaking either.

Fate and Ade must've known this was coming, and that's why Ade took Ella upstate to the Barnum and Bailey's Circus. With Kristal's fingerprints out of the system, only Fate could have let them in. I want to hurt them yet kiss them for it– bitches.

Standing on my bed, I hop off, not caring that I'm naked. My newfound confidence has nothing to do with Marc's practices or Cort's humiliations, and everything to do with the eight weeks of constant swimming and healthy food that have hardened my body.

There isn't an ounce of fat on me, because I no longer have the *'I sit in a chair 24-7'* body. Queen wanted to be strong inside and out– mentally, physically, and emotionally. I've never felt as empowered as I do standing naked before my fellow Masters of Restraint. I look them each in the eye through their goggles, saving Marcus for last. He flinches when our eyes connect. As sick in the heart as that makes me feel, it's like a minor victory.

Stalking toward my closet, I smooth my hand along my shorn hair, and I hear several gasps of surprise when they take notice. I take this exercise of restraint one step further, by setting my pile of clothing on the edge of my bed and by forcing them to watch me dress.

If we're going to do this, we're going to do it Queen's way.

Humming along to the song I was listening to when I was invaded, I pull on a bra and panty set. Leaning forward, I settle my huge tits into the cups with no shame, and I face my invading hazers while I do it too.

Queen says they're beneath us– I wholeheartedly agree. We've evolved.

Pulling on a pair of skinny-jeans, I marvel over the fact that I can slide them over my hips, ass, and thighs. I'm not skinny by any means, but I'm physically fit now. I top the outfit off with a punny t-shirt I picked up at a tech convention last year. *Nerds Do IT Better.* I do it to spit into their faces, because before me stands the elite in their thousand dollar socks. My outfit cost less than a hundred dollar bill, and the shirt was free with the cost of admission.

Smirking as I hum, I have more money than most of them combined, and I live like a normal person– as they should.

I pull on my indulgence– a pair of boots that fall just beneath my knees. They're killer, but still not as pricy as the socks on the feet of the men and one woman before me. Next I tug on my leather bomber jacket, and then I make a show of pocketing my new cellphone.

"Am I driving myself, or are you bitches going to do this right and kidnap me properly?" I infuse myself with Cort's snark. I've heard it for a year and a half, and I'm highly proficient now.

Smirking in challenge, I fist my hands on my hips.

They attack as a unit. Swarmed, my hands are zip-stripped behind my back, and a burlap sack is unceremoniously shoved over my head. I'm tossed over someone's shoulder with my ass in the air. Bobbing out of my bedroom to the hallway, several hands smack my ass in passing.

Whoever is carrying me walks with smooth, graceful elegance, and I instinctively know he must be Pretty Boy. Ezra and Cort are exactly my height, but lanky. Dexter is too short to carry a six-foot-tall woman. Syn is out, because she must be the intruder who is barely brushing five-feet. Marcus won't touch me, even though he could easily maneuver me. By process of elimination, the man carrying me must be Pretty Boy. As I learned on the night of his initiation, he and I are the same height, and he seems strong.

"Are you allowed to speak this time, or are we still doing tap-tap?" I flirt, and have no idea why since I never flirt. "I guess you could always smack my ass in response."

A sense of euphoria descends from no sleep, no food, stress, and adrenaline. I'm in the mood to fuck with their initiation process. Really, what can they do to me? Fuck them! I need respect, not friends. If I can't earn it, I'll demand it.

In response, I receive a throaty chuckle and a smack to my ass. "Oh, I can speak tonight, Queen." Voice dark and smooth, Pretty Boy is beyond confident. "Misbehave and make my night." Beneath his amusement is a silent threat.

A premonition roars to life, causing a wave of panic and uncertainty to roll along my spine.

"Are we driving a blacked-out rape wagon?" My voice takes on a taunting edge. "Or did you all bring separate cars?"

"I don't remember you being so sarcastic." Pretty Boy swats my ass again. "I like it– give 'em hell, Queen." Laughter floods my ears as I'm tossed into someone's lap.

An erection bites into my hip, and I immediately feel at ease. "Ah, Cort... I'd recognize that exquisite cock anywhere." I tease my long-lost buddy.

Snickering, Cortez settles me firmly into his lap, with his arms cradling me protectively. Two distinct growls echo around the abduction vehicle.

Since I have a death wish– "Cort, your fan club isn't too happy about the fact that I know your cock good enough to recognize it prodding my hip." I chuckle in mock-amusement. "Marcus and Ezra are positively possessive of you, ya lucky bastard."

Inside it hurts to hear Marcus upset that Cort enjoys my company, but no one can see the expressions crossing my face because of the hood, so it doesn't matter if I show it on the outside either.

"I think you're misinterpreting that sound." Cortez replies, shifting our weight as the vehicle lurches forward.

A hand brushes my hair where the hood rides up in the back, and it's not Cortez's touch. I ignore the fingers playing with the short, curling ends.

"If you were really going to be all scary, you should have gotten a delivery van. An expensive SUV just doesn't have the same thrill factor. Plus, I'd love to have seen you all roll around for twenty minutes." I taunt the lot of them, hoping they'll chat with me. If they talk, I won't feel so nervous and scared out of my mind.

"Hmm... let me use my powers of deduction. We're riding in a black Escalade registered to the owner of Restraint. C'mon, am I right? Admit it, I am."

"Why'd you cut your hair?" Marcus asks, voice pitched low. Since I can't see his face, I can't determine his mood.

"It's not like it was doing anything for me– ugly is ugly, short or long. It was time for a change." I let a moment pass. "Cortez, did you notice Marcus didn't deny my ugly claim. I wasn't fishing for a compliment, but it's quite telling."

"What's going on Reg– Queen?" Cort wasn't smooth enough to cover up my name with the Queen, but it's not like anyone in the vehicle doesn't know who I am, seeing as how they invaded my home.

"Why nothing at all," I drawl out. "I've been enjoying my newfound independence for the last two months." Turning a bit, I cuddle into Cortez's arms, luxuriating in the comfort after so long of having no one touch me.

"I've missed you, by the way." I snuggle in deeper, and Cort squeezes me tightly in return. "You could have called, or at least sent me an email or something. I've seen you almost every day for a year and a half, and then no calls." I turn flippant, trying to bury the hurt. "You'd think we had a one-night stand, and you didn't call after you said you would."

Stilling beneath me, Cortez demands, "What's Regina talking about, Marcus?"

"Don't bother. What did I say that wasn't true? Two months– eight weeks with no contact with any of you, except when Marcus commandeered Jamie's cellphone."

Marcus tries to explain, "Regina, I–" but I cut him off because I don't want to hear his excuses.

"Yeah, it really makes me want to join your little group," I mutter snidely. "Ignoring me and cutting me off makes me feel *so* welcome."

"What's going on?" Ezra's cold voice echoes around the vehicle. "What's Queen talking about?"

"*We're your shelter from the storm, your shoulder to cry on.*" I mock Marcus by twisting his words. "I guess I wasn't dealing with any important issues these past few months. Frankly, I was pretty sure I'd never hear from any of you again." My voice breaks as I admit my biggest fear.

"What's Regina talking about?" Cort growls near my ear, as Pretty Boy adds in his two cents. "What did you do, Marc? You promised never to fuck with Queen's emotions."

"We're here," an uneasy female voice announces from the front. Syn must have been delegated as driver. Her voice wavers slightly, like she's scared to interrupt. I can't see anyone's facial expressions, and no one is speaking. I don't feel their gazes on me, either. Something must be going on that's unseen and unheard, or the notorious Syn wouldn't be so uneasy.

Cort's body thrums with pent-up energy, and I want to calm him. A wound-up Cortez is a menace. "Easy, killer. Let's turn that down a notch. You're making my hair stand on end, and no one wants to see that."

A collective breath is released and the tension lessens. I have a feeling this initiation isn't going as planned. I wonder why.

Hands wrapping around my shoulders, "I'll take Queen again," Pretty Boy demands, voice tight with anger. He isn't cocky like Cortez, because he assumes you'll just do as he says. I wonder how old Pretty Boy is. If he's young, we should be terrified of him, because he could rival Marcus when he reaches full maturity.

"NO!" Marcus bellows in the SUV, until our eardrums reverberate with his violence, to the point they feel like they're going to rupture. "Don't touch Regina!"

Cortez recoils, holding me tightly, and his breathing is loud against the burlap covering my head. The vibrations strengthen the sound.

"Marcus?" Pretty Boy tries again, sounding reasonable. "I would enjoy some time alone with Queen. If I don't get what I requested, this will be all I get."

"I said no," Marcus barks out. "You'll get more than Regina's prepared to take, and I don't give a fuck what you want at this moment."

There's a single heartbeat in the car, and it beats frantically as we all wait to see what will transpire between Marcus and Pretty Boy.

"Go into the dungeon, and wait for us," Marc commands in a deadly quiet voice.

Pretty Boy can't leave well enough alone, "Marc–"

"Dexter, get him out of my sight, because you have no idea how badly I want to annihilate him. But I fear what Regina and his father would do to me if I did."

"Marcus, you don't mean that." Pretty Boy's voice drops low, sadness evident.

"Regina would rather subject herself to your reward than see you murdered. But I'm not Regina. So heed my warning, Pretty Boy, because I'm not above murder at this point."

"C'mon, kid." I'd forgotten how Dexter's voice flows like the beat of a drum– deep and resonating. "Marcus would regret hurting you on so many levels, but you're pushing your luck. I don't know what you did to get him to agree with your demands, but you better quit while you're ahead."

My hearing intensifies, picking up the whisper of clothing and the stride of footsteps on pavement by my soon-to-be fellow masters, leaving just Marc, Cort, and me in the car.

"Get out!" Marcus orders roughly.

"Sir, you're not going to hurt Regina, are you?" Cortez's voice sounds unsure, and he never treats Marcus with respect. The fact that he is frightens me. Arms enveloping me protectively, Cortez pulls me closer to his chest and leans toward the right. I can feel the night air through the open door, as if Cortez is considering lunging us to safety.

"Just take the bag off my head, and stand outside the car. Please," I whisper through the burlap.

"If it wasn't for the fact that what you just said made sense, I'd be even angrier that Cort is considering it." Marc's voice is chilling. "Cortez, I'm your master, lest you've forgotten. Drop your arms before I rip them off, and then get the fuck out!"

Marcus screams– Marcus never screams.

I don't want Cort to move his arms because I can't see and I'm bound, and I need him for protection. I have no idea what I did to anger Marcus so badly. Tears well up in my eyes and start to moisten the sack. The trembling starts at my toes, and works its way upward, until I'm a quivering mess.

"You're upsetting Regina," Cortez bites out, suddenly protective of me.

"Cort." Marcus sighs, sounding calmer. "Just wait by the door. I only need a moment of privacy with Regina before her initiation. It's important, and between her and I. I'm calm." Marcus may sound reassuring, but I don't buy it. Cort must, though, since he releases me, and then crawls out from underneath me. A moment later the door closes us in.

"Regina, are you all right?" Marcus asks in concern with a calm voice.

"Peachy." I use bravado to hide the trembling in my voice.

"I'm sorry," is whispered softly.

"For what?"

"For scaring you," Marcus replies without missing a beat. But it's not good enough, because there are so many things he should apologize for, scaring me the least of them.

Tugging me forward, Marcus presses me down to the floorboard until I'm kneeling between his feet. The bag is raised, air hitting my damp cheeks, and I sigh in relief.

Left staring up into Marc's whiskey eyes, usually they're warm amber with flecks of gold and bronze swirling around, but tonight they darken to chocolate.

"What did I do?" I sound meek, but determination laces my voice. "What did I do to turn you from me for so long? Worse is the fact that I feel it was without provocation."

"I brought this." Marcus produces the scarf I used on Fate during my final– the one I used to control her breathing. "That was one of my proudest moments, watching you with Fate. You were wonderful." I should have known he'd be watching. "Alive. Powerful. Queen."

"What did I do to garner your disappointment?" I ask again in a new way.

"It's only fitting that I use this to blind you tonight, and it will be very pretty with your new haircut." Marc's fingers sweep my hair, and then he sighs. "It suits you. And your hair is not, nor ever was, ugly."

Leaning down, Marcus wraps the scarf around my head, pulling it taut over my eyes, and then knots it in the back where I can't reach. Kneeling on the floor between Marc's feet, I wait minutes while he doesn't speak or move. The only sound for the longest time is his labored breath… and then a noise I would recognize anywhere– a zipper being drawn down.

Something moist taps my bottom lip, asking me to open. My tongue darts out on its own accord, and returns to my mouth with a taste. I don't know what Marcus is doing, or why, but I shudder from the earthy taste of his ambrosia after so long being denied.

Coaxing, Marcus pushes his length between my parted lips, and it's a struggle with his girth, and then he palms the back of my head. I wait for the skull-fuckage to begin, knowing he's angry with me and my punishment is finally being delivered.

As bizarre as it is to admit, I want to cry because Marcus is giving me something he's always denied me, and it feels like a goodbye.

Opening my mouth as wide as it will go, I breathe through my nostrils. Surging downward, cock so thick it steals my breath away, I struggle to move vigorously up and down the column of his cock.

Palm stilling my movements, Marcus murmurs, "Slowly."

Calming, I give Marcus a blowjob in the way Grant taught me– gentle sucking, while exploring with my tongue and lips. Scraping my teeth tenderly over his cockhead, Marcus bows against the seat, and I wish I could see his facial expression.

"I've often wondered what it would be like to enjoy this with someone." Marc's low voice sounds unbelievably intimate in the dark of the car.

"My first blowjob was when I was still a virgin– married but untouched. I was sleeping, and I thought I was dreaming a wet dream, as most young men often do. I woke as I came. Then when

I glanced down, I was horrified to discover it was no dream, but rather a living nightmare I've never recovered from experiencing."

Startled by his words, I still my movements, but the palm resting on the crown of my skull urges me to continue. It's like Marcus can't continue to speak until I'm preoccupied with his cock.

"My next oral experience was when I was captured and training with Olivia. The first few times she tried to have sex with me– and make no mistake, Olivia got my dick in her –I couldn't get hard. I don't classify anything during my time in Vegas as consensual, so I don't add it to my sexual history."

Tugging free, "Marcus?" But a gentle pressure to the back of my skull urges me back down onto his cock.

"Olivia is vain, an otherworldly beauty. But since I couldn't be aroused by her, when she didn't realize it was because it was forced, not because she wasn't the most sensual creature I've ever seen, she would tie me down and force her whores on me. If I managed to get hard, not that I stayed hard until completion, Olivia would turn furious and beat me because I thought another woman was more arousing. So I learned to hate the act, seeing it as humiliating, a form of submission."

Yet again, I try to pull away so I can speak with Marcus, maybe reassure him, but he doesn't allow it.

"Olivia's conclusion was that I was gay, which was a way to comfort her bruised ego. I'm not gay, or straight, or bi, or whatever. I'm attracted to the person, not their sex parts. First came the male whores, who couldn't even get my dick to twitch. Olivia knew the secret to how I lost my virginity, so she sent her son to me, night and day, and never in a sexual way for months on end. Leviticus was seducing me at his mother's bidding, but neither of us realized it... then Levi's grandfathers came, and it all changed for the worse."

Resting both palms on the back of my skull, Marcus guides me to take more of his cock down my throat. In the silence, he lifts his hips, gaining a better angle, until I taste the bitter tang of impending release on the back of my tongue. Sighing, Marcus lets up to delay his release.

"I will never give the details, other than to say Olivia got what she wanted out of me. Finally finding a way to milk my cock. Unlike most, my time in Vegas wasn't spent being trained in BDSM, even though the same tenets were used by my fellow trainees. I was held captive, but it was of my own choosing because

I went there freely, even if I didn't know what I was getting myself into. I've had countless mouths on my cock, all trying to drain it into a condom that would be delivered to Olivia. None by choice, except for two."

"Cort?" I mutter from around Marc's cock.

"And you." Marcus brushes my hair back, palms curving around my skull. Then he rises and lowers his hips a few times, getting into a rhythm. "It's different with Cortez. He balances my need like the perfect submissive. Cortez needs it rough, craves it, and Ezra can't stomach doing it because it terrifies him– in case you were wondering why my son allows such intimacies to take place. But it's *my* punishment– a way of fighting my demons." My heart aches for Marcus, especially for the lost tone in his voice.

"I love your mouth on me." Hips rising, Marcus presses as far down my throat as he can go, pubic hair tickling my lips and covering my nostrils, with his balls curving against my chin. "I knew I would enjoy everything with you, but I was too frightened to find out."

Tears stream down my face as I give Marcus pleasure, and I can sense he's fighting for control– control over his fears. I'm shocked as much as pained to know Marcus has endured rape. It explains so much, and yet so little at the same time.

"I apologize, Regina. I was angry and hurt. I received disturbing information, and my pride got the better of me. I was told you'd been intimate with Roman, and it took me two months not to kill him. This morning, I finally worked up the courage to ask Roman, and of course he denied it. Then I asked you on Jamie's phone, and you denied it. You both responded with the exact same thing. At first, I was leery of your reply, and I didn't believe you until I saw your face and heard you speak with Cort. I'm sorry."

The man who never apologizes, apologizes twice in one night. Betrayed, I begin to cry in earnest. Pulling away from Marcus, blowjob the last thing on my mind, I sob with my face resting against his thigh. The pain of betrayal wracks my body.

Sniffling, I long to reach up to tug the scarf from my eyes, needing Marcus to see all the betrayal and loathing pouring out, but my hands are restrained. "Bullshit," I snarl. "I smell your bullshit, fuckface. I'm not saying you did or didn't hear that, or that you wouldn't put it past Roman. But after the past year and a half, where I came to you for everything, pouring my heart out and laying every secret I have at your feet, you know damn well that's bullshit. Total fucking bullshit."

"Regina, I can't think clearly around you. I lose all focus, and that isn't a good thing for a man in my position." Whispering so quietly, I'm not sure I hear him, "How I feel about you terrifies me."

"You're the master of all those who were in this car." Crawling back into the seat beside Marcus, I refuse to rest at a lower position than him. We are equals. "Stop being a pussy."

"Regina, you don't get it." Marcus has never looked weaker in my eyes. "I'll explain in detail after your initiation. Please take me back into your body. I need you. I need you to forgive me, even if it's just a lie."

Pointing a fingertip into the center of his chest, I let Marcus have it with both barrels. "I've trusted you infallibly, even knowing you held secrets from me. I've never given you a reason not to trust me, Marcus. I need to know this won't happen again, but I won't be able to believe you if you say it won't."

"It won't," Marcus protests.

"Bullshit," I snarl. "I've had a difficult two months. The loneliness killed me, and I can't do this again."

"Regina." Marcus tries to capture my hand, but I won't allow it. "You have no idea what's been going on inside my goddamn head since the three of us made love. I feel like an interloper, holding onto secrets I wish you knew, knowing when you learn the truth you'll leave me."

"Here's an idea." I kneel in the seat, needing to be taller than Marcus. "Tell. The. Truth."

"I can't!" Marcus shouts, tears threatening to fall. "Don't you think I want to? I would only keep these secrets for one person, even knowing it's going to ruin my life. There's one of two possibilities: you're either going to leave me for him, or you're going to leave me for not telling you, but both options have my heart broken."

"Goddamn you, what the fuck are you talking about?"

"You're not mine!" Marcus bellows. "I wasn't supposed to fall in love with you. Don't you fucking get that? Don't you?" Getting up on his knees, Marcus curves over me, having to be in the top position. "You're going to leave me anyway, so I used Kristal's lies about Roman fucking you as my early way out, so it wouldn't hurt so fucking much when you leave *me*!"

Palms landing in the center of his chest, I push Marcus hard, until his ass lands back on the seat and his head knocks against the side window.

Glaring up at me, Marcus is seething. "No one is as blind as you are, if you don't have a fucking clue who Pretty Boy is, but your guilt and grief have made it so you can't see." Pointing at Restraint. "He'll destroy what we've built, and he's the least of our problems, Regina. *The least.* But Pretty Boy is a pretty big fucking problem, which should tell you how motherfucking HUGE our actual problem is."

Deflated from confusion, "What are you talking about?" I breathe.

"You." This time Marcus stabs a fingertip in the middle of my chest. "I'm just waiting for you to figure it out, working on borrowed time and sucking up whatever love and devotion you're willing to give me. Tonight, I have to stand by and watch the first layer of our relationship dissolve during your initiation."

"I love you," I admit for the first time.

"I know," Marcus growls.

"I mean, I'm *in* love with you."

"*I know*," Marcus stresses, tears betraying him. "You have no clue how fucked up we are. I've never been in love with anyone but Grant before you, and what we did…" Marcus turns away from me. "You have no idea how much it meant to me the last time we were together. No idea."

Slumping back into the seat, I'm at a loss on how to continue. "You won't be able to respect me, and I won't respect myself, if I continue to allow you to treat me like garbage. You say you're my partner, yet you spin more mind fucks than my worst enemy would."

Marcus is quiet for a few minutes, contemplative. All I can hear is Marc's labored breathing and Cortez's movements as he tries to get comfortable by leaning against the outside of the SUV. I know Cortez can hear us in here, but I'm not embarrassed for once.

"Okay." Marcus shifts, putting his game face on. "Pretty Boy is playing his own game tonight, and your initiation is going to turn into wild kingdom. Master of the Masters of Restraint, or not, it's out of my hands. Everything you do or don't do is up to you, and I hope you kick Pretty Boy's ass once the night is through."

"Pretty Boy can get at the back of the line, because I want to kick everyone's ass."

"Good luck with that, because you're going to need it." Sighing, Marcus looks utterly defeated. "Do you really want this, Regina? Because the cost is high."

"Yes, I need it." I pour my guts out, just as I always do around Marcus. "Work is work. My daughter is my greatest joy. But I need something to keep me alive, and Restraint is the ticket. I don't want to *play* BDSM in the dungeon. I want to run the whole fucking place and *own* everything and everyone in the dungeon."

"Then you'll get fucked tonight," Marcus warns. "Mentally, emotionally, and physically fucked. You've been warned."

I didn't think it was possible to be numb yet exhilarated at the same time, but I am. "Do I have to fuck them all?"

"That depends entirely on your definition of fucked, Regina."

"Fucked in the head?" Marcus snorts, thinking I'm being cute. "I need this. I need something for me, only for me, Marcus. I'm sick of feeling like everyone's pawn, and I know I have been since I received my scholarship to Hillbrook when I was months shy of fourteen. Everyone around me is lying, and I need to feel in control of something."

"Understood." Marc's voice turns wry. "I can't believe we told each other we loved one another while screaming into each other's faces." Marcus shifts, a sad smile playing along his lips, then he opens his arms in invitation. "Now get your ass over here and hold me, let me kiss you for a minute before you're finally Queened."

Chapter Thirty-Three

I feel bad that Marcus made everyone wait as long as he did. He held me for over an hour, trying to stall the inevitable.

Initiation wasn't always a hazing. In the beginning, it was just Marcus and Dexter drinking whiskey and playing cards. Ezra joined them, and they continued to do this weekly as they told humorous stories of what happened at Restraint during the week. The change occurred when Cortez and Syn were inducted. I've heard stories about this, even before I ever set foot into Restraint. Ade looked crazed as she recounted parts of the story that Ezra allowed to slip. Cort, trying to frighten me, told me in greater detail of that night.

After that clusterfuck, everyone was scared shitless of the Pretty Boy's initiation. But I guess it turned out like the original times. They ate pizza, got drunk, and played poker. Pretty Boy won the game, and his reward was a freebie jerk off session with Cort. Surprisingly, Cort didn't complain, which I found strange. I wonder what Cort did in another life to piss everyone off.

Now it's my initiation, and I feel it in my bones that it's going to be bad. Marcus was shivering in the car, which I found strange since he's the one in control and calling the shots.

Marcus left me so he could put his *Master* face back on, whatever that means. Cort and I stand silently in the predawn light, shivering as the frigid air whips around us.

"Ready?" Cort's eyes twinkle with excitement. Hopping on his heels, he flashes me a cocky smirk.

"What are you so happy about, mister?"

"I've never been to an initiation where I wasn't the one offering pleasure." He pointedly looks at me. "First there was my own, then there was Pretty Boy's initiation." Rubbing his palms together like a villain, Cort's eyes are bright. "I'm excited."

"Oh, so you're hoping you'll get to sex me up?" Raising an eyebrow, I turn sarcastic. "Just so you know, I'm not a virgin anymore."

"Really?" Cortez grabs his chest, gasping. "I'm shocked senseless. I guess I imagined all those times I watched Marcus plow into you."

"I can't believe Marc's going to do this," I grumble. "Especially after everything we said in the car. I don't think I could suffer through watching Marcus touch other people."

"Marcus has no other choice. It's going to be horrible for him to watch you with Pretty Boy. It'll be easier if it's a progression."

Taken aback, I try to get a read on Cortez's expression. "What do you mean?"

"Prepare for an orgy, Regina. Pretty Boy has Marcus in a mood, and I can't wait for you to disobey." Cortez's voice takes on a cadence of mischievous evilness.

"You're fucked, Cort, but not by me."

"Ha-ha! By the way, the problem won't be you disobeying Marcus– it'll be when you disobey Pretty Boy. It was his checkmate on Marc. No way will you do as he asks."

"You can't know that," I mutter in denial.

"Okay, if you agree to all of Pretty Boy's demands, make sure you have an icepack ready. Syn hits hard– my crotch was black and blue last time."

"What?" I gasp in shock.

"Nope! Come on, Regina. I'm horny." Cortez whines, hitching up his pants to show off an impressive bulge. He laughs at my frightened expression.

"It's time to put the scarf back on." Cortez ties it quickly, blocking out all available light. I like the scarf a whole lot better than the burlap sack. At least my mouth and nose are uncovered.

I worry about walking through Restraint without sight, but Cort swings me up into his arms, and then strolls through an eerily silent club. "My... my... my... what big arms you have," I purr, impressed.

"Regina, you're my favorite person ever." Cortez flirts back, affection thick in his voice.

It's almost four in the morning, lending to the hollowness of Cort's footsteps on the flooring. I concentrate on the sounds around me instead of how my heart is threatening to beat out of my chest. Beeps, clicks, the opening and closing of doors, and Cortez's footsteps.

"You'll be fine. Pretty Boy won't do anything to harm you of all people. This is a dominance challenge between the Master of the Masters of Restraint and our youngest master. But at its core, it's all about you. Neither one of them will ever hurt you intentionally," Cort promises.

"I'll never hurt her," rings in unison, followed by an angry growl.

I don't have a fucking clue what's going on. Setting me on my feet, Cortez stabilizes me before letting go, then I wait.

Using my senses, I get a feel for what's around me. The room is vast, judging by how it doesn't feel as if anything is closing in around me and how I'm unable to sense the walls or furnishings. My hazers are within arm's reach, because I can hear their breathing and feel their body heat. The air is humid but cold, proving the space is cavernous and closed off with no windows or access to fresh air. Every movement echoes in the dungeon I've never seen but am destined to run.

"Welcome, Masters of Restraint!" Marcus projects, voice echoing off the walls. "This night is of great importance as we induct our seventh Master of Restraint. I also want to announce how I'm training two others: Dalton Thompson and Roman Alexander. It's humbling to see how we've grown from three men bullshitting to a true charter of Maître du Jeu. Okay, enough business. Let the fun begin. Strip!"

"What?" several shouts of outrage bellow, bitch, and complain. I stand frozen since Marcus wasn't speaking to me. I have a cable-tie holding my wrists behind my back, so clearly that is an order I can't obey.

"Don't test me, children." Marc's voice is scary calm. "Do as I say." The whisper of several articles of clothing dropping to the floor is eclipsed by the metal on metal sound of zippers and the jingle of belt buckles.

"But not as you do?" Cort snarks.

"You won't strip." A belligerent female voices, one who I assume is Syn. "Why should we?"

"Did you not just hear our master, you little sneaky snake of a cunt?" Cortez turns into a different person, voice low and seething with bitter loathing. "Do as Marcus says, not as he does."

"You have no need for shame, little one," Marc patronizes. "I wish I could strip and join the hedonistic fun, but someone has to remain in charge."

"Lucky you," Dexter murmurs underneath his breath, but the dungeon is not forgiving and all sound echoes. Loudly.

"Do you really want to see me naked, cousin?"

"No, but I also don't want you to see me," Dexter mutters, causing Cortez to snicker.

"I've seen your show since birth, Dex, and you with me, so stop feeding into your protégée's disgruntled behavior."

"Fine, but I hate taking orders from my *little* cousin."

"Duly noted, dumbass." I can hear the eye roll in Marc's voice. "I may be a few months younger, but I am bigger."

Dexter turns arrogant. "In height, but not cock size."

"Zeitler fight!" Cortez shouts, while clapping echoes around the dungeon. "Not you, Ezra. You're technically a Holden. Plus, Dexter's cock is the rock, Marc's the scissors, and I'm paper. Everyone else has thumbs for dicks."

"Oh, will you?" Pretty Boy begs. "Will you please play rock, paper, scissors, but have Ezra replace Dexter with me as scissors? Pretty please."

"Jesus Christ, does he really want to have a sword fight with those two idiots?" I whisper to myself, and Cort laughs in answer.

"You did not just say that!" Syn snarls, sounding on the verge of gagging. "We need some more members, because this incest shit is for the birds. I'm so sick to death of hearing about Cort's dangly meat. It's not exquisite, cocksucker. It's just a dick, and half of the population has one."

"It fucked you well enough, bitch!"

"Cortez?" Ezra calls softly. "Behave. Our dicks are identical."

"They are not. Mine's bigger."

"They *are* identical," Syn interjects. "And I'm the only one here who'd know. In the dark, you guys are interchangeable."

Whoa...

"Bullshit," Cortez snarls. "That was when I was a teenager. Your opinion doesn't count."

"I'm going to have to go with Syn on this, Cortez." Marcus chuckles sardonically, probably because of Cort's reaction.

"Traitor!" Cort snarls.

"I'm willing to test the theory," Pretty Boy offers. "I'll fluff the Ezes and measure them with my mouth."

"Oh. My. God." Syn sounds revolted. "I'm going to fucking puke. Marcus, I swear to God, you promised I didn't have to see anything sick tonight."

"I'm flattered, Pretty Boy." Blindfolded, even I can hear the blush in Ezra's voice. I expect Cortez to throw himself, but he releases a satisfied masculine chuckle instead.

Smiling like an idiot, I'm finally at ease. The Masters of Restraint are just normal, fucked up people who have a common interest. If anything, they all fight like siblings. They're not going to hurt me. Once I get to know them, they'll probably let me boss them around because they sound like they don't know jackshit.

"No one is going to interact with anyone else but Queen," Marcus promises to smooth Syn's ruffled feathers. "So get undressed. The nakedness is not sexual in nature, just a way to level the playing field and make everyone comfortable, or uncomfortable as the case may be.

With my arms tugged slightly, a snip and my hands are freed. I rub my wrists and sigh in relief. "Thank you, Marcus," I say in his general direction.

"And you knew it was me, how?" Marcus whispers in my ear. He brushes his lips against my neck, and I relax even more under his affectionate touch.

"I'd recognize your scent anywhere," I whisper underneath my breath.

"And I, yours," he breathes against the side of my neck.

Marcus slowly divests me of my clothing, with his fingers continuously lingering on my exposed skin. I know the other masters are watching, because I can feel their gazes burn into my flesh with every pass of Marc's finger over my skin.

I gather strength from an unknown source, finding myself no longer frightened or worried. They've already seen the show when they abducted me, so getting naked before them is no issue.

My body trills with power. Wild and freeing.

"You've slept with Queen?" Ezra accuses.

"No comment," rumbles from Marcus, which is answer enough.

"Whoa, Ezra. You seem to accuse me of screwing someone every time we meet. Last time it was Cort, this time Marcus. You have some serious boundary issues, my friend. My sex life is none of your concern."

"Sorry," is mumbled in apology. "But Cortez and Marcus *are* my business."

Ezra is going to be a problem for me, I can bet on it, especially with that possessive, pissy attitude he's emoting.

"This is Queen." I can't see him, but I can sense Marcus is presenting my naked form to my fellow masters. His pride in me in unmistakable. "Please greet her in order."

I wait for handshakes.

I'm a moron.

I'm a *huge* fucking moron.

Tentatively, lips struggle to touch my cheek. It's Dexter, and he must be on his tippy toes. "Hello, Dexter. It's nice to see you again, and I hope you're not sneering at me as you did the last we met." My voice is friendly, but it's laced with annoyance.

"I apologize for my asinine behavior. I was having a bad day," Dexter offers lamely. "You've kept Cort off my hands, and I can't thank you enough for that. Considering I nearly killed him mere minutes before I met you."

"Apology accepted. Cortez may be an acquired taste, but I'm rather fond of the naughty asswipe."

The next set of lips leaves me gasping. Ezra kisses me, and I freak the fuck out with hands rising to ward him off. There goes the sister-code!

"Regina, it's okay." Marcus tries to soothe me. "What happens in the dungeon doesn't leave the dungeon. The only rules that apply are mine." Marcus knows exactly what to say to me since he and Jamie were the ones to shoulder my burdens with Kristal.

The kiss returns, and it's intense, questing, and punishing. Ezra bites my bottom lip hard enough that I hiss in pain. The instant my mouth opens to release the plea, Ezra's tongue dives in and tastes me. Pulling away abruptly, he releases a hiss of his own.

"Marc's mouth has been on yours." Ezra mutters in awe, in the creepiest tone I've ever heard.

"Yes, we've kissed before." I speak underneath my breath because I don't want anyone else to hear us, but it's for naught. I can feel the pack of lusty masters hovering inches from us.

"Have you had sex with him?" Ezra issues his angry demand, then presses his body to the length of mine. Grinding his rock-hard erection into my belly, I freeze in shock.

Where's the calm, sensible man who's engaged to Ade? The doctor of psychiatry? The *gay* man? The person before me is more animal than man. Voice sounding different, deep and as smooth as glass, I feel as if I could sip it and savor it as a fine whiskey.

OH! I'm a moron. Snippets of conversation snap into place, along with Marc's constant reminder that his son is not sane.

"Master Ez?" My voice lilts in an upward inflection, realizing Ezra's dominant being may be driving the bus with Ezra nowhere in sight.

"Yes, Queen?" Master Ez breathes against my mouth from lips turned up into a sneer. "Did you sleep with him?"

"No, I've never had sex with Cort." I shake my head and my voice is strong with truthful denial.

"I'm not speaking of Cortez. Our master, you're his lover. I can feel it."

"No," I lie, leaving absolutely no trace of deception.

"You lie," Master Ez accuses. "Master's taste is in your mouth, and not the kind from his *tongue*." He enunciates the word tongue, and it's beyond creepy.

"How would you know Marc's taste?" I don't deny it, but I turn it back around on him. What sick shit has Ezra been up to? "Are you a connoisseur of semen?"

"You lie. This explains much. Welcome to the family, Regina Regal– mother of the Whittenhower heirs." I freeze when Ezra says my name. My heart pounds and my blood rushes to meet its beat. Suffocating, I start to gasp for air.

"I didn't recognize you at Restraint when you were dressed as you were. But when I came to the brownstone, you were dressed in jeans and I recognized you immediately."

Leaning deeper into me, Master Ez kisses me roughly, almost as if he's trying to remove all traces of Marcus from my mouth. Squirming, I whimper when his warm testicles press against my mound and a trickle of precum dampens my belly.

Master Ez is fucking scary.

"Tell my fiancée that time is ticking. In a few months, Katya will be here. Tick-tock… Tick-tock." Master Ez threatens in a sing-song cadence. His body leaves me cold in more ways than one. I'm flushed with fright and with a creepy form of lust that popped out of nowhere.

I'm able to relax because I know who's up next. I patiently wait for Cort's lips, but I'm taken by surprise when a set of small hands frame my hips instead. Syn struggles to her tippy toes, just as Dexter had, but more so.

"Syn, do you wish to kiss me on the cheek, or would you prefer something else? I'd suggest a hug, but we're both kind of naked." I'm shy from embarrassment.

"May I have your ear, please?" Syn's voice is soft, barely projecting, and at complete and total odds with the instigating tone she took on with Cortez.

"Okay," I draw out as I bend at the waist.

"Why are they saying you're a lesbian when I know you're not?" Syn accuses.

"You know nothing," I bite back at her.

"Regina, you love cock more than I do. I'd rather hurt things than fuck them," she says with a strange feminazi sort of pride.

"Why do you think you know me?" I whisper-argue in Syn's direction.

Instead of answering me, Syn hugs me even though we're both naked. Her body is small, compact, and curvy. Her high, round breasts press into my belly. I turn my cheek at the same time she offers me hers, but I can't see, so I end up kissing the corner of her mouth. Syn makes an impatient sound as she walks away.

"Nice to meet you too, Syn," I mumble after her.

"Syn has a terminal condition otherwise known as being a judgmental, bitchy cunt." Cort informs me as he moves forward in greeting. "If you'll let Syn whip you, you'll have a new best friend."

"Was Syn's terminal condition brought on by too much Cortez Hunter exposure?" Voice light, I take on Cort's cadence.

"I believe Syn would agree with that," he muses. "Believe it or not, a long, *long* time ago, Syn was a beautiful, innocent girl, who thought I walked on water."

"Fuck you, cocksucker," the smoky voice sneers at him. "No, get fucked!"

"If yours was the last cunt on earth, I'd get Carpal Tunnel Syndrome, Syn." Cortez says her name in a way that makes you want to punch him in the nuts. Cortez's art is antagonism. "Lest you forget, I've fucked that used up pussy of yours hundreds of times. I wasn't impressed then, and I'm not impressed now. On the other hand, you always screamed for me– *begged* for it. Thanks for teaching me everything I ever needed to know about pussies."

"Cortez, that's enough!" Marc's voice projects, and I can hear struggling in the background.

"Behave," I chastise while reaching for the bastard.

"After you see Syn, you'll never let me name-call her again." Cortez proves he's an expert at whining and pouting. "It's so unfair. I have notebooks filled with insults."

"Are you going to greet me, or are we going to be standing here when Restraint opens its doors in the evening?" I try to pop a brow, but the scarf across my eyes impedes my snark.

Expecting Cortez to inhale my mouth, he starts gently instead, with only his lips touching mine. Our tall bodies are more than a foot a part, like kids at a junior high dance. I can't even feel his body heat from the wide distance. As we build into the kiss, Cortez begins to draw closer and closer, until we're perfectly aligned.

I don't mean to make a sound, but I can't help the moan that bubbles up my throat and spills from between my parted lips. Cortez returns the sound with one of his own. Warm, strong fingers grip my ass and lift. My choice is either to wrap my legs around his hips, or endure his struggle to hold me inches off the ground. Automatically my legs hook around Cortez's waist with my arms around his shoulders. The hard exquisiteness slips between my thighs to seat itself snugly against my slit.

We attack one another. For almost a year and a half, we have been subjected to training without release. We flogged, spanked, restrained, and did humiliating acts to one another every other day, and never did we get this pleasure. Our long denied bodies go on autopilot as we moan and groan and grind against one another. It isn't about love or affection. It isn't about friendship. It's pure, unadulterated lust.

I never thought Cortez wanted me– I was wrong.

"Master, stop them!" A deep, authoritative voice bellows.

"Why? Regina will fuck Cortez before the night is through. She'll fuck all of you." Marc's voice sounds hopeless. "Just as you planned."

"How can you do this?" Pretty Boy sounds very upset. "How can you watch?"

"You have a choice to make, son. We can eat pizza and get drunk, then the winner of cards can pick their victim. You're the smartest of us here, so you'd probably win anyway. Or you can watch Regina screw everyone in this room, not knowing if you'll get the chance."

"That's not what I want, and you know it!" Pretty Boy protests.

"Think wisely and steadfastly, young man. Do you wish to see Regina as a whore? You've placed her on a pedestal for so long, it probably shocks you how she would gladly fuck Cortez. Even I've ignored that fact, because I was worried it would bother me. But I rather like how they look pressed together– pleased with themselves and *very* aroused."

"Don't ever call Queen a whore, Marcus." Pretty Boy threatens, voice quivering with rage. "You'll regret it."

"Oh, I'm not," Marcus mutters snidely. "I'm not a Whittenhower. I don't see Regina as a disposable whore that you fuck and hide behind closed doors."

I suck in a sharp breath as Marcus unleashes my dirty secret and years upon years of resentment.

"Take that back!" Pretty Boy's calm demeanor snaps, and he lashes out viciously.

"Why, it's true. Is it not?" I've never heard Marcus sound so arrogant, and considering he's the most arrogant man I know...

"Marcus, no more," I cry out, more than done with these theatrics. I drag a hand through my hair in frustration and sigh loudly.

SHIT!

"It's what Pretty Boy wants, Regina. He wants to take you into the Whittenhower room and fuck you. But at least Grant let you look him in the eye as you took him into your body." Marc's voice seethes, but I can hear the hopeless quality to it.

"Don't make what I want sound nasty." Pretty Boy's frustrated voice echoes throughout the dungeon. "It's my right."

"Your right, you entitled asshat? What of Regina's rights? Why doesn't she get any?" Marcus asks the question I've been asking myself for ages.

"No more," I protest, putting my hand up to halt the oncoming fight. "Fine. I wanted to have a haven where people didn't know my secrets, and would just get to know me for me, and respect the person they learned. Fine." I yank the blindfold off my face and scream to the ceiling "So fuck it! I'm Regina Regal, forever known as the Whittenhower Whore. Happy?" I spit.

Glaring Marcus down, I try to stop the tears threatening to track down my cheeks by holding my eyes impossibly wide, but they fall anyway. Betrayal. I wanted to be respected while in this building. It's why I trained so hard and suffered through things I didn't enjoy.

"This was supposed to be *my* night– about *me*. Not about Cortez and Faith fighting their lovers quarrel from their teenage years. Or a cock measuring contest. Or the fight between Marcus and Pretty Boy over who gets to possess me. Tonight was supposed to be about *me*. *MY* initiation. Where I was afforded the respect I deserve– the respect I've earned.

"But you guys are narcissistic assholes, which is why I need to be here in the first place. Someone must be your checks and balances before you destroy each other. I'm a mother, so by God, I'll fucking mother you into behaving, especially since you all think that's the only thing I'm good for– birthing the next generation of Whittenhower heirs."

Ashamed and humiliated, I'm more furious than anything. I am more than *that*, so much more. If they loved and respected me as much as they say they do, they'd stop throwing that fact into my face and only seeing me as Niel and Ella's mother. I close my eyes and count to ten, and then to twenty, and thirty, and beyond. I use the shocked silence to center myself, and then I rip the motherfucking Band-Aid off.

"Whitt, get your ass over here." I croak out. "Now!"

In the back of my mind, I've known this entire time, but I was too frightened to admit it for many reasons over. The green-eyed monster tattoo Whitt designed is inlaid on Kristal's décolletage. Admitting Whitt was Pretty Boy would have led to the fallout between Kristal and me– I can't let her go knowing she needs me. I can't give up on my friend. But she's been fucking around with Whitt for the past two years, and that shit can't stand. Then there's how Whitt touched me on the night of his initiation, and the things he's wanting from me on mine.

It also explains Syn's outburst about incest and not wishing to see anything sickening. Whitt doesn't even realize he's in this dungeon with his older sister.

No one else would dare speak to Marcus like that without a vested interest in me. No one else would get under Marc's skin enough for him to completely break. No one else would have Marcus afraid I'd cut him from my life when I learned the truth of who he was keeping away from me. No one else would think they had any rights to me.

Everyone always wants something from me, using hidden agendas to get it. They drain me dry, never filling me back up.

Squeezing my eyes shut, I keep them closed, even after I'm engulfed by a set of arms and pressed against a hard chest. I can smell him. It's Whitt's scent that is my ultimate undoing.

The dam bursts.

Sobbing hysterically, I tighten my arms around Whitt as I shake with a plethora of pent-up emotions in need of release. Whitt's chest is moving erratically, so I know he's crying too.

I haven't seen Whitt since I screamed '*shut up!*' to a room full of my loved ones. Whitt was pacifying Niel and Whitney by playing Candy Land. Seconds later, we got the call saying Ezra, Cortez, and Aaron were safe but mentally broken. I walked from the room with Grant, and when I opened my eyes that same evening, my life had burnt to the ground.

"I drew the portrait so you'd recognize me," Whitt whispers softly against my hair, hands running in a continual circuit up and down my back. "I wanted to make sure you knew it was me."

I laugh and sob at the same time. Five sets of eyes stare at us with a mixture of confusion, shock, awe, and understanding.

"Whitt," I choke out. "I would've recognized you immediately, anywhere– obviously even while blindfolded in the dark. The voice isn't anything I would've thought, though. You sound nothing like Daniel or Grant, not even Jackson."

I finally look at Whitt, only to discover his eyes are tracking across my face as mine do the same with his. The moment I met Whitt, I knew he'd be breathtaking when fully grown. Grant was… words cannot describe Grant. It hurts to look at Whitt because he's nearly identical to the Grant I once knew.

The only difference is in the eyes and the mouth. Both are shaped and colored the same, yet it's the set of Whitt's lips and the knowledge and confidence pouring from his eyes. Whitt is just as playful, I'd bet my life on it. His scent is muskier, and I can feel the immense power rolling off of his skin. Whitt has the same suffocating presence his namesake has. When these men walk into a room, the room revolves around them. All eyes seek them out, and then look to the floor because they feel unworthy.

I step back when I remember we aren't dressed. Shock fills me as I think about how Whitt touched me intimately as a reward before his initiation and how I flirted with him as he carried me to the SUV. I blush bright red in embarrassment, and then lash out in discomfort like a wounded, wild animal.

"What the hell, Whitt? Why would you want to have sex with me?" My voice quivers in confusion and hurt. It makes me angry that our reunion is being ruined by this fiasco of an initiation. "Oh, my God! I'm going to kill that fucking cunt," I hiss. "Kristal's ass is dead."

I turn to Marcus, and watch as understanding dawns in his eyes. I have to do something about Kristal, even if I don't know how or what. At the same time, I have to deal with Marcus keeping secrets from me as well.

"You're a grown man– you can fuck whoever you want." Who am I to judge at this point? "But Kristal has broken every promise she's ever made to me. If she touches my son, I'll bury her in the backyard where she was fucking Roman tonight."

Screaming a song of intense mourning and betrayal, the sound echoes throughout the dungeon. The betrayal, frustration, and pain pours out of my throat to fill the air with my agony. My body tingles and my skin tightens against the sensations engulfing me. All I can see is red– the color of unadulterated fury.

"Kristal's... I'm at a loss. I don't know what to do, Marc."

Everyone looks between Marcus and me, as if they're viewing a tennis match volleying back and forth, or watching an argument between their parents.

Marcus nods, and then finally speaks. "You know Kristal was the one who said you were intimate with Roman, and that she's the one who was playing with young Daniel... among other things. I tried to warn you, but I don't think you were ready to come to that conclusion on your own just yet."

I seethe. If Kristal were to materialize in front of me, I would tear her to shreds with claws formed from my bare hands.

"I didn't sleep with Kristal, Queen." Whitt whispers shyly. "I was only practicing with Kristal, because she obviously has had experience. I'm still a virgin."

"You're what?" I gawk in shock.

"I'm still a virgin." Whitt announces proudly. Men his age would find it humiliating, while Whitt seems to wear his innocence as a badge of honor.

"Why the hell would you want to have sex with me?" I ask in utter mystification.

"It's what I want," Whitt answers with no shame.

Whitt takes on an expression I remember he used as a child, the one when he was feeling petulant and was determined to get what he wanted at any cost. I laugh and shake my head, because it's so fucking bizarre.

"Don't laugh." I've insulted Whitt, judging by the way he scrunches up his crystalline blue eyes. "My body's nice. I know how to please a woman."

Standing in front of me, I try not to *see* Whitt. I close my eyes against the vision of a man who looks like Grant, but better in some ways and different in others. Never would I want to admit that Whitt is bigger, and not just in muscle mass.

Leaning in, I whisper in Whitt's ear so no one else can overhear, explaining how I wasn't laughing at his male form. "I'm not your type if I recall, Sunshine. I may have been blindfolded, but I wasn't deaf. I heard you flirting with the Ezes. So how come you want to play with ladies? Older ladies. How did you develop mommy issues, because Priscilla is a wonderful mother?"

"Mommy issues? Yes, but not because of Priscilla or you–honest." Whitt has the decency to blush, the flush rising up his chest, across his neck, to fill his dimpled cheeks. "The gay population is rather thin," he whispers back. "Okay, so it's prominent in this dungeon, but they don't want to play with me because they see me like their little brother."

Whitt laughs a sound that breaks my heart while simultaneously filling it with pure joy.

"You have Grant's laugh," flows from my lips without thought.

"Thank you– Daniel has this thing where he has Niel make me laugh on purpose, just so he can hear it. Then he has Niel read to him because the kid's voice has broken already, and he sounds just like Grant did. It's bizarre, but when Niel laughs, he sounds just like you."

"Oh, God." I whimper, hand clutching at my chest.

Leaning back into me, not giving a shit that he's naked, Whitt holds me while I'm assaulted from all sides by emotional pain. "We're going to get our family back, Queen. I promise. It's one of the reasons why I've been practicing with women, because it will be a necessary evil we'll have to perform and I want to make it good for you– not awkward. Besides, women are soft and pretty, and they smell nice. I love pleasure, both giving and receiving, so playing in this dungeon wasn't a hardship."

"Why Kris? Why me?"

"Kristal knows me, so she was safe. I've played with the other submissives, too. I just didn't have sex yet. I wanted to do that with *you* first." Whitt holds my eyes, imploring me to understand what's left unsaid.

"I'm not going to be your lover," I deny him.

"I know. I can tell that position is filled." Whitt glares at Marcus. "We can all tell Marcus is batshit for you."

"I'm not having sex with you, Whitt," I warn, voice stiff with anger. "It's not going to happen."

"You will once you realize why it's necessary. But until then, I have a contingency plan set in place. If anyone knows how stubborn you are, it's me. So you may still disobey the orders I've created for you during your initiation. In fact, I know you will." Whitt's voice takes on the note of a cocky swagger, and I don't even know how that's humanly possible. "Disobeying means I get one time in your bed. It'll only have to be once, unless we both like it."

"Why is this so important for you?" My voice is muddled with confusion.

"Not here," Whitt breathes. "We'll talk in private. But first, let me prove to you that I'm a grown man."

Moving fast, before I register what's about to happen, Whitt surprises me with a passionate kiss. My lips freeze underneath his, remaining passive until he proves how much he's practiced for this moment. I don't want to respond, but my traitorous body does as it pleases. I don't want to enjoy it, but my nerves don't give a shit. It feels incredible to be consumed by someone I've missed and longed to touch.

Exercising restraint, I pull away before the kiss turns into more, and Whitt is left smiling in satisfaction because of my reaction.

Tears drip down my face as his dimples indent his cheeks. "It's okay, Queen. You can cry. I knew it would be hard for you to look at me and see Grant. I miss him so much, too. Being around you makes me feel closer to him, and I hope it'll be the same for you." Whitt's thumb catches my tears on his fingertip as his own glide down his cheeks.

"Since Regina has been formally introduced to everyone in attendance, I think it's time she goes through her rites of passage," Marcus announces. A slight quiver in his voice is evidence of his unease.

"Oh, do we get pizza and beer now?" I use Cort's snark to remove that tone from Marc's voice. "I'm quite the card shark, as Whitt can testify. I taught him all he knows."

As I wipe the tears from my cheeks, I know Marcus has been terrified I would kill him once I discovered who two of the Masters of Restraint were. I feel pity for Marcus, because I know how painful and suffocating it is to keep secrets that aren't yours to tell. A part of me feels betrayed, but the empathetic, non-hypocritical part understands. Marcus is full of secrets, and I know deep down he wishes he didn't hold that burden.

"No beer and pizza this time, Regina." With a deep breath and terrified eyes, Marcus issues the first of many demands I won't enjoy, all of them coming from the young man who shouldn't be forcing me into this position.

Voice hollow and strained, Marcus commands, "Regina, kneel before Dexter and suck his cock."

Chapter Thirty-Four

My eyes never leave Marc's as I drop to the floor. I don't feel the biting pain of the slate shocking the nerves in my knees. I understand why Marcus called this a rite of passage. I know I will end up in that room with Whitt, even if I do everything commanded of me. Whitt's going to ruin me or heal me, maybe a combination of the pair.

"Marcus, are you sure?" Dexter's voice is uncertain. "Why don't we all acknowledge the fact that Regina is your lover, and get it over with? Do you really want to share her with me?" Gesturing to everyone in the dungeon, "With them? You having a lover is a pretty big fucking deal, cousin. You've never had one before."

I realize we aren't fooling anyone. Marcus is very reserved and self-contained, and his out-of-control behavior around me isn't his norm.

"Whether we are or aren't lovers is irrelevant. I assure you I'm not monogamous or exclusive with anyone," I state unemotionally, while a part of me is waiting for Marcus to speak up and claim me as his– a test he fails, when I shouldn't test him like a coward. "No one owns me, and I'll do what is necessary to get what I need."

A blowjob with Dexter is just about gratification, and I do love the empowering feeling I get when performing oral sex. Sex with Ezra would be uncomfortable for both of us. Sex with Cort would be like going to an amusement park– it's always fun until it becomes too much and you get sick from the rollercoaster ride of thrills.

Whitt– I can't even imagine what emotional torture sex would bring to the surface. It wouldn't be about fun or lust. It would be about love and pain, and shame and guilt.

We share a look, Marcus and I, when we've never been able to accomplish that feat before. Silent communion. It's that potent look Grant and Ade shared. The look Grant and Whitt shared. It's the ability to communicate without speaking. Marcus and I finally click– irrevocably connected through good and bad.

Pragmatic and tenacious, stubborn even, since Marcus doesn't stop this, I do whatever is necessary to survive this moment and move forward.

"I have to have a taste of the legendary Dexter," I drawl in a flirty tone I picked up from Kristal. "I wouldn't miss this opportunity, even though I prefer a pretty, pink cunny to a big, nasty cock. I hear you're hung like a stallion, stud."

I easily slip into lesbian mode– a mode I won't relinquish. Tonight is a onetime deal. From now on, I'm a one-woman kind of gal. Restraint for me is about power and respect, putting wrongs to rights. It's not a place where I go to get fucked. If I have to say I'm a lesbian so I can get that respect without leering eyes and loose tongues, then so be it.

"Have you sucked much cock, Queen?" Dexter sounds serious, but his eyes are dancing with mirth, no doubt realizing I'm playing a game. Dexter's also pointing a middle leg at me. Eyeing it, I blink and swallow hard.

Jesus. Dexter's cock could play Rock, Paper, Scissors with itself.

"Um…" I swallow again, then moisten my lips.

Dexter's cock jerks as his eyes latch onto my tongue swabbing my bottom lip.

"I've only sucked two cocks." I don't know why I answered like that. I shake my head, trying to clear the fogginess away. It was three, not two. I didn't forget Jamie. I don't know why I said it. I feel disoriented. Maybe it's because having Marcus in my mouth was so new, and not to completion. My odd admission pleases Marcus for some reason– his smile is brilliant.

"Well, I think it's about time we add another to that very short list, don't you?" Dexter appears shocked as he glances over his shoulder at Marcus. The look screams '*how can you allow this?*'

I don't think, knowing that is the last thing I need right now, because it will bring about regrets and desires I shouldn't have. Sucking Dexter's cock into my mouth, I go as far as I can, and end up stopping like I hit a brick wall with my mouth wide open.

Girth nearly choking me, I only manage a quarter of Dexter's length. I hope to God he isn't into skull-fuckage like his cousin– he'd suffocate me. Enjoying the feel of a dick in my mouth and the flavor riding my tongue, I lose any decorum I possess. Drool pours from my mouth, sliding in a trail down his huge cock, and trickling to my wrists. With my hand, I use my saliva to smooth the path of my stroking.

I'm a big girl, not fat but large like a man. I'm tall, big boned, and have large features. My mouth and hands are proportionate. With that being said, my mouth barely contains Dexter's dick, and my fingers don't meet around his girth.

Did Dexter's mom eat growth hormones when he was in the womb?

Raw and dirty sounds erupt from my mouth as I work. This truly is a blowjob. *A job.* It's difficult and taxing, and I can barely breathe. I've given one blowjob and a small taste of one in the past decade. Even if I had been on my knees every day for a decade, I never would've had enough practice for Dexter's behemoth cock.

Pulsing in my mouth, I suck the head as one hand wraps around the base and strokes, and the other massages Dexter's balls. I'm so thankful he isn't a marathon man.

Grunting and groaning like an injured animal for my efforts, Dexter isn't as loud as I am. But he is softly moaning in pleasure with every suck I take. He wants to grab the back of my head, I can tell by the way his fists clench and release with every moan. I smile around Dexter's cock, allowing the vibration of my delighted laughter to add another level of pleasure.

Power.

I'm the one who's making Dexter insane, and I'll be the one who forces him to release. I've learned a lot by watching the dance between Marcus and Cortez. Release is a total loss of control, and we dominants don't like to be out of control, even if it's for ten to fifteen seconds. It's the dance between a dominant and submissive, but Dexter and I both long to be in control.

This blowjob isn't about anything but dominance– if Dexter comes, I win.

Dexter's eyes snap down to connect with mine, and I gaze up at him in challenge. Eyes widening, he recognizes that I get it. Knuckles turning white, Dexter tries to stay his release.

Inhaling deeply, I push the air from my nostrils as I abruptly sink Dexter's cock down my throat. I only need a second, even if it hurts like a bitch. But I manage to force my throat to accept Dexter's dick until my mouth meets his pubic hair.

With a beast of a cock like that, there's no doubt Dexter has never experienced the forceful pleasure of deep-throating. Screaming to the ceiling, Dexter fires down my throat. Pulling back enough to breathe, wave after wave of semen floods my mouth, but

I can't swallow it fast enough. The fluid drips down my hand, my chin, and slides down my body, speckling my breasts.

Dexter yanks from my mouth with a grimace and a sharp hiss, knees almost giving out.

"Ah… ya couldn't take anymore." A wicked grin curves my cum-splattered lips. "I win!"

After flashing Dexter a very serious facial expression, I start to laugh at the ridiculous nature of my initiation. My lover– no, the man I'm *in* love with –just watched me suck his cousin off, yet he looks proud of me. Meanwhile, the boy I thought I would get to raise as my own, not realizing that even at six Whitt was an adult posing as a child, just watched me suck off a man.

Eighteen-year-old Regina, the one who had yet to graduate Hillbrook, the one who was taking care of her dying mother, would be shocked at the level of depravity I display.

I may be jaded, but I feel fucking alive!

Heart racing my blood through my veins, with my nerves rapidly firing power throughout my entire body, I experience true empowerment– finding power and pride even as you kneel with cum covering your body. If you can feel empowered while you're on your knees, no one can tear you down when you're standing.

Swiping my hand down my bare breasts, I smear Dexter's sticky spending around, and then I show him my hand. Fighting back a smirk. "Do you want this back?" I ask innocently.

The tension in the dungeon collapses and is replaced with camaraderie. We are a pack. We may not like each other, but we're in sync.

"Well," Marcus clears his throat. I worry he's upset, but he looks thrilled. My attitude is affecting him, and he keeps stepping from foot-to-foot in discomfort. I arch an eyebrow in question. Chuckling sardonically, Marcus turns his back to all of us, where he adjusts himself in relative privacy, and then turns back to us.

"Well," Marcus tries again. "That was impressive. Let me see a show of hands– who wants to be next?" Flashing a devastating smile, he shows off predatory teeth.

I watch as Syn shrinks into the background. I already know she doesn't like sex, especially with me. I think I'm one step above Cortez in her eyes.

Whitt looks bored, but I know it's feigned. He's just biding his time like the calculating, patient boy I remember him to be. I don't want to notice that no matter what expression he's faking, his body is showing a different reaction. My mind screams that I mustn't look at Whitt like that, but my body refuses to release my eyes from his erect cock. Is there anything on him that isn't pale, rosy perfection?

Cort and Ezra are staring at each other, doing the silent communication thing that I finally understand. Cort leans over and whispers in his ear. He tries to reassure his partner while he looks like he's ready to jackhammer concrete.

They negotiate.

With great patience, I wait for what's next, trying to ignore my heartbeat tattooing the inside of my chest. Kneeling on the cold, slate tiles, I can't see much around me. I'm in the center of the dungeon with only a single bare bulb glowing above my head. The other masters flank me, blocking all view of the dungeon.

I decide to communicate silently with Marcus. I miss him already, even though he's right in front of me. Maybe five feet away, but an insurmountable chasm lies between us. He knows it, I know it, but we can't do a dang thing about it– yet.

"Regina?" Cort's voice snaps my eyes from Marc's gaze. Cortez looks uncertain, and it gives me confidence. "Do you trust me?" he whispers.

"Do you even have to ask?"

"Yeah. Actually, I do," Cortez mutters bashfully.

I crick a finger, beckoning Cortez down to me, then I whisper in his ear. "Marcus trusts you infallibly, so who am I to discount his judgment?"

"I wasn't sure. Most people just think I'm an asswipe." Cortez flashes me a self-deprecating smile that's genuine.

"Yeah… but you're *our* asswipe," I tease Cortez.

"Good, I like that." A grin breaks free across Cortez's lips, erasing all traces of insecurity. "I think it's time we fuck, don't you?"

"Sure. Why the hell not?" I gesture to the dungeon around us. "Right time, right place, with an audience that doesn't want to be here anymore than we do."

"I know, right?" Cortez releases a carnal laugh– the sound a man makes when he knows he's about to get laid. "I'll even let you be on top." Cortez sits on the cold tile next to me, nudging my thigh. "I know how much you miss that." He says in challenge to Marcus, tone expressing how ridiculous it is that Marcus is a one-trick pony with the no foreplay or different positions during sex. "You begged enough for it during training."

"HA! I'm not the one who would spontaneously come whenever the Violet Wand popped out of the toy box." I taunt him because it feels light and freeing. "Cort, don't temp me to spill the dirty details."

Eyes bright with anticipation, "I have a wand in my room– do you want me to run and get it?" Eager, Cortez reminds me of a kid on Christmas morning.

"No." I huff a laugh. "I want this to be about sex. You'd blast off in a second if I started electrocuting your ass, you twisted motherfucker."

Shutting my mind off, I try to be in the moment without regret. Pushing my palm against Cort's chest, I make room on his lap for me. Straddling his hips, our eyes connect, and it changes this from fun banter that was meant to make us feel comfortable, into an uncomfortable situation. Intensity overpowering us, it's time to feed the beast.

Settling firmly into his lap, Cort's cock eagerly rises to greet me. "I've wanted this since we were in the Vanquish," I reluctantly admit. "I'll never repeat that, so enjoy the revelation."

"I've wanted this since we met." Cortez contributes his own odd revelation. "You were the only woman to look at me like I wasn't suave enough."

"Sorry, I didn't mean to hurt that massive ego of yours, buddy boy." Enjoying our banter, I shift to allow Cort's cock to notch along my slit. Eyelids shuttering, it's hard to ignore the hard press between my thighs. The exquisiteness is burning my flesh. "No fault of your own, but my body didn't wake up until later that night."

"What changed?"

"Not what– who."

"Who?"

My eyes seek Whitt to find him looking at me knowingly. Whitt and Marcus stand side-by-side in a strange state of aroused misery. They both hold the same facial expression– infinite patience.

Placing my palm on Cortez's shoulder to stabilize myself, I grip his cock in the other. Lowering slowly, "Grant woke me up," I whisper as my body engulfs Cort's.

Crying out in a mix of emotional and physical pain, tears flood my eyes, but I fight them back. What am I doing, and why am I doing it? This isn't me, but it's too late in the game to change my mind.

This is different than having sex with Marcus. Marcus and I felt right, almost as perfect as it felt with Grant. The night I spent with Jamie was as effortless and freeing as breathing. The blowjob with Dexter was a test I had to pass, and I felt high from a job well done.

But Cort is different. I'm not in love with him, but I do love him as a friend and ally. The emotions that are involved make me feel as if I'm betraying someone, but who? The hell if I know who, but my soul doesn't like it one bit.

"It's okay." Cort murmurs, trying to soothe me as I hide my face against his neck. Taking over, he rocks me against his hips. "Just pretend it's not me." The lost tone in his voice makes me cry harder.

"It's not that it's you– it's that it *is* you." I cry out, frustrated and hurting. "I can't explain it."

"I understand, Regina." Cortez wraps his arms around me, trying his damnedest to comfort me. "I know everyone sees me as an arrogant asshole, but I do know how you feel right now. I've felt it every time I've had sex– Every. Fucking. Time."

Getting a clue, I lean back to look into Cortez's eyes. "Because it's not Ezra?"

"Because it's not Ezra," he whispers, a storm of sadness brewing beneath the surface. "Who do you wish it was?"

"I don't know, that's what makes it worse." Closing my eyes in defeat, I breathe, "I just don't know."

"I'm so fucking sorry, Regina," Cortez mumbles into my ear.

Holding onto Cortez tightly, I peek out over the masters who are watching. Marcus and Whitt are looking at the floor, either out of respect or sorrow, but I can't tell which. I catch the gaze of the one I was seeking, because while I don't know who I need, I do know who Cortez needs.

I try to communicate with Ezra– and it is Ezra, because Master Ez fled when he heard the words Cortez was whispering to me. Understanding the position Kristal has been placed in, I break my sister-code with Ade for Cort.

Ezra doesn't belong with Adelaide, no more than Roman or Whitt belong to me. Ezra belongs with Cortez, and Cortez belongs with Ezra– they always have, and they always will.

Adelaide doesn't even fit into the equation.

If sex can heal, it's worth a shot.

Ezra's eyes drift over us, while a shy smile flirts with his lips. I've never seen Ezra smile, and I instantly understand why Cortez loves him so much.

I assume this is second nature for Cortez and Ezra, because I'm not the first woman who was their conduit. Faith– sweet, innocent Faith was just a girl. Listening to Syn, I understand her fury directed at Cortez, but what I don't understand is why none of it is sent Ezra's way.

I wasn't the first, nor will I be the last, not with Katya Waters on her way to Dominion to complete the Ezes' circuit once again.

Closing my eyes, I focus on Ezra's light footsteps as he walks over to us. I squeeze my eyelids tighter as he kneels behind me. Leaning forward, Ezra kisses my shoulder, and then Cortez's cheek.

With a gasp of surprise, Cortez's eyes open slowly, the fringe of his lashes clumping with unshed tears. The gunmetal gray eyes look silvery as they glisten in anguish. Here and now, I know without a shadow of a doubt, that even though Cortez moved back into his apartment with Ezra, they haven't touched, not even with simple affection.

"May I join you?" Ezra asks his partner, voice reverberating along my flesh, causing me to shiver in trepidation.

Cort sobs in a breath, and then nods yes emphatically. Long fingers grip his chin, steadying him. Pupils blown, to the point the black eclipses Cortez's irises, I watch as they shrink back to pinpricks. Cort's breathing accelerates, even though the second Ezra kissed his cheek we stopped having sex.

That intense reaction was just because Ezra looked Cortez in the eye while touching his chin. I learn something else in that second– Ezra is Cortez's true master in every way imaginable.

Marcus interrupts by pressing something into Ezra's palm. Cort snorts, lips curling into an asshole smirk. Ezra rips the package open with the corner of his front tooth. Huh? I didn't want Ezra to go bare either, but why the hell didn't Marcus hand one to Cort?

I flash Marcus a quizzical look, but he just shakes his head in reply, and then his eyes dart to a blushing Whitt.

This time, Marc doesn't look down at the floor as he had when Cort entered me. Instead, Marcus stares right into my eyes, anchoring me. It's like when I met him outside of the brownstone for the very first time– Marcus sees right into my soul. It's the same sensation as when he stared at me through the crack in the panel of the secret passages at Whittenhower Estates.

Lending me strength to endure by completely captivating me, I can't break away, not even as Ezra pushes into my ass. I gasp in pain, but I can't break free from Marc's capture.

The partners have sex *through* me, as if I'm just a conduit for their connection. I maintain my connection to Marcus as Ezra and Cortez embrace each other through me. Kissing each other over my shoulder, they grip my hips– Ezra's hands over Cortez's.

I experience the rush as Master Ez roars back to life, all because Cort is chanting a never-ending list of why he loves Ezra. It's reminiscent of Marcus at Lake Serenity, as he said the strangest things just because he could.

I know I'm being used, but I can't help but smirk as Cort growls about how incredible it feels to touch Ezra again. Cortez nearly screams how much he has missed Ezra. He rambles on and on, every word more emotional and salacious than the last. Cortez won't shut up, so I have to bite my lip to stop my silent laughter from interrupting them.

Dexter sits on the floor, drawing a pattern on the tile with his fingertip, a funny smirk plays along his lips as he listens to the lovers reconnect. Syn sits next to Dexter, wrapping one of his tight ringlets around her pinky. The sadist mentor and his protégée both seem uncomfortable with the adoration pouring from the love-starved men.

They're uncomfortable?

I'm the cream in this fucked up *Oreo* sandwich.

I focus in on the building hum Whitt is emitting, instead of the grunts and growls of Ezra and Cortez's professions of a love. Whitt finally gives up on standing next to Marcus like he's in charge, and decides to join Syn and Dexter instead.

Secrets and lies coming back to haunt me, a dark flash of fear streaks through me when Whitt touches Syn, until I realize he's studying a tattoo on her shoulder. Whitt continues to hum as his fingertip outlines the art on his unknown sister's flesh. Syn is covered in ink, to the point no unmarked flesh is visible, and I bet some of it is Whitt's doing.

Startled, I look up and nearly gasp. Marcus is standing at Cort's back, hovering over the three of us. Marcus wants my eyes back on his, demandingly so, and it terrifies me.

Suddenly naïve, I look to Marcus, feeling completely out of my element. I fall into the snare of his whiskey eyes as Ezra and Cortez seek their mutual release. Marcus holds my sanity in the depth of his gaze as Cortez floods me with his warmth and Ezra pulses in my rear. I feel no pleasure other than the knowledge that I was the conduit for their affections.

Hands hooking beneath my armpits, Marcus pulls me from between them. Cort immediately curls around Ezra's legs, resting his head on Ezra's thigh. Then he issues a sigh of contentment that echoes around the dungeon.

I close my eyes, hoping to God that that was all I have to endure for the night, because I don't know how much more of this I can take. The loaded look Marcus gives me speaks volumes. I sag in his grip, spent and emotionally exhausted.

"No!" I shake my head listlessly. "No, Marcus– no," I plead in denial.

"Syn?" Marcus calls, causing her head to snap up– she grimaces instantly.

"NO!" We shout in unison, in the same disgusted cadence.

Whitt continues to hum as he traces his sister's shoulder, but the sound gets interrupted by a set of dimples denting his cheeks. With a taunting quality, Whitt looks up at me with the same expression he would give me when we disagreed. It's the '*I always get what I want*' look.

It's devastating on his manly face, even if I want to bitch-slap it off him. Whitt's tawny eyebrow lifts in silent challenge, then he continues to hum. The sound takes on an edge, a taunting quality.

Syn was Whitt's trump card. This was the demand he knew I'd disobey, gaining his one time in my bed.

"NO!" I hiss obstinately, sounding more like a child than the grown idiot who came up with this diabolical plan.

Whitt's a genius, way more intelligent, manipulative, cunning, and calculating than I'll ever be, and he knows it.

"Syn?" Marcus sighs in defeat. "I command you to perform oral sex on Queen." He commands, but he doesn't mean it.

We all know it's never going to happen.

"My God, you're a Whittenhower, aren't you?" I shake my head in utter disbelief, but my tone is impressed.

"Hey, don't put the name down. Your children are Whittenhowers." Whitt retorts, flashing me a shit-eating grin. "Someday, somehow, it'll be your surname as well."

Marcus and I, and everyone else in the dungeon, level our eyes on Whitt, but none of us have the balls to comment.

In that moment, the trickle of Cortez's semen makes itself known. What comes up, must always come down, which is why this has been a continual fight between Marcus and me over the past year and a half. Knowing it's Cortez's spunk makes it all the worse.

"You–" I point at Whitt. "You are a diabolical bastard, and I feel sick praising you over that fact."

Bowing at the neck, "Why, thank you, Queen." Whitt is beyond pleased with himself.

"You made sure than even if I agreed to let Syn go down on me, she'd never do it because of Cort's spunk. You know I can't do it– I'd have sex with you willingly, before I made Syn touch me unwillingly."

Looking down at Syn, all I see is a ten-year-old child with dirty blonde pigtails and crooked front teeth. I remember Faith chattering excitedly in a West Virginian drawl as she played Barbie and I played Ken, while Fate directed the scene.

I could never touch Faith in a sexual manner– ever. She was my little sister for four years, and then she disappeared. My daughter is the same age Faith was when I first met her. It doesn't matter if Faith's hair is asymmetrically razor-cut and dyed blue-black, or that she has tattoos covering every inch of her body, or that there are piercings in places no metal should ever venture. It doesn't matter that Faith calls herself Syn and gets off on hurting people.

Faith will never be *that* woman to me.

"Faith, Syn– whatever you want me to call you, I'll make a deal with you. If you forgive your big sister, I'll walk away from this. If you refuse, I'll make you suck the cheating bastard's cum from my cunt."

Queen's voice delivers the request, and I notice several masters shiver at its tone, recognizing the power building inside of me.

"I know they both hurt you, but you don't know your sister the way I do."

"I know Fate better than you ever will, Regina," Syn challenges me, but her voice is softening from how it sounded when she spoke to Cortez.

"Fate is one of the most submissive people I know. Compassionate and caring, your sister is the mother hen in my house, taking care of my daughter with a soft maternal instinct I lack. I'm the mother lioness, but there are things only Fate can provide my daughter."

I look away, not wanting to say this out loud, because it borders on what Roman demanded I never say. "Faith, your sister needs you– she spends way too much time with your mother."

"I thought Lara was dead?" Whitt and Dexter say in unison, staring at each other in confusion. "Didn't she kill herself years ago?"

Flinching hard, as if Whitt and Dexter struck her, Faith gives in but not much. "I'll try, but no promises."

"One hour. Once a week. You'll have a meal with Fate. I can buffer if you'd like. You don't have to be best friends, but you *will* be sisters. You don't have to like each other, but you have to love each other. Do you understand?"

"If I say yes, that little peckerwood is going to hurt you." Syn points at Whitt. "I'm having a difficult time deciding. I can endure two minutes of unpleasantness, but I don't know if you can handle having Whitt inside your body, and we both know why." Hiding her face against her knees, Syn places the decision in my hands. "I'll reconnect with my sister, because the Regina I used to know wouldn't do shit Whitt asked unless she wanted to, so good luck."

As always, Whitt gets his way.

I'm proud to say, Whitt doesn't gloat, or even smirk. He sits stone-faced and doesn't blink.

"Do you really want to have sex with me that badly?" An incredulous look is passed his way.

"Yes," Whitt answers without missing a heartbeat. "I really do, Queen." He looks away, and in his profile I see his cheek dent.

The little shit's trying not to smile.

"You could've just asked me instead of playing this therapy bullshit we've all had to endure tonight. None of us are unscathed– well, except for Dexter, I guess."

"You would've never said yes. I needed you to see it's the right thing to do, so I had to trap you because you're stubborn." Whitt manipulates me flawlessly.

"Do you honestly think that if I love the sex that much, I'll keep doing it?" I bait him.

"No," Whitt mutters defensively, but that's exactly what he thought.

"I can't believe I'm really going to do this." I scrub my face with both hands. I'm going to regret this, but there's no going back now. "What's next, since Syn and I are calling a pass?"

Marcus looks like he wants to hold me, or maybe he wants to kidnap me and never come back. Frustration etches his face, with fine lines making an appearance at the corners of his brown eyes for the first time.

This is Marc's greatest fear— Whitt rolling over me.

"You will be Queened." Marcus says with pride, then his lips twitch. "Queen."

As if by some unspoken cue, Whitt stands and walks over to a cart that I hadn't seen earlier. He pushes it over, refusing to meet my eyes. At least Whitt has the decency to be embarrassed over his shitty behavior. Whitt's still so young— he thinks like an adult and his body is built as an adult, but he doesn't own or understand the consequences of his actions, much like a child.

"Time to ink your M, Queen." Grin gleeful, Whitt's holding a tattoo gun in his hand like it's a magic wand.

Looking around in confusion, I try to figure out what's going on. I can't take much more. Putting me out of my misery, Marcus shows me his hand, stretching the webbing between his thumb and index finger. Inked within the webbing is an intricate M.

"What's the M mean?"

"Master or Mistress is what an outsider will think it means," Marcus answers. "My two idiots get a big kick out of telling everyone that I'm such a possessive asshole, I have to brand them with my initial."

Cort snorts from his position in Ezra's lap.

"What's it actually mean?"

"Maître du Jeu," Marcus says without inflection, and I notice everyone but Marcus, Dexter, and Whitt shiver like death just drew a finger down their spine.

Masters of the Game doesn't sound like a BDSM organization. It sounds more like egomaniacal founders using all of Dominion as its pawn.

Chapter Thirty-Five

After I was tattooed, I was shown to a blank slate of a room, and was told it was mine to do with as I saw fit. Energy waning, Marcus took pity on me by escorting me to the Zeitler private room, which was four times larger than mine, and supped out as an efficiency apartment and dungeon combo. For the past twenty minutes, I've been sitting on the edge of the bathtub while staring into the mirror.

I don't recognize myself.

Marcus had delivered me to this bathroom, where he then placed a pile of my clothing on the vanity, with my cellphone resting on top. He didn't ask me if I was okay. Instead he handed me a disposable douche.

Since that moment, where I was left alone in silence, I've split my time between staring at myself and staring at that box. Both feel like an accusation.

On autopilot, I'm dialing my cellphone, then placing it on speakerphone. I wait for it to stop ringing, signaling the call has been received, and then I dump every emotion I possess at my confessor's feet.

"Hi," I breathe, voice uncertain. "I just… everything I did tonight was wrong. Every single goddamn thing was wrong, and I don't know how I'll ever handle it." Voice wavering, I cry out, "Oh, God!"

Sliding off the edge of the tub to land on the cold tile bare-assed, I rest my head in my hands. "I don't even know where to start, except to say I don't know who I am anymore… everyone's a goddamn liar, including me. Somewhere between blowing Dexter and allowing Cortez and Ezra to fuck me, I realized I was a horrible person.

"I cheated on you," I admit without hesitation. "Just thinking about it, I want to vomit. It wasn't the same as when you and I and Marcus joined as one. That was special, about love and affection and acceptance– connection. I allowed myself to be used until there was nothing left of me.

"Drained. Selfish. I was drained for their tortured form of therapy. Everyone here is so fucked up– they need help. Serious goddamn help. Every. Last. One. Of. Them. There's this spot deep inside me that thinks I can help them, but the rest of me is screaming that I flee. Because what if in my quest to help them, they drag me down with them until I don't recognize right from wrong? I can't leave them to their own devices, though– fuck, I sound like Albert.

"I'm already terrified for that Katya Waters woman the Ezes are dragging to Dominion. What kind of person sits back and watches that shit? Not me, that's who. Someone needs to protect her, even if she doesn't realize she needs to be protected.

"Then there's Marcus. I appreciate the ability to make my own decisions, but he's the driver and we're all the passengers. Not once did he step in tonight. He didn't try to stop me. He allowed it to happen, and I don't know how I feel about that. Who says this shit had to happen? Marcus, that's who. He was the only one who could stop it. I could have walked out, but what I've been working toward for nearing on eighteen months would have been for naught.

"Not counting the fact that for over a year Marcus kept Whitt and me separated. But I do get that, because I don't know if I was strong enough to battle Whitt last year. But at the same time, it was a year longer that the boy got stronger himself. Jesus Christ– that kid.

"But you know, don't you? You know how Whitt is, don't you? Whitt is not the weak boy Jackson and Daniel thought he'd become. He's like someone merged those brothers and Whitt is the product.

"But you also know me, and you know how Whitt and I were together. Marcus actually thinks I'm going to have sex with Whitt tonight. You should have seen the way he looked at me before he left me alone in this bathroom. I can't even describe the look, but it disappointed me. Maybe Marcus doesn't recognize me anymore because I don't recognize myself.

"I'm not going to, in case you're wondering. Sure, the brat is up to something. Hell if I know what, but I'm about to find out. But I can assure you that it won't be sex. I don't even know if I want sex with anyone anymore. It's too complicated. What happened to communing in bed with someone you loved? When did sex become political? When did it become about therapy, fighting ones demons, and machinations? Marc's touches are a way for him to battle his demons, when that's not how I want to be touched. You should have seen all of them in the dungeon. You know, don't you? That's why you're not here, too.

"I'm so angry at everyone. Everyone. But I'm being a hypocrite. Because when I looked Whitt in the eyes, I didn't tell him the truth then, but I will once he comes for me. Maybe not all of it at once, because it's a lot to take in. I know you don't want me to tell him about Maître du Jeu, but I'm going to. Be pissed if you want, but you know how Whitt and I were together. I know you had Roman tell me to back off, because I've been talking to you about this one-sided for months. There's no way your enforcer didn't rat me out immediately.

"I know you want me to leave it alone, and I get that. But I can't pretend to be ignorant any longer. I can't. That's not me. If you thought Marcus and I made a good team, just wait until I have Whitt by my side... Marcus can't be a partner right now, because he's too divided, he's too invested in you. And you don't want us involved.

"I'm going to be selfish. Whitt won't roll over me, because we're going to meet halfway. Someone needs to keep all of these people from destroying themselves. I know I sound manic right now, but you're the only person who has ever known me at my baser form.

"When it comes to you and me, *Jamie*, I'm going to keep ignoring the truth. Because I don't think I can survive not having you in my life as you are. I need you. Someone needs to be my mirror– the person who tethers me to reality. It wasn't Marcus, or BDSM training, or Restraint that had me sparking back to life. It's you.

"Don't take this away from me, because I'm not ready to suffer the burden of the truth. Not yet. I need to focus on what's to come, on getting our family back together. I need Whitt almost as much as I need my children. I need Marcus because he makes me feel high. But Marcus needs you *and* me, because his biggest nightmare is me knowing the truth.

"But at the core of everything, it isn't that I believe ignorance is bliss. It's because I need to get stronger to survive the truth, because my greatest fear is that you and I won't survive it while still intact."

Hanging up as quickly as I dialed, I have no idea what gibberish I just spilled. When I don't get a text message whistle alert within seconds of disconnecting, I scuttle across the tile floor to vomit more than a decade worth of pain into the toilet.

I can't go there. I don't have the luxury to feel the betrayal and fury– I can't survive living without him again just yet, and my self-respect would demand I do just that.

Crawling into the shower, I turn it to its hottest setting, then I curl up into a ball on the shower floor. I allow the water to cleanse my skin while it purifies my soul, washing the dirty taint to swirl around the drain before disappearing forever.

Douching has become commonplace in my life, because Marc's seed in my belly doesn't feel right– it never has and it never will. But this time, I'm on the edge of hysterics as I flush Cortez from my body. I've never felt so dirty in my life, and it has nothing to do with Cortez and everything to do with how I'll never get over Grant.

Sobbing, I'm not sure how I'll survive. But as usual, the text message alert whistles because Jamie always has perfect timing, always knowing when I need him the most.

Jamie: *Check your email. What I had to say was too long to type in a text message.*

Chapter Thirty-Six

To: regina_regal@empowerment.com
From: author@jamesatwater.com

Echo,

I'm just going to pour it all out. If ignoring the truth gets you through the day, then I'll let it be. I know in this instance the truth won't set you free, but only turn you away from me.

You're upset and thinking about what others think of you, instead of worrying about how you feel about yourself.

It doesn't matter what I want from you, or what Marcus wants, because we shouldn't want anything you're not willing to give. It shouldn't matter how we see you, because we should accept you as you are.

When you started this journey of training for Restraint, I understood to an extent, knowing that aspects would not sit well with you. The deviancy, the hedonism, while on the surface it looks enticing, it's not for someone like you. That is neither insult nor compliment. You are you, just as those who already frequent Restraint are who they are. Neither is right or wrong, only right or wrong for the individual.

Even with knowing what happens in the dungeon isn't for you, I understood why you trained, because of the structure and your thirst for knowledge, and in hopes of wielding your power for the greater good. Control and empowerment. The events of your initiation were the cost of admission, your tuition for becoming a Master of Restraint.

Whether the price was too high to pay is up to you. Accept what happened at your initiation and move on. If you're unhappy with what happened, make strides to change it. But don't stew and bleed guilt over something that has already come to pass and can't be changed in retrospect.

My thoughts on whether or not joining Restraint's ranks was a good idea is a moot point, because it was only your decision to make. Sometimes we have to walk alone to learn what we're made of and who we are. If someone is always holding our hand, or talking in our ear, we're not walking on our own two feet or listening to our inner voice.

I'm a firm believer in personal growth, and I don't think that's possible while living in a bubble where you don't live at all. I also don't think it's possible if you go from your parents to your spouse. I think partners should meet each other head-on, as individuals who bring everything to the table, not as emotional leeches who force their partners to live a pattern of abuse thanks to the baggage they drag into the relationship with them.

Yes, that is a comment about Marcus, because his actions toward you are not out of love, but reactionary from those who harmed him in the past. It's arrogant of anyone to think they are the savior in a relationship. Moreover, it's naïve.

You are not arrogant or naïve, Regina. Marcus doesn't need a savior– he needs professional help. Love can be tainted and warped, while a sane, clinical psychologist cannot.

A partnership is made up of equal parts. Not one part wounded party who abuses because he cannot help himself, and one who gives all of themselves to the point nothing is left.

The leech and the victim.

To throw your own word back at you: drained.

I'm fighting my own demons as well, Regina. Ones I don't want to taint any other part of my life, and I won't take them out on others. The fight is hard. While I may be submissive in nature, I'm not weak. I will conquer said demons before I face my partner again.

You're not capable of facing your partner yet, either.

For more than a decade, you were in stasis, neither evolving nor devolving. You were stuck at the age when you had Ella. You had a support system in place that acted as your own personal bubble wrap.

You told me time and time again how you dubbed this past era Apathetic Regina.

You felt alive again once you set foot into Restraint, and then bloomed with life when Marcus called you in from the sidewalk in front of my home. I will be honest with you, Regina. I, too, dubbed this current period of time for you.

Destructive Regina.

You were reactive instead of proactive. Your choices were influenced by others, even when I tried to clear your mind and get you to think. This is no excuse for not owning your decisions. You made the choices, whether they were directed by another's hand, or not.

You've been so worried about who your friends are and how to keep them, that you've never asked if they deserve your friendship. Kristal seeks validation from sex, when validation can only come from within. What do you call it when you keep friends around who treat you worse than enemies? When they lie to your face with every breath they take? When they epitomize the green-eyed monster?

I can only hope your initiation was a wakeup call, and you'll put Destructive Regina back to sleep, stifle Apathy Regina who will no doubt try to rise in the wake, and just be YOU.

You named your business Empowerment, for Christ's sake. Own it. Own who you are, and accept it.

Queen is not a product of BDSM training, or an entity who rises to the fore in hopes of playing at Restraint. Queen is YOU. The only true version of yourself who isn't numbed by the past sense of guilt, shame, and grief, you hang onto like armor. The only true version of yourself who isn't being reactive to the actions of others.

All of Marc's secrets are ones I've forced him to keep. Blame me, but realize every lie he tells is a choice he makes to keep those secrets. I placed him in this position, as did you inadvertently, but only Marcus can remove himself from the situation if he doesn't wish to be there in the first place. Marcus is no victim. This same philosophy pertains to every other liar in your life, including you.

When you speak to Whitt, no doubt he will throw the fact that you kept secrets from him that would change the course of his life. Hang on to why you kept those secrets in the first place, ask for forgiveness, and then remember this lesson when others do to you what you did to Whitt.

No one held a gun to our children's head and forced you to lie to Whitt by omission, but you did because you felt it was right. So when your friends and loved ones are discovered to be liars, try to remember how you felt when Whitt attacks you for being a goddamn liar too.

Don't be a judgmental hypocrite— be human.

Remember it, and use it to grow as a human being. I know you're not Catholic, but remember only God has the right to pass judgment. Your only recourse is maintaining your self-respect in the face of others' sins, including your own.

You have to live life to gain life-experience. I've made mistakes every step of the way. I've made impossible sacrifices that hurt my soul, but I did them for the greater good while everyone will see me as a weak, spineless coward running away. When in reality, I wanted to run forward and toward, not backward and away.

A sacrifice by definition is giving up what you want most. I wanted, I had, and I gave it away to protect it. But like a cosmic joke of a boomerang, it came back to me, and I'm not letting it go again.

Do you hear me, Regina?

I will tell you this, the sacrifices were for naught. Had I known things would play out as they have, I would do everything differently. I walked away from my life to save those I loved the most, only to have those same people be drawn back to me, drawn into the taint I tried to protect them against.

I own this, Regina. I own the fact that all the sacrifices I've made took me full circle, making all the agony, pain, loss, and torment for naught.

To put this in terms you can understand. Kristal Harris. You met a girl, and you wanted to protect her and help her reach her full potential, and you accomplished it. Only after fostering Kristal for the better part of a decade, her true nature would not relent, and she fell back into destructive patterns.

Regina, Kristal hurt you. Your sacrifices were flipped around and thrown back into your face, to where in Kristal's mind she's in the right. This left you feeling frustrated, hurt, and lost.

I hear you, Regina.

Ignorance is bliss? Once my loved ones find out the truth, they won't see my sacrifices as anything but a betrayal and cowardice, because they've never lived through what I tried to protect them against. Worse, the frustration of knowing I can't explain when and how the storm will hit, nor the intensity. So after all those sacrifices, where I tried to protect them from the storm, I have to sit back in agony while it rolls over them, and pray they are strong enough to survive the aftermath.

I realize you don't understand what I'm trying to say, at least not now. But you will in the near future. I just hope you will remember this email, and reread it, again and again and again.

There are a few things I need to get off my chest. While I ask nothing of you, that doesn't mean I don't have feelings. For the last year and a half, I have listened and heard you, without passing judgment. I've offered comfort, understanding, and a soft place for you to fall. I did this without an expectation of anything in return. I did this because I needed to feel useful and to offer the only support I can.

I may not be strong, domineering, and possessive, but that doesn't mean I'm not a man. You've asked me time and time again why I wouldn't reveal myself to you, and the answer is you.

You, Regina.

Just as you admitted earlier, you aren't ready. Even when we made love, I took the supportive role when Marcus arrived, but not because I'm submissive in nature. You didn't see me as a man then, nor do you now.

I know you better than you know yourself. Meanwhile, your head has been so far up your own ass, you're not hearing me or seeing me, and I don't mean that in the physical sense. Without a voice, I can't share my physical form with someone so unwilling to 'see' or 'hear' me.

I'm in love with you, as I know you are with me. If only you would open up your mind, you'd see me. Truly see me.

I waited for you, Regina, and when you didn't come, I used the only form of communication I had at my disposal. Our texts. When Marcus turned his back on you two months ago, you never came back. But what you failed to realize is that you turned in a key to MY home.

You failed to return to MY house.

You left ME behind.

From day one, I never once told you you couldn't enter MY home, or walk up MY stairs, or enter MY bedroom. I waited for you to see me, to see me as a man, to come back home.

I waited in my bed for you, not for sex, but because I was willing to hold you while you cried, while you released all those pent-up emotions, and then I was waiting to hold you so you could sleep all night. I waited to be your rock, your support system, to give myself to you while everyone else wanted to take something away from you instead.

I waited.

I still wait.

And I'll wait forever.

In the meantime, you have to find yourself. While you do, your reflection shouldn't be how I see you, or how Marcus does, or society at large, only how you see yourself. Because no matter who you partner up with, they don't need a list of how everyone else on the planet sees you, Regina.

Your partner just needs you.

Until you realize who you are, whether it be the apathy or destructive version of yourself you're living through, I'll be waiting…

—J.

To: author@jamesatwater.com
From: regina_regal@empowerment.com

Jamie,

Thank you for the reality check. Thank you for being the only person who ever asks how I am, and for not having an agenda for whatever my answer may be. Thank you for always listening, for hearing me, and for being there when I need you.

Someday I hope I'll be there when you need me the most, because I realize now how one-sided our relationship has been.

You give me your all. I give my all to Marcus. If I had to hazard a guess, Marcus is giving most of himself to you, while spreading the rest out amongst the masses, myself included.

Our relationships are off-balance.

Now I have to get something off my chest. I'm ignoring the truth because it's the most devastatingly miraculous truth imaginable. But with the depth of the betrayal and the sense of abandonment, no matter how much I may love you, my self-respect would dictate unadulterated fury and loathing to develop. That is why ignorance is bliss. That is why we are on borrowed time. I'm not ready to lose you just yet.

What are you waiting for exactly?

The epic ass-kicking you have coming? Because given time, be rest assured, it's headed your way.

It will take a long time to digest everything you said in your email for me to truly hear it. So I won't send you platitudes, because we both know I'll be dealing with Whitt in a few moments, and you deserve to have my undivided attention.

I make no promises about what direction my life will take… but I can promise you this, from now on, I'll listen in the silence, and truly hear what I'm trying to tell myself.

I've never denied it, and I never will. I love you unconditionally and without reservations.

To: regina_regal@empowerment.com
From: author@jamesatwater.com

Reggie from the block,

If physically hurting me is what you need, go for it. I'm stronger than I look. Every punch thrown will sound like an 'I love you' from your lips. At least you'll be touching me, right?

Word of advice, one I hope to use on you in the future: handle Whitt head-on. Be honest. Admit you lied, explain why, and then move on. When the time comes, it's exactly what I'll be doing.

Word of advice on Marcus: Nothing you do is a betrayal of me, but be careful. His jealousy and possession over me had him hating you at first. His love for you is what saved us both from his wrath.

Slap Whitt upside the head for me, because he was acting like an ass.

–J.

To: author@jamesatwater.com
From: regina_regal@empowerment.com

I'm never going to be forced into anything ever again. I just endured a trial by fire, where I was Queened.

Checkmate

Mistress & Master of Restraint #7

The long-standing Mistress & Master of Restraint series is dark and mysterious, with a warped sense of morality. Erotic romance fans, would you prefer something just as twisted, but not as dark? Try the Blended Series, beginning with Good Girl. For a mix of both styles, try the Rusty Knob series.

To purchase any of Erica Chilson's titles, please visit her website (ericachilson.com) for details.

Acknowledgements

A lot of work goes into writing a novel, and it isn't just by the writer herself. **My parents:** for their unconditional support. **My readers**: thank you for reading my twisted words and spreading my books to the masses. For without you, no one would have ever heard of my stories. My readers are my lifeblood. A shout out to the members of the **M&M of Restraint Group on Facebook**: thanks for the endless entertainment and inspiration. Thank you to my street team: **Erica Chilson's Deviants!** You guys ROCK! **Wicked Reads**: (in all its incarnations) **Angela G.**, thank you for taking over and making Wicked Reads better than I could have done by myself. & thank you for helping promote my work and the work of other authors. Angela? Have I told you lately how much I appreciate you? A huge thank you to the **Wicked Writer's Betas** for keeping me grounded and encouraging me to keep trudging along when I get frustrated. Your thoughts and observations are invaluable. ((Hugs)) Beta readers: **Kris | Suz | Darcy | Sandy | Di | Angela | Diane | Jacki | Linsey | Alexis | Billie Jo | Tassie | Caroline | Judith | Jodi Lynn | Jodi |** Someday, I'd love to meet you all in real life– it would be the experience of a lifetime.

About the Author

Erica Chilson does not write in the 3rd person, wanting her readers to *be* her characters. Therefore, writing a bio about herself, is uncomfortable in the extreme.

Born, raised, and here to stay, the Wicked Writer is a stump-jumper, a ridge-runner. Hailing from North Central Pennsylvania, directly on the New York State border; she loves the changes in seasons, the humid air, all the mountainous forest, and the gloomy atmosphere.

Introverted, but not socially awkward, Erica prides herself on thinking first and filtering her speech. There are days she doesn't speak at all. If it wasn't for the fact that she lives with her parents, giving her a sense of reality, she would be a hermit, where the delivery man finds her months after expiration.

Reading was an escape, a way to leave a not-so pleasant reality behind. Reading lent Erica the courage she gathered from the characters between the pages to long for a different life. Writing was an instrument of change, evolving Erica into the woman she is today– a better, more mature, more at peace thinker.

Erica has a wicked mind, one she pours out into her creations. Her filter doesn't allow all of it to erupt, much to her relief. Sarcastic, with a very dark, perverse sense of humor, Erica puts a bit of herself into every character she writes.

I love hearing from readers. If you would like more information on release dates, works in progress, teaser chapters, and random bits of madness, please visit my Facebook Fan Page:
https://www.facebook.com/thewickedwriter my website:
ericachilson.com or please contact me via email:
wickedwriter.ericachilson@gmail.com
DEVIANTS ONLY, if you'd like to join Erica Chilson's closed Facebook group, M&M of Restraint:
https://www.facebook.com/groups/MistressandMaster/